CHASING TODAY

THE PERIPHERALS: BOOK THREE

MARK ALDRICH

Wallace Street Press • Kill Devil Hills, NC

Cover Design: Chris Sorensen
Proofreading: Gretchen Douglas
Formatting: Chris Sorensen
Editing: Amy Gillespie
Author Photograph: Justin Patterson Photography

ISBN#: 979-8-9871069-2-1

Published by:

Wallace Street Press
P.O. Box 211
Kill Devil Hills, NC 27948

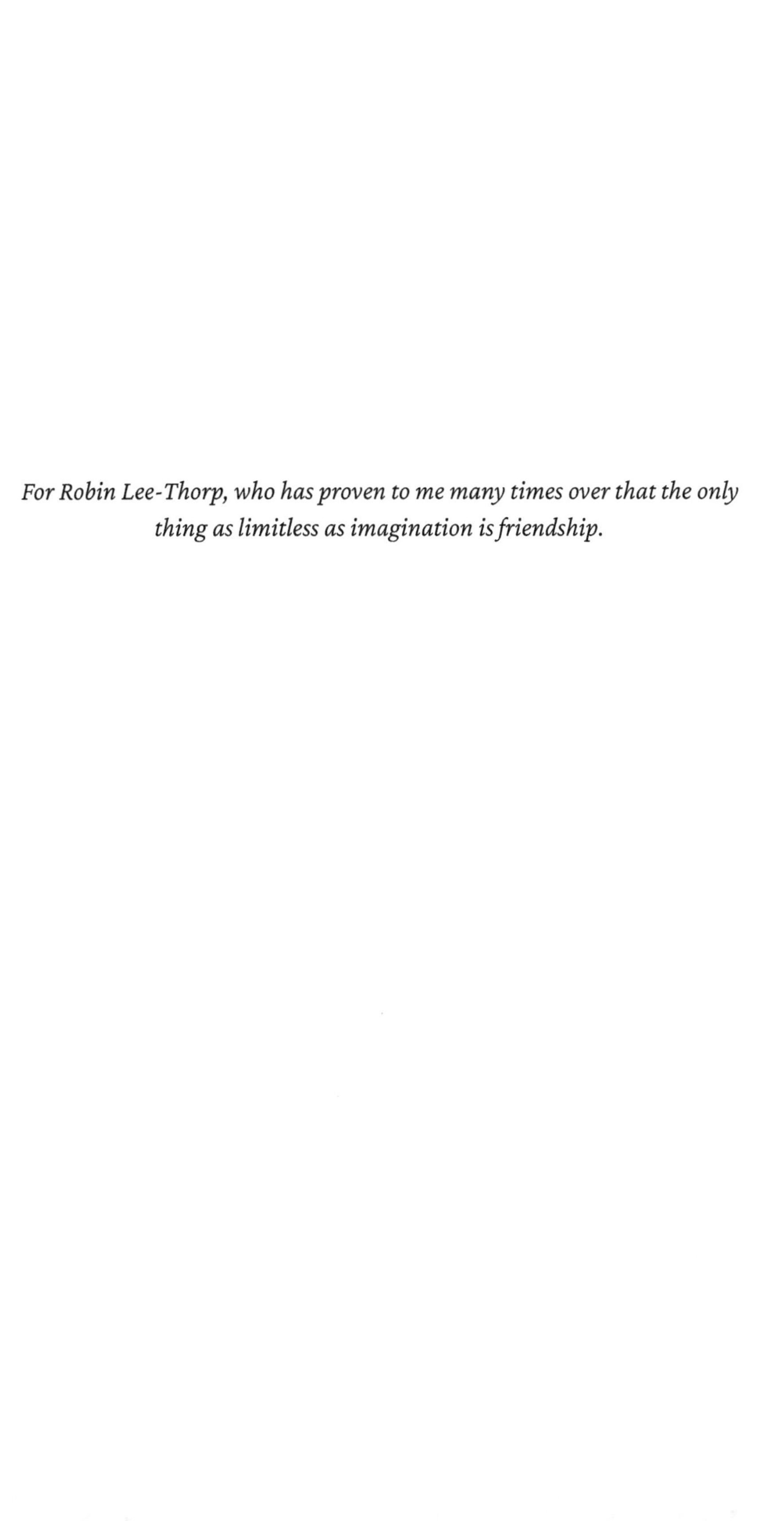

For Robin Lee-Thorp, who has proven to me many times over that the only thing as limitless as imagination is friendship.

CHAPTER I

Marcello Pettirosso stood at the window in his spacious office above Prince Street in Lancaster, Pennsylvania. It was a quarter to five and the sun was nearly set, throwing shadows across the block. As he watched, the antique gas lamps flickered to life, and their dancing flames made the shadows seem even darker. As he peered out, Pettirosso felt suddenly exposed as darkness settled outside and the light at his back left him silhouetted for passersby to see. He reached behind him and pushed a button just under the lip of his desktop. With that, the floor-to-ceiling windows along the façade of the Fulton Theatre became opaque, and he allowed himself to breathe easier, knowing that the headlights from the passing cars could not pierce the dark tint now protecting him. But it wasn't the street traffic that had set him on edge.

He had been in place as the Executive and Artistic Director of the theatre for well over a decade by now. He was in the final days of overseeing a massive renovation of the nineteenth-century opera house. It was a Victorian jewel box, stunning in its beauty and a snapshot of what life had been over a century and a half ago.

It had not always been the Grand Old Lady of Prince Street. In the earliest days of America, the site had been home to a jail, with many of the original walls still visible in the interior of the theatre. It had also been the scene of unimaginable tragedy, in addition to playing a part in the sweep of history throughout the new country as the nation struggled to discover itself. The Fulton had overcome those early dark days and served as a meeting hall, a community center, and eventually a performance venue. With the advent of film, the building added a movie screen, but over time fell into disrepair and second-rate status. The community eventually rallied around the theatre and fundraised to retore her to her former glory. Over the years, she continued to reclaim her place in the immediate area and then, finally, as a treasured institution presenting the finest in theatre, music, and dance in the region and gaining national attention.

Pettirosso had used his tenure to take the valued hall into the twenty-first century as no one had dared imagine. His appearance on the Lancaster scene was shrouded in rumors of a storied career in his homeland of Italy, but little evidence of his exploits could be found online. No matter. There was no denying the impact he'd had on the institution. The historic spaces had remained pristine. What had been added were facilities of the highest caliber around those cherished areas. A lobby that could function as a world-class concert hall. A backstage that surpassed nearly every Broadway space in New York. Apartments for visiting artists were created mere steps from the stage. It was an unprecedented explosion of progress, creativity, and expansion.

The community at large was excited about the changes and eager to reap the benefits of this exquisite facility in their midst. If they saw the Fulton as Pettirosso's domain, he knew better. The theatre was his charge, his ward. He had been sent here to safeguard it and all who crossed its threshold. To honor its history, even the most difficult episodes, and propel it forward, leaving the darkness behind. It was a bridge. From the past, to today, and on to tomorrow. A bridge where thoughts and feelings were shared, often between people who would likely never cross paths otherwise. It was a haven where the spirits of the past could rest easy. The venerable stage was a palette, where the greatest creative minds could create new worlds and share them with hearts and minds watching in wonder from the darkened auditorium.

As such, Pettirosso knew that it would also be a target. That there would always be those who found such freedom and creativity threatening. That was why he had been sent here. That was his calling. His duty. He had been in this world for longer than he could remember, and this sacred space had given him a sense of purpose like none he had known. He knew the darkness was gathering, and the deepening shadows below him brought forth a grim determination in him. He was well aware that tomorrow everything would change. He was ready as only he could be.

A tap on another button under his desk lowered the shades on the windows. He turned to a large monitor on the wall opposite his desk and spoke it into life, a camera pointed on the stage from the grid high above flickering to life. The ghost light sat alone center stage, casting its glow to the lip of the playing space, but leaving the corners of the space in shadow. Although the crew was long gone for the day, the darkness seethed with movement and Pettirosso allowed himself a wry grin. The spirits knew something was coming. They stood watch over their home. Pettirosso took solace in the knowledge that he was never truly alone here, but he knew the defense of this place would ultimately fall to him. As it was always meant to be.

Darkness beyond the walls. Darkness within the walls. And all of it paled in comparison to the darkness that would soon arrive.

***

Packing days were always fraught. No matter how many times Sean Curley left New York City to start a new show out of town, the process of leaving was complicated. How did one pack for ten weeks? With many suitcases, duffels, backpacks, and coolers. And no matter how much or how little was packed, it would somehow seem that you had both packed too much and left vital items behind. Today was no different.

Sean stood in the middle of his small living room and scanned the absolute chaos he had unleashed upon the room. Most of his luggage sat half full. Someone entering the room now would have a hard time deciphering if he was coming or going. He had one bag that consisted solely of chargers and cords—phone, computer, Kindle, electric toothbrush, AirPods, headphones...and he was somehow sure he had left something out.

Despite the clutter surrounding him, Sean was relieved to be leaving for a bit. The last two months had been stressful, to say the least. He was on his way someplace he knew well, Lancaster, Pennsylvania, and the Fulton Theatre. This would be his eighth show there. Or was it his ninth? In any event, it was a home away from home for him both artistically and personally. Every new show felt like a clean slate. New friends. New colleagues. Old friends. Old stomping grounds. New show. New role. New chance.

Lancaster was only 180 miles away, barely three hours if the traffic gods were kind (which they rarely were these days), but it would be a welcome change. He needed a chance to catch his breath, and to just be... Sean Curley, actor. But first—packing.

He'd be there for a change of seasons, late fall into the first whispers of winter. That made packing more complicated. Layers. Think layers. Versatility. Workout clothes! He'd forgotten them. Okay, they could go into the large rolling duffel. There was a corner in the bag that looked to have some space remaining. Light jacket. Check. Heavy jacket? Probably not needed. Unless he didn't pack one. Then he would definitely need one.

He heaved a sigh. It was always fine once he got out the door. It was everything up to that point that was tricky. He sat heavily on his worn and sagging sofa. Maybe after this job he would splurge and finally replace the couch. He was in his mid-forties. Time to stop living like a college student.

Okay. No slacking. Another good half hour and he should be ready. Another glance around the room. Would it all fit in his new car? Talk about splurging. He'd gotten fed up with relying on his friends for rides and he spent far too much time out of town to go on any longer without wheels of his own. His buddy, Dan Trout, would probably be relieved not to be his personal chauffeur. Although, honestly, Sean would miss some of the road trips. And he would definitely miss Trout's tricked-out 1996 Ford Bronco. The most comfortable antique he'd ever experienced. He loved his slightly used Subaru Crosstrek, but it didn't have seat massagers, personal headrest speakers, and a cooler compartment. It was his, though, and there was a lot to be said for that.

He checked his phone. Just after five o'clock. If he put the finishing touches on this chore, he would have plenty of time to meet his friends for what they called their "Happy Trails Happy Hour." Every time one of them left town for a show, no matter how long the contract, they would gather to raise a glass and wish each other well. They'd all been in the business too long to still cling to silly traditions like that. On second thought, no they hadn't. In fact, the older they got, the more important the lasting friendships seemed.

This particular gang had been together a long time. They were all of similar ages. Give or take. Middle-aged seasoned Broadway performers who had been dubbed "The Grumbles" because they almost always played cranky, middle-aged characters. Rather than take offense, they embraced it. Had actually come to love it. Most of them had recently finished a year-long run in a Broadway show together, and they were missing the opportunity to see each other six days and eight shows a week. Even the tempestuous experiences of the last few weeks hadn't dampened their genuine affection for each other. Well, for the most part.

Sean pushed those thoughts away. Thinking of the last few weeks would bring Breena to mind and he was just not ready to think about her. He'd genuinely believed that, despite some large issues to overcome, they would find a way to be together. Now he didn't think so at all. But it was too raw. Still too painful.

Okay. Focus. Brain off, packing instincts on.

Thirty minutes later he sat back down with a relieved grunt and a slightly louder crackling of his knees than he had ever noticed before. The bags were full and stacked by the door. Two compartments remained open in the backpack—one for toiletries he would need tonight and one for the chargers he would use overnight. That was it. Done.

He thought, not for the first time, of the absurdity of the life he had created. Fallen into? Hs early years had been spent discovering his love for music and performing. As he moved through the school years, the enjoyment became more serious and so did his studies. He worked—hard—to put himself in a position to compete with the best. The logical progression had led him here to New York. To push himself in hopes of creating a career and reaching the stages of Broadway. He had done all of that, surprising even himself more than once along the way. But no one ever told you what happened *after* those things. And what had happened, at least for Sean, was that the struggle continued. Broadway shows end. Contracts end. And then what? Well, back to the grind. Auditions. More lessons. More goals and more crushed dreams. Or dreams realized, depending on the day of the week. There is no finish line. Things didn't progress neatly from one phase to the next. The history of Broadway is littered with wonderful performers who were riding high for a time, only to fade and disappear from the spotlight. Literally and figuratively. So here he was, with a birthday approaching that would put him squarely in his late forties, still auditioning for—hoping for—contracts like the one he was lucky enough to be starting. Contracts that took you away from the city you had striven so long and hard to reach. Contracts that would take you away from the life you had built. Contracts that saw you leave behind friends and loved ones, even if it was only for six weeks. Or eight. Or twelve. Those friends still represented your roots. Your chosen family. The life of an American mid-level actor was a tease of a hamster wheel that made you think you had achieved something only to snatch it away from you when you weren't paying attention. Round and round it went. And he was one of the *lucky* ones. Sheesh. "Lighten up," he told himself. He always felt this way before leaving for a gig. He'd be happy as a clam once he got to Lancaster.

Okay. Time check. Good to go. Twenty minutes until he would head to midtown Manhattan.

He cocked his head, thinking he had heard something from the direction of the refrigerator. The apartment was small enough that he only had to crane his neck to glance into the galley kitchen. Nothing. Weird. He had good reason to not ignore these sensations, but this time he found nothing. The refrigerator motor kicked on and he allowed himself to believe it must have been that.

He heard a sound come from the bedroom in back and did force himself to get up and check that out. One strange noise? Possibly nothing. Two? Definitely should be looked into. Entering the back room, well insulated against sound of all kinds by the full-to-bursting bookshelves on every wall, he heard the sound again. A low rumble that suddenly grew in volume and felt as if it would shake the walls.

The motorcycle club in the alley out back was finishing their Sunday get-together. Apparently, their lease on the industrial garage they occupied was up soon. They were nice folks, but he wouldn't miss the noise.

But wait. They were even louder than usual. He crossed to the window and peeled back the shade. It was open and a cool November breeze hit his face. Now, that was weird. He never opened that window, especially this time of year. He slowly closed it, then took another look around the room. Nothing was out of place.

He crossed back into the living room and paused to listen. Still nothing. He was probably just jumpy after recent events. But a strange noise *and* an open window? He didn't like it but had to admit that the apartment was too small for anyone to be hiding in here. Chill out, Sean.

He went to the bathroom, splashed some water on his face and took a good look at himself in the mirror. He looked older. Tired. Time to see some friends, clear his mind, turn the page to a new job and a new experience.

He headed for the door. Keys, wallet, phone. Good to go. And so, he went. Friends healed everything. Usually. Well, most of them.

It was after midnight when Sean finally made it onto the train to head back home. These were the sort of friends that made time seem to disappear. Friends that, no matter how much time had passed or what had happened in their lives, were as comfortable as your favorite concert t-shirt from college. And yes, he still had a few of them in his closet. Third Eye Blind still got some wear, but that Creed shirt had fallen out of the rotation.

The N train rolled into the Broadway stop in Astoria and slowed with an alarming squeal of brakes. Sean waited patiently for the door to slide open and exited into the brisk late November air. The group had chosen to meet at The Pony Bar on the east side of Manhattan, a departure from their normal theatre district haunts. The original Pony Bar had been in that part of the city and visiting the newest incarnation had been a nod to their early days of friendship. It was different, but familiar and homey. Just what they needed.

He was tired, but it was a good tired. The tired that comes from laughing too much, having one too many beers, and far too many fried cheese bites. They were delicious but could never replace the late lamented fried green beans that had been removed from the menu. At least they had been able to pretend there was some nutritional value in those. The cheese bites? Not so much. Calories on packing days don't count. That's what they had stated repeatedly, with little conviction.

The Grumbles had been in rare form. Brandy Johns, the spark-plug tough-as-nails rock at their center, had complained all night about having to actually take a subway to meet them. A compact figure, standing under five foot four, she made up in attitude for her lack of stature. She was letting her hair grow longer, and her shoulder-length brunette tresses brought with them a feminine air at odds with her colorful vocabulary and base sense of humor. She could have easily been a longshoreman if her life had gone a different way. Living in midtown, she was used to walking a few blocks to Beer Culture, their usual haunt. Despite her griping, she had grinned from start to finish. She had actually just been cast in the show that Sean was leaving to perform, so they would be working together again. Her patient, saint-like husband Mick had been happy to see her cast. She always did best when working. With their daughter, Donna Vanessa, working in D.C. for an oceanographic research group, Mick was due for some solo time in their apartment, but he didn't seem fazed by it one bit.

Sullivan Nichols, who went confusingly by the nickname Nick, had traveled in from his new house on Cranberry Lake in New Jersey. Bald as a cue ball with keen blue eyes that missed little and gave away even less, he was the group's intellect. The inquisitive one. He was nearing completion of his first novel, and his agent had managed to create a bidding war for the manuscript. A handsome paycheck lay just around the corner for him and there were whispers of Hollywood sniffing at his historical bodice-ripping book. He had added a supernatural element to it, and more than one A-lister was jockeying for the lead role. Nick picked up the tab for the entire night.

Stewart Garland, the lone Black Grumble, had appeared more relaxed and happier than they could remember seeing him in quite some time. A tall, elegant performer, he had enjoyed quite the early career as a leading man, breaking barriers for so many actors who came after him. As he got older, he found himself less enamored of his place in the industry. Surprisingly, he had discovered a talent for healing and natural remedies. He had been studying with Sandy Dale, an unofficial Grumble, who had retired from her successful life on the stage to open a holistic shop in the beach town of Montauk on Long Island. Stewart had only recently come back to the city, lured by a new romantic entanglement with a very influential PR agent, Gwyddion Evans. Along with that relationship had come offers for very lucrative solo performances in some of the best nightclubs in town. *Just goes to show you*, Sean thought, *when you stop caring too much about something, good things will find their way to you.*

Dan Trout, their larger-than-life pal who hailed from Montana and carried himself as if he was still prowling the open country there, had come over from his apartment in Bayonne. He cut an impressive figure at over six foot four with a massive moustache that practically demanded that he star in westerns. Ironically, he never had. Despite that, Trout was the most accomplished of them all, with so many Broadway shows to his credit that he couldn't remember them all. He lived a low-key luxurious life. A plush and well-appointed apartment, a souped-up classic Ford Bronco that had more bells and whistles than most top-of-the-line new cars. He lived life full-out with no apologies. He'd recently fallen—hard—for a woman who lived an interesting life back in the Outer Banks of North Carolina. Complicated didn't begin to cover it. In that regard, Sean and Trout shared something. Sean's potential relationship with Breena was also complex. That, and the intense time they'd shared recently, had formed a bond between Sean and Trout that saw them enjoying a deeper friendship than ever before.

Last, there was Ken O'Carroll, likely the trickiest relationship at this point amongst all the friends. He had climbed quickly, startingly so, some would say, to the heights of the New York theatre scene. He was tall, thin, and remarkable like Sean in complexion and hair color. The primary differences were that Ken's eyes were green to Sean's blue, and he stood a good three inches taller than Sean. Less obvious at first glance, was his copious consumption of cannabis, although he swore he was cutting back. With the help of a high-powered public relations firm, Evans and Attay, Ken had been poised to ascend to the highest levels of celebrity. However, ego and ambition had gotten the better of him, and a particularly disgraceful moment of road rage had been captured on video and gone viral at the worst possible moment. He had lost it all. He'd lost his one-man show. He'd lost his newfound PR team (and yes, the Evans involved was Gwyddion Evans, Stewart's new partner). He'd lost the trust of his wife, Anne, and their two children. He'd also severely damaged the bonds between himself and the other Grumbles, but they steadfastly, some thought foolishly, had stuck with him. They continued to call him, invite him out, and coax him back to the Ken they had known before all the mess. This night, Sean's final before leaving town, they had finally convinced him to join them. He was sheepish, embarrassed. But he showed up. And by the end of the night, he'd even allowed himself to relax a bit and had finally smiled. The first smile any of them had seen him wear for weeks.

Even their old friends Paul Campanelli and David Marquez had put in appearances. Paul had added The Pony Bar to his résumé and was now managing there in addition to his duties at Beer Culture across town. Dave, co-owner of the uptown Gunhill Brewing, had even appeared bearing a gift: six bottles of Gunhill's barrel-aged Void of Light Imperial Stout, aged for three years in his personal beer fridge.

"This one's a good one!" Dave had announced unveiling his contribution. "Three for tonight, and three for when you get back, Sean. Call it an enticement to make sure we don't lose you to Amish country down there in Pennsylvania."

They had all happily downed those three bottles. The entire gathering had the vague sensation of what Sean's ancestors had called an "American wake"—saying farewell to someone sailing across the sea from the homeland. In years past, emigration was almost equivalent to dying. Everyone knew the relation would begin a new life in America, but for all intents and purposes, they would be dead to those left behind, likely never to be seen again.

Even though Sean and Brandy were leaving for only two months, everyone knew they would be heard from little and seen not at all while they were gone. A temporary American wake, of sorts. However, the events of the last few weeks had taught them that life could take unexpected turns. Safe to say, no one present assumed anything these days.

If at moments, Sean stared out the window trying in vain to banish thoughts of Breena, or Trout peered into his beer glass as if it could reveal how to solve the complications in his relationship with Eleanor, the others chose to give them the space they needed. And as Ken seemed to shrink as far back into his seat as he could at times and looked at the others with a mélange of regret and shame, the others gently assured him with every shoulder pat and shared memory, that they were simply happy to have him there with them.

They all worked hard at keeping things light. Reveling in the shared friendship. Celebrating Sean's job, and their shared existence in an insane industry while living in a challenging city. The one thing they assiduously avoided, spent so much time sidestepping that it loomed over them throughout, was the fact that they had discovered a race of otherworldly beings who lived just beyond human senses. Descended from the Tuatha De Danann, an ancient Celtic supernatural race with counterparts from cultures around the world. They called them "The Peripherals," due to their hovering on the edge of human perception, but they had become anything but peripheral to the Grumbles and recent events. The actors' involvement with the Peripherals had led them, more than once, to the cusp of disaster with ramifications in the balance for more than just themselves. In their hunger for normalcy, they all steered clear of those memories. But it was foremost in all their minds. And none of them believed that things were settled. For good or ill, there was another reckoning on the way. But not that night. Not in the warm and cozy Pony Bar.

And so, they drank their beers, basked in friendships that ran deeper than they could explain, and eventually scattered into the night.

Sean exited the subway at the elevated Broadway stop. The platform was remarkably quiet, even for after midnight on a Sunday night. The city that never sleeps was surprisingly drowsy as he made his way through the station and down the stairs to the sidewalk at Thirty-first Street and Broadway's northeast corner. Parisi Brothers Bakery perched on the corner was closed tight, but light snuck out from the kitchen in back. The smell of fresh bread wafted over Sean, a testament to the late-night baking going on in preparation for the early morning opening. It was one of Sean's favorite things about getting off the train in his neighborhood. It always felt as if the entire neighborhood was welcoming him back with a baguette and some black-and-white cookies. As excited as he was to spend some time in the relative quiet of Lancaster, there were definite pangs of regret at leaving his home.

As he stood with his nose almost pressed to the window, silhouetted by the glow within the shop, he felt the hair on his neck stand on end. He felt a chill run down his back. He'd recently become used to the sensation of being watched. The Peripherals had taught him that not everything was evident to his five senses. This felt different. A primitive piece of his brain was crying out a warning. His first thought was that he felt as if he was being stalked. As if something unseen waited in the deepest recesses of the darkened doorways. He glanced west along Broadway, his path home, and was distressed to notice just how many of those darkened doorways he must pass. He glanced around him. There were a few pedestrians to be seen, but no one nearby and the emptiness of the sidewalks struck him again, this time more ominously.

He pulled his jacket closer around him, hoisted the backpack higher on his shoulder and started home, more quickly even than his usual Big Apple pace. A breeze kicked up and Sean felt it at his back, pushing him along. It was almost as if the wind itself sensed something wrong and was warning him, hurrying him. He pulled his collar up, his neck suddenly feeling exposed. He realized as he picked up his pace even further, that many of the bars that used to dot the street had closed over the last few years of gentrification. Broadway Station remained, but sat two doors from the bakery, and beyond that—not much. The pizzerias were long closed for the night. More than one parcel of land sat empty, piles of rubble beyond plywood fences where buildings had been torn down to make way for luxury condos. Each time he came across one of these construction sites, Sean felt the maw of emptiness beyond the fences and couldn't help peering through the cutouts in the plywood, almost expecting to find someone, or something, peering back.

As he crossed Crescent Street, he heard a scuffling behind him and turned his head to catch what it was. He laughed quietly to himself as he found it to be a tabby cat slipping under one of the construction fences, no doubt on the hunt for rodents. He shook his head at his own foolishness and was brought up abruptly by the screaming horn of a yellow cab that had sped up to try to make the yellow light. It was in vain, and it ended up running the red light while also nearly taking Sean down.

He cursed under his breath and made sure to make note of the cab number. He often did that, vowing to call the taxi commission to lodge a complaint when something like this happened. He'd never followed through, but it somehow made him feel less powerless in the moment to swear retribution.

He took a moment to gather himself, then proceeded across Crescent and toward his apartment. The breeze had quieted as had his sense of dread. The air had gone out of the moment, and he forced himself to walk more slowly. He'd walked these blocks thousands of times over the years. He had never—not once—had a problem. Tonight was no different, he told himself.

Five minutes later, he let himself into his building, and as the metal fire door closed behind him, he leaned back against it and heaved a sigh. An overactive imagination, one beer too many, the anxiety/excitement that came with going away in the morning. Any of them could have sent him into his mild panic. He started up the stairs. Into his apartment. He made sure both deadbolts were in place and put the chain across. Normal, commonplace big-city precautions that tonight seemed to take on added importance and seemed somehow inadequate, given what he had dealt with over the past few weeks. He was home now. Safe. Ish. Check the mail. Set the alarm clock. Drink a glass of water. Then get to sleep and start a new fresh adventure in the morning.

As soon as the door to the street had closed behind him, the breeze picked up again and a shadow flitted past the window cutout in the front door. Across the street, a deeper shadow seemed to crouch on the top step of a stairwell to the basement of the facing building. A pair of eyes caught the gleam from a streetlight and reflected briefly before winking out and disappearing. Sean was already in his apartment and saw neither of them.

CHAPTER 2

S ean awoke five minutes before his alarm was set to sound. This was something he'd done as long as he could remember. If he had to be up for something, some lizard part of his brain kicked in before the alarm could do its job. On this morning, getting out of bed was a relief. He'd slept fitfully, with dreams of vague shadows pursuing him down city streets, through corn fields, past lakes. His sheets were damp with sweat, and he felt more exhausted than when he had arrived home after his night out.

Swinging his feet over the edge of the bed, he gave a joint-cracking stretch and padded into the kitchen. He'd brewed coffee the day before and he grabbed his now-iced coffee, took a swig, and turned to face the mountain of luggage and bags that awaited him by the door. This was going to take more than one trip down to the car.

He decided to forgo a shower, reasoning that all of the packing and unpacking ahead of him would leave him in need of one at the end of his journey south. He knew it was a bit of justification. The truth was, now that the time had arrived, he just wanted to get on the road. He wasn't good with change, even change that would last only a few months. (Not for the first time he acknowledged the irony in his career being one life-change after another.)

He dressed for comfort. He'd be sitting behind the wheel for a few hours, at least. No one would see him. No one to impress. He popped his favorite Milwaukee Repertory Theatre hat—he had a habit of collecting things, one of those things being baseball hats—on his head. Turning to the assembled bags, he made a plan of attack. First, he would load the clothes and other soft items. They would be on the bottom, safely cushioning everything on top. Next, he would bring down the electronics and various cables and chargers. On top of those he would stack the perishables, the few things he had to bring from the fridge because they would be long spoiled by the time he got back. He knew folks who essentially brought their entire kitchen along—spices, condiments, produce, even frozen items packed in ice packs. He wasn't one of those people. He had every intention of getting to know the local restaurant scene very well.

A half hour later, his new Subaru was packed. As he wiped his brow, he was glad he'd postponed that shower. It was unseasonably warm for November and the multiple trips up and down the stairs to the parking lot in back of his building left him eager to get started and blast the air conditioning. He headed to the chain-link gate, but before he unlocked the padlock, he thought better of it and dashed back up to the apartment to make sure he'd turned everything off. Fans? Off. Wi-Fi? Off. Lights? Off. Toilet not running? Check. Toaster unplugged? Check. Gas stove, that hadn't actually worked in years? Off. Good lord, he was turning into his mother with all of this checking things were off.

Out the door he went. Again. Locked both of the deadbolts. Double-checked them. Shaking his head at himself, he trotted down the stairs and out back to the parking lot he went. Unlocking the gate, he struggled to slide it open. Probably should join the gym in Lancaster, given how hard that gate had become. He started the Crosstrek, affectionately named Scooby, and paused only slightly to glance up at his window before he pulled into the alley, closed the gate behind him, and pointed himself toward Pennsylvania. The panicked run home the night before almost forgotten in the conflicting feelings of excitement, fear, anticipation, curiosity, and relief.

<hr>

As always, once he was clear of the city, his shoulders relaxed and he settled into the seat and his just over three-hour drive, according to his GPS. The George Washington Bridge had been a nightmare, as always, but not long after that he turned west onto Route 78 and set the cruise control. He had plenty of time. Checking in to his apartment couldn't happen until after two, and he wanted to arrive later than that to give the house management folks longer to get things cleaned and set up, so he took the more scenic route. This came with the added benefit of avoiding the Jersey Turnpike. That alone would make his day significantly better.

More than once, he had the unsettling feeling that he was being watched. Ridiculous. He was in his car, and no one even knew when he had left or even exactly how he was getting to Pennsylvania. Still, he found himself checking the rearview mirror, which made him feel even more foolish. Despite his prolific viewing of British police and mystery programs, he had no clue how to spot a tail. Especially on the packed roadways of New York City. No denying the goosebumps on his neck, though. If he'd learned one thing recently, it was to trust his gut. Even if it made little sense.

To distract himself, he set his satellite radio to the Lyle Lovett station and sang along to "This Is It" followed by The SteelDrivers' "Where Rainbows Never Die." Songs that never failed to make him smile. The anxiety of leaving home started to drip away. Music, man. It could work wonders.

A few minutes later, he decided to test out his new hands-free feature, and tapped the dashboard touch screen to call Brandy. She was coming from Manhattan and would take a different route, but he figured he'd check in.

After three rings, the line opened, and he heard muffled sounds of a phone being dropped. Sure enough, a moment later he heard Brandy shouting from somewhere not close to her phone's mouthpiece.

"What?" she yelled. "This better be an emergency, Ginge. I'm just getting out of the Lincoln Tunnel, my AC is broken—which means my window is down and the car is full of tunnel fumes, and I could get pulled over for answering my phone while driving. So, I repeat—what?!"

"Okay, then," Sean answered. "Figured you'd have hands-free by now. My bad. Just wanted to see how you were doing. I'll just see you in Lancaster. Take a deep breath and chill, B."

"Hands-free?" she replied. "What have you been smoking? Is this Ken I'm talking to? I'm lucky the old Chevy Cobalt even started. In fact, if it dies on the way, I'll be calling you and asking for an emergency pickup. Hands-free. Who do you think I am? Trout?"

"Yeah, yeah. I get the picture. Drive safely. And don't break down. I'm packed to the roof. I'd have to strap you on top. Or use you as a hood ornament."

"Oh, nice," Brandy seethed. "Short jokes? I expect more of you, Ginge. Whatever. See you down there. Drive carefully in that fancy new car of yours."

Sean laughed. "You, too. Hey, Dispensing Company tonight?" he asked, referring to their favorite Lancaster watering hole and restaurant.

"Well, duh," she answered. "Have you met me? Dipco tonight. And you be careful out there, Ginge. This is going to be fun."

"Absolutely," Sean said, chuckling. "You be careful, too."

Hanging up, he turned up the stereo. Squeeze. "Pulling Mussels (From the Shell)." Perfect driving music.

* * *

Three and a half hours later, after one gas stop and one farmstand stop to pick up his annual decorative gourds (miniature ghost pumpkins were a particular favorite), Sean pulled up in front of The Fulton Theatre on Prince Street in Lancaster, Pennsylvania. The newly digitized marquee was flashing the photos of cast members of the currently running hit,

Man of La Mancha. Sean had been up for the role of the Padre, but it had gone to some other ginger tenor. He'd been a bit put out, at first, but everything works out for a reason, and he was very happy to be starting rehearsals for *A Christmas Carol* for the holidays.

As he slipped the car into park, he saw a familiar face emerging from the front doors. Deborah Bialasek. Deborah had been working in and around the theatre since Sean's first show there more than fifteen years earlier. She had, at one time or another, seemingly worked every position in the administration. A tall, elegant, and impeccably mannered woman, Deborah was the perfect ambassador for the theatre, both to arriving employees and to patrons. Despite her many talents, she chose to remain largely out of the limelight. The smooth running of the theatre was reward enough for her. Today, she seemed to be welcoming incoming cast and steering them toward their housing, though Sean had no idea if her job title now included Company Manager.

She approached the passenger side of Sean's Subaru as he lowered the window on the side and greeted her with a heartfelt smile.

"Deborah," he enthused, "I couldn't ask for a better welcoming committee. So great to see you. All well?"

"Right back at you, Sean," she answered. "It's always a good day when I see you pull up for a new show. How was your trip down?"

"Smooth sailing once I got out of the city. I could feel my mood getting better the closer I got to Lancaster."

"That's what I like to hear," Deborah responded. "Hey, look, I hope you don't mind, but we don't have you in the new housing. The *La Mancha* cast doesn't move out until the end of the week, so we've got you up at Dremmel. You know the one on Orange Street? Beautiful apartment. Top of the stairs when you enter. Number six. That cool?"

"Of course, it is. No worries," Sean said. "I like that walk. Ten minutes each way. All good."

"See how you like it," Deborah continued. "We can always move you down here if you'd rather next Monday when the *Mancha* folks are gone."

"I'm sure it will be fine, Deb," he assured her. "Can I just park around back there?"

"Yup, you got it," Deborah replied, handing him an envelope with keys and a parking pass. "You're space number seven. Good luck, there. Oh, and Marcello wants to meet up later. Maybe come on down around five, or so? He'd love to give you a tour of all the renovations."

"Every single thing you just said sounds perfect," Sean said, grinning. "You're the best. Great to see you. Say, has Brandy Johns checked in yet? She's a buddy from the city."

"I assumed as much when I got a look at her résumé. She's not here yet. And just so you know, she is staying down here in the new apartments. Don't be jealous."

Shaking his head, Sean assured her there would be no hard feelings. "But I will," he said with a chuckle, "give her grief about it."

"I'll leave that between the two of you," Deborah continued. "Give a shout if you need anything, yeah? I think you'll be happy up there."

"I have no doubts," Sean said. "I trust you completely."

He pulled away from the curb, honked the horn in farewell, and turned left on King Street. Five minutes later he pulled into an alley off of Lime Street that led to the small lot behind Dremmel House. He found space number seven, pulled in and sat for a moment before turning off the car and grabbing his backpack from the passenger seat and heading up the side of the house to the front door.

The outer door opened easily to Sean, but he had to fumble with the keys he'd been given to get inside the inner doors. He passed the laundry room on the right. Duly noted. In the foyer, he paused to take in his surroundings. The stairway up lay just in front of him and a corridor to the left of it led to some first-floor apartments. He knew he was on the second floor, so up he went.

Apartment Six lay directly at the top of the worn and obviously well-traveled stairs. They had seen better days, but obviously had been incredibly posh in their day. In fact, the entire building gave the impression of faded glory and Sean couldn't help but wish he'd been able to see it when it was shining and new. One of the aspects of working out of town he had come to love was discovering nuggets of history and windows into the past of a new city. While Lancaster wasn't new to him, this house was, and he was drinking in the atmosphere.

He fumbled with the keys until he found the one that opened the front door and heaved both his backpack and a sigh of relief when he finally made it inside. The pack he set on the floor by the side table by the front door and he proceeded into the living room. A small and surprisingly new television sat on an end table to the right, while a writing desk faced the window to the left that looked out onto an exterior walkway that he assumed led to other apartments.

Through the living room, he found the bedroom. It was small but well-appointed. The brass bed was tall and luxurious. He jumped up onto the mattress and was pleasantly surprised to find it so comfortable. He was tempted to stretch out and relax for a moment but didn't trust himself to stay awake. He still had a full car to unpack.

Sitting up, he scanned the rest of the room. There was another, smaller, TV in the corner of the room behind the doorway. Nice. Opposite corner was a deep maroon chaise lounge, or as he had recently discovered, chaise longue in its original French. How could he have known? He took Spanish.

Through the bedroom, he found the kitchen. Large and stocked much better than his kitchen at home. There was even room enough for a full-sized dining table. Not for the last time, he shook his head at the confines of his—and most—New York apartments. Standing at the sink, he glanced out the rear picture window and was pleased to see it looked out over the parking lot and he had a clear view of his car parked below. Even better, he discovered a door to his left opening out onto a landing and, upon investigation, a steel stairway that led down to the lot. Excellent. That would save a lot of steps in the back and forth of unpacking.

Looking through the length of the apartment, he was pleased. It felt antique, filled with rich colors—deep ruby, rich royal blues, emerald green. The tapestries were thick and elaborate. All in all, it fit perfectly with the Victorian nature of Lancaster itself. And the show he'd be doing. He just knew he would be happy here.

As he headed down to the Subaru through the back door, he thought he heard something in the living room and stopped to see what it was, expecting a new neighbor or someone else from the theatre staff stopping by with supplies or a friendly welcome. Instead, he found nothing but the deep blue curtains swaying lightly in front of the open window by the writing desk.

Had that window been open when he arrived? He couldn't remember, but he was sure he hadn't opened it himself. He closed it and set the latch, some of his earlier feelings of being watched returning and setting the hairs on his arms to sound the alarm.

Rubbing his eyes, he realized how tired he actually was. Even the short three-hour drive had taken something out of him. It rankled. He remembered twelve and fourteen hours behind the wheel when he'd been on tour. Had he really gotten so old so fast? He scolded himself for overreacting and headed once more for the back door.

As he reached the Crosstrek and began pulling the luggage out, the window by the desk began, ever so slowly, to inch its way open again. It would be late that night before he would even take note.

Brandy Johns pulled up to the front of the theatre a full hour after Sean had arrived and forty-five minutes after the check engine light had come on in her Chevy Cobalt. The last forty miles had been a white-knuckle affair. The last thing she wanted was to have to pull off and get a tow to Lancaster. Luckily, that hadn't been needed, but there was a decidedly unpleasant knocking sound coming from under the hood by the time the drive was done.

She pulled up to the loading zone in front and before she was able to get out the doors opened and a young man with the friendliest smile she had seen in ages trotted across the sidewalk, waving. He was tall, just over six feet with jet-black hair, sensitive deep-blue eyes, and a sartorial sense that had Brandy shifting uncomfortably in her ten-year-old *Newsies* t-shirt.

"Howdy!" he called, staying a few feet away, under the awning of the marquee. "You must be Brandy, yeah? I'm Drew. Drew Brindig. Been waiting for you. Was just starting to get worried." He glanced at his watch. "But all good! You have plenty of time."

His energy gave off the "most open, genuine, earnest guy in the universe" vibes. Brandy mistrusted him instantly.

"Yeah, that's me. Sorry to keep you waiting," she mumbled, trying to hide her stretched-out shirt and baggy jeans.

"Oh, no, no, no! Not at all. Just wanted to be sure your trip was a smooth one. Well, that and Marcello—that's Marcello Pettirosso, the big boss here—was hoping to give you and Sean—you're friends with him, right?—a personal tour around five o'clock. Luckily, you're staying here on campus, so no problem."

"Okay, slow down there, Bucky. Walk it back a bit. Let's start with where I can park and go from there."

"Whoops. My bad. Of course," he answered, with genuine regret. "I get too excited sometimes. To park, just cross King Street"—he gestured to the next intersection—"and park in the first garage on the left. I've got a pass for you here. You can enter the apartments through the side or the back door on Water Street. I'll give you the code for the door. You'll be on the third floor. Brand-spanking-new apartment. Thirty seconds to the stage. You can drop off any of your bags here and I'll watch them. Or take them up for you. Whatever works for you. Sorry. There I go again. I just get so darned excited to meet the new cast members. Questions?"

He flashed her another smile and she did her best to approximate it in return, but suspected it was more of a grimace.

"I think that'll do for now. I'll drop off my bags and then park. Probably will think of some questions along the way. No need to carry my stuff up. I can do that. Just keep an eye on it, if you don't mind."

"Okey dokey," he enthused. "Not a problem. It's my job. Well, one of them. I do a lot of everything around here. You'll see. Wanna pop the trunk? I'll get your things up and out."

Brandy popped the trunk, slipped the car into park, and before she could get out to handle some of the bags, Drew had emptied the trunk and the back seat.

"All set!" he cried. "Just go through the light, and first garage on the left. Park on the second level. Plenty of space there this time of day. I'll be here!"

Brandy gave him a slow nod of the head as she settled back into the driver's seat.

"I can give you the name of a good mechanic, if you want. That engine sounds a little iffy to me," he said, as she pulled away from the curb.

"Jeez," Brandy muttered to herself as she waited for the traffic light to change. "I hope they're not all so helpful here. I feel like I'm on a sugar high."

Checking her rearview mirror, she saw Drew waving her off as if they were lifelong friends and couldn't get the image of Forrest Gump out of her head.

***

Unseen from the street, Pettirosso and Deborah stood at the tinted office window watching the proceedings.

"Bless his heart," Deborah said. "Maybe we shouldn't let him greet the New Yorkers from now on."

"Nonsense," Pettirosso replied. "He's the perfect introduction to what they should expect. She'll thaw. Everyone loves Drew eventually. Just those two for now, yes? Curley and Johns."

"Exactly right," Deborah said. "The others don't even know they'll be brought here. These two are all that's required right now. We need to suss these two out first."

"As it should be," Pettirosso agreed. "Let's get ready for that tour. I'll want your genuine impressions."

"I would never insult you with anything less," Deborah said.

A touch of a button and the shades lowered, as the two of them turned back to the work at hand.

CHAPTER 3

Sean sat up suddenly in his tall, too-comfortable bed. It took a moment for him to remember where he was. The sun had set while he dozed after unloading his car. The apartment lay in darkness, a single light from the parking lot out back sent an orange glow through the space, barely reaching the living room beyond the bedroom, leaving it shrouded in shadow.

His heart was beating fast. Too fast. He gulped air and steadied himself, grabbing the side of the bed until his equilibrium settled. He'd been dreaming. Vividly. But the full dream was being coy, eluding his consciousness, running to hide every time he drew close to recalling what it had been. This was unusual for him. He normally could hang onto his dreams, especially anything as impactful as this one had clearly been.

The only thing he could recall was a sense of being pursued. And a forest. His pursuer, or pursuers, had remained unseen, but their footfalls had been distinct. He had awakened before he had been captured. At least, he thought so. It was the chase that had given him the palpitations.

He checked his phone. Still forty minutes until he was due to be at the theatre for his tour. Plenty of time to settle down.

He swung his legs over the side of the bed and headed to the kitchen and poured himself a glass of water from the tap, making a mental note to fill his water purifier pitcher when he had unpacked all of his bags. Actually, the water was surprisingly fresh. Still, better to be safe.

He peered out the back window. The Subaru was safely parked up under the overhead light. The very one that bathed the apartment in its copper hue.

As he was woolgathering, something caught his attention out of the corner of his eye. Turning, he was surprised to see the shadow of a man crossing the kitchen wall. He turned to the door, expecting to see one of his fellow actors passing by on the walkway outside. He stopped short when he realized that the curtain was drawn. There was no way a shadow could have been from that direction.

Confused, he turned back to the shadow. It was still there and traveling along the kitchen wall toward the other end of the apartment. It was distinctly male and seemed to be wearing, incongruously, a fedora. Not just a hat. A fedora. And a long coat, calf-length.

As he turned back to the window at the sink, he caught glimpse of some...thing. Another shadow. This one with less distinct form, seemingly peering over the edge of the window at him. It was gone almost before he could register what he had seen. He cautiously leaned over the sink to get a better look and realized that there was no porch outside the kitchen here. It was a two story drop to the small backyard. So not possible for anyone to be standing there looking in.

Sean settled back in his heels. Both shadows were now gone, and he instantly began to doubt himself. It must be the residual feelings from his dream and abrupt waking. He was very used, at this point, to things hovering on the edges of his perception. His discovery of the Peripherals had been a shock at first, but he quickly became acclimated to them, and his senses had sharpened to the point where he thought even they would be hard-pressed to avoid his detection.

So, what exactly was happening here?

He crossed to the kitchen door. The curtain covering the window was thick. A heavy, deep blue, almost velvet fabric, similar to those in the other rooms. Nothing could cast a shadow through that. Then what had he seen? Or who? Wearing a fedora, long coat, and sliding smoothly across the wall?

He opened the door and stepped outside to the walkway running along the side of the building. Sure enough, it ended at the staircase to his right that led down to the yard. Peering around the corner, he confirmed that there was no place for anyone, or anything, to stand outside the kitchen window. Curious.

After all he'd been through lately, he was nowhere close to panicking, but he was baffled. He opened his senses, hoping to find one of his Peripheral friends nearby but sensed nothing. He would get no help from them. Not yet anyway.

He reentered the kitchen and made sure to close and lock the door behind him. He pulled the curtain tightly shut. Taking in the kitchen, he saw nothing out of place or unusual. He didn't entirely dismiss what he had experienced, but he was determined not to overreact. He wanted so much to have some simple, normal time to himself, he refused to be drawn into negative thoughts.

Sometimes, being in a new place was unsettling, at first. No matter how many times he had done it—and he had done it many times with many shows around the country—it never became second nature.

Shrugging it off, he crossed into the bedroom where he picked up his backpack to take to the theatre. He didn't really need it. He took it out of habit. Tomorrow, with the start of rehearsals, he would need his pack. Tonight? No. He forced himself to put it back on the chair by the bed. This was more of a social meeting. He thought.

He crossed from the bedroom into the living room and turned on the lamp that sat on the writing desk by the window. He didn't like coming home to a darkened apartment. Especially one that he didn't know and had already given him more than one start.

As he turned to leave by the front door, his heart leaped when he saw a large shadow climbing down the front wall. He paused. Shook his head. It was his own shadow, thrown by the lamp he had just lit.

"Stop being an idiot, Sean," he muttered. "Just let things be normal. For once."

He exited and headed down the stairs to the building's front door and into the night. Turning left on Orange Street, he was determined to have a pleasant, leisurely walk to the theatre.

He never saw the shadow on the front wall that remained after he left. The curtain over the desk billowed as the wind picked up outside. The lamp extinguished and the apartment was dark once again.

Brandy thanked Drew for his too-eager help, although she noted that he'd not carried a single bag, instead leading the way, and shut the door to her new apartment behind her. She turned to survey her home for the next two months. It was new. Newer than any New York apartment she'd seen for quite some time. The floors were a hardwood, new, and done in a light finish. The furnishings were all brand new. She wondered if anyone had ever used them before her. It didn't look that way.

By the entrance to the bedroom to the right, halfway through the space, stood a massive washer/dryer pair. She couldn't believe her eyes. She hadn't had her own home laundry since she'd moved to New York over twenty-five years ago.

She left her bags by the front door and moved into the bedroom. The king-sized bed was massive. She had a hard time actually climbing up onto it. Once there, she felt lost in the expanse of the thing. She could turn herself a full 360-degrees and never come close to touching the edge. The comforter was blindingly white. She actually wondered if it would keep her up at night. She laid her head down and it gently nestled first into the comforter and then, when she shifted, onto the softest pillows she had ever experienced. What did that? Goose down? Definitely not the sale pillows she and Mick had picked up at Marshall's. The theatre was definitely not scrimping on the actors' housing. They might have to pry her out of here when the show was over.

She jumped down from the bed, careful to land as gently as possible. Her tiny frame would need to get used to that. She crossed back into the main living area. To the right was an expansive room with a large flat-screen television mounted on the wall. She picked up the remote and checked out the channel guide. Whoa. Full package and, apparently, subscriptions to some streamers she had only heard rumors of. She checked her phone. Forty minutes to her meeting with the head honcho, Pettirosso. No time to get sucked into anything. Plenty of time for that later. She could do with a shower and a freshen-up.

Back at the front door, she realized she had passed right by the bathroom when she came in. She entered and stopped short. It was fully tiled —floor, walls, ceiling. The whole thing. And it was big. Easily bigger than her bedroom back home. And *that* was considered large by NYC standards. There was no tub; the walk-in shower was spacious, with not even a lip on the floor to step over. That explained the tiled floor. The tiled everything. She also made note that the entire bathroom was accessible. Floor space galore. Hand bars on the walls. Bright fluorescent lights.

Emerging back into the entryway, she made a quick scan of the kitchen space. Fully stocked. More pans and pots than in her own home. She noted that someone had even stocked her fridge with some local apple cider, some fresh produce (also local, no doubt), and what she would come to realize was a local delicacy, Lebanon Bologna, a cured, smoked, and fermented beef sausage, and not pork, despite its name. She sniffed it tentatively and was pleased to find it closer to salami than she had expected. A plate of that, along with some cheese and a local beer would close out this day nicely. She'd see if Sean wanted to join her after their tour.

Turning around, she noted her own rather pungent scent. She'd driven that last leg of the trip with her window open in order to keep a close ear on the troublesome noise coming from the Cobalt's engine.

She'd made it okay, but not without feeling she had a film of exhaust, road dust, and random detritus thrown up by the semis that had barreled past her ailing Chevy.

Scanning her luggage on the floor, she spotted the plastic shopping bag she had drafted into use as her toiletries bag. Pure class, that's what she was, she thought as she laughed and hoisted the bag. She could deal with the rest of her things after the shower. Or even after the tour, if that shower was as relaxing as it had looked at first glance.

She left a pile of slightly crusty clothes behind her on the floor and eagerly headed in for what ended up being a near half-hour long, steam-filled, muscle-relaxing, therapeutic rinse. Her body and mind both finally feeling refreshed, she felt a mild panic at the thought that she could have loitered too long and could be in danger of arriving late for the meeting with the big boss man.

With more than a little regret, she turned off the water and toweled off. The fan in the ceiling hummed loudly, and most of the steam had been drawn out, so she could easily check herself in the mirror.

"Damn, Brandy," she said aloud to herself. "You still clean up okay."

Before she could laugh at herself, she heard something in the living room. Figures. She knew it had been too good to be true. They'd probably put her in the wrong apartment, and the correct actor had just shown up. Made sense. This place was way too nice for her.

"Sorry, sorry!" she called. "Is someone out there? They put me here but obviously someone screwed up. Just let me dry off and we can get it all cleared up!"

She pulled the incredibly soft towel tighter around her, checked herself in the mirror one more time, and opened the bathroom door an inch.

"Hey, there?" she said. "Just an honest mistake. I'll be gone in just a —" She stopped speaking abruptly and stuck ger head cautiously further out the door. "Hello?"

She emerged fully from the bathroom, confused. The room was empty. But she had clearly heard someone moving out here. Right?

She crossed into the bedroom. Checked behind the door. Under the massive bed. She even opened the armoire. Empty. All empty.

She shook her head and padded back into the bathroom. Maybe noise carried between the apartments more than she expected. She had heard something, and while standing back at the mirror drying her hair, she had the unmistakable sensation that she was being watched. She closed and locked the door then, even as she knew she was behaving foolishly. It was a new space. She had to get used to its idiosyncrasies.

Sounds. Light from King Street beyond the window. Even the chime of the elevator just outside in the hallway. All of those would take some getting used to. So why did she feel as if she wasn't alone?

Damn. Too much dragging her feet. It wouldn't do to be late to her first theatre call, especially since she was living in the building itself. She was only thirty seconds away. If that.

She rushed out to her bags in the entryway and found one of her nicer outfits in the large plastic trash bag she had used to pack. Casual, but clearly showing an effort. That's about as good as it got with her.

She did a quick brush of the teeth and a last look in the mirror. That would have to do.

She grabbed the keys to the apartment from the table by the front door. The instructions left for new occupants warned against leaving them behind. The entrance from the street was via a keypad, but not the apartment itself. She was determined not to be one of *those* actors calling company management at odd hours to let them in due to a forgotten key.

As she stepped into the hallway, she paused to scan the entire apartment once again. Definitely empty, but sure didn't feel that way. Well, if there was something rattling around in there, it didn't feel negative. In fact, it almost felt reassuring. Friendly. That would be a welcome change after recent events.

She was certain, though, that there were no Peripherals in there. She had grown comfortable enough in their presence that she didn't think they could entirely evade her. At least she liked to think so, although Sean was much more in tune with them than she was.

She remembered after the door closed that she had left the fan on in the bathroom. No time to go back now. She'd get it when she returned.

The sound of the fan drowned out the quiet hum of the upscale washing machine. Which is probably why she didn't notice that the machine, which she hadn't started, was running, and her dirty clothes were gone from the floor.

CHAPTER 4

At five minutes to five, Sean turned the corner from Orange onto Prince Street and wandered up to the front door of the theatre. He wasn't exactly sure who would be meeting him. Checking his phone, he saw no messages so tried the doors. All were locked but the one nearest to the box office. He wandered the lobby, scanning the posters and plaques commemorating shows from years past. Considering the ephemeral nature of live theatre, Sean was touched at the respect given to those who had trod the boards here before him. He stopped in front of one poster from nearly seventy years past and paused, noting one of the actors with the last name Bialesek. The same as Deborah's. He made a mental note to ask Deborah if Karl Bialesek, credited on the poster, was a relative. Surely, he must be. Bialesek is anything but an ordinary name.

Sean thought, not for the first time, about legacy. One of the aspects of life in Lancaster he had always appreciated was the sense of history. Not just the buildings and the events from years gone by, but the heritage passed down from one generation to another, by families that had settled here and remained for centuries. That was something he missed in New York. Success in the big city was fleeting. He had seen so many personalities—actors, singers, artists, politicians, writers, pundits, journalists—reach the dizzying heights that only New York could offer, only to see them fade into obscurity in the blink of an eye. Meteoric flashes in the glittering sky of the metropolis, but so easily and blithely burned out and forgotten. "Whatever happened to…?" was a question he and his friends found themselves asking each other often.

While theatre was here and gone so quickly, something about the Fulton made it feel more permanent. It wasn't just the old posters on the wall. It wasn't even just the age of the building. As Sean stood in the old lobby, he could almost sense the past still swirling through the space, around him and filling the hall. The ghosts of years past seemed real. Alive. Not literal ghosts. Sean didn't really believe in them. At least he never had before recent events. He may have to revisit that. More to the point, he could *feel* the energy they had left behind. Theatres were mystical places to him. They always had been. The emotion, the energy, the commitment, the beauty that had lived within these walls lingered and each one added to the sense of depth he now experienced. He closed his eyes, feeling all of it sweep around and through him. Theatres were, at their best, magical. Sacred places, to those who truly listened.

That was one of the reasons Sean had never aspired to stardom. He'd become an actor because he loved it. The collaboration. The passion. The friendships. If he could find a way, and he had, to simply maintain a career and life, he would feel fulfilled. It had always been more about the shows and his colleagues than celebrity. He chuckled to himself. Very easy to convince yourself of that when celebrity was not on offer.

He thought of his friend Ken O'Carroll. He'd never have believed that Ken, one of his nearest and dearest, would ever fall victim to the lure of fame, but he had succumbed in no time at all. In fact, it had corrupted Ken almost beyond recognition, threatening every relationship that had ever meant anything to him.

At least, Ken had found his way back to himself. His fall from grace had been very public and very humiliating, but his friends, the fellow Grumbles, had welcomed him with somewhat open arms. Who could blame any of them if they had been somewhat cautious in their approach with Ken. But so far, so good. Hopefully, his relationship with his wife Anne, and their children could be salvaged, as well. That would surely be a bit more complicated, but Ken had so far displayed a willingness to do what must be done.

Sean literally shook his head to move on from his contemplation of the transitory nature of art and fame. Sheesh. Lighten up. A few weeks of adventuring with paranormal beings and he'd turned into Aristotle. Sometimes theatre was just entertainment, escape. And that was perfectly okay. If there was one thing he desperately needed right now, it was escape. From danger, complicated love, mystery, and evildoers wanting to harm him. In that regard, this show in Lancaster would be the perfect salve for his wounded psyche. Some happy tunes, children's faces alight with wonder, good friends in a beautiful theatre, and maybe an eggnog or two? Yes, please.

He tipped his Red Sox baseball cap to the antique show poster. "Thanks for the chat, Karl Bialesek. Nice to meet you. Let's do it again soon, yeah?"

A rattling of the doors behind him broke his reverie and he turned to find Brandy working her way along the row of doors trying to find her way in. He chuckled and noted it was three minutes past five. Brandy was late, but not *too* late. A specialty of hers. He motioned her along the bank of entries, miming an attempt to open each one for her as they proceeded. When they reached the last door, the one closest to the box office that Sean knew to be unlocked, he pretended it, too, was locked. He held it closed with one hand below the window and shook his head helplessly and mouthed, "No luck. You have to go around."

Brandy threw her hands in the air. "Around where? I have no idea how to get in!"

Sean laughed and pushed the door open for her. "Ah, quit yer whining! Get in here. I was just kidding. But maybe you deserve it. How can you be late? Aren't you actually staying *in* the building?"

"Yeah, yeah, real cute, you soulless ginger," Brandy retorted. "Not funny. And yes, I am staying in there, but it's like a rabbit warren. I tried to walk here through the building and got completely lost. So, I had to come around on the street. That's why I'm," she paused to check the time, "four whole minutes late."

"Fair enough," Sean said. "Just teasing. Deborah met me when I got here. You meet her?"

"No, sadly," Brandy answered. "I was met by *Drew*, the single nicest human being ever to cross my jaded city self."

Shaking his head, Sean laughed. "You must have hated that."

"You know it," Brandy answered with a grimace. "I hope this whole city isn't like that. I'll have trouble keeping my food down for the next two months."

"Chill out, Scrooge. You'll be fine. I'd actually like to meet him. Sounds great. Deborah was nice, too, by the way, so you may have to just accept some kindness."

"Yeah, well screw that," Brandy said, shaking her head. "Nothing can move this heart of granite I have."

"And you call me soulless," Sean noted.

"Yeah, I chose my compassionless state. You were born with yours."

Before Sean could respond, one of the doors to the auditorium opened and Deborah poked her head into the lobby.

Ah, there you are," she said, nodding to the two Grumbles. "Perfect. Let's get started, shall we? Marcello will meet us in his office."

She held the door open, and Sean and Brandy passed her on their way further into the theatre. She locked the door firmly behind her after they had entered and gave it a firm shake, making sure it held fast, before turning and leading them up a wide, elegant stairway and to an elevator behind a curtained doorway and pushing the button to take them to the highest floor.

Exiting the elevator, Deborah led them down a corridor of dark, rich wood. At the end of the hallway, they paused outside a massive door made of oak. Sturdy, solid. It gave the impression of a castle gate more than the office of an arts administrator. Heavy iron hinges bordered the portal, a heavy iron ring the only sign of a doorknob.

Deborah gave a gentle rap on the door and, without seeming to wait for an answer, lowered a shoulder into it and shoved it, slowly and with great effort, inward just enough for them to make their way inside.

The office was expansive. More old wood and intricately embroidered tapestries ringed the walls. Four columns, made of dark, aged wood, formed a square in the center of the room. They seemed more ornamental than functional, adding to the old-world feel. Those tapestries and columns were at odds with the clean, contemporary window treatments looking out over Prince Street. The glass in the windows frosted, opaque. The room was filled with books. Floor-to-ceiling shelves filled every bit of wall space between the tapestries. The books were substantial. Many leather-bound, giving the impression of being very important. The posters were from theatres around the world, with a seeming emphasis on works both here at the Fulton and in Italy, which Sean took to be Pettirosso's homeland. While Sean had worked at the theatre previously, he had never been directed by Pettirosso himself. In fact, he'd had little interaction with him at all. The Artistic Director had proven somewhat elusive, giving rise to a Willy Wonka-esque mystique around him. His incredible success in recent years both onstage and in reshaping the institution had done nothing to dispel that.

So it was with surprise that Sean found himself greeted by a diminutive figure, who seemed almost engulfed by the massive desk behind which he sat. Pettirosso rested his head in his hands, leaning forward, and the smile that greeted the group upon entering was as winsome as it seemed genuine. The twinkle in his eyes was obvious from across the office. Sean was surprised to find himself liking the man instantly. Not at all what he had expected.

Pettirosso was a compact figure, less than five and a half feet tall, but somehow elegant. As he rose and moved around the desk, his background as a dancer became obvious. His close-cropped dark hair and creamy white complexion seemed at odds with his Italianesque surname. He was wearing a knee-length Victorian Steampunk jacket, black with large brass buttons lining the full length. The impressive jacket was paired with simple black pants and chunky boots straight from London in the early nineties—the 1990s, because the ensemble could have leaned into the nineteenth century easily. On anyone else, Sean thought the outfit would have come across as inauthentic. Not on Pettirosso. The tail of the coat billowed behind him as he crossed the office floor, hands outstretched as if he were greeting his oldest friends. His deep brown eyes were alert with intelligence, and while every move he made was earnest, there was no mistaking that those eyes were soaking in everything about the new arrivals.

"Sean and Brandy! Welcome! May I call you that?" he asked, taking their hands in his one after the other. "I feel as if I know you already, but I in no way want to be presumptuous."

"Oh, wow. Not at all. It's my pleasure. We've met, but only in passing," Sean said, suddenly self-conscious of his faded jeans, Montauk t-shirt, and sneakers next to the sartorial splendor of their host.

Brandy was clearly feeling the same thing, especially given her well-worn outfit had clearly seen better days. "Yeah, Brandy is great. Nice knocker," she blurted, gesturing back toward the massive oaken door, before suddenly realizing what she had said. "Oh, jeez. That was a *Young Frankenstein* reference. Stupid. Totally inappropriate."

Pettirosso laughed easily. "Not at all, there's nothing Abby Normal about that, at all." The wink he shot toward Brandy was so sly she almost missed it.

Sean, never having seen Brandy so flummoxed, tried to rescue the moment, while giving her the gentlest of digs with his elbow. "So, Mr. Pettirosso, what should we call you?"

"Oh, my," Pettirosso replied, clapping Sean on the shoulder. "Mr. Pettirosso was my father, and he's been gone a very long time. Very. No standing on ceremony here. Call me Marcello. Actually, just call me Cello. Easier, and I think we're going to be friends."

"Cello," Brandy said, desperate to redeem herself. "You got it."

"It's always been one of my favorite instruments. Such a soulful tone." He clapped his hands. "All right, the introductions out of the way, let's have a little tour, shall we?" Pettirosso turned from them and headed toward the windows on the far wall facing Prince Street. "This is one of my favorite new things in my office." He tapped a button under the lip of his desk and the windows, as if a sheet of ice suddenly melted and slid away, became clear, offering an expansive view of the street below and Lancaster stretching out beyond.

"Whoa. Very cool," Brandy muttered, impressed.

Sean took a moment to scan the street below, the café across the street, and surrounding shops. "It's changed so much since I was here. So many new businesses. I remember it being much slower. Not less developed, because so many of these buildings are the same. Historic. But new businesses. Interesting."

"True, Sean," Pettirosso agreed. "I think, in general, people have discovered our little gem of a city, here. Close to New York, Philadelphia. In some ways a gateway to the East Coast. We have so much to offer. History, culture, cuisine, commerce. I suppose it was only a matter of time until we were dragged into the present."

"I think you're being modest," Sean said. "Looks like what you've done here with the Fulton has created a downtown anchor. A hub. Not many cities this size can boast something this impressive. And along with the theatre, restaurants, and hotels, retail...it all benefits from increased traffic. Literally. Look at the parking lot across the street. Packed. I don't remember that from before."

"Yup," Brandy agreed. "I actually just read somewhere that theatre in New York brings in more revenue than all of the professional sports teams. Combined. Blew my mind. Seems like you have something similar going on here."

"You are too kind, both of you," Pettirosso said. "It does my heart good to think our little home here could spill over into our community in some small positive way. Really, our only motivation was to restore this old lady's past glory. Perhaps burnish it a bit." He ran his hand down the wall next to the window and glanced around the room fondly. Turning, he indicated the four columns in the center of the room.

"Those may seem familiar, Sean," he said. "They were reclaimed from the massive original beam that used to be stage right. The renovation called for it to be removed, but I thought this was a fitting new home for them."

"Oh, wow," Sean replied, crossing to the nearest beam and running his hand along it. "I remember. Touching that as we entered backstage was always a little personal ritual. A bunch of us used to do it. Love this."

Deborah cleared her throat from behind them. "I'm so sorry, sir. You do have that meeting in a bit and there is so much still to show them."

"Right you are, Deborah," the diminutive Italian replied. "What would I do without you to keep me focused. So true! Let's get this tour moving. My meeting is less important than getting the two of you off and out to enjoy your night."

Deborah seemed pleased, if a bit nonplussed, by the compliments.

There's a story there, thought Sean. *None of my business, though.*

"Right then," Pettirosso pushed off from the window. "So much to see, so little time. This here"—he pointed toward a framed print of Basil Rathbone—"really is my favorite. Good old Basil performed here in his day, and we do like to remind everyone of our history, but that's not the best part." He pushed another unseen button under the edge of the desk and Rathbone's image morphed into a massive flat screen television. Another button pushed, and the screen sprang to life showing the stage, four floors below them. "Live view of the stage. I love it! Very helpful when I have work to do during the run of a show. And"—he tapped the screen on his smart watch and the view shifted—"I can keep an eye on any part of the theatre space with a simple tap. Backstage. Up top in the grid. Lighting rails. Or talk to stage management. I can even access the exterior security cameras, and view outside the theatre. And I can view on this little screen. Wherever I am. I love the twenty-first century."

"So, so cool," Brandy whispered, stepping closer to the screen but seeing no visible cables. "I need one of these for home."

"Strictly for public workspaces, of course," Pettirosso noted and chuckled. "Believe me when I say that is more than enough to keep me busy."

"Very impressive," Sean said. "I don't think I've ever seen anything quite like it."

"Not surprising," came a new voice from the far corner of the room. "Pretty sure that there is the first of its kind."

Sean and Brandy both jumped, startled by the newcomer. Turning, they found themselves a few short feet from Drew Brindig, who had been in the far corner of the room, unnoticed, all along.

"Sweet lemony Lincoln!" Brandy blurted. "Where the hell did you come from?"

"Gosh, I'm so sorry," Drew apologized. "I've been here the whole time. Just letting the formalities get done, first." He turned to Sean. "Drew Brindig. Pleased to meet you, Sean. I was on staff when you worked here before, but I don't think we had the pleasure of meeting."

Sean, hand to his chest as he waited for his pulse to slow to normal levels, nodded. "No, I don't think we did. Great to meet you." He laughed again. "Whew, I did *not* see you over there."

"I tend to blend into the background at times," Drew said. "Folks around here are used to it and sometimes I forget newcomers might not react quite as well."

Sean raised a hand to stop Drew from further apology. "Not at all, not at all. Clearly, we just didn't take in our surroundings. Must have been blinded by all the bells and whistles. Not your fault in the slightest."

"Too kind, I'm sure," Drew demurred. "Say, boss, since you have that meeting, why don't I go ahead and show our new friends around? I'd be happy to."

Pettirosso and Deborah shared a brief but pointed look. Brief, but not so brief that Sean didn't notice.

"Well, Drew, that's a very good idea and a nice gesture," Pettirosso replied. "I don't want the two of you"—he nodded to Sean and Brandy—"to think I'm trying to pass you off. The truth is that Drew probably knows even more about this old lady than even I do, and that's saying something."

"Gee, boss, thanks. Really glad to lend a hand."

"I know you are, Drew. Much appreciated. But, please, no need to call me boss. I think you've known me long enough to just call me Marcello. Actually, call me Cello. I think it's safe to say we're friends, by now, wouldn't you?"

"Whatever you say, Bo—sorry, Marcello."

Pettirosso turned to the two Grumbles. "Honestly, he'll be calling me 'boss' again in ten minutes. We've been going around on this for years. Please, enjoy the tour. Drew is an excellent raconteur. If you are planning on the Dispensing Company later, and I hope you are, please put your tab on our company account. Deborah, would you mind tagging along on the tour? Just in case any administrative issues arise?"

"Of course, sir," she said. "Delighted to."

"Thank you so much...Cello," Sean said, extending his hand as Deborah held the office door for them. "I'm looking forward to working with you finally."

"I share the sentiment, Sean. We have some good, honest work ahead of us." Pettirosso held Sean's hand just the briefest moment longer than expected, and the searching look he gave Sean was surprising.

The moment passed and Sean turned when Brandy called for him from the corridor beyond the office door. "Ginge! Step to it! These folks have places to be."

"Right, right," Sean said, hurrying to catch up. When he reached Brandy, he muttered, "Lemony Lincoln? What the hell was that?"

"What? Too soon?" Brandy quipped.

"Well, yes, too soon. But also, probably best not to invoke Lincoln's name in an old theatre. Or any theatre, really."

"Oh, good point. My bad."

The two dashed for the elevator, where Drew and Deborah had already pushed the button for the ground floor.

Pettirosso, when the office had cleared, turned to the screen and with a tap on his watch the view shifted to the first floor and the elevator doors.

Just under an hour later, the little tour group found themselves back at the stage door, which sat in a side street near the back of the theatre. Deborah held the door for them, while Drew held back within the doorway and gave Sean and Brandy a broad, open smile.

"Well, I feel like I need to thank the two of *you*," he said. "I haven't given one of these tours in a while. Just so nice to remind myself of all the wonderful new things here. And all the meaningful old things, too, of course,"

"Not at all. We definitely owe you for that," Sean replied. "Amazing stuff. Such a history and now with all of the modern improvements? Safe to say there's no place quite like it anywhere else."

Brandy, still shaking her head at what she had seen, agreed. "Not even close. I mean...that rehearsal room is as good or better than anything I've seen in New York. I can't wait to get to work in there. And that LED light wall? Come on!"

Deborah chuckled. "I agree with Drew. Sometimes, when you spend all day in the midst of something, you forget just how wonderful it is. This was nice for me, too."

Sean considered Deborah and Drew for a moment. "They're lucky to have you two. And we're lucky to work with you. You made our night."

"I second that," Brandy said. "Hey, just curious. How long have you both been here? You seem like part of the place, at this point."

"Oh, goodness," Deborah answered. "I've been here, off and on, since the sixties. I've always found an excuse to be here, even when there wasn't really a job here for me. Stuck around so much, they finally realized they couldn't do without me."

"And, well, for me"—Drew seemed nonplussed at the question—"I've been around a long time, but I've been around more since all the improvements happened. More work to do."

"Well, Drew," Sean said. "You don't seem nearly old enough for that to be true. Must be all your clean living. Hey, we're heading over to Dipco for a quick bite if either of you is up for it?"

"Aren't you sweet to ask." Deborah was clearly pleased at the invitation. "Unfortunately, I still have some work to finish up and a day-end recap meeting with Mr. Pettirosso. I do hope you'll invite me next time?"

"Of course we will. I'm going to need all the female time I can get, I have a feeling," Brandy said. "Drew?"

"Gosh, that's so nice. I—I don't think I can." He shot a slightly panicked glance toward Deborah.

"Oh, that's right," she jumped in. "I'm sorry, but we still have a few things for Drew to finish up before he knocks off for the night."

"Another time then," Sean assured them. "And, again, thanks so much. Whatever they pay you two, it isn't enough. I can't wait to start tomorrow, after that tour."

Sean and Brandy waved goodnight to the two and as the door closed behind them, Brandy looked expectantly at Sean.

"Lead on MacDuff," she said. "I have no idea where this Dipco is."

"Man, you are really pushing your luck today, aren't you?" Sean asked.

"What? I have absolutely no idea what you are talking about. I've been on my best behavior all day."

Sean grabbed Brandy's shoulders and forced her to look at him. "First, the crack about Lincoln in the theatre, and now you quote the Scottish play less than ten seconds after we step out of a theatre? And not just any theatre, one of the most haunted theatres. Anywhere."

"Oh. Ha! Yeah, didn't even cross my mind," Brandy answered. "My bad. Again. But wait, haunted? You never told me anything about that. Haunted how?"

Sean shook his head in disbelief. "Did you not read up at all on where we'll be working?"

"Didn't think I had to. Just another theatre, I thought. So, what gives?"

Sean started across the street. "Yeah, let's get away from here first. And I could use a beer for this conversation."

"Okay," Brandy said, hustling her shorter legs to keep up. "I still don't know where we're going."

Sean pointed across the street. At the rear of the parking lot directly opposite lay a large brick building, clearly Victorian in origin. Bright, golden light streamed from its windows.

"Not far," Sean said.

⁂

The two Grumbles climbed the steps to the Dispensing Company. They were oddly placed, straddling a corner of the Victorian building, bisected by a column at the top. It all came flooding back to Sean. He always felt a bit precarious entering the restaurant, as if he'd had one beer too many before he'd even entered. Brandy held the door for Sean and the two stopped just inside to take in the atmosphere.

Although it had only been a restaurant since the 1970s, the building was Victorian, and the establishment leaned into that pedigree. Dark wood and yellow lighting gave the impression of stepping back in time. Two rows of tables stretched the length of the dining room, but it was the massive oaken bar that dominated the scene. It ran almost the length of the building on the left. Dark and tall, the bar top itself was marble with a wooden, scrollwork edge around it. Tall, lattice-backed barstools ran the length, and three bartenders, all wearing long aprons, patrolled the bar, chatting with a patron here, topping up a glass there, and making sure that every customer felt pampered.

"Jeez," Brandy said, whistling. "Nice joint. More Victoriana. This entire town makes me feel like I stumbled into a Dickens novel. And I don't mean that in a bad way."

Sean nodded. "Yup. It's a unique place. Just wait until we're out late at night sometime. You'll definitely feel like you stepped back in time. Bar okay?"

"Do you need to ask? When was the last time you saw me at a table?"

"Just checking. You know, in case you had a Victorian lady urge, or something."

"Bite me, Ginge," Brandy growled, as she stomped toward the bar.

As they crossed the room, a voice called out. "Sean? Sean Curley, is that you?"

Sean stopped and scanned the room. He noticed a table of three tucked into the back corner where one of the occupants facing him was waving.

"Hey, just a sec. I know these folks."

"Of course, you do," Brandy muttered, following Sean toward the back.

They arrived tableside and a mountain of a man stood to welcome them, thrusting out a beefy hand for a shake, then forgoing it to wrap Sean in a suffocating embrace, especially since Sean's face reached only to the man's shoulder.

"Sean Curley! I heard you were going to be here. How long has it been, pal? Don't answer. The only correct answer is too long." The man mountain turned to Brandy. "And who might you be? You must be a castmate because this joker could never rate a girl like you. Name's Dante. Dante Gugliomo. Like the inferno. I'm French. Kidding. Italian. Well, Italian descent. You get the picture."

With his face pressed into Dante's pectoral muscle, Sean managed a muffled, "Brandy Johns, meet Dante." He managed to pry his face away from the pecs, caught a breath, and continued. "Dante and I have done —what?—four shows together here? Five? I've lost count. He's a Fulton favorite. You're still living in Chicago, though, right?"

"I am, indeed. Probably a lifer, at this point. Pleasure to meet you, Brandy. Please excuse my enthusiasm. Excited to see my buddy."

"Not at all," Brandy answered. "Pleasure is mine." She turned to Sean. "I like him. I always respond to flattery."

The other two occupants of the table rose and extended hands in greeting. The first, a sandy haired man with hazel eyes that flashed blue when the light caught them just right, laugh lines that promised a good time would be had, and a head of matinee-idol hair swept back as if he'd just climbed off of his yacht, shook Sean's hand before turning to Brandy. "Bobby Smalls. Nice to meet you, ma'am. And you! So good to see you, Sean. Glad we get to do this together."

"Bobby, great to see you. I like our little gang. This is going to be a heckuva show," Sean said, shaking the proffered hand.

"I like this one, too!" Brandy declared. "*Ma'am!* Much nicer than what I normally get called. Looking forward to working with you, Bob."

The final person at the table stepped around. She was tall, graceful, with a fall of light chestnut hair that reached halfway down her back. Her bright blue eyes spoke of a keen intelligence. Her movements were precise, controlled. Everything about her announced her as a stage manager. "Hi, Sean. Welcome back. Brandy? So nice to meet you. Rebecca Chapel. I'll be your stage manager for the show. Any of these jokers give you a hard time, you come to me." She gave a light laugh, but the steel in her eyes was unmistakable. This was not someone to be trifled with.

"Wow," Sean said. "So great to see you all. Now it's starting to feel real."

"Very real. Just wait until you see the amount of music you have to learn," Dante clapped a massive hand onto Sean's back.

"Oh, yes," Rebecca was suddenly all business. "There has been some reassigning of songs. Nothing to worry about. We can clear it all up tomorrow morning."

"Okay," Sean sounded just a tad nervous. "I'll mentally prepare myself. Looks like you all are just finishing up, so I won't keep you. We're gonna park at the bar and grab some wings, if you don't mind."

"Go to it," Bobby said. "I think Dante is probably about done after his drive in today."

"I am that," the big man agreed. "Not as young as I used to be. Enjoy those wings. Ten in the morning will get here soon enough. Great to see you, Sean."

"It really is good to have you back, Sean. Get some rest. You at Dremmel this time? I think I heard that." Rebecca lightly placed her hand on Sean's arm. A movement which did not go unnoticed by Brandy.

"I am," Sean said. "Nice apartment. Number six."

"Ooh, yes. Very nice," Rebecca agreed. "Enjoy the peace and quiet tonight. I think you're the only one up there until tomorrow."

"Good to know. You have a good night. I hear some wings calling our names."

Sean and Brandy ambled over to the bar, while the others reseated themselves as they settled their tab.

Brandy turned to Sean with a grin. "So, that Rebecca seems nice. Very...friendly."

Sean shook his head. "Nope. Don't even go there. Good friend. Excellent stage manager. End of story."

"Whatever you say," Brandy replied, eyeing the menu. "So—what's good?"

Sean paused just a fraction to make sure the subject had changed. "Well, pretty much everything. But for your first visit, I think wings are in order. Bourbon glazed is what I always do."

One of the bartenders strolled over. "What can I get you?" she asked. "Oh, hey! Sean, right? Welcome back."

"Thanks," Sean replied. "Surprised you remember me. It's been a while. Kat, right?"

"Yes, indeed. So...?"

"Right! Sorry. Can I do a lager?"

"No worry! All good. Lager it is. And for you?" Kat asked, turning to Brandy.

"Any local IPA you have would be great."

"Absolutely. Be right back."

Brandy turned an incredulous look on Sean. "A *lager*? Just—a lager? You, the master of craft beer, just ordered an unspecified lager?"

"Okay, settle down, cupcake. We're in Pennsylvania now. Yuengling is king. If you order a lager here, they know that's what you mean."

"Really? Huh. Learn something new every day." Brandy shook her head.

"Just a personal tradition. My first beer when I get to town is a Yuengling. Just as a nod to local history."

At that point, Kat returned. Her tight blond curls bouncing with each step.

"Okey dokey, then. One lager and one Glow from Cartel Brewing.

They're just down the street. About as local as you can get. Any food tonight?"

"Please," Sean said. "I'll do a half dozen bourbon glazed wings."

"Smart man," Kat answered. "My personal favorite."

"Well, I guess I have to do the same then," Brandy announced. "Always trust the bartender's recommendation."

"And a smart woman." Kat laughed, and it was a light, open, joyous sound. "I like smart customers."

"I'm so sorry," Sean interrupted. "Bad manners. Kat this is Brandy. She's in the show with me. Brandy, meet Kat, one of my favorite bartenders on the planet."

"You silver-tongued devil," Kat raised an eyebrow toward Sean. "It's all coming back to me, now. I love it. Don't stop. Let me get these in for you. Need anything, just shout." She headed toward the kitchen, holding their order over her head as she walked away.

"I like her," Brandy announced. "Spunky. Lots of spunky people here." She took a sip of her beer. "Holy...that is some amazing beer. I like her even more now. She knows beer. This place is just down the street?"

"It is," Sean said. "We'll go. Don't worry."

"Lancaster is growing on me," Brandy said, considering her beer mug before taking another swig of the beer.

"Yeah, it does that." Sean paused, gave a quick look to Brandy, before deciding to continue. "I have to say, I'm really looking forward to tomorrow. After everything we've been through, and I know we haven't talked much about it today, but I just want to sing...to sing. Does that make any sense?"

Brandy looked at him in the massive mirror behind the bar. "It does. I get it. It'll be nice to not feel like the fate of the world hangs on every note."

"Exactly right," Sean agreed. "Singing, music. Has always been an escape for me. Something that came naturally and brought—not peace so much as, calm? I don't know how to explain it. And then, over the years, it became my job. It took on new weight. Sing or starve. Or find a new job. Then when the Peripherals came onto the scene...it became even more heavy. I wasn't just taking care of myself, I had to use my voice to save you. All of us."

"I know, Sean," Brandy said. "I'm sorry so much of it fell to you. We tried to help. As best we could. But in the end, it came down to you more than once. I wish we could have lightened that load for you."

"No, no, no," Sean protested. "I don't mean that, even. I mean, yes, it was a lot, but I was glad I *could* do something. I'm sorry you missed it, but when I got up and sang with Trout in that bar in North Carolina, it just felt—so different. It was spontaneous, and goofy, and real, and…it felt good. It reminded me of why I fell in love with singing in the first place. And now I'm hoping that will carry over into tomorrow. I think it will. It felt like some sort of reset button got pushed."

"I hope you can hold onto that. I really do. I think I get it. In my own way."

"I have a feeling you do." Sean stared back at her in the mirror. "I don't want my voice to become about violence. I always saw music as a healing thing. A bridge between people. I want to feel that again."

"Then you will, Sean. You will."

Sean turned and raised his glass in a silent toast and Brandy returned the gesture.

An hour later, Sean and Brandy settled their tab and headed toward the exit contentedly.

"Well, jeez o flip, Ginge," Brandy patted her belly. "Those were some of the best wings I've ever had."

Emerging into the night air, they perched at the top of the awkward stairs. It had rained while they were inside and a light, drifting fog had settled over the city.

"There's a reason we all come here. Okay, I'm over this way." He gestured right through an alley. "Up Orange, and you, oh spoiled one, are across the street, so see you in the morning?"

"You will," Brandy agreed. "Get up early and warm up. They'll be having you hit some very un-masculine notes in the morning, I bet."

"Yeah, yeah," Sean said. "I just want to crawl into bed, right now."

"Copy that. Sleep well, soulless ginger." Brandy gave him a playful punch on the arm as she turned to the left and headed across the parking lot toward the theatre.

"'Night, Brandy," Sean said, his arm raised in farewell as he wandered down the alley.

As he headed toward Orange Street, the cobbled alleyway and the gas lamps fluttering in the fog made him feel as if he'd slipped backward in time and with each step headed further into Lancaster's Victorian past.

CHAPTER 5

Sean wandered up Orange Street, in no particular hurry. He was looking forward to testing out the massive bed in the apartment, but beyond that, he was more than happy to stroll anonymously through the city. For the first time in weeks, he felt as if he could breathe easy. He missed Breena, more than he was willing to admit to even himself, but he'd come to accept that, whatever happened next, he would have little influence over the outcome. Her otherworldly family, the Tuatha De Danann, had decided that she was to be married to another influential family in their world. As a pedestrian, and mistrusted, human, he was seen as inconsequential and far below the station her mate should occupy. Not much he could do about that.

He dug into his jacket pocket. All his talk of music with Brandy had put him in the mood for a walk with accompaniment. He tucked earbuds into his ears. They never fit quite right. He supposed he was one of the few whose ears weren't suited to the shape. Normally, he used them only at home to make sure he wouldn't lose them, but this moody, foggy, daguerreotype night seemed to call for a soundtrack.

He paused to pull up some music on his phone, making sure he connected to his earbuds. If he hadn't stopped just there, at the mouth of one of the many brick alleys that dotted the rabbit-warren downtown area, he likely wouldn't have heard the muffled steps. The raised voices and the solitary cry of pain.

Peering into the gloom of the alley, he couldn't see a thing. He took a step closer. Still nothing, but something had disturbed the low-lying fog, and he saw it eddy and swirl. Another muffled cry was all it took to draw him further.

Someone, or something, was in distress down there. So much for his peaceful trip home, but he knew he couldn't just pass this by. It just wasn't in is nature to turn his back on a situation like this. Maybe it was nothing. But maybe not. And something deep inside him was telling him it was something.

"Hello?" he called quietly, very aware of the apartments surrounding him along the row houses lining the narrow lane.

Nothing.

"Hello? Is there someone there? Is everything okay?"

There it was again. A quiet, almost inaudible, voice. The cry was fading. It had almost become more of a whimper, and Sean had a sense that time was of the essence.

"Hang on, there," he called, louder this time. "I'm headed your way."

He walked slowly into the fog. The golden light from the streetlights on Orange Street was swallowed surprisingly fast and he found himself reaching out to run his hand along the rough brick of the building to his right to keep his bearing.

Halfway down the alley, he spotted a light. Not the rich hue of the gas lamps, but the cold, white glare of an LED light mounted above one of the garage openings. As he approached, he spotted three figures huddled around something propped up against the wall.

"Hey," he called again, "Is everything okay there? Someone sounds in trouble—" He stopped suddenly as one of the three figures turned to him.

The face that turned toward him was flushed and angry. A young man, dressed entirely in black, with a worn denim jacket tied around his waist. His eyes took a moment to focus. He was obviously in the throes of some sort of chemical influence. Something glinted in his right hand as he noted Sean's presence and turned fully to face him. His two companions, similarly dressed and equally sluggish and feral in their altered states, followed suit and Sean found himself the object of their ire.

"Get out of here, buddy, unless you want to be next," the first figure growled. His voice was slurred and gravelly. It matched his movements, but there was a sense of menace that nearly overwhelmed Sean, even though they remained ten yards apart, at least.

As they turned, Sean saw that the object they had pinned against the wall was another man, slumped to the ground and with his arms covering his head as if warding off blows, and, judging by the crowbar he spotted in one of the other figures, Sean thought that must be exactly what was happening.

"Sorry, gentlemen, and I use that term very loosely, I can't do that." He placed his backpack gently next to the wall and made sure he removed his earbuds. Not going to lose those. Not for the likes of these thugs.

"I'd say it's time we even these odds a little bit, yeah?" He stepped purposefully toward the group. "Why don't you let that fella there up and we can all go our separate ways with no harm done."

"Not gonna happen, buddy," the first figure answered. The object in his hand flashed again and was shown to be a very nasty looking blade, a good twelve inches long. "We very much plan on some harm, and you barging in where you don't belong just means we'll double our haul tonight. So, thanks for that, loser."

"Won't happen. And I'm not your buddy," Sean said calmly. He began to hum quietly to himself, and felt his power begin to rumble deep within him. He'd never tried to use it without his friends nearby, He had no idea what might happen, but he knew doing nothing was not an option.

The three figures began to approach, and upon hearing Sean's note, broke into raucous laughter. "You are shitting me," the leader scoffed. "Are you going to sing us to death? Can you believe this?"

He turned to his friends, who had moved to flank him but paused when he saw a look of confusion, and then fear, cross their faces. He turned back to Sean and froze. Sean had begun to glow a dim golden hue. At first. But as the would-be muggers watched, the glow intensified, and Sean's eyes flashed brighter than the rest of him as his volume rose. The alleyway was flooded with light. In moments, the attackers were shielding their eyes and backing away.

The one with the crowbar dropped his weapon and turned tail, running in the opposite direction as fast as he could. The second culprit began to shout a nonsensical stream of not-quite-words.

"Wha—da—nah," he stammered, and then he, too, was moving away, first backing up to keep an eye on Sean, and then finally turning to follow his accomplice into the far reaches of the lane and away from the brilliant light.

And then there was one. The last assailant tried to put on a brave face. Credit where it was due, he managed to stand his ground and form complete words, but that wasn't saying much.

Still clutching his knife, he spat at Sean. "Whatever, dude. So, what, you have what a mag light? Something like that? I'm not scared of some glowing crap. I'll take you down, and then come back to finish this loser off."

He managed to lift one foot off the ground in an apparent attempt to reach Sean, but a flick of Sean's wrist sent his knife in one direction, where it clattered harmlessly to the ground, and him in another. Another slight flick of his wrist, and the mugger found himself hovering three feet off the ground, encased in a bubble of brilliant light.

"Okay, okay, okay," he shouted. "I give. Put me down, you freak. What the hell are you?"

Sean closed his mouth and the thug fell abruptly to his knees. Hard. He started to scramble away on all fours, before finding his feet and sprinting in the direction his friends had taken.

Wow, thought Sean, *that was a lot easier than I thought it would be. Never did that on my own before.* He tried to ignore the niggling feeling that maybe that wasn't a good thing.

He crossed to the figure still huddled against the wall, offering a hand to help him up. Slowly, the young man raised his face to finally take a good look at his rescuer. He was thin, with shaggy brown hair, mutton chops nearly the length of his jawline, and deep brown eyes. It took a second glance from Sean to confirm that they weren't actually black. When he finally stood, he was taller than Sean would have expected. Lanky. His worn brown pants and deep green woven shirt were covered in dirt from his time underfoot. He bent to retrieve a very faded blue corduroy jacket, which he brushed off before folding it under one arm.

"Thank you," he said quietly. "I wasn't exactly sure how I was going to get out of that one. They've been bothering me for years, but never took it this far. I'm lucky you happened by." He paused to step back and take a good look at Sean. "What exactly happened? I had my face buried, but even so I saw the bright flash. Was that you? It must have been to move them off like that."

"Just an old parlor trick I've picked up. Nothing all that impressive," Sean replied.

"Coulda fooled me. I'm Duncan. Duncan Wulliver. Thanks again. I've never seen you around here before."

Something in his tone told Sean that his story about a parlor trick was not entirely believed, but Duncan, clearly grateful, chose to let Sean hold onto whatever he was hiding.

"Yeah," Sean answered quickly, moving the conversation along. "I just got into town. Sean Curley. Doing a show down at the Fulton. Say, if you know those jerks, are you going to be okay? Will they be back after you?"

"Probably," Duncan admitted. "But not tonight. Your *parlor trick* spooked them pretty good."

Duncan reached and pulled his sleeves down past his wrists, and Sean wasn't sure, but suspected he may be hiding something. Had he been hurt worse than he let on? Or something more innocent? Tattoos? Scars? He couldn't be certain.

"If you're sure. I mean, I'm just up Orange here. Happy to make sure you get to wherever you're going."

"That's generous of you, but I promise you—"

Duncan's next words were drowned out by an enormous roar and a flood of light filling the entire alleyway from top to bottom.

"Looks like your buddies are back, after all—" Sean began.

His voice trailed off as the light extinguished itself to reveal a massive Harley-Davidson, taking up nearly the entire access to the street. Astride the bike sat a wiry, lithe figure dressed entirely in black leather. Jacket, pants, boots, gloves. Even the helmet was black with a full, tinted visor.

A muffled voice reached them from within that helmet. "Thought I saw something unusual going on back here. Seemed worth checking out it. Everything good?"

Duncan visibly relaxed at the sound of the voice. In fact, he nearly laughed with relief when he responded. "Yeah, all good. Thanks to my new friend, Sean, here."

"Yeah, I've already had the pleasure," the rider said. The helmet came off and a shower of tight, blond shoulder-length ringlets sprang forth, eager to escape the confines. A pair of bright blue eyes turned to the pair of men.

"Hiya, Kat," Duncan said. "You just missed all the fun."

With the arrival of Kat, Duncan seemed to relax even more and agreed to let the two of them walk him to his apartment over on Shippen Street, not too far past where Sean needed to go. Kat dropped her bike off in front of Sean's place, Dremmel House, and walked with them the rest of the way. They turned left on Shippen and strolled toward Walnut Street.

"I got the feeling," Sean said, "that there was a bit of history between all of you back there?"

"Well, yeah, I guess you could say that," Duncan replied. He seemed even younger in the brighter lights of the main streets, maybe even still in his teens. "My family has been here for a long time. Like, a really long time. They came over from Scotland, oh I don't know exactly, sometime in the nineteenth century. Problem is, those other families have been here a long time, too."

"And they are?" Sean prompted.

"Those three specifically were Michael Verdun, Pierre Burgot, and Peter Stubbe. Man, I hate to even say their names. For whatever reason, their families and mine have always had a beef. Something just raises the hackles whenever any of us are near each other. No clue where it started or why, but they picked right up where the generation before them left off. They've been harassing me since grade school."

"That seemed like more than schoolboy bullying to me, not to minimize bullying, but they looked like they were out for blood," Sean said.

"Wait, what?" Kat interrupted. "What were they up to now?"

Sean shot a look to Duncan who seemed disinclined to answer at that moment, so he responded instead. "Well, they had Duncan here down on the ground and surrounded. I saw a crowbar and definitely saw a knife. Not schoolboy stuff, if you ask me."

"Duncan," Kat said, concerned. "How long has it been like this? They were always annoying, but nothing more than that. This is much more serious, dude."

"Yeah, I know," Duncan said quietly. "The last few months they've picked it up a notch. Maybe two. But this was by far the worst it's been."

Kat shook her head. "The whole city feels like it's been on edge lately. I mean, the theatre expansion has been great for downtown—Dipco has seen business boom since it came online, but...the streets seem unsafe at night. And tensions are high even during the daylight hours. Never felt like this to me before."

"Me, either," Duncan agreed. "Although, what happened back there is a new level. Even between our families."

"Well," Sean said, "coming from New York, I didn't notice a thing, but I only just got here. I'm really sorry to hear that. I always think of Lancaster as sleepy and quaint. Charming."

"And it is," Kat answered. "Usually."

"This is me," Duncan said, pointing to a row house on their left. "I have an apartment up top in the back. Thanks for the walk. I'll be okay." In a response to a pointed look from Kat, "Really. I'm fine."

"If you say so," she said. "Just don't take any long walks alone at night for a while, yeah?"

"I won't. Promise. Hey!" Duncan turned quickly to Sean. "Can you hang on a sec? I want to grab something for you."

"Duncan, there's no need for that," Sean said. "I'm just glad I was in the right place."

"No, really," Duncan insisted. "It's just a little something."

Without waiting for an answer, Duncan ran up the front steps and into the building.

"Hey, if it makes him feel better, let him do it," Kat said. "He's a good kid, but he spends a lot of his time alone. Probably happy to have a new friend."

"Man, that whole thing was too close for comfort," Sean replied. "If I hadn't been walking past—"

"But you were," Kat said, placing a hand on Sean's arm. "You were. And he's okay. Let's celebrate the small victories when we can."

"You're right," Sean agreed. "Noted."

Duncan reappeared at the door and dashed back down the stairs, slightly out of breath. He was holding what looked to be a scarf, but not like any scarf Sean had seen before. It was a deep brown, almost black, and seemed to be woven with a rich, dense fabric. It was clearly hand-made, and the usually warm-blooded Sean immediately guessed it would make him uncomfortably warm. Th gesture behind it, though, was earnest and kind.

"It probably seems silly, to you," Duncan seemed apologetic handing it over to Sean. "My family have been craftspeople as long as any of us can remember. Weavers, saddlers, girdlers. This is a special design from one of us—a long time ago. Guaranteed to keep you warm. Or cool, depending on the situation. It would mean a lot if you accept it. Just a token. Wullivers around the world will know you're a friend if you have this on."

"Thanks," Sean said. "It's beautiful. It's totally unnecessary, but I'm touched. Really."

Duncan, well-pleased by Sean's reaction, looked at his feet before scanning the street, a gentle grin on his face.

"Looks like the coast is clear," he said. "I'm going to take myself upstairs, check for bruises, maybe catch up on *Shetland*. Great show."

"You give me a call if you need anything, yeah?" Kat called as Duncan headed inside.

Duncan gave a half turn and shot her another grin and gave her a thumbs up before he disappeared.

———

Sean and Kat turned away from the row house and began the stroll back up Shippen Street toward Orange and Dremmel House where Sean was staying.

"This is the most I think we've ever actually spoken," Kat observed, taking a peek in the windows of The Corner, a bar at the intersection of Shippen and Chestnut streets. She saw a familiar face and gave a nod. "I remember when this was Molly's. I loved that place. Need to give this new spot a chance."

"Oh, Molly's. I had some great nights in there. Probably too many," Sean said with a chuckle. "And, yeah, this is definitely the most we've spoken. I'm usually on one side of the bar and you're on the other."

"This is better," Kat replied. "No manager looking over my shoulder. No tab waiting for you at the end."

"Yup," Sean agreed. "Definitely better. I'm here for the next seven weeks. Let's do this again? I mean, not the saving a kid from getting beaten, we can leave that out. Just the talking like normal people."

"That sounds good," Kat answered. Then she suddenly changed gears, nodding at Duncan's scarf that Sean had draped around his neck. "That looks good on you, actually. His family really is known for their crafts. Wullivers have been around a long time. Used to have a store out on Lincoln Highway."

"Used to?"

"Yeah," Kat said, pausing to consider. "Haven't thought about it in a while. Duncan's parents were in an accident years ago. Shop went away not long after. The parents survived but haven't been seen much since. I think the grandparents are still around, too. Don't see much of them, either. They must really be up there by now."

"Sounds like Duncan's pretty much on his own then," Sean said. "Maybe we can include him in one of our normal-people nights out?"

"I bet he'd like that. Like I said, a good kid," Kat answered. "This is you, yeah?" She lifted her chin toward the darkened Dremmel House as they approached it.

"It is, indeed," Sean answered. "A little weird being here with so many empty apartments. I'll be glad when some more folks move in tomorrow."

Kat stood next to her motorcycle and slipped her helmet onto her arm. She looked up at the darkened windows, a contemplative look crept over her face.

"Not to freak you out, but this place always gave off bad vibes to me. I ride past every day. Shivers down the spine every time. I get feelings about things, sometimes. This is weird, though. My grandparents lived here way back when. Before my time. You'd think this place would give me good feelings. But no."

"Well, it's already been a bit creepy, but I'm sure it's just being here alone that had me on edge," Sean said.

"Mhm." Kat turned to Sean. "You know what, I'm giving you my number, just in case it gets dicey in there. No funny ideas, mister. Just looking out for a friend. Call if you feel like it. Anytime. I'm a night owl, so no hour is off-limits."

"Thanks," Sean replied. "And trust me. I rarely get funny ideas. Just ask my acting coach."

With a shared chuckle, they exchanged numbers and Kat climbed aboard the Harley and started it with a rumble that chased the silence away from the block.

Sean watched her pull away from the curb and her bike shook the neighbors' windows as she sped off home.

A man wandered past on the sidewalk, barely veering aside at the last moment as he passed Sean. Sean, startled, jumped back and shot the retreating figure a dirty look. He bit back a flippant remark. He'd had enough confrontation for one night. He did make a mental note of the man's bright red woolen knit cap in case he saw him again. Lancaster was a small city.

He took a deep breath before turning to face the entrance to Dremmel. He pulled his new scarf tighter around him and was surprised to find that his feet were sluggish heading up the stairs, as if they were getting a message from his subconscious that he wasn't privy to. The black upper floor windows seemed to stare balefully down on him, their emptiness easily mistaken for malevolence in his current mood.

He began to hum some Jimmy Buffett to himself, in a vain attempt to take this odd edge off of his nerves. He opened the front door, and it swung wide like the maw of an angry spirit and swallowed him as he reluctantly entered.

***

He let the door swing shut behind him and stood in the vestibule, taking in the darkened and quiet house. It was too big to be this silent. There was one bulb burning faintly in the entranceway and another on the stair leading to his apartment that flickered and sputtered intermittently. Despite the stillness, the feeling that he was being watched returned to Sean, and he moved quickly up the stairs and his apartment door at the top.

At one point, he was sure he heard something following him as he climbed. He paused and the sound stopped. He turned, but saw nothing, so he resumed climbing through the slow strobing effect of the sputtering lightbulb. As soon as he moved, the sound returned. He stopped quickly again. So did the sound. A thought struck him, and he took one step up.

Stopped. Another step. Stopped. The sound mimicked his motion. He flexed his knee and, sure enough, the sounds crackled forth. He shook his head at both his advancing age and his advancing paranoia. His knees sounded like a bowl of breakfast cereal, and he'd literally spooked himself.

Shaking his head, he took the remaining stairs two at a time, mostly to prove to himself that he still could. Letting himself into his apartment, he felt some relief in closing the door behind him. Leaving the rest of the building to itself for the rest of the night and claiming the apartment as his own. At least for the next month and a half. Leaning on the door from the safety of his living room, he never saw the bulb on the stairs flicker out and remain off. Nor did he see that darker shadow, hidden amidst the normal household shadows. Didn't notice it follow him up the stairs. Didn't notice the fedora on its head. And he certainly didn't see it slide smoothly under the door to his apartment. Apartment Six.

He slipped his shoes off without untying them and flopped himself down on the chaise lounge. He was weary. Not just tired, but actually weary. He was so tired, he didn't notice the window by the desk was open again, despite his closing it when he left earlier. So tired that it didn't occur to him that the lamp he had left on was darkened.

It had been a day of extremes. The drive down, exploring the new, yet old, theatre space, quality time with Brandy while also reconnecting with some old friends. All of those seemed relatively normal. Normal. Something he was craving. But normal had flown far away as soon as he made the decision to intervene with Duncan.

It wasn't just the physical violence that had sent the night careening into a strange and dangerous place. He hadn't felt much threat from Duncan's attackers. That alone was new and unusual. The old Sean avoided confrontation. Had no confidence when it came to defending himself, let alone standing up for others. And yet, he had waded into the confrontation with no hesitation whatsoever. And the power he'd called had been almost instantaneous. It bothered him that he fell so easily into that place—violence, or the threat of it. It would have taken no effort for him to unleash his voice, his power, on the assailants. And he'd given them no thought at all. It was clear to him from the first moment that Duncan was the victim. He'd somehow just *knew* where the evil flowed.

Even more than this new confidence and sensitivity, something deeper felt off, now in hindsight. There had been more to the assault than simple long-simmering antagonism. Something deeper was at play between those families. Along with the other heightened senses he was experiencing, Sean felt—knew—that all was not as it seemed.

Normal. He was beginning to fear it was a thing in his past.

Spread out on the lounge, he suddenly felt ridiculous. Splayed dramatically across the upholstery, like a silent movie damsel in distress. And also, that pinprick of dread that told him he was being watched made itself felt again. More paranoia. Or was it? He had just been taking note of all the new senses he was experiencing. It might be wise to listen to these inner voices. With that thought, he felt exposed. Vulnerable.

He rose and settled into a blue easy chair in the far corner of the room. He remembered the advice of the master spy, Thufir Hawat, from one of his favorite books, Frank Herbert's *Dune*—"Never sit with your back to the door." So he sat facing the door.

He turned the television on and starting flipping through what was available. He was surprised—the theatre had maintained a cable package—but was grateful. He couldn't settle on one thing to watch. His mind was restless. Ping-ponging from one subject to another. If *Doctor Who* couldn't hold his attention, nothing could, so after a few minutes, he turned the TV off and went into the bedroom, climbing onto the ridiculously tall bed. He snuggled down into the comforter and turned on his Kindle. Maybe reading would settle his nerves. Quiet his frantic mind.

Plugging his phone into the charger by the bed, he brought up a music app and settled on a John Gorka album. Acoustic. Gentle, but not cloying. Hopeful, but honest. Perfect for this moment. He turned off the bedside lamp. He would read until sleep pulled him down into the so-thick mattress.

Back to the Kindle, he remembered that he had been reading Chris

Sorensen's *Bee Tornado*. That was a tad tense for the night, so he pulled up *Dune*. He hadn't read it in ages. Maybe another world, another galaxy, could help him escape. He'd already taken one piece of advice from Frank Herbert. Maybe there would be more to mine.

Hours later, Sean awoke suddenly. He'd fallen asleep with the Kindle open, and it sat on his chest, the screen darkened. He ran his hand across his eyes, trying to rub some of the blur away. He had been deep in his subconscious. Something must have startled him awake. A lifelong light sleeper, Sean knew that the slightest noise would pull him awake. Shaking the cobwebs away, he sat halfway up in the bed and peered around the room. Nothing jumped out at him—literally or figuratively—and he allowed himself to relax slightly. Maybe it was simply being in a new bedroom.

Then it hit him. A scent. A deep, musky cologne. Sean didn't wear cologne, so there was no way it came from him. His arms broke out in gooseflesh. Was someone in the apartment with him?

He swung his legs over the bed and hopped down. Something felt off. Not just the scent that still floated through the space. Something... else. More. He walked into the living room and finally noted the open window. He paused and considered it. He was sure he had closed it earlier. Right? He closed it again and made sure the lock was latched. Then he double-checked.

He moved to the front door. The deadbolt, chain, and knob lock were all secure. If someone had come through there, they had locked up behind themselves.

He turned to consider the writing desk by the window. Nothing was disturbed on the desktop. All was as it had been. But wait. The lamp. He always left a light on when falling asleep, and he *knew* he had left it on earlier. Was he really that tired?

He thought of his friends the Peripherals. Beings from myth that existed on the edge of most people's senses. Could one of them have visited? Or still be here? He opened his mind, let his senses flow through the apartment. He had become very attuned to them in their time together and was reasonably sure he would be aware of them, but their plane contained beings and creatures he had not encountered yet. Could it be one of them? Possible. But unlikely.

He switched the lamp back on and scanned the room again. The scent was fading, but what lingered proved to him that he hadn't imagined it. The only places he hadn't checked were the bathroom and the kitchen. First, he opened the door to the bathroom. Nothing. He even went so far as to pull the shower curtain back. He felt foolish but allowed himself a small breath of relief when the tub proved empty.

Last, he entered the kitchen. It was a big room, and the linoleum lent it a hollow echo with each step he took, even in his bare feet. The door leading out to the back staircase was shut and locked. The sheer white curtain that covered the window in the door was hanging limp, no breeze to stir it. The window over the double sink looking out over the parking lot was fastened firmly.

He took a moment to glance out and make sure his car was safe in its space and gave himself a quick nod when he saw it was. He turned at the sink to look around the room. Still nothing. At least nothing that his eyes perceived. Still, something at the edge of him was alert. He sat for a moment in one of the kitchen table chairs. Was still. Listened.

Turning, he glanced up at a print on the wall above the table. A jaguar. What a strange and incongruous thing in an apartment filled with mostly photos and paintings of Lancaster over the years with a healthy dose of Amish tableaus sprinkled throughout. He knew that often the apartments were furnished and decorated with donations from patrons and supporters. It could be as simple as that. Something about that jaguar, though, drew his eyes back to it. Great. It was one of those creepy prints that looked as if its eyes followed you wherever you went. Not what he needed tonight. He made a mental note to ask Drew or Deborah where it had come from.

He'd had enough. It was late. After two, now, and he needed sleep before his first rehearsal, which was now less than eight hours from beginning. He rose and passed back into the bedroom. He was tempted to doomscroll on his phone but knew it would only keep him up. He fired up the Kindle again. Maybe some time with the Bene Gesserit would distract him enough to fall back to sleep. At least the cologne smell had left. That had been strange. An olfactory illusion? He'd look into that later. Definitely not a rabbit hole he wanted to disappear into right now.

Twenty minutes later, as the words on the screen in front of him began to swim and make little sense, he made sure to close the cover of the tablet and settle in to sleep.

The sleep that found him was not peaceful. It felt oppressive. His dreams were angry, vivid, relentless. He felt trapped in them. He knew he was dreaming, but he could find no way out. It was as if he were underwater, and despite kicking off the bottom and pulling as hard as he could for the surface, he could never break free. Never reach air. Drowning. Desperate. Even worse, he couldn't escape the thought that he wasn't alone. That someone, or something, was inside his dream with him. Hovering just beyond his ability to detect.

The last dream sequence he remembered he was crossing a street at a busy intersection. Not one he recognized. As he began to cross, he saw an elderly woman crossing in the opposite direction, moving toward him. It had clearly just rained, and the gutters were running fast with water. As the woman passed, he saw with alarm one of the puddles gaining shape, growing. It crested, as a wave, and began to sweep toward both him and the elderly pedestrian. The water reached his ankles, his knees, his waist. The current, increasing, threatened to pull him under.

There was no one else nearby. He watched as the woman faltered. She lost her footing and began to slip under the rising water. She turned panicked eyes to him, pleading, and he saw that she had no mouth. She couldn't call out for help. Or even scream in fear.

He turned and rushed as quickly as he could back in her direction. He was her only chance. He reached her and clutched at her arms just as she was about to disappear under what was now a rushing river, the street entirely submerged. He threw her over his shoulder in a fireman's carry and tried to go toward the curb he had just left. The closest and best chance to escape. The water rose. His stomach, his chest, now his neck were under. He stretched his neck, desperate to keep his face above water. To breathe. To save her. Save them both.

He saw a massive wave forming, rushing toward them, and he knew with certainty that they would not make it. Feeling the adrenaline coursing through him, he lifted her above his head. He told her he was sorry, and then hurled her with all his might, which, dreamlike, proved to be considerable, toward the sidewalk and safety. Incredibly, she landed safely on the verge of green beyond the road. The grass almost seemed to reach up for her, to welcome her back to earth. To cushion her fall. It was the last thing he saw before the water closed over his head, the last air in his lungs was forced from his body and he felt himself pulled down, far below where the pavement should have stopped him.

He heaved himself up in the bed, gasping for air. It was light out, but still early, barely seven. His heart was pounding, and he held tightly to the edge of the mattress, getting his bearings. Even for someone who often dreamed vividly and remembered those dreams, that had been... intense. He leaned forward. Shaken. What had it meant?

There would be no more sleep this morning, so he rose and began to get ready for the day ahead. He desperately hoped that the joy of singing and working with friends would help erase the terror he had just felt. At that point, it seemed unlikely, but the day ahead was long.

CHAPTER 6

The dream had unsettled Sean. More than he would have expected. He showered and wolfed down some yogurt, dropping some blueberries into the cup. They were a superfood, he had read. He made himself a cup of coffee, but it was poorly done. He would make a horrible barista if he ever needed a survival job.

In the shower, he let the water run over him, hoping it would help loosen the tension in his shoulders. It didn't. In fact, when he rinsed his hair and opened his eyes, he was sure he had seen the shadow of something passing by through the shower curtain. With that, he quickly shut off the water, wrapped a towel around himself and tore open the curtain. Nothing. Of course, there was nothing. He was just still on edge.

Brushing his teeth, he leaned on the sink and paused to consider his reflection. He looked tired. And, he thought, older. His ginger hair was beginning to show signs of fading. He knew redheads went white, not grey, but he was in no hurry to test that theory. For the first time, he noticed crow's feet next to his eyes and deep lines—he refused to call them wrinkles—on his cheeks. The last weeks had taken a greater toll than he'd realized.

He dressed quickly, but with care. He always tried to make a good impression on the "first day of school," as actors tended to refer to the first rehearsal. He would know many of his castmates, but not all. Only one chance to make a good impression. He sat on the edge of the bed and dangled his feet above the floor. The creeping sensation had not disappeared with the light of the day, which somehow made it all the more unsettling. Despite his positive first impression, he had an unavoidable negative sense about this apartment. He really just wanted to leave. He packed his backpack—pens, pencils, highlighters, script, protein bar, a full water bottle. Snapping his fingers, he returned to the bedroom and grabbed his phone charger. He would be recording a lot of music today and would need a recharge at some point. Checking the weather on the phone, he stuffed an extra t-shirt into the bag, in case he needed to layer later. He grabbed his jacket from the front closet and, just before he headed out, remembered the scarf Duncan had given him and wrapped it around his neck.

At half past nine, Sean began his walk down to the theatre. He left plenty of time, so that he could dawdle along the way and peek into the windows of the shops along the way. Likely pick up a coffee at the café across the street from the marquee.

He was surprised at the volume of traffic on Orange Street. Sleepy Lancaster really had done some growing since he last worked here. He tripped slightly over a loose brick in the sidewalk and caught himself before he took a tumble. He felt his face flush in embarrassment and made a quick check of his surroundings, relieved to find no other pedestrians nearby.

He sorted himself and walked on before hearing a somewhat familiar rumble drawing near behind. Sure enough, a moment later a massive Harley swung up to the curb and Sean felt his blush deepen when he turned to find Kat idling next to him. She flipped her visor up and greeted him with a lopsided grin and remarkably white teeth.

"You city folk just aren't used to our brick sidewalks, I guess," she said, but the playful note in her voice softened the statement. "Nice scarf, by the way."

"Thanks," Sean replied. "It's definitely growing on me. And so glad you were here to witness my near wipeout. Not embarrassing, at all."

"Hey, I'm impressed you didn't faceplant. Nice catch. Trust me, even the locals take tumbles on those bricks. Impossible to keep them always in order. Need a lift?"

Sean looked dubiously at the motorcycle. "I can barely walk, and you want me to climb on that thing?"

"Well, on this you just have to sit quietly. I do all the work."

"Fair point," he said. "But I'm actually early, so I think I'll just wander down. Appreciate the offer, though. Any chance you're working tonight?"

"I am indeed," Kat answered. "Five o'clock 'til close. Did I ever tell you my granddad worked at the theatre? Not sure what he did there. I never knew him. Funny, haven't thought about that for a while."

"I never knew that. Wild. Would love to hear more about it. Maybe later? Hopefully, I'll get to see you after rehearsal."

"Not if I see you first," she quipped with a wink. "I joke. Come by. Tell me how it goes. And try not to go rescuing anyone in the alleys on your way down there. I won't be around to bail you out." She was laughing as she slid her visor into place and gunned the engine before slipping neatly into the flow of traffic.

Sean watched her go and considered how much had happened to him in just the half-day he'd been in town. He hoped things would quiet now. All he really wanted was some peace and quiet.

The cool morning air helped wake him up and shake off the creeps the apartment had given him. Ten minutes later, he emerged from the café with an iced coffee in his hands and crossed Prince Street for the stage door down the alley to the right of the main building. If the man in the red cap on the corner seemed to be watching him a little intently, Sean chose to let it go. When he glanced back, the man had gone. Just jittery.

At the door, he opened his email to check for the entrance code to open the door, punched it in, and heard the door click. He gave it a test push, felt it give and pushed it open. Something made him pause before he entered the theatre. There it was, again. That feeling of—being watched? Foreboding? He glanced up and down the alley but saw nothing out of the ordinary. No Peripherals. No Breena. Nothing. Just a gnawing in the pit of his stomach. He turned to the theatre and walked in. Hopefully, the music would settle his nerves. It had always been able to do that. At least, it had before.

The stage door swung shut behind him. He hadn't noticed that some of the alley shadows were darker than others. Or that they slipped along the pavement and away down Water Street after he was gone.

***

Sean caught his breath when his eyes adjusted to the light in the hallway. What he remembered as an older, well-worn interior had been transformed. It was now cool greys and whites. Sleek. Modern. He shook his head in disbelief as he wandered the hallway toward where he remembered the dressing rooms to be, only to find that nothing was where he thought it would be. He turned, dumbfounded, and realized that he was already lost.

"Don't worry," a cheerful voice called out. "Everyone gets lost their first time in the new space. You'll get used to it in no time."

Sean turned to find Drew Brindig, the theatre handyman and jack-of-all-trades, following him down the hallway. He hadn't passed him on the way in, he was sure of it.

"Where did you come from?" Sean asked. "I just came that way but didn't see you."

"Yeah, lots of nooks and crannies in the new design. It's like one big English Muffin. You must have come through a cranny while I was in a nook." He laughed quietly at his own joke. "Easy to miss each other back here. Come on, I'll show you to the elevator. That'll take you up to the rehearsal space."

Sean shrugged his shoulders. "Guess so. It's all so different. Appreciate a point in the right direction. I remember when we used to rehearse in the clubhouse across the street."

Drew breezed past Sean and called over his shoulder. "Yup. Those days are done. I have a soft spot for the old space, but, trust me, you're about to be knocked over by the new facility."

Sean hoisted his backpack higher on his shoulder and took off after the briskly moving Drew. They turned the next corner and Sean almost ran headlong into Brandy, standing in the middle of the hallway looking very lost.

Drew was already past her and sent a lighthearted laugh back to the two actors standing behind him.

"And we have another lost sheep! Come on now. Just one more turn and—" He stopped and pointed to a gleaming chrome elevator door. "Voilà. Your chariot awaits. Just take it to the top. You'll see a door in front of you. Through that door, you'll find what you're looking for. Have a great first day! I can't wait to see what you all come up with. Whole staff feels the same way!"

With that, Drew turned, shot them a quick and slightly awkward wave, and headed past the elevator and around the next corner, hustling toward what used to be the stage entrance.

"Thanks for the—" Sean began, but Drew was gone before he could finish his sentence. "Such a nice guy," he said, turning to Brandy. "And you—how did you get lost? You live in the freakin' building."

"I do. Trust me, it's easy to get lost back here, no matter where you live. And yes. He is nice. Very. Don't trust him one bit."

"You are a ridiculous human being," Sean shot back, and, eyeing her usual outfit of jeans, a t-shirt, and sneakers, added, "Nice of you to dress for the occasion, by the way."

"Yeah, yeah. Bite me, Goody Two-shoes. Not all of us feel the need to brownnose on the first day."

Sean laughed. "Good to be here with you, as always, you charmer."

The elevator door closed behind them as Brandy punched him on the arm. "Don't get all sappy on me, now, Ginge. Time to make the donuts."

Moments later, the elevator opened onto a small alcove. Assorted tables were taped on their surface and labeled for props to be stored there in the coming days as rehearsals progressed. Plain black rehearsal blocks, sturdy wooden cubes used to stand in for set pieces, were stacked in one corner. The atmosphere was utilitarian and familiar. All the simple trappings of a theatre rehearsal bid them hello. Sean felt instantly at ease. This was home to him. Every theatre, everywhere, had these simple and basic elements. He could walk into any theatre and be comfortable. He felt the tension of his sleepless night and anxious walk that morning slipping away, and he heaved a sigh that earned a sidewise glance from Brandy. Brandy snuffed audibly.

"I don't know," she said. "Looks pretty standard to me. Not so special, after everything we've heard." She laid an arm gently, and uncharacteristically, across his shoulder. "But yeah. I get it. Feels good to be back."

"Yeah, it does," Sean agreed. "Didn't know how much I missed it. Think the rehearsal room is through there?" He gestured to a plain door directly ahead of them.

"The one with the plaque that says 'rehearsal room' on the wall next to it? I think there's a good chance, yeah."

"Okay, okay. I didn't notice that. Just having a moment over here," Sean replied. If it were anyone but Brandy, he might have been embarrassed.

Together, they crossed to the door and Sean opened it while bowing low and sweeping his arm ahead for Brandy to proceed him. He followed her and almost ran her over when she stopped abruptly as soon as she crossed the threshold.

Brandy whistled long and low, and when Sean caught up with her and took in the rehearsal space, he understood why. The room before them was enormous, with a ceiling at least twenty feet above them. Two of the walls were made entirely of glass and steel, offering an expansive view of downtown Lancaster, the Victorian rooftops of nearby buildings on Water Street giving a magical, almost otherworldly charm to the entire experience.

If the view outside gave a sense of antiquity and nostalgia, the room itself was distinctly modern and well-appointed. The ceiling was a latticework of pipes and beams, all designed to allow set pieces to be flown and stored overhead. The floor, already taped to indicate where the set would be, gave slightly beneath their feet as Sean and Brandy crossed to the center of the room. They shared a glance.

"You feel that?" Sean asked.

"Yeah. This floor is sprung. Majorly," Brandy said. She bent her knees and bounced lightly up and down. "Wow. Dancers are going to *love* it here."

"Yup. This floor will add years to a few careers, I'm sure. Happy dancer knees," Sean answered, giving his own little bounce to test the floor.

They continued to take in the room. Chairs were lined along two of the walls, waiting for the rest of the cast to arrive. The wall facing the largest window held a production table with two laptop computers, rolls of multi-colored tape, an array of pencils and highlighters, copies of the script, bags of cough drops, and a massive plastic bucket filled to over-flowing with various candies. Behind the table were seats for the director, Pettirosso, and the stage management team, Rebecca Chapel and her assistant, Dani Landau, another familiar face to Sean, who crossed to greet her.

"Dani! I didn't realize you were on this! I'm so happy!" Sean cried.

"I am, indeed," Dani replied, turning with a hundred-kilowatt smile. "Been looking forward to it. This room is going to be filled with a whole lot of my very favorite people. Throw in some holiday magic, and I'm a happy camper. I'm staff now! Finally found my artistic home. Couldn't be happier."

"Oh, wow. That's wonderful! So happy for you. I know how much that means to you. Congratulations. Wings are on me later to celebrate." He turned to Brandy who still stood in the center of the room. "Brandy! Come meet your new best friend. Brandy Johns, this is Dani Landau, stage manager extraordinaire."

Brandy walked to the table with her hand outstretched. "Nice to meet you, Dani. Excited to get to work."

"You and me both," Dani answered, shaking Brandy's hand. "I feel like I know you just from following Sean's social media. Happy to meet you in real life."

The room was beginning to fill up. The door opened and Dante, Bobby Smalls, and Rebecca entered. Rebecca approached the production table and shook Brandy's hand while giving Sean a quick hug.

"Marcello will be here in a sec," she said. "Grab a seat. We should have the full cast any minute. Couple of last-minute additions coming in. We'll take care of the Equity business after our welcome talk, cool?"

"Of course, whatever you say, boss," Sean answered with a grin, earning a shake of her head in response.

Brandy began to tug on Sean's sleeve, lightly at first and then with greater urgency.

Sean finally turned to her. "What?"

Brandy pointed to the far corner of the room, where a piano sat facing them. Behind it were two figures, seated on the bench and hunched over the keyboard, almost hidden from their view, which is why Sean hadn't noticed them sooner.

"Um, is that Haydn and Page behind the piano?" Brandy muttered.

"What? No. Of course not. Wait..." He turned to Rebecca and Dani, a question in his eyes.

"Yeah, sure is," Dani answered.

"So, like I said, some last-minute additions. We're going to have some original music, so Marcello brought them in," Rebecca said.

"*Brought them in?*" Brandy said, her voice rising with excitement. "How exactly does one just bring them in? They're the hottest writing team on the planet right now."

"I mean, *Bottom of the Barrel* is shattering box office records in New York, right now. I don't get it. They're huge. Bigger than huge. Mammoth."

Rebecca laughed quietly. "All true. But Marcello knows them and sold them on the show and what he wants to do here. Both this piece and the theatre as a whole. They were happy to join up."

"Unbelievable," Brandy muttered, turning to take in the duo working at the piano.

Jeff "Jiff" Haydn was the composing half of the pair. He sat at the keyboard, oblivious to all around him. Entirely focused on what his fingers were creating as they flew across the ivories. He had a shock of dark, curly hair, bright eyes with more than a little twinkle to them, and a ready smile that lent lines and character to his face. He'd earned the nickname "Jiff" because of his legendary energy and talent for multi-tasking. He was known for creating some of the most memorable and catchy melodies in the theatre over the last ten years.

Will Page, standing slightly behind Haydn and eyeing the musical score on the piano, was the lyricist and book writer of the team. He was taller, lanky, with a sweep of dark hair that insisted on flopping onto his face and covering at least one eye at all times. From time to time, he would lean over to make a note on the music. He had a pencil in his mouth, one behind his left ear, and one in his hand. Apparently, he'd forgotten all about them and was using a pencil that sat in front of Jiff on the music stand. As deft as Jiff was with a melody, Will was his equal when it came to turning a phrase.

Before Sean and Brandy had a chance to approach them, Marcello Pettirosso swept into the room, a dervish of energy and enthusiasm. He was dressed elegantly, almost as if he'd stepped into the room from a bygone time. A cutaway jacket, a colorful pocket square, snug pants that emphasized his background in dance and his every fluid move-ment. He even sported a sharp fedora. Blue with a green feather stuck jauntily in the band. Rebecca and Dani barely had time to usher the actors to their seats before the director sprang front and center on the taped-out rehearsal room floor and began his welcome speech. For those who had worked with him before, the words were familiar, but the sincerity of them was not diminished by their having been used before. Even after a long career in the theatre, Pettirosso oozed excite-ment and bonhomie. For those who didn't know any better, it would be easy to assume that he was a newcomer to the theatre, so abundant was his joy.

"Welcome, everyone!" he began. "Welcome. Welcome to the Fulton, welcome to our new Castagna rehearsal space, welcome to day one, and welcome to the first day of what I know will be an explosion of creativity and goodwill, spreading from you, across our stage, and into our community and beyond. I can't thank you enough for being here. Truly. I know how much you're making to be here. I sign the checks. You all deserve more than you're getting. What we don't provide in dollars and cents, I think you will find is more than made up in other ways."

Sean and Brandy shared a look and a shrug. They both thought they were being paid pretty well.

Pettirosso turned in a circle, taking in everyone in the room. He insisted they all stand and introduce themselves and their place in the production. Everyone—cast, creative team, staff, stage management, crew—all took their turn. Sean found his heart beating ridiculously fast, and his palms grew damp. Nerves. What a strange thing to be nervous about when you spend your career onstage in front of thousands of people. But first impressions only happened once, and it was vastly different to stand on a stage reciting lines someone had written for you than to speak your own words in front of new colleagues.

Sean tried his best to commit the names of anyone he didn't already know to memory, but there were too many and he knew he was doomed to fail. Still, had to make the effort. And of course, there were the old friends—Dante, Bobby Smalls, Rebbeca Parish—and the renowned writing team that needed no introduction, although they stood and announced themselves as if they were unknowns.

"Right," Pettirosso continued after the introductions were complete. "First, don't get used to seeing me turned out in my finest." He indicated his outfit. "Most days I'll be wearing sweatpants and a Disney t-shirt, but first days are important. Also, there will be a photographer in later shooting some PR shots. Before we begin, I do have a few things I'd like to share. So, settle in for a mo'. We'll be hard at work soon, but let's get to know each other a bit, shall we?"

Sean took a furtive look around the room. The group ranged widely in age. Roughly half of the performers were local residents, some he'd known for years. The stage crew and administrative staff ringed the room. Sean spotted Deborah a few feet behind Pettirosso—Cello, he reminded himself—doing her best to avoid too much attention. In a far corner, he spotted Drew, standing alone and doing all he could to go unnoticed.

"I think *A Christmas Carol* is quite possibly one of, if not the, most original and moving story ever written," Pettirosso said. "From start to finish, not one word is wasted. Its universality is undeniable, as witnessed by it being a staple in theatres and on screens every year. With that in mind, I want you all to know that we will be creating our own unique take on this. Given the perfection I mentioned, we won't be reinventing the wheel, but we will allow our creative instincts some free reign. As I'm sure you've all noticed, we've been joined by no less than the team of Haydn and Page, who will be creating some musical magic to add." Sensing some unease in the room, he plowed on. "But it will be done respectfully. And entirely in keeping with the tone of the source material. Also, this is a safe space. I *want* you to try things out. Not every idea will work. Don't be afraid to make mistakes. You all have the job. Stretch your performing muscles. One of my mottos is: the best idea wins. Doesn't matter whose idea it is. If it makes the show better, it's in. So don't be shy.

"We also will have some additional company members joining us. More coverage and understudies. It's a good thing! More on that later. There will also be a new work debuting in our black box theatre. Details to come. The new Fulton is aiming to be full of art and creativity and connection at all times. I hope you will embrace that attitude and reap all it has to offer. We are on our way to becoming a nationwide force. Right. I'm tired of hearing myself, which means you certainly are, too. Rebecca? I turn it over to you."

Rebecca stepped from around the table with a clipboard in hand. "Okay, everyone. We will need a few minutes with the Equity members. Just some housekeeping and electing a deputy. The rest of our company is welcome to step outside into the upper lobby," she motioned to a door behind the production table, "where they will find coffee, bagels, dough-nuts. All the necessary breakfast staples. Once we're through, we will get down to it."

As the non-union actors, staff, and crew ambled out to grab a bite, the remaining folks gathered closer around Rebecca. As they did, Pettirosso gestured for Sean and Brandy to step aside and join him across the room. Sean shot a startled look at Brandy before the two of them followed the director over.

"So, I want to let you both know of a few new developments. As I mentioned, we will be adding some added coverage for the show. With the new music, we'll need to be sure we have appropriate voices and understudies, blah blah. You've both been through it before. You know the drill. The aspect I want to let you know is—one of the understudies we've hired is someone you know. Ken O'Carroll will be covering you, Sean, and a few others. Dante, Bobby. I just don't want it to come as a surprise. It's well known there has been some friction amongst you. I hope you will find it possible to work together?"

Sean took a breath and released it slowly. Processing. "Uh, well—yeah. Of course. Ken is...was...is a friend. I'm sure he's happy for the work." Then, with a glance to Brandy, "No problem on our end. Will be nice to have him around. I'm hoping."

Brandy nodded in agreement if her smile was less broad than Sean's. "Appreciate the heads up, Marcello." In response to Pettirosso's raised eyebrows, "Sorry. Cello. Ken can be a good guy, and he's definitely talented. He'll help the show. For sure."

"I appreciate your professionalism. I also hope the chance to work together again may heal some of the ill will," Pettirosso continued. "Although that aspect I will leave to you to address." He paused and fixed Sean with a piercing look. "Nice scarf you have there." He gestured to the scarf Duncan had gifted him the night before. "Very unique."

"Oh, this," Sean said, glancing down as if he'd forgotten it was there. "I made a new friend on the walk home last night."

"That's one way to put it," Brandy mumbled under breath.

"Well, that is a well-known local design," Pettirosso noted. "Wullivers have been crafting and selling those around here for generations. I'm guessing it was Duncan Wulliver you met?"

"It was, actually," Sean confirmed. "Nice guy. Seems a little at loose ends."

"Indeed he is," Pettirosso agreed, then pivoted quickly to take in the full company returning behind them. "You'll have to tell me more about that meeting later. Now, if you are both amenable to Mr. O'Carroll joining us, we should reconvene."

Sean and Brandy shared a glance. This Ken thing could go either way, but only one way to find out.

"And one last thing," Pettirosso said, still facing away from them. "We have commissioned a play from another of your friends, Sullivan Nichols. He will be here tomorrow. And another of your Grumbles, Daniel Trout, has been cast in the still-developing piece. So, you see, your little group will be largely reunited. Sadly, Stewart Garland is otherwise committed, and I was unable to lure him down."

"You seem to know an awful lot about us and our friends," Brandy replied, her eyes narrowing as she stared at Pettirosso. "What's up with that?"

"Nothing nefarious, I can assure you," Pettirosso answered. "Your social media reveals quite a bit, and our HR team always checks that to see if there are any local connections we can highlight. And Mr. O'Carroll's—shall we say *incident*?—was very well documented. The rest was not hard to deduce. We believe in second chances here. And friendship. Personally, I've found those two ingredients can often lead to sublime artistry. Simple as that. Shall we?" he asked, motioning toward the company members and walking away briskly.

As they headed back to the reassembling group, Brandy pulled Sean's arm to hold back a step.

"Well, there's a whole lot about us he can't find out from our social media. Wouldn't he be surprised to know the truth of the last few weeks?"

"I'm not sure," Sean said slowly, eyeing the retreating diminutive director. "I get the feeling he has a few surprises in his past, too."

"I guess we'll find out!" Brandy answered. "Or not. Don't care much either way. Just want a quiet couple months doing a sweet show at a beautiful theatre. Easy peasy. And added bonus? Being in the principal's office for that tête-à-tête just now means neither of us could be elected deputy. Can't elect us if we aren't there. Today is a good day."

As they rejoined the group, Dani, the assistant stage manager, approached Brandy and handed her some completed forms and a folder full of papers. "Congratulations! You were elected union deputy in absentia."

"Wait, what?" Brandy stammered. "But...I thought—that's not—man, sonofa..."

Sean stifled his laugh, but not quickly enough to escape a withering look from Brandy.

With the paperwork and introductions out of the way, the theatre staff went back to their respective departments and the cast broke up into groups. The dancers stayed put in the large rehearsal room where Pettirosso led a choreography rehearsal and blocked the ensemble into the first songs and scenes of the show. Sean and Brandy were dispatched to a smaller rehearsal room to learn music with Haydn and Page.

Sean couldn't believe his good luck. Spending a morning in the company of a legendary composing team while they quite literally wrote songs to suit his voice. All with one of his closest friends at his side to both share the experience and bear witness. He floated through the rehearsal, recording everything on his phone to rehearse with later on his own. The entire experience was a bit of a blur. A blissful blur. He even allowed the events of the night before—the violence in the alley, the disturbed dreams—to fall away as he remembered why he had become an actor in the first place.

He and Brandy shared more than one "pinch me" glance. Sean was playing the put-upon Bob Cratchit and would need to learn a number of numbers. Brandy, much to her chagrin, was playing Mrs. Dilber, Ebenezer Scrooge's long-suffering housekeeper. She insisted she was far too young and glamorous to be playing such a role, but her contract said differently, as Sean enjoyed reminding her. Her songs were comic, and biting, and brilliant. Sean sat back more than once to watch her and remind himself how talented his friend was. All of his friends, actually.

An hour into their rehearsal, Dante, who was playing Scrooge, arrived to join the music rehearsal. Not long after, Bobby Smalls, playing Scrooge's nephew Fred, also arrived. They all quickly fell into their old ways—making jokes at each other's expense, freely offering compliments, and diving headlong into the learning. Sean reveled in flexing muscles that had been overshadowed by the supernatural events he'd dealt with recently. He almost felt—dare he think it?—normal.

By eleven o'clock, Sean was called into the large room to be put into the opening numbers. Brandy had a short break but decided to tag along to watch the cast putting it together.

As they headed down the hallway from one room to the other, Brandy turned to Sean and, with a quizzical tilt to her head, asked, "Trout, Nick, even Ken, all coming. Something feels...I don't want to say 'off.' It feels...contrived. Yes? Manipulated?"

"Ah, jeez, Brand. Don't make me think about that stuff. I was just beginning to feel like I was coming back into myself. I mean, that rehearsal was—mind blowing. Yeah? New Haydn-Page songs? Written *for us*. Written *with* us. With us *in the room*. Can we just sit with that for a bit? Besides. It's just coincidence. We're in Lancaster. Pennsylvania. Nothing bad happens here. I mean, all of that old history stuff aside. And look at this theatre. State of the art. We're here to do a show. Nothing else. Can we just do that?"

"You're right," Brandy quickly answered. "My bad. Just a show. An amazing show, with amazing people. I will be amazed. And that is all."

But her words rang hollow, and she kept her eyes on the floor on front of them as they reached the next room.

"Dammit, Brandy," Sean muttered. "You're right. Something's up.

Nothing good happens by sticking our head in the sand. Let's keep our eyes open. But I'm going to enjoy as much of this as I can. No matter what."

"I'm with you there, Ginge. After you?" she asked as she held the door for him. But both of them felt things had shifted. Just a bit. Because once those kinds of words are shared, they can't be unsaid. And something was definitely up.

The rest of the day sped past. One rehearsal bled into another, with groups moving from the music room to the staging room. Even with that nagging suspicion building in the back of their minds, Sean and Brandy were able to remain distracted. At lunch, they went to the café across the street with others, and enjoyed simple conversation—recent auditions, theatre gossip, changes in Lancaster. They stuck close to each other, alert to anything unusual. But the remainder of the day was a blur of creativity and friendships renewed. By the time things wrapped at six o'clock, they had almost convinced themselves there was nothing to worry about.

They wandered out the stage door and up to Prince Street. Both were exhausted. First days, with their combination of nerves, concentration, and adrenaline, were always tiring, and this one seemed doubly so to them.

"I'm stopping by Dipco to see my friend, Kat," Sean said as the reached the street. "Up for it?"

"Kat, huh?" Brandy replied. "After what you told me about last night, I wouldn't miss it. You, my copper friend, are a trouble magnet, so I'll sit a few feet away, but I'd love to hear her version of things."

"Well, okay, then," he answered. "Wings and maybe a beer? And thanks, so much for the name-calling. You've caused your fair bit of hassle, too, you know." And then with a sigh, "But you have a point. I can't get out of my own way, lately."

"Yeah, yeah. I'm sorry I said anything. Put the sad sack away and let's go take a deep breath."

She gently pushed him ahead of her and into the crosswalk. The stream of traffic stopped as soon as the drivers saw them.

"Definitely don't get that in New York. We'd be dodging them to get across," Brandy noted.

"See what I mean? Lancaster," Sean said. "Sweet. Charming. Harmless. Safe. Lancaster!"

If either of them noticed the shadows behind them deepening, they chalked it up to the setting sun and the flickering to life of the gas streetlamps. None of that explained the deepest shadow, that moved differently than the others. And seemed to be wearing an incongruous fedora.

Marcello Pettirosso, however, standing in the window of his darkened office gazing out over the street below, saw. And his brow furrowed with just the slightest concern before he pushed the button to shade the windows and shut out the street. And the noise. And the shadows.

CHAPTER 7

One-hundred and sixty-five miles northeast of Lancaster, while Sean and Brandy crossed Prince Street after rehearsal, Stewart Garland was having a pinch-me-to make-sure-this-is-real moment. He sat in the star dressing room of the Nederlander Theatre on Forty-first Street in Manhattan. The lights were dimmed. The theatre was nearly silent. He could hear Paolo, the doorman and his friend, rustling papers down the hall at his station, but he was fairly certain he was the only other person in the building.

Broadway theatres are much in demand. There are only forty-one of them, and they are booked well in advance by shows—whether new or revivals—hoping to score big in the bright lights of New York. Stewart was still in shock that his new manager and romantic partner, Gwyddion Evans, had managed to secure the space for a one-man show starring Stewart. It had been some time since he'd played a starring role in New York. In his earlier career, his dashing good looks and velvety baritone voice had catapulted him to the top of most casting directors' lists. As he aged, however, he had settled into more supporting roles and, truth be told, he'd found that he preferred it out of the blazing lights and attention that came with New York celebrity. For such a big city, it was a small city, and the sense of being watched and judged had worn on him. He was far more comfortable being an actor. Not a star.

He scanned the room. Taking in the bamboo flooring, full personal bar, top-of-the-line sound system, plush leather furniture. All of it had been installed mere weeks ago by his fellow Grumble, and hopefully still friend, Ken O'Carroll, before Ken had buckled under the pressure of a meteoric rise to stardom. His fall from grace had been spectacular and included a very public, and recorded, road rage incident at the Lincoln Tunnel where he had berated and threatened an elderly couple.

The scorn had heaped onto him almost immediately, and his own one-man show, also shepherded to the stage by Gwyddion Evans, had been pulled from the theatre's schedule within hours, thus the availability. If he didn't trust Gwyddion so completely, he might have qualms about how things had worked out. He still considered Ken one of his dearest friends and would never wish him ill. He also knew that he, himself, had nothing to do with events. He hadn't even considered a show of his own until Gwyddion suggested it one night over dinner.

Despite initially rejecting the idea, the seed had been planted. He couldn't shake it, and as it took root, he realized he had things he would like to say. Music he wanted to make and share. At his age, with more of his forties behind than in front of him, he knew this would likely be his last shot at something on this scale. With gentle nudging, he'd come on board.

And that's how he found himself sitting in the star dressing room of the theatre he'd shared with his fellow Grumbles during their year-long Broadway run. It somehow felt odd to be here without any of them by his side. But he knew that Sean and Brandy were in Pennsylvania, rehearsing their *A Christmas Carol*. He'd gotten texts earlier in the evening that Nick and Trout would be heading to the same theatre for a different project. Not long after, another text had arrived telling him that Ken would be heading down, too, to cover a few roles in the larger show. That Ken found himself grateful for that job, after the heights he had very nearly reached, was a lesson not lost on Stewart. Showbiz is a fickle thing.

He also felt just the slightest bit left out. After the last few weeks, the Grumbles had been through so much together. From Ken's disappearance to the friendships made with the otherworldly Peripherals, to the danger posed by the evil Dullahan and its minions, they had emerged closer than ever, with the exception of Ken who had ridden his ego into a dark space where they could not follow. Given all of that, it seemed a bit too coincidental that all the others would be reunited in Lancaster, and he would be checking in regularly to make sure they were in no danger.

Truth be told, despite his twinge of envy, it was somehow appropriate that he found himself here alone. He suspected that one of the things that bound the Grumbles so closely to each other was that they had all felt themselves to be outsiders. Not uncommon for actors in general, who were often far more introverted than the public would suspect. But the Grumbles had all seemed misfits in an industry of misfits. With all of that, Stewart had always felt his difference keenly, even from the other Grumbles. It had nothing to do with him being Black, although that had certainly been an obstacle on more occasions than he could count. He supposed it was that his heart seemed just a bit more vulnerable than the others. He was more sensitive, open, more easily hurt. He disguised it with naughty jokes and a willingness to give as good as he got, but it always hid a delicate disposition.

He'd been forced to acknowledge much of this during their recent adventures. In the midst of the violence and peril, he'd been taken into the confidence of Kelphit, an ancient wandering Native healer. In learning some of Kelphit's secrets, Stewart found a deep longing to heal others. And with that came an equally profound aversion to violence and harming anyone. He'd held back from the most vicious moments of their dealings, but his talent for soothing angry situations had saved them all more than once.

And it was this discovery within himself that had ultimately moved him to accept the responsibility of the one-man show. He wanted to share his optimism, his desire for peace and connection, with audiences. Ken's show, borne of his desire for fame at all costs, had been angry and fueled by the belief that narcissism was the path to fulfillment. Stewart's very different path was not meant to be an indictment of Ken. He just thought the world...needed this. Even if it was delivered to small audiences one night at a time. He wanted to be the pebble in the pond that sent ripples to the farthest shore.

Happy. Something Stewart had almost forgotten. And here it was. A chance to make a positive difference. A chance to be heard. Really heard. And a partner in Gwyddion who valued him and wanted to see him succeed on his own terms. He wasn't ready to use the word "love" just yet. Not even to himself. But he could feel it skulking around and waiting to pounce. Gwyddion. So much good there. So much unexpected. Stewart chose to believe that it was of no importance that Gwyddion was the Welsh God of Mischief. Real was real. And this was real.

Sean and Brandy found themselves on the same barstools as the night before. Dipco was slow and Kat allowed herself to loiter by them at the bar. She patiently listened to them recounting their first rehearsal and couldn't help smiling at their enthusiasm as they explained the shock at finding Haydn and Page working on the show.

"I mean, I use one of their songs from *Patriots* as an audition piece," Sean shared, gushing like a teenager. "I think that one song has gotten me more work than just about anything else. And they were writing a song for *me* today. Just mind blowing."

"Yupper. I did not see that one coming," Brandy agreed. "This is a ridiculous business, and it never stops surprising me. Hey, I see Dante and Bobby Smalls coming in. I'm going to say hey. Gonna have to make some friends other than you, Ginge, if I'm planning on having fun here." With that, she hopped down from her stool and wandered toward the front door where the newcomers were waiting to be seated. There were a few other cast members with them, and Brandy sauntered along with them when the host led them to a large table in the far corner.

Sean watched the group settle in and when he turned back to the bar Kat was still there giving him a quizzical look.

"What?" Sean asked. "What did I do to deserve that look?"

"Deserve?" she volleyed back. "Nothing. But I just sorta sense there's something on your mind. I do that. I pick up on things a lot."

"Oh, you do, huh?" Sean chuckled and ducked his head to take a sip of his beer. This time the Cartel beer Brandy had enjoyed the night before. "Well, your antennae must be on the fritz, because I'm happy as a clam. Did you not hear everything I just said?"

"Oh, I heard," Kat replied. "But I also could tell there was something you *weren't* saying. But look. You don't need to tell me anything. I'm just letting you know you *can*. If you want to. I get that you have Brandy and other friends here. Just putting it out there."

"Thanks. I appreciate it. I'm good. I really am. Promise."

"Whatever you say," Kat tossed her bar towel up over one of her shoulders and gestured to a patron at the end of the bar that she'd be right there. "You do you. Just an observation."

As she wandered to the other patron, Sean watched her go, and cocked his head to one side. She did seem intuitive. He'd give her that. He already felt like he knew her better than he had from his previous time in Lancaster. And how exactly had she just happened to be there last night when the fight in the alley had broken out? And then this morning, just passing by when he was walking to rehearsal. He knew Lancaster was a small place, but those were a lot of coincidences in a short amount of time.

And, while he didn't want to admit it to himself, there was a small seed of worry that had taken root. The encounter with Duncan and his attackers. The vivid dream last night. The sudden inclusion of the other Grumbles. He desperately wanted to just have a normal, quiet experience here. Do his show. Enjoy it. Let all the upheaval of the Peripherals and the evil they were fighting drift away, even if only for a little while. But Kat may be on to something. Maybe she had even sensed it before he was fully aware of it. There were too many things swirling around him. Dammit. He glanced down the bar at her and caught her looking at him. She shot a knowing grin and turned back to her work.

A few minutes later, Brandy returned and jumped up onto her

barstool. "You know, Ginge, you should really cruise by to say hello. They're all asking after you. Man, they are all still flying from today. There's talk of a get-together back at Dremmel House in a bit. I was thinking might be fun. Whaddaya think? Up for it?"

"Hm. Maybe so. Could be a good way to get to know some of the newbies. But, if we're doing that, I need to get back now and put in some homework. I definitely won't do it after a party." Sean waved to Kat and motioned for their check. She gave him an exaggerated sad look followed by a grin and a thumbs up.

Sean mentioned the party to Kat as he settled up, drawing a raised eyebrow from Brandy that he chose to ignore. Kat was noncommittal, but said she'd see how early she got off of work.

Sean and Brandy stopped by the large cast table on their way out the door. Dante had volunteered his apartment as party central. He had moved his things in just an hour before. He was just down the hall from Sean, so there really was no good reason to miss out. With promises to see each other shortly, they headed for the exit.

Outside the front door, Brandy started back toward the theatre building and her apartment.

"Good call on the homework," she announced as she walked away. "I'll tag along with some of the others and see you in a couple hours. You can show me your nightmare apartment."

"Careful, there," Sean called after her. "Don't take any bad juju back with you. On second thought, take it all back with you. I could use a good night's sleep."

He watched Brandy disappear across Prince Street before turning down the alley leading to Orange Street. Once again, the gaslights flickered and danced in the night. He paused to listen but heard nothing. No following footsteps. No calls for help. Just a normal autumn evening in little, normal, safe Lancaster.

He found himself hoping that Kat would drop by the party. Maybe she had a point. And just maybe, he would confide in her. If he could figure out for himself what he was thinking. Or feeling. Or both.

It was nearly three hours later that Sean finally lifted his head from the script on the desk in front of him. Dusk had slid into night without him noticing, despite being seated by the window. He'd actually been comparing notes with his old, dog-eared copy of the Dickens source material, something he hadn't done for any show in quite some time. Clearly, he really wanted to immerse himself in being an actor again. There was something liberating about being away from the commercial motivations of the city. Something freeing about doing a show for the simple sake of telling the story. No eye on the weekly grosses. No tallying up the empty seats in the audience when the curtain rose at top of show. Just...telling the story. Stripping it all back down to the things that had led him to a life in the theatre in the first place.

He took off his reading glasses, another begrudging acknowledgment of his current age, and rubbed his eyes, hearing his mother's voice in his mind, 'Don't rub your eyes. It's bad for them.' He stretched his neck and noted the popcorn crackle as he let his head roll in a circle. He really hadn't moved much for the last few hours.

He became aware of the voices drifting down the hallway outside his front door. Dante's get-together had kicked off and he had been so focused he'd completely missed it. It seemed more a steady burble of discussion. Nothing crazy going on, which was perfect in Sean's opinion. Ten o'clock rehearsals felt early these days, a point driven home by the creaking of his knees as he rose to stretch properly.

Shadows danced across the wall behind where he had been sitting. The streetlight streamed through the skeletal winter tree limbs that shuddered just outside the window. For just a fraction of a moment, it looked as if something, or someone, was reaching toward him. The room was dark, and he flicked the nearest light switch to chase the shadows and his now-returned sense of unease away. At least the shadows disappeared.

He really should bring something with him. It must be after nine, by now. He padded into the kitchen and, perusing the meager contents of his refrigerator, some English muffins, six eggs, and half a Dunkin' iced tea. Underwhelming. He glanced at his phone. Oops. Almost ten, meaning no place would be open. He thought for a moment, before texting Kat, asking her to bring some beer if she was planning to stop by, with a promise of repayment and being forever in her debt. Within two minutes, she responded in the affirmative, with a vow to hold him to both conditions.

He stepped into the bathroom, ran a wet comb through his hair to rid himself of a wayward curl, brushed his teeth, splashed some water on his face to clear the cobwebs, and headed for the front door.

Dante's apartment was only two doors down from his, and he was at the door in just a moment. He could hear Brandy holding court through the door, her voice cutting through the general din. He couldn't help a smile. She always landed on her feet.

He ran a hand down his face, flicking any remaining water off and knocked on the door.

***

Sean was surprised at how much he enjoyed himself at the cast party. He normally shied away from large groups, and parties were not traditionally his thing. However, as he made the rounds from living room, to kitchen, and back again, he was struck by what an exceptional group of people Marcello Pettirosso had assembled. He was sure they were all consummate performers; that had always been his experience at the Fulton. But tonight, not having seen most of them at work, he sensed they were kind. Deep. Engaged. He allowed himself a second beer, checking his phone to see if there was any word from Kat on her ETA. He met Adriane, a dancer from Chicago whose every move was a lesson in grace and who was eager to discuss literature. And wildlife, in particular her current fascination with stoats. He met Cory Jones, a local actor who had bounced back and forth between New York and Lancaster, doing stints at Radio City, before realizing finally that home was where his heart truly was. The gleam in his eye told Sean that he had made the right choice. He met Lina, a diminutive actress and dancer who, despite being in her late twenties, was playing one of the Cratchit children. In other words, she was playing one of Sean's onstage children, which did nothing to ease his feelings of encroaching age.

Lina was telling a gathering crowd that she had stayed in Dremmel House the last time she worked at the theatre. In fact, she had lived in Apartment Two, on the first floor to the left of the stairs up to the other floors.

"I was really hoping I'd be there again, but no luck. With all the new housing down at the theatre, I'm in one of the fancy new spaces," she told the ever-growing group of listeners. "There was this one time I had forgotten my keys in the dressing room. It was during tech, and the last thing I wanted was to walk all the way back to get them. Someone suggested I ask the apartment ghost, Mum, to let me in. Well, this was the first I'd heard of any ghost in my apartment, and I was less than excited about it, but I gave it a try."

Brandy had joined the conversation and couldn't hold it in any longer. "You asked a ghost to let you in to your place? Just, what? 'Hey, ghosty, let me in'?"

Lina turned a withering eye on Brandy. "Not exactly. I was very respectful and just asked Mum to let me in so I could get some rest."

"How'd that work out?" Brandy persisted.

"Funny you should ask," Lina continued. "I'd barely finished speaking when I heard a click, and the door began to swing open. I wasn't sure whether to run away or say thank you."

"And which won out?" Sean asked.

"I went into the apartment, said, 'Thank you very much, Mum,' and slept like a baby. Every night after that, whether I had my keys or not, I asked Mum to let me in. And every night, she did."

Dante, leaning against the mantel with a full wine glass in his hand, poked his head into the circle of listeners. "Have you said hi to Mum since you got here?"

"No, actually," Lina answered. "I felt bad that I wasn't down there this time. I don't think anyone has moved in yet. Do you think…?"

"Yes, I do think!" cried Dante, fueled by the two Malbecs he'd already had. "Everyone top off your drink! Let's go see if the door is unlocked and pay Mum a visit."

Sean shared a look with Brandy. A few months ago, both of them would have scoffed at this and dismissed it as tipsy party talk, but recent events had taught them to keep open minds. They shrugged to each other and grabbed drinks from the kitchen before following the others down the stairs to Apartment Two.

Halfway down the staircase, Sean's phone pinged, and he checked his texts. Kat would be here soon, armed with a variety of beer courtesy of tonight's manager at Dipco. That manager just happened to be Kat. Well, her timing was good, thought Sean. She should get here just in time for the Mum investigation.

The group, eight strong, took a sharp right when they reached the first floor and proceeded to the door to Apartment Two. Suddenly faced with the actual doorway, they all awkwardly paused, unsure what to do and feeling just a bit foolish about the mission. They glanced amongst themselves, and no one moved until Lina stepped out from the ring of onlookers and approached the white door with a brass "Two" affixed to it.

"Well, it was my place and I'm the one who knows her, so I might as well be the one to give it a go. We're sure no one has moved in here yet?"

"Not as far as I know," Dante answered.

"Okay, well, here goes," Lina squared up to the apartment and tried the doorknob. It didn't budge. Clearly locked. She turned to the group. "Locked tight. Of course, it is if no one is here yet."

"Let me give it a try," Dante said, rubbing his meat-hook hands together and stepping to Lina's side. He placed a hand on the doorknob and gave a turn. Nothing. He doubled down and leaned into it. "Maybe it's just stuck. Been locked for a while." Despite his increased effort, nothing happened. "Huh," he said, disappointed. "Thought I could get that. Really is shut up tight. Bummer."

As the others turned to head back upstairs, Sean stepped forward and tried the door. It was definitely locked, but for some reason felt warm to the touch.

Kat walked in through the front door in time to hear Sean turn to Lina and say, "This door is warm. Weird. Maybe you should just ask her to let you in, Lina. You know, like old times."

Kat stepped quickly to Sean's side, arms full of beer cans, and said, "Um, Sean, that might not be the best—"

Lina spun on her heel. "Great idea! Should have thought of that myself." With a shy grin she approached the door and laid a hand on it. "Mum? Hi, it's Lina. From a few years back? I'm here with the new show, but I'm staying at the theatre this time. I wanted to say hi, though. Maybe introduce you to some of my new friends. Any chance we can come in?"

She stood, hand on the door, and everyone held their collective breath. This was already not a typical cast party. Was it about to get even more remarkable? One moment stretched to another. Then another. Nothing. Lina sagged against the door, deflated. The others followed suit, and a few turned to head back upstairs.

"Thanks, anyway, Mum," Lina whispered through the door. "I just hope you're doing well. Thanks again for everything. Hope the new person is nice to you."

Kat leaned closer to Sean and handed him a Cartel Brewing can. "Listen, this might be for the best. I told you I sense things, and—"

Before she could finish her sentence, the door to Apartment Two very clearly and distinctly gave the loud click of its doorknob unlocking. As the group collectively, and almost as one, did a slow burn turn back toward it, the door began to swing slowly and inexorably inward until it stood wide open. As they looked into the space, the light in the entranceway flicked on to reveal the interior.

The shouts from the assembled actors could be heard on Orange Street outside. Cory screamed and threw himself behind the considerable bulk of Dante. Adriane threw her hands in the air. Unfortunately, the wine glass in her right hand followed suit and emptied its contents in the vestibule. Bobby Smalls stood stock still, grinning from ear to ear. Dante let out a roaring laugh. Lina stepped into the doorway, almost shyly.

"Thank you, Mum," she nearly whispered. "I knew you wouldn't forget me."

Brandy looked at Sean raised first her eyebrows, then her shoulders. "So much for quiet, huh?"

Sean, mouth agape, nodded slowly. "Yup. That's not gonna happen, now."

Kat put a hand on Sean's shoulder. "Yeah, forget what I was about to say. Guess we'll find out what's what soon enough." She grabbed and opened one of the Cartel beer cans for herself, took a deep breath, and followed the gang as they filed cautiously into Apartment Two.

<hr>

Apartment Two sported a more modern and eclectic décor than Sean's apartment that looked as if it had been plucked out of the nineteenth-century and deposited on the second floor. Apartment Two was more Ikea comfy. The furniture in the living room, to the right of the front door, was covered in a sturdy cotton of deep royal blue. Lina perched in an overstuffed chair in the corner and tucked her legs up under her. She looked as if she had just come home after a day at work. She snuggled deeper into the cushions and smiled as she closed her eyes and rested her head on the chair back.

Others perched around the room, and when the seats were taken Cory and Adriane sat on the floor. They all looked to Lina and began to pepper her with questions. Who was Mum? Had she ever seen her? Was she the only spirit in the apartment? In the house? Had she ever been scared?

With everyone occupied, Kat grabbed Sean's arm and motioned

toward the kitchen in the opposite direction and said, just a bit too loudly, "I'm going to put the beer in the fridge. Give me a hand?"

Sean, slightly confused, agreed, and started to follow her. Brandy took note and headed in the direction.

"Nope, you don't get away that easy," she called. "Not after what we just saw."

As the three entered the kitchen, Kat placed the cans in the refrigerator and turned to Sean and Brandy, leaning against the door of the fridge.

"Look," she began, "I was trying to give you a heads-up that something felt off here. Clearly, didn't get that message out fast enough. Now, I don't know what happened here, and I'm not getting particularly negative vibes from this apartment. In fact, weirdly the opposite. This room feels—safe. But like I told you, this house has always struck me as—off, somehow. Now I've seen that? I know I was right."

"There is definitely something weird here," Brandy jumped in. "How do we know there isn't just someone in the front bedroom and it was all a big joke on us?"

She stomped through the doorway at the far side of the kitchen. Three was a small bathroom to the right and she paced into it, checking behind the door and then sweeping the shower curtain quickly open. She craned her neck to take everything in and seemed almost disappointed to find no one lurking.

With an about-face, she left the bathroom, and before heading into the bedroom to her right fixed Sean with a meaningful glare. "Well, come on, Ginge. You going to let me take on these pranksters alone? I mean, I can take care of myself, but that doesn't seem very gentlemanly in front of our new friend, Kat."

Sean shot an apologetic look to Kat and followed Brandy.

"You're not leaving me here by myself," Kat exclaimed, and walked behind Sean. Then more quietly, "But I don't think you're going to find anyone back there."

Brandy stopped inside the bedroom. She approached the closet and flung the door open. Nothing. Just a few wire hangers, swinging from the force she had used. Next, she went to the armoire in the corner and opened the doors. Nothing. Lastly, she got down on the floor and examined under the bed.

"Dammit," she said. "A few dust bunnies, but that's it. Sean, check that window. Unlocked? Could someone have gone out that way?"

Sean went to the window and gave it a heave. It didn't budge, and he confirmed that the latch was on.

"Nope. Locked from the inside. No one went out this way."

"Yeah," Kat said. "There's no one else in here. No one corporeal, anyway."

Brandy turned and sat down with a thump on the floor by the bed.

"I was sure it was a gag. Pick on the new kids, type thing," she said. "Otherwise, what just happened...really happened?"

"Looks like it," Sean answered.

"Hey, Ginge, could it be any of our friends? You sensing anything, if you get my drift?"

Sean pretended he didn't see the questioning look that Kat shot him. "No, I don't think so. I'd pick up on that."

"Well then things just got even more interesting than they were. And I didn't think that was possible. Damn."

They all looked to each other before gathering themselves and joining the others in the living room.

Lina stood crossed to Kat when she, Sean, and Brandy entered the living room.

"You're Kat, right? Someone said you're behind the bar at Dipco now. You used to be—where?"

"A few places," Kat answered. "Spring House for a while. Was up at the old Molly's. Now it's back as The Corner I may look at going back."

She was answering Lina, but trying to keep an eye on Sean, with little luck. Brandy took the chance to pull Sean back into the kitchen, away from the others.

"You're telling me you didn't sense any Peripherals here? You're more in tune with them than I am. I just figured you were keeping it on the down-low, what with Kat right there and all."

Sean looked at Brandy, clearly at a loss. "That was my first thought, too. I tried everything I knew, but nada. If there's a Peripheral nearby, they don't want me to know it and they are much better at hiding themselves than anyone we've met so far. Good or bad."

"In other words, no Peripheral," Brandy concluded. "You would know if there was someone here. So...what was that? Do we have to deal with ghosts now? Spirits, whatever. What does that mean? Are they different from our friends? I mean, Sean. What the hell? Enough is enough."

"Okay, calm it down, Brand. I know how you feel," Sean said, trying to push his own foreboding aside to calm her. "Our friends aren't spirits. They live. Are flesh and blood. They just occupy a different space than us most of the time. Different plane. If they can be real, is it really such a stretch that spirits could find a way to hang around? Far as I'm concerned, anything is possible, at this point."

"Yeah, I get it," Brandy said, sagging against the counter. "It's just a lot. Mythical bad guys are one thing. Dead people, though? I just can't."

"Let's just see this play itself out. So far nothing bad has happened. Just a door opening and a nice warm apartment for us. Maybe this is a good thing."

She fixed him with an incredulous look. "Good thing? Come on, buddy. Have you not seen the movies? It always seems harmless at first, and then—things turn ugly and the spirits demand something. Revenge, a sacrifice, blood. It never works out."

"Well, lucky for us this isn't a movie," Sean answered, putting a calming hand on her arm. "Not much we can do now. How evil can a spirit named 'Mum' be?"

"I'll remind you that you said that when we're hanging from ropes upside down in a dungeon somewhere soon," Brandy huffed.

"Come on," he gently led her into the living room. "Let's go hang out with some living folks."

They reentered the den to find a number of hushed conversations underway. Adriane and Cory were huddled in one corner, intently discussing the day's rehearsal. Bobby Smalls and Dante were on the sofa, deep into discussion of the New York Mets' offseason moves, which both agreed were underwhelming. Kat and Lina both sat cross-legged in the middle of the room, deep in discussion. From what Sean could gather, Lina was a bit of an empath and had picked up on the sensitivity in Kat. They were finding a lot in common.

Sean turned to Brandy a moment after they entered. "See?" he asked. "Totally normal. No blood on the walls. No freezing breezes. Just friendly banter."

"For now, sure," Brandy said, unconvinced.

Lina checked her phone and let out a small yelp. "Folks, it's late! Almost twelve. Where did the time go? I need to get back to the theatre and get some sleep."

"That's the most sensible thing I've heard in a while," Brandy agreed. I'm going that way myself."

Dante pushed his bearlike frame off the sofa and stretched. "Yup. Time to call it. I have my car here. Happy to take a few folks back down. Adriane, come with me. No one walks alone. Five minutes, tops. Let's just grab your things from my place upstairs."

Bobby rose next to him. "I'm headed the other way. Cory, I know you're only a couple blocks, but I can give a lift."

"I never turn down a ride home at midnight," Cory said. "Thanks, Bob."

As the group headed for the front door, Lina stopped and closed her eyes in a silent thank you to Mum. Whoever Mum was. Kat watched and gave a small nod of approval.

While filing out, Kat caught up to Sean and stopped him with a hand on his chest. "Sensing friends?" she whispered quietly but intently. "You have something you need to let me in on?"

Sean paused. He felt sure he could trust Kat. He wasn't entirely sure why, but he just knew. But he also knew this was not the time or place. "Look," he matched her whisper. "I do have some stuff I can share with you. Just not here or now. Not after all that and with everyone here. But I will. Just keep an open mind."

"That's the best kind of mind to have," Kat said. "But I'm going to hold you to that. Something weird is up. This town is going through something, and whatever it is, it seems to have hit high gear when you all got here."

"I promise," Sean swore.

Dante leaned in between them with a grin. "Kat, like I said, no one walks alone. Need a ride?"

"Much appreciated, Dante, but I have my bike here," she replied. "I'll be home before you even get this lot piled into your car."

"Okay, then. Safe home."

"Same to you, good sir," she answered.

"Right, if everyone is sorted," Sean announced, "I'm off to my apartment. 'Night, all!"

Brandy shot him a warning look as she followed the others to Dante's. Kat shot him a similar look as she left through the front door to her motorcycle. He heard her rumbling up Orange Street before he even reached his door.

He stood just inside his apartment and scanned the living room. The rich Victorian décor seemed somehow austere and cold after the relaxed feel of "Mum's place." He thought he might ask at the theatre tomorrow if he could move down there. Sure, it was smaller, but it just seemed—friendlier.

But that could wait until tomorrow. Tonight, he would get ready, climb into his very fluffy and too tall bed, and hopefully sleep well. Another day of hard work tomorrow. And he was looking forward to it.

Sean's eyes flew open. It was dark. Very dark. The only light in the apartment filtering in from the streetlights around the drawn shades. Something had woken him. Something was in the room with him. Shadows flickered. The damn shadows again. He opened his eyes just a fraction. He was perfectly still. He held his breath. He wasn't alone. He just knew it but couldn't see anything. Or anyone.

His first thought was Mum, but this was different. There was none of the gentle warmth of her space here. Next, he cast his senses throughout the room. Could it be one of the Peripherals? But no. They would make themselves known, and even if it were a Peripheral with ill intent, he was confident he would know. Their presence had become familiar to him. This was something else.

The shadows shifted. He thought. The far corner of the room seemed...darker. He noticed the room was filled with a strong scent. Perfume? No. Cologne. A musky men's cologne. It seemed old. Something his grandfather would have worn. Had it been there when he woke? He didn't think so. But it was here now and growing stronger.

The foot of the bed shifted. It felt as if someone had sat down. He felt the comforter shift. All intention to keep his eyes closed vanished, and he tried to lift his head. But he couldn't. And try as he did, his eyes refused to open fully. They were stuck barely open. He felt—paralyzed. There was no other word for it. He felt panic rising in him. His chest struggled to heave a breath, but the air came in shallow gasps. And they were growing shallower.

Whatever had perched at the foot of the bed began to move toward his head. For all the world, it felt as if something were crawling up along his bedclothes, closer to his face. As that happened, the musk grew heavier. It filled his nose until it was all he could smell. Through his slitted eyes, he saw a darkness settle over the bed. A blackness encompassed him. It filled his mouth, his eyes. With no breath, he couldn't even release the scream that was trying so hard to escape his embattled lungs. Air grew precious. And scarce. The dark covered his face, smothering him. The mattress below him began to bow downward. He felt himself being pulled into it, unable to lift his arms to try to stop the descent. In another moment, he would be gone. Consumed by the dark. And he was helpless to stop any of it. His thoughts turned to Breena, the beautiful Peripheral. The otherworldly Tuatha who had captured his heart before disappearing. His heart ached at the thought of never seeing her again.

Of succumbing to whatever this evil was that would steal him down and away.

There was an enormous battering crash. A wild cold wind shook the room. Shook the bed. And shook the darkness from his eyes. They flew open and he found himself able to move. His arms flailed around his head but met no resistance. The dark swirled and danced about. Crashing toward the ceiling, away from the door to the living room.

He levered himself halfway up. A bright light streamed around the bedroom door, which suddenly blew itself inward with such force that it dangled from one of the hinges. In the middle of the light, a female shape stood, arms outstretched.

Sean's first thought leapt to Breena. She had come to his side when he most needed her. But as he looked closer, he saw that the figure was of a woman. Her silhouette showed her to be wearing an older style dress, squared shoulders with a defined waist and flared skirt. This was not Breena.

A woman's voice broke what had been an unearthly silence. "You do not belong here! Go! This house is under my protection, and you will not harm this man!"

Sean had by now struggled to a sitting position and saw the black shape ooze and slide along the ceiling and out into the kitchen. With it gone, Sean now saw a familiar shape, the shadow of a man wearing a hat, slip along the wall toward the kitchen, stopping to doff the hat at the woman in the doorway before exiting to the faint sound of a deep rumbling laugh. Before Sean could vault from the bed, he saw two more figures crouched in the opposite side of the room. He rubbed his eyes, disbelieving what he saw, but when he looked again the sight of a jaguar and grey fox remained crouching there. The jaguar turned to the woman in the doorway and spat at her. The two creatures then simply fell through the floor and were gone.

"Now, Sean," the woman cried to him. "This will not hold. Come with me. Quickly."

"Mum?" Sean stuttered, as he did his best to reach the floor and head toward her. He felt the cold wind that had preceded her pushing him from behind, almost lifting him along the room.

She turned and led him out of the apartment and down the stairs, her feet never touching the floor below her. She moved swiftly and without a sound. The door to Apartment Two lay open when he reached the first floor. He stumbled inside and the door closed emphatically behind him.

When he turned, he found himself facing a lovely middle-aged woman, clad in a classic emerald-green dress reminiscent of the early 1960s. Her dark hair was rolled tightly up and away from her face. She looked as if she had stepped straight out of the history books.

"You will be safe here for tonight," she said in a rich, deep alto. "Sleep now. You must recover. You will need strength tomorrow and going forward."

"What the hell was that?" Sean asked. "I couldn't move. I couldn't—anything."

"A great evil is here, but we will talk about it tomorrow. Pettirosso will know and have a plan. Sleep now."

Sean felt an irresistible fatigue take hold of him. This time, as he felt himself being drawn down into the overstuffed sofa, he felt safe. Secure. The last thing he saw before his eyes closed was the figure of Mum, stationed by the door and safeguarding both Sean and the apartment. His eyes now closed; he knew nothing until the morning light through the window startled him awake. Awake and alone in Apartment Two.

CHAPTER 8

Sean's eyes fluttered cautiously open. The terror of the night before was the overwhelming sensation flooding him as he shook his head lightly to clear the cobwebs and nightmares. He peered through to the kitchen, seeing that it was just after nine. He had almost an hour to steady himself, get ready, and make it to rehearsal.

He swung his legs off the sofa and worked some kinks out of his back and shoulders. The couch was surprisingly comfortable, but just a little too short for him and he had spent the night curled in a protective ball. He woke in exactly the same position as he fell asleep. He sat with his head in his hands and recapped what had happened.

It had been far more than a dream, that much was clear. But it had somehow grown out of his dreaming, and that was where his confusion mostly settled. He took in the cozy interior of Apartment Two. That part was clearly abundantly true. Mum had burst into his apartment and whisked him away to safety.

"Mum?" he whispered into the empty room, feeling more than a little foolish. His normally reliable senses found nothing in the room, and crossing to the kitchen, he found nothing there or anywhere else in the apartment. He sat, more collapsed, into one of the chairs at the table by the refrigerator. The vinyl tablecloth, with its brown and gold floral pattern, stuck to his fingers when he placed his hands down. He could swear his grandmother had had the same one in her home.

Thinking of getting ready, he realized he had none of his belongings with him. His toiletries, backpack, phone, chargers—even his script— were all upstairs where he had dropped them the night before as he got ready for bed. Damn. He really didn't want to go back upstairs. Even in the light of day, the desperate struggle to breathe was far too fresh in his mind. Sadly, he couldn't think of any alternatives. He didn't even have a change of clothes. Just the sweats and t-shirt he had slept in.

No choice, really. He tapped his forehead lightly on the tabletop in resignation and rose to his feet. He crossed to the front door and paused. He realized he didn't even have the keys to his apartment on him. Well, hopefully the door didn't lock behind them when he and Mum had rushed out. He wasn't optimistic, though. Not given everything else that had happened.

His bare foot kicked something lying on the floor by the door and with a muttered curse, he grabbed his toe and hopped back a step. The curse died quickly when he saw what he had stubbed his toe on. There, on the floor by the door, was his backpack. On top of it was a change of clothes, his keys, and his phone. He checked the phone. Fully charged. Opening the pack, he found his shaving kit, script, and everything he would need at rehearsal today, including his phone charger.

On top of the script was a handwritten note.

I hope you will have all you need. Do not under any circumstances go upstairs. Ready yourself here and go to the theatre. Trust no one until you speak to Marcello.

Sean shook his head. Mum was clearly living up to the name Lina had given her. The discovery of his pack felt like the weight of the world had lifted from his shoulders.

"Thank you, Mum," he said into the empty space. This time with no trace of embarrassment. "I owe you. Everything Lina says about you is true."

Fifteen minutes later, he had showered quickly and readied himself to go. The fridge and cupboards were bare. Even Mum had her limitations, apparently.

He paused as he exited. It felt as if the night before was clinging to his feet, dragging him backward. He desperately wanted to launch himself outward. To catch the day that felt as if it were already galloping away from him.

He had no keys to Apartment Two, and no desire whatsoever to go back into his own apartment. Well, a bridge to cross later. The day would surely bring more change and more surprises before he faced that choice. And if Lina was right, and last night was any indication, Mum would have his back and let him in downstairs at the very least.

He left quickly, almost dashing to the front door, with the barest glance over his shoulder and up the stairs where his door looked shut tight. No sign of what had happened hours ago. But Sean knew what had happened and put distance between himself and that place as quickly as he could.

<hr>

Sean made his way into the theatre and to the rehearsal room. Gone were the first day jitters. There was already a calm ease to everyone. Dancers ringed the room, in various stretching routines. One corner saw some of the cast sipping their morning coffee and chatting. A few were scattered with their noses in their scripts, many with highlighters in their hands and focused expressions.

Sean instantly felt out of step with everyone else. He desperately wanted to be one of the gang, loose and eager. But the night before had been too intense, too terrifying, to simply ignore. He dreaded going back there after rehearsal. Feared what he couldn't understand. He could sense Peripherals. He had battled creatures from other realms with fantastic powers. Yet, whatever had assaulted him the night before had left him helpless. He likely would have perished without the help of

Mum. Why couldn't he sense them? Even Mum largely avoided his detection. How?

Brandy arrived and made a beeline for him. Plopped herself down opposite at his table and began pulling supplies out of her backpack.

"What up, carrot-man," she quipped. "Ready to face down the spirits of Christmas past, present, and future?"

Sean found himself unable to answer. Her banter hitting a little too close to home after what he'd gone through. What if these actually were spirits? Was there another plane other than where the Peripherals lived? He'd never really thought about it before. If there was one other plane, why couldn't there be others? Could there be an infinity of them, just now bleeding into his to assault him?

"Hey, Sean." Brandy stopped what she was doing when he didn't respond. "You okay? Geez. You look horrible. You actually do look like you saw a ghost. What's up?"

"Last night didn't go so well," he began.

Before he could finish, Pettirosso appeared beside them. True to his word, he was wearing sweatpants and a shirt with a Disney character racing across its front.

"My friend," he said, crouching next to Sean. "I've had word of a difficult situation. If you would be so kind, could you refrain from discussing it for the moment. Even with the charming Ms. Johns? I ask you both to join me in my office at the first break. But, Sean, know this—wheels are in motion. You are safe. And will be."

Sean nodded slowly and half-turned to the director. "Thanks, Cello. I appreciate that."

"I appreciate your understanding," he replied.

"Oh, I don't understand a damn bit of what's going on. But I trust you. From what I've been told, you're the one person I *can* trust."

"Soon, Sean. I promise." Pettirosso rose and headed to the front of the rehearsal room as Dante, Bobby Smalls, Lina, Cory, and Adriane—the gang from the night before—came in chattering about what had happened with the locked door. With everything that had happened after, Sean had nearly forgotten it.

Brandy took a close look at him. "I've learned to wait for answers in situations like this, but that crack about not trusting people better not have included me or you'll have an even bigger problem than you seem to have now."

Sean grinned, but just barely. "You know I trust you. Idiot. I meant all the rest." He gestured around the bustling room.

"Gotta say," Brandy said. "I thought the ghost and the locked door were the highlight of the night. Sounds like I missed the real action."

"You have no idea," Sean answered.

"I don't like the sound of that," she replied. "Can't let you out of my sight for a minute."

"Trust me. Be glad you weren't there."

She shook her head and rolled her eyes. "Trouble already. That didn't take long."

Stage managers Rebecca and Dani rose and called out the actors needed for the coming scene's rehearsal. Sean and Brandy were both called and rose to go to work. Neither seemed particularly focused.

***

Over the next hour and a half, Pettirosso blocked the actors into the first scene, which consisted of a group of mourners at Jacob Marley's funeral and the introduction of the central characters. Sean played the minister leading the service in a downpour, which they were told would be created with the use of a massive wall of LED lights upstage that would shift frequently to set and enhance various locations.

Sean stood center stage, facing away from the audience, leading the cast in a Latin funeral dirge. It suited his mood perfectly. He kept flashing back to the nightmare of the night before and how certain he had been for a split second that he would be the one needing a funeral.

The majority of the cast sensed nothing amiss, but those who knew Sean could see that he was not himself. Brandy tried to lighten the mood with a few well-timed goofy faces but received no response. Sean didn't even seem to notice. The stage managers shared a glance, wondering if they were in for a show full of cast drama. It was only day two, after all. Pettirosso, though, stopped by their table and gave them a quiet assurance that all was fine.

Finally, after eighty minutes, with the scene blocked and rehearsed multiple times, a break was called. Pettirosso announced that the following scene, a street scene following Scrooge through the streets of London to his office, would be staged by his associate choreographers, Adriane and Cory. The company applauded the announcement and gathered around the two to show their support.

With that taken care of and the union break under way, Pettirosso gestured for Sean and Brandy to meet him in his office. Before he left the rehearsal room, he made sure to tell them to take their break before joining him.

"I don't want to infringe on your breaktime. I hear your Equity deputy is a stickler for following the rules," he said as he passed them.

Brandy let out an audible groan. She had completely forgotten that she had been appointed to that position.

After the ten minutes were up, mostly spent with Sean staring out the windows over the rooftops of Lancaster, while Brandy buzzed worriedly by his side, the two left the room and headed toward the elevator. As he pulled away from the window, Sean thought for just a moment that he spotted the man in the red cap on the street below. But as soon as he noticed him, the man was gone. Rebecca gave them an approving nod as they motioned their intent before she turned back to the rehearsal just getting under way.

Once in the hallway, Sean picked up his speed and his face settled into a look Brandy had only seen once or twice. Normally when they had been faced with seemingly insurmountable odds and hordes of creatures determined to end their existence.

"Slow down, Ginge," she called to him. "My legs are short. Even shorter than yours."

"Sorry," he muttered. "I just really need to know what's happening."

"I hear that," she agreed, doubling her pace to match his strides.

The elevator opened and the two hustled out, stopping at the door to Pettirosso's office to knock.

"Please come in!" the diminutive director called in a voice surprisingly large and resonant.

They opened the door and found Pettirosso behind his desk, facing away from them as he gazed out over Prince Street. He turned slowly to greet them, and they were instantly struck by the change in his demeanor. The carefree and exuberant creative spirit had seemingly been replaced by a visage of steel. His brown eyes seemed almost black. The levity of earlier had been replaced by steel. The only lighthearted part of his appearance now was the animated character galloping across his shirt.

"I had truly wanted to allow you more time to settle in. To acclimate," he began, raising his hands in apology. "Unfortunately, the events of last night have accelerated things. I have much to tell you, but, Sean, let's begin with you telling me about last night. This room is safe and nothing you say will be overheard or draw attention. Please. Sit."

He gestured to the two chairs opposite him at the desk. With a flick of his wrist, he depressed a button on the desk and the windows grew shaded and grey. Another hidden button turned the massive, ornate chandelier over their heads to life and it threw a golden glow over them all.

"I've been told of what happened to you last night. I want to hear it in your words." Pettirosso sat. "Tell me everything."

When Sean finished recounting to Pettirosso the events of the night prior, the director remained still, concern on his face. Brandy, on the other hand, was anything but silent.

"What the hell?!" she cried. "All of this happened *after* I left? You've been seeing shadows since you got into that apartment? And a guy in a red hat? Why didn't you say anything? You have got to be the dumbest ginger on the planet. What if that Mum person hadn't shown up? We'd be planning your memorial! Just craptastic, dumbass."

She leapt out of her chair and paced the length of the office, barely able to contain herself. She stopped, whirled to look at Sean again, pointed at him, opened her mouth, closed it again, and resumed pacing.

"At least as far as his misadventure last night," Pettirosso said, "his silence on that was at my request. Apologies. I thought it best to discuss this in private. I do, however, agree that it would have been helpful to know you'd been watched."

"I wasn't exactly *sure*," Sean answered. "It was just a feeling. Nothing concrete. I didn't want to cause a fuss."

Brandy stopped short again and turned to him. "Really? After everything we've been through? That head of yours isn't just enormous, it must be thick, too. Idiot."

"Okay, okay." Sean raised his hands in surrender. "Not my brightest moment. I just wanted everything to be normal. Quiet. Like it used to be."

"News flash, Einstein. They're never going to be normal again. Ever." Brandy was fuming.

Pettirosso rose and crossed from behind the desk to the front door of his office where he engaged the lock. He opened a small panel next to the entrance that was nearly invisible, disguised as just another piece of the wall. He pushed a series of buttons and the air in the room seemed to buzz with energy for just a moment before returning to normal. He turned to Sean and Brandy.

"Sean," he said, "there is some truth to what Ms. Johns says. I'm afraid what you think of as normal is a thing of the past. But that doesn't mean that what lies ahead need be something to fear. If we, and I do mean *we*, react with alacrity and courage, we can create something even better than what was. But first," he looked uncharacteristically abashed, "I owe you an apology. I have not told you everything that you should know. I did it out of an abundance of caution, both for you and the others in this building, but that is no excuse. I put you in danger and that is never acceptable."

Sean sat up straighter in his seat. "I'm not following you," he spoke haltingly. "I've been a magnet for things like this for the last few months. Actually, from what I've been told, these things have been around me all my life, I just didn't know. Until recently. You haven't had anything to do with any of that."

Pettirosso sighed deeply and slowly crossed back to his side of the massive desk.

"First, I've engaged certain precautions," he nodded to the panel by the door. "We are free to say anything here. It is a safe space."

"Cone of silence," Brandy cracked to Sean.

"In a manner, Ms. Johns, yes." Pettirosso gave her a glance that was both amused and indulgent. "But much more than that."

"Why would we need that here?" Sean asked, choosing to ignore Brandy. "What could we have to say that is dangerous? Who exactly are you, Marcello? I've suspected there is more to you than we've learned. Am I right?"

"To understand me, you must first understand this place. This theatre that is so much more than that," he answered. "As I'm sure you are aware, the site of this building has a troubled past. Long before it became a cultural hub, there was a great evil committed here."

"The attack, yeah?" Brandy asked. "We know about that."

"Of course, you do," Pettirosso said. "But there is more to this place than that. The others, you would call them Peripherals, or Fae, Tuatha, or what have you, recognized even then that there was great power here. I believe you encountered some of the temporal portals that carried your adversaries, and even some of your allies, from place to place."

"Yeah, "Sean agreed. "We've seen a few. Underground in Montauk, in Buffalo City in North Carolina. Apparently, there was one at sea off Montauk, also."

"Exactly," the director affirmed. "But this location, what is now the Fulton complex, is a portal on a scale you would have difficulty imagining. That power was attractive to the Others, both with good and ill intentions. When it was manipulated to create that horrific event, decisions were made. Safeguards were put in place. To ensure that the power here would never be used again to harm innocents. Or for any malevolent purpose."

"Safeguards?" Brandy asked. "What kind of safeguards? That was hundreds of years ago."

"Two hundred and one years ago, to be precise. As for the safeguards, you are looking at them." Pettirosso spread his hands wide and presented himself to the two.

"Okay, Cello...Marcello...whatever, what do you mean? Because I'm getting some strong weirdness vibes right now, and I do not like them one bit," Brandy said, half rising from her seat.

"You just said it was over two centuries ago," Sean said quietly. "How could you have been here that whole time? We know you arrived here after your career in Italy."

Pettirosso continued. "No need for alarm, Ms. Johns. I assure you I am very much aligned with you."

"Damn straight, Skippy," she muttered. "You better be."

"You would call me a Peripheral, I'm afraid. All those years ago, my family and I decided that I would be tasked with preserving this place. Ensuring that it would never again be exploited by evil. I became something of an anchor here. Perpetually guarding the sanctity and putting its power to work for the betterment of all."

"Wait." Sean held up his hands. "You can't have been here that long. I just told you we know you came from Italy. You're a young man. That's—"

"You already understand that our kind lives at a different rate than you. Our lives are longer. Time passes differently for us," Pettirosso said. "We knew, however, that if I were to protect this place, I would need to be disguised. For many years, I existed as your Peripheral friends do. On the edge of perception. Guiding the humans who worked here. Nudging things in certain directions when it was called for but otherwise, simply a watcher. However, there came a time when that was no longer sufficient. It would require a visible and stronger presence. The strength in this place continued to grow. It attracted not just my kind and yours, it also began to call to other realms. Most notably, what you would call the spirit realm. Those, usually of your race, who wander lost between planes. The Fulton came to be known as a safe space for all, regardless of where they were in their terrestrial or celestial journey."

"That explains all of the ghost stories. This is rumored to be the most haunted theatre in the country. So, there's truth to that?" Sean asked.

"You really need to stop watching those ghost hunter shows," Brandy said, shaking her head.

"There is some truth to those stories, yes. But as that activity grew and came under more scrutiny, I knew I needed to be able to step in directly. That was when I assumed the role I now have. As I said, I'm an anchor here. Tethering this place securely where it should be, in terms of intention."

"But how?" Brandy asked, her agitation far from soothed.

"Every quarter century or so, I simply—reinvent myself. One of the gifts of my people is the ability to cloak ourselves in other forms. You could call us shapeshifters, although that falls short of the truth. So, I have been here all this time. I have been Michael; I have been Marc. I have been Christopher, and Blasius. My people vowed that, unlike its past when this place was used to imprison humans, we would transform it into something much more magical—a place where art, and thought, and music, and language would be allowed to set people free. A bridge of sorts, between those who may not otherwise come to know each other. A beacon."

"Holy shit," Brandy said, settling rapidly back into her chair. "A Peripheral. Here in plain sight all this time."

"There are very few places like this on your plane. Places of such enormous power that, if exploited, could change the course of the entire world. All of our realms, actually. As the city became more renowned, it attracted attention from all sorts. As I mentioned, we became a haven for the lost. Those who seek something other than the lot they have been handed. Spirits, to you. But also, those who would seek to exploit the power here. Lancaster itself became awash in beings from—elsewhere. Good and evil. Aimless, but also driven. They all came here seeking...just seeking. I became the peacekeeper. Not by choice, but by necessity. Until recently, it appeared that things were contained. My role was changed, but I accepted it. There are not many of my kind that would be able and willing to accept such an assignment. I am."

"There are others?" Sean asked.

"There are," Pettirosso replied. "But they will not enter into this story. They are anchored to their portals. We must never waver in protecting them. They remain where they are. No matter what happens."

"Unbelievable," Brandy said. "None of our Peripheral buddies ever said anything about any of this to us."

"Nor would they," Pettirosso agreed. "Likely, as they are relatively young by our standards, they know nothing of it. At most a rumor or suggestion. But even if then, they would be sworn to secrecy. This is one of our greatest secrets. We protect against the evil in our own kind, yes. But I am also tasked with protecting this space from the rash and impetuous of your kind. Your lives burn so swiftly, that power of this magnitude could be an irresistible call to the weaker willed."

"Come *on*," Brandy said, clearly having difficulty digesting all of this.

Sean leaned forward across the desk. "Okay. It'll take a while for me to process all of this, but while I work on that, I have one pretty important question: why did you bring us here? Because that was no accident. Are we here to help or are we here because we pose a threat?"

"Interesting question," Pettirosso replied.

Pettirosso rose from his desk and crossed to the door, stopping to disengage the precautions he had put in place earlier.

"I fear we must return to rehearsal. Our absence will be noted if it goes on too long. It's imperative that we maintain a semblance of normalcy. Our cast and crew have all been impeccably vetted. We are safe in their company. But tongues tend to wag when rehearsal ends and the less attention we attract the better."

"Whoa, whoa, whoa, mister," Brandy said, not rising from her seat. "That question needs to be answered. We're all on the same side, here, yeah?"

"Actually, she has a good point," Sean agreed. "It would help to know exactly why you brought us here?"

Pettirosso paused at the door, his back to them. "The answers to your questions are layered. You are here because you have drawn the notice of some powerful members of our realm. As we learn more of who is involved, we realized that having you here, one of our most secure locations would be of service to all. Further, your particular strengths, shall we say, make sense here. If it comes to an assault on you or the Fulton, you will be well looked after here and likely will prove a powerful ally. If you were to fall into the hands of our adversaries...well, the repercussions would be catastrophic. So, you see, the answer is both."

"And here I was thinking we got these roles because we're good actors," Brandy groused. "Should have known better."

"Oh, you most certainly earned these jobs. As I said, we aim to avoid unnecessary scrutiny. You most definitely belong on our stage. If you weren't qualified, we would have found different tasks for you here."

"Well, thanks for that, at least," Brandy said, somewhat mollified.

"We're all better off together in one place," Pettirosso assured them. "But I do owe you an apology, Sean. I was wrong, something rare. I housed you at Dremmel exactly because Mum was there. She is an old friend. I trusted that her presence would safeguard you. It did, but only just."

"Wait," Sean interrupted. "You sent me there knowing it was haunted?"

"Haunted is perhaps the wrong word. I knew Mum was there. I hoped to stash you there with little attention paid, while the theatre was the focus of their scheming. Rather than focusing here, our foes seem to have chosen to pursue you wherever you went. I expected them to target me and our sanctuary. They must want you very badly. Either aiding them or destroyed. I will investigate who it was that visited you in your rooms. I will not make the same mistake again. I will have Deborah move your things down here to the campus while we rehearse. I have an apartment for you. Just a few doors from Ms. Johns. It was being worked on but is ready. now"

"Jeez," Brandy said. "Just call me Brandy, yeah? Ms. Johns sounds all kinds of wrong."

"If you insist—Brandy." He grinned at her. "For now, It seems the fight has arrived sooner than expected. I will let you know what I find. In the meantime, to work. We will make some wonderful theatre. If all goes well, we will be able to avoid confrontation, come to an agreement, and go on our ways."

"I have a feeling we won't get off that easy," Sean said, slowly rising.

"And now we just go back to rehearsal like nothing has happened? That's the plan?" Brandy asked as she slowly rose to match Sean.

"Yes, of course," Pettirosso replied, spreading his arms wide and beaming at them. "Because we are all professionals. It's what we do!"

They filed out of the office and headed to the elevator. Sean and Brandy were noticeably less enthusiastic than the director, whose passion seemingly could not be dampened.

As the three entered the rehearsal room, the cast was preparing to run through the opening number they'd been working on. Sean and Brandy sat behind the production table, happy to have a chance to somewhat ease back into the work. Their heads were still spinning with what they had learned from Pettirosso. However, once the music began, even with just the piano for accompaniment, they found their attention captured.

Sean stood to get a look at Haydn behind the piano. His fingers flew across the keys, dancing every bit as much as the actors who began to enter the rehearsal stage. Slowly, at first, and then with increasing tempo as the streets of London were portrayed waking up, and grinding into the hullaballoo of the street markets, the crush of pedestrians, the hawkers selling wares. Haydn's music swelled and the players matched it in intensity.

Sean and Brandy sat, mouths open. There were Cory and Bobby Smalls, weaving throughout the athletic choreography, two charity workers making their way to Scrooge's office. Brandy tapped Sean and pointed to where Lina and Adriane crossed the entire stage pirouetting. Joyful, fluid, contagious. And there was Dante, playing Scrooge himself, stalking through the throng, shoving aside anyone who dared slow his progress. But it was all designed and set. It fit the soaring music perfectly, and by the time the final note had played and hung shimmering in the air, Sean and Brandy had been completely transfixed. All thought of the danger beyond the building forgotten, at least temporarily.

They leapt to their feet, applauding enthusiastically. The cast, the number finished, fell to the floor, exhausted, but laughing and hugging each other with congratulations. New life had been breathed into the old play. It felt as if it had never been seen or heard before, and indeed, this version hadn't.

Flushed faces looked around the room. It was the all too rare moment of creating something new, unique. And as Sean thought to himself that it was, indeed, magic at work, he turned to Pettirosso, who was also on his feet, beaming and laughing from the sheer joy of collaboration and connection.

"Well, that was nothing less than awesome!" he cried. Jumping out from behind his table and crossing center stage, He pointed at Adriane and Cory, beckoning them to take a bow. "Last time I leave you two in charge. I'll come back and you'll have taken my job! Honestly, though, beautiful. Just stunning. And you!" He turned to Haydn and Page at the piano. "Sorcerers. Nothing else explains what I just witnessed."

The performers allowed themselves to relax. Some sort of litmus test passed and ready to enjoy the moment just a hair longer before tackling the next scene.

"And now," Pettirosso announced, "we will be moving on to the first Scrooge office scene. Anyone not involved in that, enjoy your well-deserved early lunch break. If you have questions about that, check with stage management. Those who are staying, we'll begin with Scrooge's entrance."

The rehearsal moved on and continued its frantic pace of creation and exploration. Pettirosso worked hard and fast. By the time they had reached two o'clock and lunch break, they had covered the entire scene, and run it more than once.

As they broke for lunch, Sean noticed the stage manager, Rebecca, hand Pettirosso a note. He scanned it, gave her a curt nod, and approached.

He reached Sean and Brandy where they had just hoisted their backpacks. "I hope you found that as exciting as I did. See what I meant? Professionals. But more than that. Artists. I hope you found some escape in that process. I know I did."

"You made a believer out of me, Cello," Brandy enthused, clapping the director on his shoulder before thinking better of it and withdrawing her hand. "Okay, yeah, maybe too soon for that."

"Nonsense, you silly person," Pettirosso responded and grabbed her for an enormous hug. The two were almost the same height, and Sean couldn't help but grin at the surprise and discomfort on Brandy's face.

"Sure," she said quietly. "It's like that. Got it."

"And you," Pettirosso continued, turning to Sean, and waving the note he'd just been given. "I am happy to report that your belongings have been deposited in your new apartment here. I am very sure you will find it more comfortable."

"Thank you, Cello," Sean answered. "I appreciate it."

"Deborah also took the liberty of making sure your kitchen was stocked with the essentials. And some inessentials." At that, he actually winked at Sean. "Please take your time acclimating. If you are a few minutes late coming back, I fully understand. But you," he pointed to Brandy, "have no such leeway. Your first big Mrs. Dilber scene is coming up. So—" He tapped his watch and gave her a wink, as well.

He turned to leave them, then snapped his fingers and turned back. "I almost forgot the most important thing. Your fellow Grumbles have arrived. Messrs. Nichols and Trout will be in the studio space upstairs. Ken O'Carroll will join us this afternoon. You will all be housed here in the theatre campus, for reasons you know too well. I will ask all of you to join me briefly after rehearsal to make sure everyone is up to speed. And I hope to have some added information for you then. Plans are being put in motion." With that, he turned again and was gone.

In the far corner of the room, where he had indeed escaped attention for much of the morning, Drew Brindig stood waving frantically to them. "Hiya, friends! I get to show you the way to your new place, Mr. Sean! Ms. Brandy, you can tag along. I know how easy it is to get lost around here. No need for embarrassment!"

"Who said I was embarrassed?" Brandy answered, with distinct embarrassment.

Drew stood aside, and allowed them through the door first, before giving a small skip and following them.

Just over an hour later, Sean was back on his way to rehearsal. His new apartment was, after a quick comparison with Brandy's, spacious, comfortable, sleek, and modern. He felt instantly relaxed there. Deborah had stocked both the cupboard and the refrigerator, meaning he had been able to have a quick bite—local pepperoni bread from Ric's Bread at the market across the street, a favorite—and fit in a quick nap. Much needed after the disrupted night before. His only regret was that he hadn't been able to thank Mum personally.

The rest had done him good and he was excited to get back to work. He was also excited because he knew his friends the Grumbles, minus Stewart, were arriving any minute and he couldn't wait for the reunion, even though it had only been two days since he had seen them. It certainly felt much longer than that, given all that had happened. He was even looking forward to seeing Ken.

He and Brandy met at the elevator in the hallway outside of the apartments. Down three levels, the door opened, and they spilled out onto stage right.

"Less than thirty seconds to commute," Sean noted. "I could get used to this."

"Only theatre I know of that can offer that," Brandy replied. "So civilized I almost don't know what to do with myself."

"Fair point. You and civilized don't exactly seem like the smoothest fit," Sean agreed, grinning.

"Nice to see you're back to your normal smart-ass self," Brandy said.

"What can I say, I bounce back fast," Sean answered, chuckling.

They proceeded to the rehearsal space and the afternoon passed in a blur of creativity and collaboration. Sean was shocked at what a difference it made to be in the new apartment. In hindsight, he wondered how much a drain the negative energy in his Dremmel apartment had placed on him. He even caught Brandy giving him a surprised nod more than once. He really must have been in a bad way.

By five o'clock, he was basically just watching the clock, knowing that the Grumbles must be here by now, and at six they would all meet up. The stage managers and Pettirosso also made note of his dwindling attention span, and at quarter to six Rebecca called Sean and Brandy over to her table.

She looked over some papers in front of her before looking up to them. "Judging by our current pace, we are not getting to your next scenes, so"—she glanced to Pettirosso who nodded with a grin—"you are free to go. I'm guessing you'd like to see your friends. Sullivan Nichols and Dan Trout are just down the hallway, third door on the left. Finishing up a meet and greet with their stage manager, Tim. Ken O'Carroll has just unpacked and will meet you there. Make sure to check the online schedule tonight for your call tomorrow. Good work, gang."

Sean and Brandy shared an excited look and almost ran to their things to pack their bags and go. As they quietly made their way to the door, Pettirosso motioned them over.

"Nice job, today. I just wanted to let you know that I took a few moments to fill your friends in on what has happened since you've been here and a little of our—situation—here. I have some added information for you all. I'll come down to share that when we finish here in a few minutes. Sound good?"

"Perfect, Cello," Brandy said, vibrating with excitement to see the Grumbles.

"On your way, then," Pettirosso replied, nodding to the exit.

Sean and Brandy paused at the entrance to the conference room, looked at each other, grinned, and threw open the door. Nick and Trout were seated at the far end of a conference table, Trout with his cowboy boots up on the table as he leaned as far back as his rolling chair would go. Nick, on the other hand, sat with his laptop open in front of him, a legal pad next to the computer with a simple wooden pencil laid on top of it, and a look of intense concentration on his face.

Trout, seeing the newcomers, leapt to his feet, and bellowed, "Let's get ready to Grumble!"

Sean and Brandy paused in the doorway. Nick looked up from his computer and said, "Sometimes you make it really hard to be your friend." Despite his biting remark, he couldn't suppress a grin, and before anyone else had time to comment, they were rushing to the side of the table and devolving into a mass of hand shaking, fist bumping, and awkward self-conscious hugs.

In the midst of the greeting, Ken O'Carroll poked his head sheepishly around the corner from the hallway.

"Well, if there had been any doubt about whether I was in the right place, it's gone now. Hi, gang." Ken hovered where he was, clearly unsure of how he would be received.

Almost as one, the others stopped their celebration and turned to Ken. A hush fell over them, their arms fell to their sides. They shared glances amongst themselves. The tension rose.

But then they all let out a raucous "Ken!" and descended upon him with equal, if not greater, fervor than they had shown each other.

Relief flooded Ken's face and he allowed himself to be drawn into the group.

Behind Ken in the hallway, Drew Brindig, who had obviously led Ken to the conference room, smiled openly before drifting back down the corridor.

After the salutations had finished, they each found a seat around the table and settled down.

Trout leaned his long lanky self over the table and pointed at Sean. "You, mister," he said. "Could you not go even a week without raising some sort of ruckus? What the hell are we walking into here? Spirits? Nightmares? Muggings? I mean, aren't you exhausted?"

"Exhausted doesn't even begin to cover it," Sean answered. "And your concern is touching. Really. Brings a tear to my eye."

Trout laughed. Loudly. "Concern? I've seen what you can do. I should worry about those spirits."

Nick took the moment to power down his laptop and stow it in his bag. "Sean, we are concerned. This big idiot just doesn't know how to express himself. Are you okay?"

"Yeah, I know," Sean said. "Part of his charm. And thanks, Nick. I'm good. Touch and go last night, but I'm still here. Where's Bunsen? Did you bring him?

"Sadly, no," Nick answered. "No dogs in the housing here, and he does better at home, anyway. Chris is watching him."

"I'm fine, too, thanks for asking," Brandy interjected.

"Oh, sorry, Brand," Trout said, turning his considerable height to her. "From what we heard, you were safely tucked into bed here while Sean was wrestling with demons, or ghosts, or some such. You have a story to tell?"

"No, not really," Brandy admitted. "My washing machine turned on by itself. Does that count?"

"A haunted washing machine? Heck yeah, we can give you that one. I know I hate it when spirits do my cleaning for me." He gave Brandy a gentle push on the shoulder. "We're glad you're okay, too."

Nick rose and strolled to the window looking out over the street.

"Mr. Pettirosso filled us in. Things sound different, but eerily familiar. And not to fan the flames of paranoia, but I did notice someone in a red hat watching me unload the car from across the street when I got here. Probably nothing, but then when I heard your story..."

"Wow. Okay. Let's see what Pettirosso has to say on that one. He said he had more to tell us," Sean answered.

Ken, looking at his phone, said, "Yo, any of you seen Playbill today?"

The others all shook their heads and reached for their phones.

After a moment, Brandy exclaimed, "Holy shit!"

Nick muttered, "I'll be damned."

Trout whistled long and loud.

Sean began reading the top headline out loud. "'Stewart Garland becomes the hottest ticket in town. Sold out shows extended amidst talk of an open-ended run. Feel good story of the year.'"

"Wow, that was fast. Guess it helps to be dating one of the gods of mischief," Brandy said.

"I don't think that's it," Ken mused. "And even if it is, it couldn't happen to a nicer guy. He deserves it. Maybe people just want something genuinely positive for a change."

The others nodded and grunted their agreement. At that moment, Pettirosso arrived in the doorway.

Pettirosso entered the conference room tentatively. "I trust you are caught up and it's safe to enter?"

The Grumbles nodded and muttered their assent, and the director took a seat at the table close to the door. Ever faithful Deborah entered behind him but strode to the window and took up station there, scanning the street below.

"First," Pettirosso said, "it does my heart good to see you all here. You are all most welcome and I'm excited to see what we conjure up for the stages here over the next few weeks. Mr. Nichols—"

"Please, call me Nick," he demurred.

"My pleasure, Nick," came the response. "I am excited to learn more of your project. For those of you who don't know, we've given Nick carte blanche in deciding his subject. Unusual, yes, but these are unusual times and you"—he gestured around the table—"are highly unusual yourselves."

"You got that right, Cello," Trout interjected. Suddenly, he realized his boots on the table may be a bit disrespectful and quickly put them under his chair. "I'll be curious to see what ol' Nick writes with that magic pencil of his." He nodded to Nick's pencil, which now jutted from his shirt pocket.

"Right," Pettirosso said. "Tell me about it again?"

"Well, it was gifted to me," Nick explained. "It came from the Mother Vine in Manteo, North Carolina. Oldest grapevine in North America, possibly. Has some enchantment on it, apparently. It helped us out down there."

"Helped us out?" Brandy said. "It basically saved our bacon. That's a helluva pencil there."

"Nick, I have some assorted shavings and chips from the Fulton beam in my office," Pettirosso said, considering Nick carefully. "I have a feeling you could find a use for them. Perhaps in conjunction with your piece of the Mother Vine."

"Oh, wow," Nick sputtered. "That would be amazing. Thank you. I seem to have knack for stumbling onto these writing tools. I'd love to do something with them."

"I'll have them brought to your apartment," the director said. "But that is for later. We shall address all things artistic in good time. We are off the clock right now and I have...other information to share with you."

"Good," Brandy said. "We have a lot of concerns, obviously. To begin with, are we safe here?"

"A valid question. I cannot give you blanket assurance that you are completely safe here."

"Ah, man," Ken murmured. "I don't know how much more of this I can take."

"I appreciate that, Ken. May I call you Ken?" When Ken nodded,

Pettirosso continued. "What I *can* tell you, is that you are safer here than you would be on your own somewhere else. In fact, we've placed you all in apartments here in our artist village. You will always be mere feet from each other during your stay. What you accomplished in North Carolina was nearly miraculous. But much like earlier events on Montauk, it was only a stopgap."

"We suspected as much," Sean replied. "It just seems that we haven't actually gotten to the root of what's happening."

"Very true," Pettirosso continued. "Hopefully, what I have uncovered will help us along that trail. As I've mentioned to you all before, Lancaster itself, in large part because of our presence, has become a lure for activity of an otherworldly nature. Paranormal, Supernatural. Call it what you will. We have become quite vigilant over the years. The theatre is a bit of a fortress in that regard. We watch over this space, but also the entire city."

"You keep saying 'we' and 'us,'" Nick broke in. "You seem a like a one-man band from where I'm sitting. What else do we have going for us?"

"Every person who makes the Fulton their home comes to us with certain...talents. Talents that lie beyond the scope of their day-to-day duties. You are surrounded by people of great resources. Much like your talents developed unexpectedly and continue to grow, many of the most unassuming here wield great influence. Some otherworldly. Some less so."

The table turned to look at Deborah, still quietly standing at the window. "Oh, not much to see here," she said with a laugh. "I think Mr. Pettirosso keeps me around because I've been here so long and know where all the bodies are buried. So to speak."

"Deborah sells herself well short. But let's hope we never have need of more than her organizational genius."

Sean leaned forward over the table. "You said you had more information on what happened to me last night?"

"Yes, quite right," Pettirosso said, redirecting his focus. "As I said, we are usually very aware of what happens here, which makes our being caught unawares distressing. Sean, you have indeed been followed. There are beings, commonly called Shadow People, who have long shared Lancaster with us. They are, for lack of better words, human silhouettes. Beings that live in our peripheral vision. There's that word again. Many cultures around the world report them. The Islamic Jinn and Choctaw Nalusa Chito are two you may have heard of. Some think they are souls trapped here after death. Others say they have come back from the underworld. Some even believe they are from another world. In most events, they are of ill intent. The man in the fedora, who you've reported seeing, Sean, is widely believed to be one of the strongest and most powerful. His most common behavior is to sit on his victims' chests and choke them. Exactly as you described, Sean."

"Oh, just great," Brandy interjected.

"Far from great, unfortunately," he continued. "We have never experienced activity of this kind here. And the fedora man has never been seen here. But there's more. There is also a cadre of what are, unimaginatively, called Hide Behinds that has moved into town. They are even more elusive than the Shadow People. And your very own Peripherals. Often, their presence is not noticed until they capture their solitary victim and drag them off. We believe that they have been near you. Likely the feeling of being watched you've experienced. It's one reason we want you all here and near each other. Where Hide Behinds are concerned, there is some safety in numbers."

"Well, this just keeps getting better and better," Trout said. "Feelin' as if I should just head back to Montana. Or the Outer Banks. At least we got rid of the bad guys down there."

"I wouldn't be too sure of that," Sean replied, earning a knowing nod from Trout.

"I'm afraid there's more," Pettirosso said."

"More?" Ken and Nick said in unison.

"Yes. The man in the red cap you've seen, Sean, is likely a scout, or more than one being. They are a race called Powries, often nicknamed 'Red Caps' for obvious reason. They hail from the Anglo-Scottish border. They have never been seen here. In fact, they are usually solitary. If we are lucky there is only one, but that seems unlikely given recent events. Their caps grow a darker color of red the older they get as a result of their habit of soaking them in the blood of their victims. I think that tells you all we know."

Brandy turned to Sean. "Sleepy, friendly, little Lancaster, huh?"

"What can I say?" Sean answered with a shrug. "This is all new to me."

"Sean could not have known of the changes here in the last few years, let alone recently," Pettirosso said, absolving Sean. "Now, lastly—"

"Jeez o flip, there's more," Ken said, putting his head in his hands on the table.

"Yes and no," came the answer. "The two animal shapes you briefly saw, Sean, we have not identified. We suspect they may be the most senior of the assailants. Likely from what you call South America, so we've gathered. But we will learn more. However, I must warn you. They, like the Dullahan you have encountered, are likely lieutenants for a much greater power. That power remains hidden to us. And that Dullahan is likely not gone for good. No sign of him here, but he is much trickier to vanquish than you've seen. Just a word to the wise."

"Is that it?" Nick asked, a bemused look on his face.

"I just have to ask, for what feels the millionth time," Ken said, staring intently at the table in front of him, "Why? Why us? We're just a bunch of actors. Not even overly successful ones at that. We're... nobodies."

Pettirosso turned slowly to face Ken. "Oh, Ken," he began. "Even after all you've been through, you still do not truly grasp your place in this. Release your conceptions of the place of music, and art, and poetry. Storytelling. You humans have moved so far from it over time, but in the beginnings, those things mattered more than almost anything else. They were what connected all of us—your kind and mine—to eternity. That was how we shared knowledge, and more importantly, wisdom. From elders to the next generations. Think of the simple, yet so delicate and intricate, alchemy of a single musical note in connection with—a lyric.

How it can transport one's heart from the everyday to a place of infinite possibility. Connection. No need for technology. Or tools. We hold the key to all of that, to everything, within us. We always have. My people have never lost sight of that. The writers, and poets, and singers, and, yes, jesters, all can lead us to better versions of ourselves. Show us what can be. What should be. A simple song can sway a nation. Inspire heroes. Expose fools. Reveal truths. Enchant lovers. Teach the children. The alchemy between word and note. And heart. So simple. Yet so inexplicable. So primal. You"—he looked around the table—"all of you, have found a way to tap that place inside you. Sean, you most deeply of all. If you continue to rediscover these things, imagine what can be accomplished. Why *you,* Ken? How could it not be you? You threaten the ages of ignorance those among my kind have counted on to keep you in your place. And those of us who have long awaited your reawakening thrill at the possibilities. You are so close to breaking free. No longer unaware of your own potential. How could it be anyone but you? You are the key to it all."

"Well, hot damn," Trout half rose out of his seat. "You just got me all fired up, Mr. Cello. That was some speech."

"Have you considered going into politics?" Brandy asked, decidedly more skeptical than her neighbor at the table.

"No! I have more than enough to deal with as it is," Pettirosso responded. "But remember as you go through this discovery, you are not alone. You have resources and allies like never before. Just look out for each other and we shall be fine. I won't say I promise all will be fine, but"—cupping his mouth as if telling a secret—"I promise." And there came that grin again. "Those who oppose us are formidable, but we are made of sterner stuff. And with that, I bid you all a good night! Relax. Enjoy the apartments and each other's company!"

He rose and motioned to Deborah, who nodded out the window and raised an eyebrow to Pettirosso but said nothing and followed him out the door.

The table sat in stunned silence for a moment. Then another.

"Well, welcome to Lancaster, guys," Brandy said, wryly.

"Ah, come on! How bad can it be? We've taken down worse, and this time we have warning and each other. I say we grab a beer, some grub, and come back to catch some TV before hitting the hay. Anyone game?"

Sean stood up. "Yeah, I could do that. I think we should stay close to the theatre, though, yeah? Just to be safe."

"Let me guess," Brandy said, rising. "Dipco?"

"Easiest solution," Sean answered.

"Sure," she answered. "I'm sure it has nothing to do with the staff."

"Shut it," Sean said, leaving the room.

The others shared a confused look and followed.

Halfway down the hallway, Trout shouted, "Shots!"

In unison, the others instantly answered, "No!"

Their laughter echoed off the walls as the elevator doors closed behind them.

Pettirosso and Deborah watched from his office doorway as they departed.

"They'll be fine," he said, more to assure himself than anything else.

"All but one," Deborah replied. "There is a shadow over one. I cannot see through."

` *****

The time at Dipco was relaxed and pleasant. After Sean and Brandy made the introductions between the Grumbles and Kat, they settled into an easy couple of beers, with the newcomers commenting on the quality of the heretofore unknown local offerings, and far too many chicken wings. Kat settled into an easy rapport with them, and Brandy made sure to get a few elbow digs into Sean's ribs under the bar. Kat paused more than once to look intently at each of them, none more so than Sean, who she gave special attention to. Conspicuously, there were no shots ordered by anyone.

More than once, one or the other would glance over their shoulder to take in the room. Nick at one point turned entirely around in his stool to keep an eye on the room. Other than that, no one would have known that five of them were in fear for their safety. And the safety of everyone else there, too.

As things were wrapping up, Kat beckoned Sean to the end of the bar under the guise of asking a question about his tab.

"Something happened today," she said. It was not a question.

"Well, a lot happened," Sean replied. "Great rehearsal. Happy reunion. Lots."

Kat leaned across the bar and fixed him with a pointed stare. She didn't say a word but held his eyes.

Sean wilted. "Yes, you're right. A lot is happening. I just can't talk about it here. Damn, you weren't kidding when you said you picked up on things."

"You have no idea," she said. "How about I stop by your creepy building when I get off work. You can fill me in."

"That's one of the things that happened, actually. They moved me down to the theatre housing today. We'll all be there together."

Kat cocked her head and considered him again. "That's good," she finally announced. "I think that's a good thing. Like I said, Dremmel House has weirded me out for a long time."

"I get that," Sean agreed. "But it's not all bad. I found that out, too."

"I'm glad to hear that," she said. "Very glad. Look, why don't I give you tonight to settle in and hang with your buddies. Maybe we can talk tomorrow. Lunch, dinner, whatever?"

"Yeah, that'd be good. Might be nice to have someone outside of the theatre and these jokers to talk to."

"Great. Text me," she said, moving away. "You'd better get back. Your friends look ready to move."

Sean returned to the others further down the bar.

"Everything okay?" Trout asked, checking out his own tab.

"Oh, yeah," Sean said. "They just added something to my tab accidentally. All good."

Brandy shot him a disbelieving look, but he was spared further scrutiny when Nick stood up and announced he would wait for the others out front. "I need some air. Long drive today. Lots of fumes. Just want some fresh air."

Ken shot him a look. "You drive a Prius. What fumes?"

"You have a better memory than I thought. Okay, then, I just want some air, then. You all right with that?"

"Go to it," Ken said, lightly. "Breathe away."

Nick left, and Trout made note that he and Brandy still had beer to finish. "You guys can just go ahead if you want. We'll be right behind you."

"Absolutely not," Brandy insisted. "We stick together, remember. Let's finish up."

"Well, if we're supposed to stick together, should we get Nick back in here?" Ken asked.

"Probably not a bad idea," Sean agreed. You guys drink up, I'll drag him back."

Sean walked out the front door and paused at the top of the unusually precarious steps. He took a look around the entrance but didn't see Nick. Glancing right and left down the alleyway, he still saw nothing.

With a rising sense of unease, he descended to the sidewalk and continued looking. There was no one in the parking lot immediately in front of him. Something was wrong.

He heard a rustling behind and to the left, where another alley broke off up the side of the historic market next door. He turned the corner and stopped dead in his tracks trying to make sense of what he was seeing. Nick was halfway down the passage, between overhead lights, but easy enough to see.

Two large, dark, animal-like forms had grabbed him from behind. They were indistinct, hard to focus on. Sean immediately rushed forward and confronted the creatures. Nick was struggling to make noise, presumably to use his voice to defend himself as they all had learned to do. Unable to produce sound, though, he was helpless and being dragged away.

Sean instinctively shouted, "No!"

The figures around Nick turned to him. He saw them for only an instant before they were suddenly out of sight, now positioned on the far side of Nick.

These are the Hide Behinds, Sean thought. He began to sing, making the tone that had served him well in the past. A glowing white light filled the alleyway, pulsing with Sean's vibrato. He gestured and the Hide Behinds were drawn from where they sheltered. They were large, over seven feet when upright, covered in a shaggy dark pelt. Their eyes were dark and piercing. Despite their helplessness, they seemed unafraid.

It was then Sean sensed something behind *him*, and turning, he caught a glimpse of a host more of the creatures approaching from behind. They scattered when he turned, but he sensed them continuing to surround him in the shadows.

At that point, the door to Dipco swung open and the remaining Grumbles appeared. Trout and Brandy still held their unfinished beers in their hands.

"What in the blazes is going on out here?" Trout called. "It's like someone turned on a dozen spotlights—"

He stopped as he took in the situation.

"Oh, no," Brandy shouted. "Not again."

She, Ken, and Trout began their own song, and their golden light slid down the stairs and enveloped Sean. However, before the light had even reached him, the closest Hide Behinds clawed the air before them and pointed in terror at the drinks in Brandy's and Trout's hands. They scattered and were gone in an instant.

Sean turned his attention back to the two creatures still held in his power. Now they appeared afraid.

Sean gathered his hands before him and with one full-throated blast of song flung them along the alley and out of sight, shouting, "Leave my friends alone!"

The others came down to his side. Ken and Brandy placing their hands on his shoulders while Trout rushed to Nick's side.

"You okay, Nick?" he asked.

"Yup, all good," Nick answered, catching his breath.

"We better get home," Ken said, looking into the shadows around them in the intersection of alleys.

"Most definitely," Brandy agreed. "I'll bring these mugs in and off we go."

Kat, who had been standing behind them in the open doorway, stepped down. "I can take care of those. You should get going."

"Thanks, much appreciated," Trout said, bringing them to her.

Sean seemed to be the only one that realized she had seen it all. Judging by the look she was giving him as they crossed toward the theatre.

The group piled through the side door into the artist village housing at the theatre. To their surprise, Drew Brindig was waiting for them just inside, as if he had been expecting them.

"HI there friends," he said, cheerfully beckoning them inside. "Mr. Pettirosso is aware of what just happened. He suggests that, for tonight only and mostly for your peace of mind, you stay in one apartment together. He stresses, again, that you are safe here, but that you may find some comfort in being together. Sean, your apartment is the largest, so I've taken the liberty of setting it up for a little slumber party."

"Of course, that's fine," Sean replied. "Why is Cello not here himself?"

"He's upstairs doing some homework on how that happened. He'll be up all night, I'm sure. But you folks shouldn't be! Go get some shut eye if you can. Sean, I did leave a note for you from the man himself. Now, I'd best get off to work."

"At this time of night?" Ken asked. "Cello is a slavedriver. You should be getting home."

"Oh, not tonight, my friends," Drew answered. "So much to do. My choice, trust me. Mr. Pettirosso would never force anyone to do anything."

"If you say so," Ken said, dubiously.

"Thanks, little buddy," Trout said. "Appreciate the gesture and I think we'll just head upstairs. Heckuva night."

"By all means," Drew agreed. "I really do hope you can rest a bit. Rehearsal tomorrow. And we are here to make sure nothing further happens tonight."

The Grumbles took the elevator up to Sean's apartment and tumbled through the door, exhausted. The sofa had been pulled out and made up. In addition, an air mattress had been similarly arranged. With another overstuffed chair big enough to sleep in and Sean's bed, there was plenty of room for all.

As they arranged themselves about the rooms, Nick lay with his phone in hand, and Brandy stood by the living room window, watching King Street below, where all seemed quiet.

"Would ya listen to this," Nick announced. "A simple search online says that one of the few things that can defeat Hide Behinds is—alcohol. Ain't that a hoot."

From the window, Brandy responded, "I'm not sure we should take our cues from Google. Seems like there is a lot at stake here."

"You know, I kinda agree with that, but they did scatter pretty durn fast when we appeared with our drinks on the stairs. Might be somethin' to that," Trout said.

"A question for Cello in the morning, I'd think," Sean said. "How's everyone feeling?"

Despite the close call and the receding levels of adrenaline, all agreed that they had come out of the encounter fairly unscathed. All things considered, it could have been much worse.

"Sean, thanks for saving me," Nick said. "Not sure what would have happened if you hadn't shown up when you did. I was going down fast."

"Hey, not a problem. We're in this together. As Cello said, we're better together. And I don't know what would have happened if the rest hadn't come out when they did. Important thing is we're safe now."

"Are we safe?" Brandy asked. "I'm staring at the street as if I could see something, but Shadow People and Hide Behinds aren't going to be obvious from here. And there's not a red hat in sight."

"Good," Ken answered. "Let's hope it stays that way."

Sean wandered into his bedroom where he found an envelope on his pillow, with a florid *MP* embossed on it. Opening it, he drew out a page of heavy linen parchment. He unfolded it and read:

Sean, again, I seem to have been caught off guard, and for that I am, once more, in your debt. Please meet me in my office thirty minutes before rehearsal tomorrow if you are able. I have some things to discuss with you that I hope will put us all in a more favorable position. Things continue to escalate in a way unprecedented, but I am not without resources. Sleep well.

Yours,

Cello

Sean placed the letter back in the envelope and stowed it in the drawer of his bedside table. He looked through the doorway where his friends were ranged around the living room, and a sense of dread and fear for their safety nearly overwhelmed him. Putting on his best face, he emerged from the bedroom.

"Right, who's up for something to eat and some TV? Let's get our minds off of things."

The others agreed, but the response was tepid, at best. The settled in with a table full of crunchy snacks, but the unease hovered over them all until one by one, they allowed themselves to drift to sleep.

The last one awake, Sean considered these friends, who had risked so much for him so often, and the sense of responsibility kept him up most of the night, until, finally, sleep crept over him and pulled him gently down and away.

He was asleep. Yet his eyes flew open, and he found himself standing on a stone jetty, peering out over an ocean. The vast body of water lay still and even. A mirror. The gunmetal sky was reflected on the surface and the two met somewhere indistinct, making the horizon impossible to pick out. Even with the heavy cloud cover, the sky was bright, and he needed to cup his hands over his eyes to shield them.

He knew he was asleep, but he felt so present, so conscious. His feet were rooted to the stone beneath him, forcing him to stare out to sea. At the very limit of his vision, something appeared, a tiny speck of darkness breaking the monotony of the skyline and sea. It moved slowly but steadily toward him. Eventually, he could see that it was a small boat, a skiff, that had no business being in open water. It crept closer, with no means of propulsion in sight. It raised no sails. No oars carved the water beside it.

As it drew nearer, Sean could see that there were people in the boat, as it moved inexorably toward him. In fact, the small boat was filled from starboard to port, bow to stern, with figures, all motionless and facing him. They were frozen, their eyes fixed squarely on him.

He grew uncomfortable as the boat drew near. He tried to move, but his feet remained planted on the jetty, forcing him to await whatever the passengers were bringing his way. When they were within hailing distance, he realized the boat was carrying his closest friends to him. They were all there. Brandy, Trout, Nick, Ken. Even Bayard, Kallan, Alara, Odette were there. The Peripherals he had come to know. He craned his neck. Someone was missing. But then his breath caught as he spied her in the center of the boat. Breena. All of them completely still. Trance-like. In the back, he spotted Duncan Wulliver. And next to him was Kat.

When it was less than a hundred yards out, he spotted a small white creature dashing back and forth from side to side. The sound of barking reached him a moment later, carrying over the water. It was a little terrier, the only creature seemingly aware of what was happening. Yapping a warning, or a greeting, but active and alert.

When the boat seemed just beyond reach, a sudden swell appeared and crested over the gunwales. Sean's breath caught as he watched the little craft struggle to stay afloat, but it listed too far to one side and, without a whisper, each of his friends slid silently into the water. As they reached the surface, and the waves lapped over them, they each turned an alabaster white, their bodies becoming stone, and began to sink quickly. The only creature who remained flesh was the small terrier, who landed in the water and began to thrash about, its cries becoming more and more frantic.

When Sean turned his attention back to his friends, they had all turned their faces toward the surface and raised their arms above their heads. To Sean. Their mouths stretched into silent screams as the deep pulled them down. Staring out of the depths. Down. And down. And down.

Sean felt his feet release from the jetty, and he found himself moving as fast as he could toward the edge, where he launched himself with all his strength into the air and far into the water. Even as he was airborne, he realized that he would have one chance to save someone. Just one. The figures were all stone now and would soon be lost to sight. Even the dog had finally begun to succumb, its snowy fur slowly turning to stone, and as it did, the terrier turned panicked eyes to Sean.

He didn't know what to do. He didn't know what he *would* do, *should* do, even as he flashed through the air. He almost felt himself lifted into the air, felt himself hanging, perched aloft, before he knifed toward the surface.

Without any conscious thought, he moved reflexively and grabbed the dog in his arms. He struggled with the now-heavy animal, pulling them both back to the jetty where, with considerable difficulty, he dragged them both onto the stones. He glanced at the dog, who had already begun to restore to itself.

He immediately whirled back to the water and threw himself into the waves again, but even as he hung in the air again, he searched for his friends, desperate to find at least one more close enough to be saved. But they were gone. They had sunk beneath the water, out of sight.

He dove, willing himself to the sandy bottom and finally, it appeared. There they were. A forest of white statues, reaching in vain for the world above. His friends had settled to the sand, stone still. Their arms remained raised high, aimed at the surface. Their expressions, so recently beseeching for Sean to rescue them, now bore expressions of sadness, of surrender, and in more than one case, reproach.

Sean found Breena and tried to raise her up, but even with the buoyancy of the water, the alabaster statues were too heavy for him. He tried Trout. And then Brandy. Nick. Bayard. Finally, his breath gave out and he felt his heart hammering in his chest. If he didn't kick toward the surface, he would be lost, too. With an agonizing cry that was almost instantly swept away to nothing by the deep, he pushed off and desperately clawed toward the air above and away from his friends.

His head broke the surface, and he screamed in frustration even as he gulped air and coughed out mouthfuls of sea water. His arms thrashed against the water, but he knew there was nothing left to be done. His instinctual choice had doomed those he loved. A dog. He'd saved a dog. Defeated, he slowly stroked toward the jetty. The little dog sat there, watching him approach. Its eyes shone with gratitude, but also pity, as if it understood the price Sean had paid to save its life.

He sobbed as he lay half on the jetty and half still in the water.

He was asleep. Sean knew he was still asleep. But what had happened felt as real as anything that had ever happened to him and his tears mingled with the sea water that still slipped along his face.

———

Sean was up and out of the apartment before the others had even stirred the next morning. The dream stuck to him. Nothing would shake it loose and he felt a great foreboding. It was too early to visit Pettirosso, so instead, he took to the streets around the theatre complex. He felt restless, cooped up. He needed to move. To think. To consider all he knew.

The air was brisk. A sharp, cool autumn morning, with a brilliant blue sky hanging over it all. Traffic was light and pedestrians were even lighter, so Sean gave free rein to his wanderlust and moved. At one point, a mother and child passed him, and the child was wearing a pink knit cap. Sean took note and watched carefully as they moved by. He stopped under the guise of window shopping to keep an eye on them as they made their way in the opposite direction. He cursed himself for once again being in a position of unease. Danger. Unknown.

He had simply wanted to be his old self. With no cares more than learning his lines, auditioning for new shows. The life of an actor was rife with difficulties. The last thing he, or any of his friends for that matter, needed was to be weighted down with a responsibility he had neither sought nor craved.

He resumed his walk up King Street. At one point, the relative quiet was disturbed by the sound of hooves. He paused again and took note of a horse and carriage clopping along. The Amish had long been an integral part of life in Lancaster, yet another ingredient in its feel of a city in a time all its own. He remembered his manners as the carriage neared and averted his stare, knowing it was considered rude. Much like the taking of pictures without permission granted.

As the horse disappeared on its way, he envied, for a moment, the simplicity of the life it and its Amish family led. Free from technology, complications. Clear in its pursuit of an uncluttered existence. But just as quickly, he reminded himself that people are people under it all. No matter the outward life they lead, no one can truly know what is seething underneath, and he suspected that the Amish were no different. The grass only *seems* greener elsewhere. It rarely is, in actuality.

He checked the time on his phone, and realized he'd best think about getting back to meet Pettirosso, so he turned left on Duke Street, then left on Orange Street again to make his way to the theatre.

What could the director have to discuss with him that couldn't be shared in front of the others? He trusted that it would be something of substance, much as Pettirosso seemed to be. Once again, he found himself feeling as if he had a target on his back. As if his being here risked the safety of all his friends. All his colleagues. Perhaps even the city itself.

He was jolted out of his reverie by a voice calling to him.

"Nice scarf you got there!"

Sean paused, startled, and turned in a circle to find the source. There, on the other side of the street, was Duncan Wulliver, smiling and waving. He seemed genuinely happy to see Sean and began crossing the street in the middle of the block. He dodged a passing car before jogging up to Sean.

"Hey, there," he said. "You're out early. I thought you theatre folk were night people."

"Normally, we are, "Sean answered with a laugh. "But we're still in rehearsals and I needed some air. So—"

"So here you are. I get it," Duncan replied. He pointed at the scarf he had given Sean which was slung over his shoulders. "I'm so glad you're wearing it. It's not much, but it means a lot in my family."

"I hear they're known for it," Sean said. "Marcello Pettirosso spoke highly of your entire family. And your scarves!"

"Really?" Duncan seemed surprised at that. "That's awfully nice of him. Didn't even think he knew who we were. He's a big deal around here."

"Well, he thinks you're all a pretty big deal, too." Sean gave Duncan's shoulder a gentle squeeze, remembering the fright he'd gotten not too long ago. "You okay? Everything settled down?"

"Oh, yeah. All good. Really," Duncan said. He seemed embarrassed to even acknowledge the near mugging in the alley. "Thanks again. You really came along at just the right time. Still don't know how you did that thing..." He eyed Sean, hoping for an answer.

Sean avoided the topic. "Just trying to lend a hand. Old theatre trick. Voice control and all that."

Duncan clearly didn't believe him but decided to leave it alone. "I gotcha. Look, I really would like to hang out with you and Kat sometime. If I'm not crashing the party or anything."

"Not at all," Sean said. "Let me get a couple rehearsals out of the way and we'll make a plan. You don't mind late nights, do you?"

"Not one bit," Duncan chuckled. "The Wullivers are night creatures from way back. Just let me know. Great to see you."

"You, too," Sean said, and realized he really meant it. Duncan was a good guy.

Then that good guy did something Sean hadn't expected and wrapped him up in a big, lanky hug. Breaking the embrace, Duncan loped off down the block with a wave over his shoulder. Sean smiled and shook his head. Just when you feel overwhelmed and put upon, sometimes a hug from a stranger can make more of a difference than you would think.

He continued on down Orange Street, turned left on Prince Street, and was approaching the theatre again when a familiar rumble came up from behind him. He stopped and turned to see Kat on her motorcycle pull over next to him.

"Hey there, sunshine," she called, resting her feet on the ground, and pulling her helmet off, letting her mop of curly blonde hair down. "You're up early after your big night. How're you doing?"

Sean stopped and really looked at Kat. He couldn't explain why she felt so familiar to him, as if they'd known each other longer than they really had. As he considered that, he realized just how attractive she was. He immediately steered away from that. Life was complicated enough without allowing thoughts like that in. And he still had to come to an understanding with Breena, though the longer he went without seeing her, the more he felt the possibility of being with her become less likely.

"Yo, Sean, you in there?" Kat poked him in the chest.

"Sorry, yeah," Sean pulled himself back in to the here and now. "Sorry. Million miles away. Yeah, I'm fine. Just out to clear my head."

"Understandable," she replied. "So—about what happened last night. I know what I saw. And it makes what I *thought* I saw in the alley the other night make a little more sense. You going to come clean with me?"

Sean glanced at the sidewalk below him and froze, unsure how to answer before deciding the truth was clearly the best approach with Kat, who was far more observant and sensitive than he had anticipated.

"Yes," he said with resolve. "I am. Later? After rehearsal?"

"Okey dokey, then, mister magician," she answered, beginning to stuff her curls back into her helmet. "You know where to find me. No secrets, yeah?"

"No secrets," Sean agreed. "Oh, Duncan wants to join us sometime. Cool?"

"Cool," she said. "Just not tonight. We have things to talk about."

"Agreed. Not tonight."

Kat pulled out into traffic, and he watched her all the way along the block until she turned onto King Street. Lancaster had some very interesting folks. He could almost see himself living here. If he ever saw fit to leave New York City, that is.

He pulled his jacket tighter around him and headed toward the stage door to make his way up to Pettirosso's office, and whatever the mysterious otherworldly Peripheral had to discuss with him.

CHAPTER 9

Sean tapped lightly on Pettirosso's door. He could see the lights were on, but when he heard no response, he tapped a second time.

"Aw, he's in there, just probably on the phone or some such. Just go on in," said a far too chipper, and far too close, voice from behind him.

Sean, startled, and whirled quickly, only to find Drew Brindig smiling amiably at him.

"Ah, Drew," Sean sighed. "Caught me off guard there. Uh, yeah, I'll just poke my head in."

"Right you are then. Have a great day, Sean," Drew said as he wafted down the hallway and out of sight.

"Never hear him coming," Sean muttered to himself as he opened the door just a crack and called quietly, "Marcello?"

Pettirosso was sitting in his desk chair, staring out the window, seemingly deep in thought. Suddenly realizing he was not alone, he spun the chair around and spread his arms wide. "You caught me woolgathering. Come, come."

Sean let himself in and, at a gesture from Pettirosso, settled into the seat opposite him.

"How was your night, Sean? Did you and the others manage to get any rest at all? I know you've all been thrown into quite the situation. Again, it seems."

"Not gonna lie," Sean said. "It was a tense evening. We'll be okay, though. Been through it before. We'll get through this."

"Indeed, you will, Sean." He leaned over his desk, leaning on his forearms. "I hope you don't mind my asking you here. I've been thinking about our situation, its implications. The pitfalls. What's at stake."

Sean nodded. "I think we're all thinking about pretty much the same things, sir. Last night was frightening. Honestly, we got lucky. A lot of people could have been hurt." He thought of Kat and all the patrons and staff who had been inside the restaurant. "People who have no idea what's happening all around them."

"Yes, I've been ruminating on that, and other things as well," Pettirosso leaned even further over the desk. "This is frightfully unfair to you, Sean. You've never sought out this power. This attention. From what I can see, you've quite deliberately tried to avoid it."

"Not very successfully," Sean admitted.

"Some things are simply not in your control, my friend. But"—the director rose from his seat and faced the window again—"some things *are* in your control. Should you choose to accept them."

"Such as?"

"Because you, Sean, seem to be the crux of so much that is happening, the linchpin that is unlocking the potential in your friends, but more importantly within yourself, your presence here could place others—all of us—at a greater risk. The question is: are we safer with you here or elsewhere, at this point."

"Wait a minute," Sean protested. "You brought me here. I thought the whole plan was to have us in one place to work together. Combine our efforts. Are you saying you want me to leave now?"

"I'm simply wondering if we should find a way to whisk you out of harm's way, conceal you, while we address the current situation in town. We may be able to throw them off your trail. If they were to capture you, as they were so clearly trying to do last night, all may be lost in very short order."

"But every time I try to get away from them, they chase me down. They seem to know exactly where I am no matter what I try."

"A conundrum, to be sure," Pettirosso said, hands behind his back.

"What are you suggesting?" Sean asked. "Could you send me to one of your realms? What about to the Tuatha? Don't they have a place in Ireland? I mean, nobody could touch me there, right?"

Suddenly, the thought of being carried off to Breena's homeland felt like a glorious plan to him, and, for the barest moment, he allowed himself to think of being near her again.

"Ah, Sean. If only it were that simple, we would have done that by now. But as you know, even the Tuatha are a divided people. Some are less sympathetic to your plight, despite what seems to me to be an obvious choice."

"I see," Sean said, unable to keep the disappointment out of his voice. "I guess I'd hoped that they'd moved past that by now. Not that I've heard anything from—any of them."

Pettirosso turned and faced him with sympathy in his eyes. "I know how badly you look for word from them. From *her*. Alas, their situation remains troubled."

"Okay, well, if you can't send me to one of your lands, and no place here is safe for me, I'm afraid you've lost me. What exactly am I supposed to do? Where can I go?"

"Bear with me, here, Sean. What if we didn't send you somewhere. What if we sent you some *when?*"

"Excuse me?" Sean asked. "What does that mean? 'Some when'?"

Sean felt a shift in the room. The air moved and, subtly, the room became charged. Not so subtle that Sean didn't know exactly what had happened. He spun in his chair and found three newcomers between himself and the door.

The first man he didn't recognize. He was tall and broad, with long auburn hair and an impressive beard that reached nearly to his chest. His hazel eyes glowed with a bright light, and he smiled broadly at Sean.

Next to him stood his friend and ally, Kallan. His golden hair and bright green eyes the same as when last Sean had seen him in North

Carolina. He was compact, as the other Peripherals were, less than five and a half feet. But he was athletic, lean, agile. His highlander mien was fierce, and he seemed coiled with barely contained violence. His countenance was stern, and though he seemed cheered to see Sean, something weighed heavily on him.

The third figure stole his breath away. She was here. Breena stood, her blond hair still cut short, but now creeping back almost to her shoulders. Her brilliant blue eyes seemed to gleam in the morning light streaming through the window behind him. She was watching him closely, the smile on her face inscrutable, and she, too, seemed to be concerned with… something. She wore a brilliant azure cloak held closed by a golden brooch at her left shoulder. It was rich, elegant. Far richer than anything he had seen her wear before.

He didn't care. He leapt to his feet and crossed the few feet to her, sweeping her into an embrace and burying his face in her hair.

"You're here," he whispered.

She hesitated for a moment, and he was afraid she would push him away, but then her resistance slipped, and she returned the embrace.

* * *

Pettirosso emerged from behind his desk, but before he could speak again, another voice rose from the far corner of the room.

"I suggest we give these two a moment alone." The voice was earnest, but laughter seemed to be barely contained beneath the surface.

Even in the state Sean found himself, the newcomer's presence made itself felt. He raised his head from Breena, but still held her close. From the far corner, another Peripheral emerged. Small in stature, as Kallan and Breena, but with chestnut hair and mirth radiating from his very being. Next to him was a medium-sized canine, her head pressed to the Peripheral's thigh.

"Bayard?" Sean said, quietly. "Oh, you all are sights for my very sore eyes."

Bayard had fallen afoul of very evil forces not long ago and Sean and

Trout had pursued him to North Carolina to give him aid. He recognized his companion, Cinder, an endangered red wolf from the wilds there. Somehow, in the unfolding of events, they had mutually adopted each other. Clearly, that affection had outlived the immediate danger. Bayard's particular talent, in addition to mischief, humor, and a knack for surprising everyone, even his friends, was the ability to communicate with wild creatures. Somehow, he was able to empathize with them in a way that proved true and worthy.

"And I am beyond glad to see you," Bayard said. "But we should leave you and Breena to yourselves for a moment. Sadly, we have no more time than that. But we shall give what we may."

Sean nodded in gratitude, and as the others, including Pettirosso, filed from the office, Sean noted that his old friends had undergone some changes. They all seemed—weary. Worn. Less naïve, but grittier than even the last time he had seen them. There were stories to be told, he was sure. Cinder, before loping through the doorway, stopped to nose Breena's boots. The wolf then let out a low whine and shot a look to Bayard, who called her to him and left.

When the door closed behind them, Sean turned his full attention to Breena, who gazed back into his eyes. No matter how he tried, he felt there was a veil between them that he had never felt before. He tried to push the thought from his mind, but his heart held onto the sensation, try as he might.

"Breena," Sean began, "how are you? What is happening? I have so many questions."

"I know you do, Sean, I know," she answered. "I feel as if I am forever telling you to wait. I am so very sorry. But I repeat that again today. My situation is still—complicated. I am betrothed, officially, but there has been a falling out of our families, and nothing is clear now. That is all I can tell you of that. For now."

"I understand," Sean replied, although he didn't. The last thing he wanted was to anger her or push her away with demands or questions. Instead, he said, "I'm just happy to see you. Your clothes...you seem different. Are you okay?"

"I am fine. I came here directly from a High Council meeting of my people. Once again you find yourself in the middle of something unprecedented. We stand on the precipice of our last hope for a peaceful resolution. At least, that is the opinion of my family and many others. Others feel the time for détente has passed, but many hope for concord. Still. Somehow."

"But why are you here?" Sean asked. "Shouldn't you be there? Talking?"

"Sean, the one thing all parties seem to agree upon is that you—your presence, your existence—put any amity in jeopardy. Those who oppose you are convinced that you are too powerful, even if you have yet to discover that, to allow you to be free. Most believe that we should imprison you. The more militant think you should be eliminated more permanently. If possible."

"This is absurd," Sean said, shaking his head. "I can make some music. That's all. Sometimes I can make things happen with my voice, but I really don't understand how. Or why." Even as he said it, Sean felt the untruth beneath the words. He had begun to awaken whatever was inside of him, and he felt shame for hiding that from Breena.

She cocked her head at him, almost as if she knew what he had experienced. "That may be so, Sean, but each time you use that gift, you gain strength. And even more to the point, you find ways to make those around you more powerful. Some now see you as the leader of humans who they have always feared would emerge. To them, if you are not stopped now...they will not be able to stop you."

"I'm no leader," Sean said. "It's not in me. Even more so, I don't want to be one. I just want to go back to the way things were. The way I was. Before."

"Oh, dear one," Breena answered, stroking his face, "the time for that is gone. Has been for some time. I imagine it was gone the moment your voice ignited the tunnels below Camp Hero. It was certainly gone by the time you dispatched the Dullahan and eradicated the Wendigo. A Wendigo that many of us thought invulnerable."

"Just dumb luck," Sean insisted. "What if I just say I won't do it anymore? Let you all work it out among yourselves? I just wanted to come here and do a show. Be quiet. Out of the way."

"I'm sorry, Sean," Breena whispered. "I would take this burden from you if I could. But they know of you now. Nothing will turn some of them aside until they are sure you are dealt with. Whatever that means to them."

"So, what now?" Sean asked. "Pettirosso told me I can't even hide in your realms, now. What can I do? Where can I go where I won't put you and all of my friends at risk? I can't live with that. If anything happened to any of them...I don't know what I'd do."

"And that unknown reaction is what so many of my people fear. But we have a possible solution. Actually, Pettirosso conceived it. Let him share it."

"Breena," Sean stopped her from turning to the door. "I don't know what will happen. If I'll even see you again or lose you to a marriage that I have no place objecting to, but I need you to know. I love you."

Breena faced the door, and without turning to Sean, she answered, "I know you do." She paused then, and he was sure she had more to tell him, but she held her silence. A breath, and then the moment was gone. She reached for the door.

Sean exhaled. He shook his head. Something felt off. She was different. Perhaps more different than he'd initially suspected.

Breena opened the door and asked the others to return. As they filed into the office, Pettirosso interrupted the procession.

"Actually, before we all get comfortable, I'd like to ask us all to head downstairs to the basement. I think if we all have a better understanding of this place, we will be better equipped to make sound decisions. Shall we?"

He motioned for the others to head toward the elevator, and along the way Deborah joined them. The group was too large for the elevator, so Kallan and Breena blinked out, with a word that they would meet downstairs. Sean felt a twinge of disappointment that Breena would leave him so quickly after being reunited, but he did his best to dismiss it as schoolboy pining.

The elevator delivered them to the basement of the theatre. This area was clearly much older than the newly renovated spaces upstairs. It felt colder, worn, disused. Sean was immediately aware of a feeling of foreboding. The basement felt dank and dark. Musty. It surprised him. He normally was not so in tune with things like that. He couldn't escape the sensation that something very powerful lay down here.

The group gathered in the center of a large room, ringed with older sofas and easy chairs. It was obviously the greenroom from earlier days. Sean paused to consider the hundreds, likely thousands, of actors, musicians and stagehands who had gathered here between shows. Between scenes. On breaks. He thought of the meals shared. The phone calls made. The friendships built and, inevitably, torn down. But this feeling of immense power in proximity was something entirely different from these theatre echoes.

Pettirosso paused and turned to point out a small door, nearly hidden behind one of the sofas.

"This," the director said, with surprising deference, "is the site of the atrocity that occurred here centuries ago. The event that led to my being here. And everything that befell after."

Sean noticed Deborah off to one side, drawing shapes on the wall and down to the floor. Before he could ask what she was doing, the conversation moved on.

"I think all of us can feel the energy here," Kallan said. "I'm not sure I've ever felt this much strength outside of our lands."

"Yes," Bayard agreed, trying to soothe the wolf, Cinder, who had become agitated and was pacing between the doorway and Breena off to one side. "It sets me on edge, and not much does that."

"It is one of very few places of such power in the lands of men," Pettirosso said, fixing his eyes on the doorway. "It has been sealed and protected for all these years. The slightest brush with what it holds would corrupt even the staunchest of humans, my apologies, Sean."

"Please, not necessary. I'm anxious even hearing about it. If it sets you all back on edge, I want no part of it."

"If only all men were so wise," Kallan said.

"Ach, I feel very 'fish out of water,' at the moment," the tall newcomer said, stepping forward and offering an enormous hand to Sean. "This lot usually has better manners than this, but this portal has them twisted in knots. Tim McCloud, at your service." His voice was deep and rumbly, and he had more than a touch of a Scottish burr.

"Yes, of course," Pettirosso jumped in. "How coarse of me. Sean, I'm pleased to introduce you to Tim. He has a very unique set of talents. We"—he gestured to the others—"very much hope he will lead us out of our current predicament."

"That's a silver tongue you've got there, Cello," the big man responded. "There's a reason he can get folks to do most anything he asks. Smooth-speaking sonofabitch, he is. But a damn fine leader of men. And...other folks." He laughed as he glanced at the assembled Peripherals.

Bayard, still trying to calm Cinder, guffawed. "McCloud, you have a way with words, yourself. And you still owe me that jaunt we discussed last time I saw you."

"'Tis true, friend. Let's make plans as soon as we get through this latest little disturbance, aye?"

"Bayard, your dance card is pretty full," Sean said. "You better not leave Trout high and dry. He's expecting to take you to Montana."

"Fair point," Bayard agreed. "Although I suspect he may be more focused on visiting Eleanor in the Outer Banks than sightseeing with me. And McCloud here offers a very different sort of journey than Trout does. What did we agree on, Tim? 1798?"

"Exactly so," McCloud said. "'Twas that or 1916. Your choice, there."

"Wait, Sean interrupted. "What do you mean? I'm very confused, and that portal is distracting me, but you have well and truly lost me know. IF there is a plan that involves me, anyone care to clue me in?"

"He's right," Breena said, quietly, from beside the door to the portal. "We need to explain."

"We do, indeed," Pettirosso agreed. "Let's have a seat and make things clear."

"Yes, let's," Breena said quietly. Her hand now resting on the small door.

The group ranged around the room, perched across the sofas. Bayard had taken a seat on the floor and Cinder had placed herself in his lap, a near constant whimper. Bayard leaned in and whispered soothingly to her.

Breena was the last to sit, and Cinder eyed her as she joined the group.

"Let me begin," Pettirosso said, once all were settled. "Sean, as you know, there are realms upon realms upon realms. So many more than mankind knows or even can imagine."

Sean nodded but kept his tongue.

"Along with those various realms, planes, call them what you will, come such as us. You call us Peripherals. And even amongst us, we each possess certain...gifts. Bayard has his connection to the natural world. Kallan, the stout warrior. Breena, who feels so keenly what others feel and is able to ease their pain."

"And you, Cello?" Sean asked. "What is yours?"

"Ah, yes," he replied. "Me. Aside from my willingness to remain here, seemingly for eternity, at this point, I am not unlike yourself. I harness power from words, music, even movement. Before I came here, I was one of the most renowned seanachie of the Tuatha. That was my *magic*, as you call it."

"Which, of course, makes you so well suited to be here." Sean gestured to the theatre around them.

"It does, indeed," Pettirosso agreed. "Temperament and talent made me the only logical choice, and I serve willingly."

"Okay, got it. Great." Sean turned to face McCloud. "So, what's up with you, then? What's your talent?"

"Ah, lad, even amongst our kind, there are certain abilities that appear only very rarely. Sometimes once in a handful of centuries. Which is just as well, because too many with my gift would alter the course of—everything."

Around the circle, the others nodded in agreement, and Sean felt the weight of the moment. All were laser-focused on McCloud.

"I'm a Timestrider, Sean. My gift is that I can move through time just the way the others can blink in and out of your perception."

"You've got to be kidding me," Sean said quietly. "You're a time traveler? Why am I surprised, after everything else that has happened."

"We think Tim offers us the best chance to stow you somewhere safe, while we try to calm the waters here, so to speak," Kallan said.

"Sean," Breena approached him and put her hand on his. "Please consider this. Let us explain it to you very carefully."

"So, you send me somewhere else—sorry, some when else—and the idea is that it will keep you and my friends out of open conflict with… whoever is behind this conflict?"

Pettirosso leaned forward in his chair. "In the simplest terms, yes. That's it exactly."

Sean scanned the faces of everyone. "Okay," he said. "If you all think it's the best path, I'm in. Now walk me through this step-by-step. I need to know…everything."

Bayard fell backward on the floor, laughing loudly. "I'll be damned, I thought this was going to be more difficult than that. On my oaths, these humans surprise me regularly. And often when I think they will disappoint. Fair play to you, Sean. You've done it again."

"Sean," Kallan said, leaning forward in his seat, "please think carefully about this. Don't jump to any conclusions."

Sean held up his hands to stop Kallan. "Look, you all know me. You know what's at stake. You know McCloud, here. Me? I'm out of my depth, just trying to stay alive and help my friends. Maybe stop a lot of innocent people getting hurt. If you think this is the way? Good enough for me."

"Your faith is humbling, Sean," Pettirosso answered. "It places a great responsibility on us. I think we are all agreed that the risk, though as minimal as we can make it, is worth taking. Frankly, it's the only course I can see working."

Breena had wandered back over to the small door and was tracing her fingers along its seams. Her head was cocked to one side, and she hummed tunelessly to herself. She felt the others' eyes on her as the conversation paused.

"Oh, by all means," she whirled a little too quickly back to the group. She crossed to Sean and sat on the arm of his chair. Absentmindedly, she ran her hand through his hair. "It's so very courageous of you to take this on. Of course, I'm not surprised one bit. No one knows you the way I do. The true Sean."

She rested her head on Sean's shoulder, and the others shared a startled look. This was—unexpected behavior.

Sean, nonplussed, hesitated. On one hand, this was exactly what he had been wishing would happen. On the other, it seemed strikingly out of character for Breena. He literally shook his head to clear his thoughts.

"Right, well, if I'm going to be doing this, someone needs to tell me all about these Timestriders. Tim, you're the logical choice. So lay it on me. What am I in for?"

"You have spirit, I'll give you that, young man. Right. Timestriders," McCloud said. "It's almost misleading to refer to them in the plural. There has only been one at a time, and precious few of those. At most— very, very most, mind you—there would be one a generation. And keep in mind that our generations are centuries in comparison to yours. I'm young by our standards, but quite old by yours. And what is it I do? It's as simple to describe as it is impossible to explain. It's an innate ability. We just—are. I concentrate and...I'm somewhen else. I can choose the time, but it is imprecise. I can go to a month. Perhaps a week. But rarely can I choose the day with success."

"Okay, sure," Sean nodded as he considered what he'd heard. "And you can take—one person with you? A crowd? How does that work?"

"Nay, no crowds," McCloud replied. "I am permitted one companion. We take the risk of temporal disruption very seriously. The ramifications are not precisely known, even to us. I cannot interact with myself in the past, although to be honest we don't entirely know what would happen if I did."

"Nothing good, McCloud. I think we can agree on that," Kallan interjected.

"This one," McCloud nodded in Kallan's direction. "He's a cousin of mine. Distant, mind you. Very distant. But family is family. Doesn't stop us from calling him a dour heilan' coo."

Kallan shook his head and rose to pace away from McCloud.

"Sadly, in this case he's nae wrong, though. We've always erred on the side of caution where moving through time is concerned. Though to be honest, I'm not above the occasional jaunt to the Middle Ages just for a personal laugh." He winked at Sean, who had no idea how to respond.

"Is it dangerous?" Sean asked. "Can I arrive in the middle of a wall or something? Can we get stuck in the past? Or future? I hadn't even thought of that. Can we go forward in time?"

"Can we? Aye, we can," McCloud said. "But we don't. And we won't, either. Too many unknowns. Too risky. And for our purposes, this will be very simple. We'll take you off to somewhen not too distant, wait for a day or two for these fine folks to set things to right, and back we come. Nothing to worry about. No fuss."

"When do you think you'll go?" Breena asked, disengaging her fingers from Sean's hair, and locking eyes with McCloud. She leaned in close to Sean and seemed to be smelling his hair. No one present missed this bit of odd behavior.

"Och, well, lass, I think I'll be keeping that to myself when I do decide," McCloud's voice rumbled and to Sean it felt much like an ominous clap of thunder. "Fewer people that know, the better. Not that anyone will be able to follow me, of course. It'll be just the two of us, Sean. We'll be fast friends in no time. My vow to you."

Breena leaned back in her chair again and resumed stroking Sean's hair, but she kept a hooded gaze on McCloud and seemed less light-hearted.

Cinder, agitated on Bayard's lap, struggled to get up and eventually walked to the far corner of the room and curled into a ball, eyes on the group.

Pettirosso rose. "Sean, McCloud will walk you through everything you need to know. I'll inform the cast that you'll be off for a day or two. Hopefully, it won't be anything longer than that before we can bring you back to today."

"The Grumbles won't settle for that," Sean pointed out. "No way they don't question me disappearing with everything else going on."

"You're right," Kallan said. "They are quite dogged in their efforts to look out for one another. They will not accept this without explanation."

"I hope to limit those who know the truth," Pettirosso answered. "If the truth is required to earn their cooperation, so be it. As McCloud so rightly noted, he and Sean will be beyond the reach of anyone. One Timestrider. Only one."

"Right," Sean said. "So, when does this happen? How much time do I have?"

"Just a few hours, friend," McCloud replied. "No sense in waiting. Remember, time is fluid for us, now. Sooner we go, sooner this lot can work their magic and the sooner we come home."

"Right," Sean heaved a sigh. "Maybe it's just as well I don't have too much time to dwell on it."

As they gathered by the elevator to ascend to the office level, Breena lingered by the doorway to the portal. She pressed her hands to it and leaned her forehead on the door.

In the corner, Cinder's fur stood up on her nape. Her hazel eyes flashed. She waited and followed Breena as she straggled to the elevator.

Bayard watched the wolf closely, and they shared a moment before the elevator doors closed behind them.

Just moments later, the group filed into Pettirosso's office again. They took up their respective positions as they had earlier. The tenor of the room though was more tense than it had been, and the director, in particular, looked as if a weight had descended upon him.

"Sean," Pettirosso began. "I do have some more information on the assault on you at Dremmel House. And who was responsible. Things are becoming clearer."

"Great," Sean answered. "Can we hold off a sec, though? We seem to have lost Breena on the way up. I'm sure she'll be right here."

"Actually, Breena was never here, and I'm so sorry to be the one to tell you," Pettirosso responded.

Sean shook his head. "I know she was behaving strangely, but I'm sure it was just the tension of the moment. She feels everything so strongly, I know she must be overwhelmed—"

"I'm sorry, Sean," Kallan said. "Marcello is correct. I had my doubts before we arrived, and everything I observed downstairs confirmed those doubts. Whoever—whatever—was with us in the basement was not Breena."

Cinder, seated on the ground next to Bayard, whined again, pushing her nose into Bayard's hand. She seemed easier now that Breena, or the Breena imposter, was gone.

"Cinder knew," Bayard added. "I had hoped it was just the proximity to the portal confusing things, but it became clear. That creature may have fooled humans, but not our kind."

"Very true, friend," Pettirosso said. "I knew almost as soon as she arrived that something was amiss. I allowed it to play out to discover what she—or it—was. I come from a race of shapeshifters, at least that's where I had my beginnings, long before I came here. I was born a Puka, in the Celtic lands. So, I am especially sensitive to others of similar talents."

"No one bothered to fill me in?" Sean asked. "I had no idea what was going on. What if she had been sent to harm me? Or us?"

"Nae chance of that happening, son," McCloud replied. "Not with this crowd protecting you. Not many places in any realm would have been safer than you with us. More importantly, what did we just encounter?"

"I believe…no, I know, that we were just visited by a Naga," Pettirosso said. "A shapeshifter from the Hindu and Buddhist traditions. They are strange and secretive creatures, who dwell far beneath the ground or even under the seas. She was a long way from home. If there were any doubts that the realms are drawing lines amongst themselves, they are gone now. The question now, is why she was here? To gather information, yes. But Naga can fall on either side of the deepening divide. Perhaps she just needed to gather information to bring to her people. Or she was sent here to discover our plans and inform our adversaries. With no way of knowing, I strongly suggest we act quickly."

"How could anyone expect to get away with that?" Sean asked. "With all of you here, it was impossible to see it being successful."

"Oh, I suspect it was successful. She discovered some of our plans and was able to sow doubt amongst us," Kallan explained. "Further, her behavior was clearly intended to confuse you, Sean. Safe to assume that your feelings for Breena are not hidden from friend or foe, at this point."

"A muddled Sean is a more vulnerable Sean," Bayard agreed. "Cinder knew immediately and was warning me throughout. Emotions are our strength and our weakness. Much like they have tried to exploit your love for your friends, Sean, they will continue to try to take advantage of your feelings for Breena."

Sean turned to Bayard. "This Naga creature. Just another sign that the worlds are drawing together, yeah? Like the Yokai in North Carolina. All of the Indigenous people we've encountered. So—what next?"

"As for the Dremmel House assault," Pettirosso rose and turned to look out the window behind his desk. "The two creatures you glimpsed, the jaguar and the grey fox, should have been obvious to me from the start, but they, too, are so far from home, it confounded me. Briefly. You were visited, in addition to the Shadow People and the Hide Behinds, by a pair of Wayob. Spirits from the Mayans, in Central America. They are devious and mean nothing good for anyone. As you learned, they enter your dreams and seek to cause you harm. That they are united with the other creatures of the shadow and dream realms is a bad omen."

"So, what happens now?" Sean felt panic rising in his chest. "My dreams seem to be the one place I can't defend myself. If not for Mum, I wouldn't be here."

"Peace, Sean," Pettirosso said. "They dare not approach you here. And soon, you will be in another place and time. Remember: only one Timestrider. No one will be able to follow you. McCloud will be your companion from this time. No one else will know."

"Okay, sure, great. Creatures from Central America, Hinduism—how many different people and cultures can align against us?" Sean looked down at the desktop. "Things just keep getting more complicated. And I came here for some peace and quiet."

"Sean, you are lifted up by friends, both powerful and those who love you powerfully. We are a long way from despair. But we are not," Pettirosso said, turning to McCloud, "a long way from sending you to a safe time. May I suggest that the two of you take a walk? McCloud, answer all of Sean's questions. Put his mind at ease. Prepare."

"What about my friends?" Sean asked. "I need to see them."

"And you will, Sean," the director said, turning directly to Sean. "I promise that. In the meantime, I will share with them some of what is happening. To prepare the way. It's past time to act. No more letting them come to us. It is our time to change the course of events."

"That's all well and good, and for the record, I totally agree with you," Bayard replied. "I do have one question, though, before we get things going. Where is the real Breena? Do *they* have her? Because I can't imagine her allowing what just happened to happen."

"A question I will answer," Pettirosso said. "And a point well made. But, Sean, put that from your mind if you can. We take care of our own and no one can exploit us. Especially an empath on the order of Breena. No harm will come to her, if she is indeed imperiled."

"Put that from my mind?" Sean said, quietly. "Not bloody likely."

Those around the table paused to look at each other. This was the group that would need to lead the way. After that pause, they swirled into action. None held it against Sean if he lagged a bit behind the others.

As Sean and McCloud made their way toward the exit, they passed the rehearsal room. The sounds of a Haydn and Page song drifted through the doorway and Sean stopped, placing his hands on the doorknob. He could hear his friends. There was Brandy's rich alto, anchoring the women's section. Jiff Haydn's fingers were cascading across the keys, weaving in and out and around the harmonies the actors' voices were creating. Sean's breath caught. He could hear Ken, now singing Sean's own lines. In fairness, he sounded wonderful, but Sean couldn't help but feel a pang. His lines. The ones he'd come here to perform. The music he hoped would restore his peace and ease his weary heart.

He lightly pounded his fists on the door. Here he was, shut out from the one thing he had believed would set him free.

McCloud held back, giving him the moment to himself. When he sensed Sean's angst, he placed a massive hand gently on his shoulder and drew him away.

"I'm so sorry, my friend," his Scottish burr rumbled. "I know your heart is there. With that music. Those people. But come with me now. Believe me, when I tell you that you are about to discover wonders you never dreamed existed. A different sort of music. Let's walk."

Slowly, Sean allowed himself to be led away from the glorious sounds. He thought he saw the golden glow of magical music seeping under the door and felt another pang. They were creating magic. Without him. Who had always led them on that path.

CHAPTER 10

Sean and McCloud emerged from the stage door into the alley and a brilliant blue late autumn sky. The cool air hit Sean square in the face and he breathed deeply. He enjoyed the tingle in his lungs. He noticed McCloud doing the same.

The big Scot stretched his arms wide. "This, now *this*, is weather made for a highlander. Reminds me of home. Shall we walk and talk?"

The two moved to the top of the alley and turned left on Prince Street. Morning business was in full swing, and the sidewalks were crowded with shoppers and students and locals making their way to work. The two of them stood against the front wall of the theatre, waiting for a break in the stream of walkers to dip out and head off toward Orange Street.

For the first time, Sean made note of the clothes McCLoud was wearing. Unlike the sleek black garments the other Peripherals had adopted, he was wearing a hodgepodge of styles. His trousers were forest green and made of a rough woolen homespun. His shirt was tartan, dark green with yellow and red. His boots were decidedly more modern. A deep, worn, brown leather with brass buckles up the length to his knees. He could easily have stepped out of a history book, or just as easily a retro-folk club down the street.

No one gave them a second look as they strolled past the music school next door, and then the record store, and on past the trendy thrift stores and boutiques.

"Is that your family tartan?" Sean asked, nodding to McCloud's shirt.

"Aye, as much as I have one, I suppose," came the answer. "This is Clan McCleod of Harris. I adopted them, so to speak. I like the feeling of belonging. With someone. Being one of a kind can get lonely, if you're prone to that sort of thing. I'm Celtic, so that's just one of many proclivities on my part."

"I can understand that. Clearly, I've got Celt in me, as well. Feast or famine with the Curleys. We're either deliriously happy or gnashing our teeth and wailing as we pull out our hair."

McCloud laughed. "You just described many a highland family reunion." He paused. "I probably should let you know what to expect when we travel, yes? There's not much for you to do, really, just stick close to me."

"Yeah? That's it?" Sean asked.

"Mostly, aye. Stay connected to me, a hand on my arm is enough. I'll give you a warning, we'll take a few steps together, and then—we'll be somewhen else. You may feel a bit queasy, but naught to concern yourself over. It passes quickly."

"And then?" Sean couldn't quite keep the concern out of his voice.

"In a while, we'll head to the outskirts of town. Better to bounce back to a site with fewer people. Fewer eyes, fewer questions. We'll find a place to settle in for a few days. Lie low. Make sure we don't attract any attention. I'll pop back after a spell and make sure things have calmed, then I jump back and bring you home here. Most people will be none the wiser."

"You make it sound so simple."

"Because it is!" McCloud boomed. "You'll just be along for the ride. And remember, I'm the only Timestrider, so no need to fear once we go where we're going. Just relax and let the others do the hard work."

"Well, that feels wrong," Sean said. "I hate to leave them on their own. I've been the one doing the hard work lately."

"Then it's high time they did their share, I'd say." McCLoud stopped when he saw Sean's eyes grow wide as he stopped walking. The big Scot followed Sean's gaze and he chuckled.

Sean stood dead still and had set his eyes on a figure a few yards further along Prince Street, standing at the head of an alley leading off to the left. The figure swayed back and forth. It wore shapeless colorless clothing, the one exception being a woolen cap pulled low over the face. A cap of faded red, almost pink. But clearly of a similar style as the other Red Caps Sean had seen.

"Red Cap," Sean whispered. "They've been shadowing me for the last few days. Pettirosso filled me in on what they are."

"Ach, that little thing? That's barely out of diapers, that one is. Look at that pathetic excuse for a cap. It's pink. That little one probably has less kills than fingers on its hands. Doubt I'll even have to roll up a sleeve to deal with this novice."

McCloud, without missing a step, proceeded directly to the Red Cap and pushed it backward into the alley. The Red Cap, suddenly aware of its danger, tried to backpedal, but its feet grew tangled in the long coat, and while it was vainly trying to keep its feet, McCloud drew back one massive arm and backhanded it down the alley. Landing nearly ten yards away, the Red Cap scrambled shakily to its feet and hissed at McCloud, but continued a retreat until it disappeared around a corner, with a last angry cry.

"Ah, haud yer wheesht!" McCloud cried after the retreating figure, before turning back to Sean. "Now that was good fun!" he crowed. "If that's the like of what they'll be dealing with here after we go, it will be a short journey for the two of us."

Sean was now catching up to McCloud and shook his head. "That was impressive. I guess there's more to you than just time travel."

"Well, I am still a Peripheral, as you call us. I have many talents," he said with a wink. "Good to stretch the old bones once in a while. Just remember, Sean. If you see a Red Cap, the deeper the red of the cap, the more dangerous the individual. They dip their hats in the blood of their victims. Light red? Not much to worry about. Dark red? Best hope for some friends to be near at hand or you'll need some fine gutties. *Or* just one friend, if it happens to be me."

Laughing, McCloud gave Sean a hefty slap on the shoulder and Sean did his best to hide his wince.

"Right!" McCloud said. "We should head back. That wee crabbit is sure to tell its mates about what just happened. Not worried about it one bit but might as well clear out before any fur flies. Off we go, yeah? Let's go visit some when."

As Sean and McCloud exited the elevator and neared Pettirosso's office, the sound of raised voices came crashing down the corridor. Sean picked up his pace, while McCloud merely cocked his head in curiosity and continued.

Sean reached the door and as he opened it, was greeted by a scene of utter chaos. The Grumbles were assembled within, ranged about the director's desk in varying postures of anger and aggression.

Brandy's voice cut through the general din, as was her wont. "What do you mean he's *going to be out of reach*?! What exactly does that even mean? You brought us here, under false pretenses I might add, and now you send him away with none of us next to him to keep him safe?"

Trout next took his turn at the front of the desk. "Now, I like to think I'm a reasonable fella with a slow fuse, but this just smacks of bad faith. If you send Sean away, we go with him. That's the situation. And if this has something to do with you worrying about your damn show, well, that just doesn't have a place in the decision for me. For us. So, you can shove that show, and your measured, reasonable tone, and tell us where our friend is. Like now!"

Sean pushed his way into the room, where he found the Peripherals, minus the false Breena, ranged around the edge of the room. They seemed, to his quick assessment, to be trying to get as far away from the confrontation as humanly, or inhumanly, possible.

"Whoa, whoa," Sean called as he entered. "Gang, I appreciate the concern. I really do. But I think you'll feel differently when you hear what I have to say. And probably more importantly, what he," he pointed to McCloud, just now arriving, "has to tell you. "

"He doesn't sound distressed," Nick said, evenly, pointedly avoiding making eye contact with Brandy.

"Why don't we just take a listen? Yeah?" Ken said. "It's Sean, if he has something to tell us, he will. And if we think he's getting bad advice, well...that's what we're here for. To make sure nothing bad happens. To him, or"—he looked at the ground—"any of us. We're Grumbles, right? It's what we do. Look after each other. Even when it's not the easy thing to do."

The Grumbles looked at each other. It seemed somehow both appropriate and chastising, that Ken would be the one to bring them back to reality. But his words struck home, and they settled.

"Just let McCloud explain," Sean said. "To that end, this is Tim. He comes very highly recommended. He's kind of a...unicorn. That doesn't do him justice. Tim, could you possibly...?"

"Aye, o' course I can," McCloud boomed. "Why don't you all just calm yourselves, and I'll let you know the plan."

"We'll listen, but that's all I can promise," Brandy said. "You'll know if we don't like what we hear. And don't even think about leaving anything out."

The Grumbles found seats or perches on windowsills around the office and turned to McCloud, who easily took center stage and proceeded to, after a go-ahead nod from Pettirosso, fill them in on the plan.

When he finished, there was a moment of stunned silence in the room. The Peripherals glanced nervously at the faces of the Grumbles and found a variety of reactions.

Brandy had turned a bright shade of puce and stood quickly. Next to her, Trout looked at the floor and was slowly shaking his head. Ken looked nervously at the Peripherals, and most pointedly at Sean. Nick, alone amongst the Grumbles, wore a broad grin and seemed ready to burst into laughter.

Brandy, not surprisingly, was the first to speak. "This has got to be the most insane thing I've heard—maybe ever. Seriously? Send the one person who everyone wants to take out alone into the past—or so you say—with this monster Scotsman, who, by the way, we've never met and have no reason to trust. Damn, Pettirosso, we barely know *you*! I've given you the benefit of a lot of doubts until now, but this...I can't go there."

"I gotta say, it does sound pretty far-fetched," Trout said. "We've only gotten this far because we've had each other. That, and Sean has saved our butts more than once. So now we're just supposed to—what? Toss all that aside?"

"I think it sounds amazing," Nick said quietly. "I mean, people have been trying to travel through time for...ever. And now, Sean has the chance? Jeez, I'd volunteer myself, if it made any sense."

"Why don't we ask Sean what he wants," Ken said. It was meant for all, but he was looking at Brandy.

Sean stepped to McCloud's side. "Gee, thanks for asking. I mean, it is me going, after all. I know it sounds crazy, but it's not the craziest thing to happen lately. Okay, maybe it is. But not *that* much crazier than some of the things we've done. And I have to say, their argument is pretty convincing. With me out of the way, maybe calmer heads will prevail. And, gang, they are coming hard for me. We just had a Red Cap come at us on the street. Broad daylight. And McCloud here took care of it without breaking a sweat."

Pettirosso stood behind his desk. "McCloud? Is this true?"

"Och, the hat was barely pink. Just a wee bairn of a Red Cap. Practically an insult when you think about it. Not a bother in the slightest."

"Be that as it may, it is an escalation," Pettirosso responded. "If you decline this opportunity, Sean, we need to devise a new plan. Fast. So what will it be?"

Bayard took this moment to push himself off the wall and approach the Grumbles. "Friends, I know this is overwhelming, but Cello and McCloud are some of our most respected citizens. You don't know them, but you do know us." He gestured to Kallan, who had moved to his side. "We would never put any of you in harm's way. We believe this can succeed. And with the least amount of hurt. Please."

Kallan nodded his agreement.

"Dammit, dammit, dammit," Brandy said, kicking the wall behind her. "Sean?"

"I trust them," Sean answered. "From what I'm told, I'll be back before you know it. And if it means fewer people get hurt, don't we owe it to everyone, and ourselves, to try?"

"Well, I'm on the record as saying I have serious reservations," Brandy said, although the fight was ebbing from her.

"Thank you," Kallan said. "If we are agreed?"

"I think we are," Trout replied, placing a hand on Brandy's shoulder. She shrugged it off.

"In that case," Pettirosso said, "I suggest we move. Now."

"Right," Sean heaved a sigh. "Let's do it. We're heading—where? Just outside of town?"

"Aye, that's my preference," McCloud concurred. "I'd like to find a bridge. Preferably something a bit older. Any thoughts?" he scanned the room.

A voice unheard before now chimed in from a corner of the room, causing Ken and Brandy to startle and jump. "I'd reckon Zook's Mill is probably the closest one of that kind. An old, covered bridge not far from town."

Everyone turned to find Drew Brindig, quietly leaning in the corner.

"Dammit, Drew," Brandy said nervously. "Don't do that to people. I didn't even know you were here."

"He's really good at that. Sneaking up on folks," Trout noted.

"I'm so sorry, Ms. Brandy," Drew said, genuinely upset. "Just didn't have anything to add until now. I'm really sorry."

"Don't worry about it, Drew," Sean said. "We're all just a little high-strung right now. Not your fault, at all."

Drew nodded, but seemed less than sure he wasn't at fault.

Sean clapped. "Right, let's take my car, yeah? I'm guessing there's a place to park out that way?"

"I'm coming with you," Brandy announced. "And no one better fight me on that. No discussion. The rest of you can go to rehearsal and act like things are normal, but I'm seeing him off."

McCloud shrugged his agreement, and the issue was settled.

"Hey, you can use my Subaru while I'm gone," Sean patted Brandy on the back. "That old Cobalt of yours is still in the shop, right? Maybe you'll even decide to finally get a real car."

"Shut up," Brandy said.

———

Five minutes later, Sean's Crosstrek pulled out of the parking garage a block down Prince Street from the theatre. Sean drove with Brandy riding shotgun. McCloud had squeezed himself into the back seat. He rolled down the windows and leaned out, allowing the wind to catch him full in the face and loving every second of it. Drivers passing by couldn't help but smile at the massive head of auburn hair, with beard to match, looking every bit a golden retriever come to life.

"It doesnae matter how many times I ride in one of these, and it hasn't happened often, but it does just tickle me to the tips of mah toes. The *speed*. The freedom. Ach, I'd be tempted to just keep going and never stop," McCloud shouted over his shoulder into the car.

"The thought has occurred to me," Sean admitted.

"Me, too," Brandy added. "But life always has a way of calling me back to reality."

"Exactly," Sean agreed.

The cabin of the car settled into a contemplative silence. McCloud's shaggy head watched every storefront, pedestrian, and eventually field, that they passed. Sean and Brandy both settled into their thoughts of the ties that called them back from a life of following the highway wherever it led.

Sean turned on the stereo. Mark Knopfler and Emmylou Harris were singing "Red Dirt Girl" about longing for more and yearning to break free from expectations. Given what they had just discussed, they both disappeared into their own missed opportunities. The mood turned a bit maudlin in the cabin until McCloud, with the largest possible grin on his face, turned to them and shouted, "Coo!"

Brandy, shaking her head, turned to him incredulously. "What?"

McCloud pointed one of his sausage fingers to a passing field and repeated himself. "Coo! Never get tired of them!"

Brandy following his gesture spotted a herd of dairy cows on the far side of the field. "Oh, for the love of...Cows? *That's* what has you worked up? Cows?"

Sean laughed long and hard when he realized what had delighted McCloud. "You know, maybe he has the right idea. I know I could use a little more childlike wonder in my life. I used to call out every time I saw a cow, too."

Brandy turned to look at him, ready to lay into him for being ridiculous, but the open smile and raised eyebrows he greeted her with gave her pause. She grinned, shook her head, and turned to look out the window.

A moment later, Sean's voice rang out. "Coo!"

Then, unable to resist any longer, Brandy rolled down her window, pointed into the distance, and as the distinct smell of dairy farms on both sides of the highway wafted through the car, she, too, called out, "Coo!"

For the next ten minutes, the drive was punctuated with all three voices calling out every time they noticed a cow. In Amish country, that meant it was pretty much a constant refrain.

As they turned off of New Holland Pike and onto Snake Hill Road, all three had tears of laughter and joy running down their faces.

As the covered bridge came into sight down the road, Brandy opened her phone and did some quick research.

"Right," she said. "Here we go. Zook's Mill Covered Bridge. Started construction in 1849. Wow. Seventy-four feet long. And that is the Cocalico Creek running underneath it. Look at it. That's one pretty bridge."

McCloud, still pulling himself together, tried to stretch his legs in the back seat of the car, wiped his eyes, and looked ahead at the structure. "That will do nicely, all right. Running water, good length, sturdy wood frame. Aye, we'll do well. Now, Sean, leave that cellular phone behind. In fact, anything that labels you from this time. Coins, bills, the lot. Nae bother about your clothes, lad," he said, seeing Sean checking his shirt for labels. "We'll scrounge some up when we get where we're headed."

Brandy, watching Sean divest himself of his belongings, muttered, "I still have a bad feeling about this."

Sean turned to her. "I know you do. I'm not completely sold on it myself, but these folks feel strongly about it. They haven't steered us wrong yet."

"You mean other than putting you in a haunted house with no protection? And leaving us to the Red Caps at Dipco? Getting us here under false pretenses? Those the people you're talking about?"

"Point taken," Sean said. "But Kallan and Bayard felt strongly about it, too."

"Yeah, yeah, I know," she answered. "It all just seems too risky to me."

McCloud stuck his head between the seat from the rear. "And your concern for yer pal is touching. We should all be so lucky. But I won't let anything happen to him. I've been doing this a long time. Never had a problem yet."

"What about you take me with you, too?" Brandy asked. "Strength in numbers and all that."

"I'm sorry, lass." McCloud reached over the seat to squeeze her shoulder. "I can only take one with me. Even I have limitations."

"I figured," Brandy said. "Worth a shot."

The three got out of the car. Sean tossed the keys to Brandy.

"Take good care of her," Sean said. "Guarantee you'll love driving her."

McCloud clapped his hands and rubbed them together for some warmth. Sean pulled his jacket closer around him and wound his Wulliver scarf around his neck a bit tighter. Brandy stood to one side, a look of concern clear in her face.

"Why a bridge, by the way?" Sean asked, turning to the Scot

"Their very nature is a help to us. They exist to bring folks from one place to another. Exactly what we need. This one," he nodded to the covered bridge in front of them, "brings its history to the table. Many souls have passed here. Each one leaves something behind. That crafts-manship there, people took pride in this. Put a piece of themselves into it. Running water below is a pleasant surprise, also. Evil has a hard time crossing that. In fact, most of it can't. Bridges are beacons of hope. Man making the way easier for his fellow man. Or woman. A symbol of kind-ness. Like a lighthouse. Or even like a theatre, as I know Pettirosso has shared with you. Beacons."

"Okay. If you say so," Sean replied, as Brandy kept shaking her head.

"Nice scarf, by the way," McCloud said, nodding toward the deep brown accessory. "I'll need to know more about that. Off we go."

As Sean and McCloud neared the span, Brandy fell back. Her head was still shaking.

"No worrying, you!" McCloud called back. "I'll be back to see you in a day or so, and right after you'll have a reunion and stories to tell your grandchildren. Always trust a Scotsman!"

His laughter echoed through the timber rafters of the bridge as they passed onto it. Their footsteps echoed off the timber around them. She saw Sean put a hand on McCloud's shoulder.

Ten steps in, they began to shimmer. To flicker. Brandy blinked to try to refocus and when she looked back, they were gone.

———

Brandy stood silently for a moment, watching the place her friend had been a moment ago. Silence fell over the bridge, and she became aware of the surrounding fields. The sound of birdsong. The breeze passing over the fallow farmland.

She suddenly felt very alone. She wondered what Sean was experiencing and sensed his absence. She had been angry at him for leaving her behind both in Montauk and the Outer Banks. But this was different. He had gone somewhere she couldn't follow. If something went wrong, not only would she be helpless to stop it, but she also wasn't sure she would even know.

Another pause. She stared onto the bridge, but there was no more shimmer. They were gone. Reluctantly, she turned and climbed back into Sean's Crosstrek. She started it and gripped the steering wheel, grudgingly acknowledging that he had a point. The was a helluva a nice car. Maybe her days in the run-down Cobalt really were at an end.

She turned the car around and headed back the way they had come, her foot light on the gas pedal and her eyes returning to the rearview mirror repeatedly, hoping for some sign that Sean was okay. Or even the two of them returning, but she knew it was pointless.

She turned her full attention back to the road and pulled up short when she saw a familiar green and white Ford Bronco idling at the next intersection. She pulled up alongside it and rolled down her window. The windows on the Bronco rolled down, as well, and she was greeted by the smiling faces of Trout in the driver's seat and Nick seated behind him. Ken was in the passenger seat next to Trout and leaned forward to give a little wave.

"Yeah," Trout said. "We figured you might need some company on the way back. Sean leaving is super weird, and we still have those shadow guys and red hat-wearing jerks to deal with. So—here we are."

Brandy was surprised at how relieved she was to see her fellow Grumbles. "Well, don't get used to hearing it from me, but it's really good to see you. He's gone. They just...went away. And not much we can do about it now."

"True," Nick called from the back seat. "But we just have to believe he'll be safe and it's our turn to take care of some business. He's saved us enough times."

"Good point," Brandy said. "Hey, one of you want to ride with me? Could use the company."

"I will!" Nick replied, climbing out of the Bronco and crossing to the Subaru. "Been wanting to check out the new ride, anyway."

"Back to the theatre?" Trout asked.

"Guess so," Brandy answered. She put the car into drive and started to roll the window up before hesitating again. "Appreciate the thought, guys. Once a Grumble—"

The others responded, "Always a Grumble."

"Why don't we give Stewart a call when we get back? Maybe a video conference? We can fill him in and hear about his stuff, too. It's been a while," Ken suggested.

"Good idea," Brandy said. "But last I heard, we still have rehearsal. So maybe after?"

"Oh, right," Trout said. "Forgot about rehearsal."

"Let's move it," Brandy insisted. "Yes, rehearsal, but also, who knows what's happening back there. "

"Another good point," Ken agreed.

"Let's hit it," Trout said, turning the Bronco around to follow Brandy.

They left a trail of dust behind them as they headed back to the highway. Zook's Mill Covered Bridge lay silent behind them. Keeping whatever secrets it held to itself.

CHAPTER 11

Pettirosso stood in his usual position, at his window, facing out onto Prince Street, hands clasped behind his back. The set of his shoulders was a clear sign that he was concerned. The strain in his voice confirmed that.

"They are gone," he said. "I felt them go, but they are lost to me now. They are truly alone."

"It was the only way," Kallan answered from the far side of the large desk. "If there is any chance of a peaceful resolution, Sean had to be removed from the equation. This is the only way to put him out of reach."

"Out of our reach, perhaps," Bayard said from next to Kallan. "We have no idea what they'll walk into wherever they've gone."

Pettirosso turned to face them. "We have to trust the two of them. Sean is not to be trifled with. I would imagine whoever or whatever they encounter will be caught very unawares by him. And it's entirely possible that they will arrive and find a perfectly peaceful scene where they can simply...wait."

"And McCloud, despite his lighthearted demeanor, is formidable. Traveling through time is not his only gift," Kallan said.

"Until we hear from them, there is nothing we can do, so I suggest we address the situation with Breena," Bayard said, rising from his seat.

"What about Breena?" Deborah asked, standing by the door. "I thought the shapeshifter left. Surely, we would know if there was any further danger."

"Oh, I agree that the Naga is gone," Bayard said. "Long gone unless it has a death wish. My point is that its presence here signals something has happened to Breena."

"Please, explain." Pettirosso emerged from behind his desk and paced the length of the office. "The impersonator indicates what, exactly?"

Bayard reached down to scratch Cinder's ears. "Breena and Sean are too closely connected. It's just not possible that a shapeshifter, in her likeness, could get that close to Sean without her sensing it and doing something. She may be dealing with her own family situation, but nothing would stop her from getting to him. Warning him. Protecting him."

"I have to agree," Kallan said. "She would never allow that to happen. But she is, essentially, Tuatha de Danann royalty. What could hold her against her will? That, in and of itself, would be provocation to war."

"Then I would say, with Sean beyond our assistance, that we should turn our attention to solving the riddle of Breena. How would you suggest going about that?" Pettirosso asked.

"I believe your hands will be full here," Kallan responded. "I think that we"—he nodded to Bayard—"should find Breena and bring her back. Either here or to her people. Somewhere safe. But I fear it will mean us leaving you now when you probably need us more than ever."

Pettirosso smiled enigmatically at them. "I am grateful for your concern. Truly. But we will be well prepared for whatever comes our way. Isn't that right, Deborah?"

Deborah, less confident that Pettirosso, nodded tightly in response.

"I'm hopeful that if we can discover who has Breena, if she has been taken, that we will reveal who is truly behind all that is happening. It is a feat of great power to imprison one of the Fae. Let alone a royal. Any Fae at all would be formidable."

"Decision made, it seems," Pettirosso crossed to the two other Peripherals and firmly clasped their hands. "Good fortune to you, friends. Come back soon and with answers. And trust me when I say that your human friends will come to no harm. The Fulton protects."

"And so do you," Bayard said with a grin. "I look forward to learning more about you, Marcello. You're a riddle to me. I'm not often stumped."

"In that case, we have something to look forward to," Pettirosso answered with his own grin.

Kallan stepped aside and glanced at Bayard. "Shall we?"

"We shall," Bayard said. He reached down to hold Cinder close to him and the two Peripherals blinked away.

Pettirosso turned to Deborah. "Will they succeed?"

She stepped to the window and assumed Pettirosso's usual stance. "I cannot see," she said quietly. "Something of great influence is moving events. Things that should be known to me are not. All we can do...any of us...is our best. And trust each other."

"I've never known you to be blind to the course of events," the director said, moving next to her. "Uncharted territory."

"Yes," she agreed. "But the Fulton will stand strong. It has for centuries now."

"Can you see that?" he asked, turning to her.

"No," she replied quietly. "But I can feel it."

They both watched the traffic passing on the street below. Standing next to each other, but miles away in their thoughts.

Back in Brandy's apartment at the theatre, the four Grumbles were perched around a laptop sharing a video call with Stewart in New York. They'd spent the first thirty minutes explaining to him everything that had happened in the last few days. They spent the next twenty minutes talking him out of canceling his solo show to come down and help. What had finally convinced him to stay where he was, was that he couldn't actually *do* anything if he traveled to them. They didn't even know exactly what the next steps would be, but seeing as it was shaping up to be some sort of Peripheral diplomatic negotiation, they guessed they would be sitting that process out. That decision made, Stewart came back around to the entire time travel episode.

"So this strange Scottish Peripheral shows up, and just—what?— whisks him away somewhere?" he asked. "What if the whole time travel thing is just a fake. How do we know he didn't just blink him away someplace, like the other Peripherals can do?"

"Well, damn," Trout muttered. "I never even considered that. Do we know for sure?"

"Look," Brandy replied. "Kallan vouched for him. And Pettirosso did, too, and he seems even higher on the pecking order than our friends. Sean believed them. At some point, we just have to trust *someone.*"

"And if anyone can take care of themselves," Nick added, "my money is on Sean. He's been up to every challenge so far."

"No, you're right," Stewart agreed. "Of course, you are. I just worry. And it's hard not to be there. I feel helpless up here."

"Well, if it makes you feel any better," Ken said, "we're pretty help- less here, too. All we can do at this point is sit and wait. And rehearse, I guess. Although that seems a little silly right now. But," he checked the time on his phone, "I think we better get over to the rehearsal room."

"I'm sure they'll cut us some slack, under the circumstances, but yeah," Brandy agreed. "We should hustle."

"And we," Nick said, rising, "should do some work, since we're being paid. Yeah, Trout?"

"Yessir, mister playwright. And director. Your wish is my command." The lanky Montanan rose from the sofa. "So, what is the show about, anyway? You never told me a thing. Easiest job I've ever gotten. No audition."

"Given everything going on around us, I decided to tell the story of the Christmas Eve ceasefire in the trenches during World War I. Thought it would go well as a companion piece to *A Christmas Carol.*"

"I love it," Trout said, clapping his hands. "I know nothing about it, but I love it. Tell me more."

Stewart, still on the video call, waved his hands to attract their attention. "Hey! I'm still here, you know."

"Right you are. Sorry, Stewart. We just should get back to the hall," Ken apologized.

"I get it," Stewart answered. "I actually have an interview in a bit, myself."

"Nice!" Trout responded. "For your show? Who's the interview with?"

"Oh, just a little TV thing," Stewart demurred. "Not a major deal."

Gwyddion Evans, Stewart's manager, significant other, and the Welsh God of Mischief, leaned into the screen. "Don't listen to him. It's with New York One and it's a very big deal. He opens in two nights, so things are happening here. Look, gang, keep us posted. Sounds like you have plenty of help there, but if you need us, or I can do anything? We can be there fast. But this performance is a very big deal for Stewart, so let's try to get him through it, yeah?"

"Understood, Gwyddion," Brandy said. "For now, we all focus on work. Not much choice."

"See ya, Stew," Trout said. "We'll keep you posted. You do the same, yeah?" Trout ended the call and turned to Brandy. "You really going to be able to focus on work now?"

"Hell no," she answered. "But you heard Gwyddion. This is a big deal for Stewart. Let's keep him on task, if we can. We can handle things here."

"You know, I think we can," Ken said.

"Once a Grumble, always a Grumble," Trout replied. "We take care of our own."

"Got that right," Nick agreed.

<hr>

Gwyddion Evans, impeccably turned out in a custom suit, turned his shockingly emerald eyes to Stewart after he had ended the video call. One eyebrow raised in an unspoken question.

Stewart, still seated at his desk, rested his hands on the closed laptop, concern etched into his face. He turned to Gwyddion. "What? Just ask, you know I can't keep anything from you."

Gwyddion smiled and rested a hand on Stewart's shoulder. "I know you can't. Actually, to be perfectly honest, no human can keep anything from me. But you, endearingly, would never *try* to hide anything. I was wondering two things. First, why did you not tell them your news? And second, would you really have dropped it all to go to them?"

"Well, I didn't want to make the conversation about me," Stewart said. "So much is happening to them, my good news seems...not so important, in comparison. Which leads me to my second answer: yes, I would drop everything to help them, if I thought I could make a difference."

Gwyddion paused and cupped Stewart's face with his hand. "You humans continue to surprise me. My kind has avoided you for too long. It may prove our undoing. And *you*, dear one, surprise me most of all. Selflessness is not a quality we have associated with humans. And yet, here you are."

"It's not a hard decision," Stewart protested. "My friends mean everything to me. One show is just a show. There will be others."

"Ah, but Carnegie Hall is a pinnacle event," Gwyddion chided Stewart. "And the promise of greater exposure after is very real."

"Won't mean a thing if anything bad happens to my friends," Stewart insisted.

"Fascinating," Gwyddion murmured, still holding Stewart's face. He broke the connection and crossed to a window looking over Tenth Avenue from Stewart's window. "I think you are selling yourself short and this opportunity has a very real chance of changing lives. I think you may find your greatest help to them will be to remain on course here and go through with this."

"We'll see," said Stewart. "I just know I will never turn my back on my friends. Ever."

"I see that now," Gwyddion replied. "Your loyalty is noted. And admired."

Stewart crossed to the window, also, and they both stood watching the flow of humanity passing by forty floors below.

As the light faded at the far end of the bridge, Sean felt his body go numb. It was as if his entire self had fallen asleep. Pins and needles. He turned to his right to make sure he was still connected to McCloud as his hand could feel nothing. The big Scotsman was still there, a look of extreme focus on his usually jovial face. He was focused on the light at the end of the bridge.

When they had stepped onto the span, Sean had noted that the opening at the far end revealed a narrow road heading west. A small patch of green separated two buildings, one small blue house to the left and a smaller white building on the right. When Sean turned to follow McCloud's gaze, he caught his breath at what he now saw. The window onto the other side was now a black expanse, fringed with a green mist. Within the void specks of light, some brilliantly glowing and some faint impressions, dotted the blackness. A universe of green, white, and yellow orbs, floating off into infinity.

McCloud raised his voice, which was when Sean realized that the bridge was filled with a sound as if a raging river was rushing around and past them. "Hold tight, friend," he shouted. "Nearly there, but don't lose your grip. I'd be hard pressed to find you here in the stream of time."

Sean felt McCloud's grip tighten on his shoulder and he returned the gesture. They pressed on, hesitating only when they had reached the far end. They stood, poised on the edge of a seeming infinity. McCloud scanned the orbs in front of them intently. He nodded once, focused on one ball of light, and stepped forward with Sean in tow.

Sean's tingling sensation intensified. For a moment, he saw nothing.

Felt nothing. Sensed nothing. He was adrift in an endless emptiness. Even the reassuring touch of McCloud's hand seemed to disappear.

And then—it was over. Light began to grow around him. He felt his feet moving. McCloud's touch returned. Together, they stepped off what they could now see was the end of the bridge. Sean suddenly found himself in the light of a brilliant autumn afternoon. The air felt crisper, cooler. Somehow cleaner. Ironically, the air was also filled with the unmistakable smell of farmland, but the lingering scent of farm animals and all that brought with it felt natural. Wholesome. The mature trees that had fringed the bridge now appeared much younger. The narrow road he had glimpsed as they entered the bridge had been replaced by an even narrower dirt path. Where the buildings had been, he now saw a mill perched on the bank of the creek. A mill that looked as if it had seen better days.

He stopped walking. Turned in a full circle, taking everything in. Looking back through the bridge, the homes they had passed on their way in were gone. One lone house was perched on the far side. It was an older, larger, single-family home. More of a farmhouse, really. It had clearly stood there for quite some time.

Sean looked to McCourt. "Well, *something* happened, right? So—where are we? Or when?"

McCloud's laugh echoed around the small dell in which they found themselves. He slipped a small disc-shaped contraption out of his pocket, opened a cover—much like a pocket watch—and glanced at a dial within. "I took it easy on you, lad. Only a sixty year jump that time. The year here is your 1964. Not too far, but far enough that we won't run into your past self. That would be messy. We should be safe, but we can always jump again, if need be." He scanned their surroundings quickly, and then turned back to the bridge they had just departed.

"Ah, I hoped for this," he said, as he moved back to the structure and ran his hand along the edge of one of the timber frames. "Remember what I said about bridges? Well, that is known widely among our kind. Now, look here." He pointed toward a lower portion of the bridge frame which seemed scratched and scored.

"Just looks like someone drove too close to the edge in that bit there. Over here, though, almost looks like a bear marked it up," Sean said, bending to get a closer look.

"No bears in these parts, but you have a good eye. It was a different sort of apex predator that stopped here. Those random-looking scratches? As it was intended," McCloud replied. "But look here. And here. There is a subtle pattern." His fingers traced along the scratches, pointing out certain marks that, when taken together, seemed to suggest a deliberate design. "To my kind, the sixty years we jumped is a blink of the eye. I suspected we may find allies, based on what I sensed in town. These markings tell me that we will be welcomed if we make our way—" He paused and examining the carvings more closely, turned and looked down the slope to the mill. "There. We go there. Our luck may be even better than I hoped. Off we go. If all goes well, this will be nothing more than a relaxing few days and a story for your grandchildren."

McCloud set his head toward the creek below and strode away. "And let me do the talking, if we meet anyone," he called over his shoulder.

Sean hustled to keep pace. "Don't have to tell me twice. My head is spinning from that time travel. Not sure I could form complete sentences with a stranger right now if I wanted to."

McCloud's laugh boomed forth again and he gave Sean a clap on the shoulder that almost sent him tumbling down the gentle hill. Sean turned to the Scot with surprise after he caught his balance, which made McCloud laugh even louder.

"Keep that scarf tight around your neck, lad. Off we go. Ach, this is good fun, this. A relaxing vacation, by my soul."

"Lead on, MacDuff," Sean said.

McCloud turned a keen eye to Sean. "I knew a McDuff once. Alastair. Such a numpty."

They shared another laugh and set their sights on the mill below.

The Grumbles headed to their respective rehearsals. Nick and Trout to the studio theatre on the fourth floor of the building, while Brandy and Ken made their way back to the Castagna rehearsal room. If anyone was bothered by their late arrival, no one said a word. Even the usually punctilious stage management team of Rebecca and Dani took it in stride without even a raised eyebrow shot in their direction.

As the two Grumbles were settling into seats on the side of the room and depositing their backpacks, Pettirosso rose from his seat and called everyone to attention.

"Before we get back to work, I'd like to introduce you to a very special guest." He gestured to a nattily dressed man sitting in the back row of the observer seats. The man was medium height, with curly brown hair, a full goatee, and bright blue eyes that twinkled with mischief. "This is the one and only Jasten Roberts. Most of you will know him by his professional moniker, Noodle."

A murmur went through the cast. Noodle Roberts was the preeminent artist chronicling the Broadway scene. Every new show in New York received an original drawing depicting the individual aspects of that show. It was a mark of distinction to receive one, and performers, producers, and all manner of theatrical folk waited long months to get a commissioned work. Getting "Noodled" was considered a sign of success to those in the know. Noodle had been dubbed the heir apparent to the legendary Al Hirschfeld and was well on his way to claiming his own place in the pantheon of Broadway luminaries. What he was doing there, in Lancaster, Pennsylvania, was a mystery to the cast, but one that gave rise to a very excited buzz.

Brandy and Ken were delighted and struggled to stay in their seats. Noodle was a longtime friend of theirs and one of their favorite people.

"Mr. Roberts has been kind enough to agree to join our design team," Pettirosso continued. "He will be drawing all of the artwork that adorns the Scrooge household, as well as providing us with the art that will be transferred to the drops and projections throughout the production."

Brandy turned to Ken. "Seriously? First Haydn and Page, now

Noodle? This guy is going for it with this show. Never seen anything like it."

"Absolutely," Ken replied. "There must be a plan behind all of this. Can they really spend like this for such a short run?"

Brandy paused to consider for a minute. "We don't have any clue what Pettirosso has acquired over the years. If he's been around as long as he says, he could have a fortune stashed somewhere."

"Fair point," Ken agreed. "But does this strike you as another case of 'too much of a coincidence'? Another one of our friends, and a specialized and highly visible one at that, is brought in? I think our director is gathering his forces in case this diplomacy thing goes south."

"But it's Noodle," Brandy answered. "He's amazing, but how could he help? He's not a Peripheral."

"No clue," Ken said. "But I do know that a few weeks ago, none of us thought we could do anything like what we've discovered. He's a pretty amazing artist."

Brandy turned and gave a stealthy wave to Noodle, who beamed a smile in her direction and gave her a thumbs up. "I guess we'll find out soon enough."

Pettirosso was finishing up his announcement. "In addition to that incredible news, Mr. Roberts has also agreed to create individual pieces for each cast member. Partially, to get to know each of you better, and partially to provide additional artwork for the show should it be needed."

Bobby Smalls raised his hand, and Pettirosso nodded to him. "Do you mean that we're all..." His voice tailed off, and he seemed struck dumb with excitement.

Pettirosso laughed and opened his arms wide. "Yes, Bobby. I'm very happy to confirm that you will all be Noodled."

The group erupted with cheers. Even Haydn and Page, in a corner by the piano, seemed swept up in the excitement.

Brandy and Ken applauded in Noodle's direction, and he bowed his head once, grinning.

Sean and McCloud approached the mill at the bottom of the gentle hill. It was a three-story stone construction, clearly made for functionality more than aesthetics. McCloud put out a hand to stop Sean as they approached the front entrance to the building. He ran his fingers along the door frame. Whatever he was searching for, he must have found it, because he chuckled quietly to himself. "No such thing as a coincidence," he muttered. He turned, glancing around the mill's yard. He approached a large stone a few feet behind and to the left of where he stood. "Must be—" He reached beneath the stone, scrabbled in the dirt with his fingers before letting out a satisfied grunt. He stood and held a large key in his hand. "Our friends steered us right." Back at the door, he placed the key in the lock and swung the door open wide.

"Definitely not just bear scratches," Sean said as he crossed the threshold.

"Not a bit," McCloud answered. "Welcome to your new temporary home. Hopefully for just a day or two."

"From your lips," Sean said.

The pair found themselves in an entryway littered with dust and disused equipment. The air was stale, as if the building had been shut tight for some time. Sean noticed that he left footprints in the dirty floor.

McCloud gestured to a doorway off to the left. "If I know anything about a fulling mill—and I know quite a bit—we should find something appropriate for you to wear through here."

They moved through the door into a small antechamber. Hooks lined the walls, with each hook holding an outfit of heavy woolen cloth.

"Ach, did I tell you so, or did I tell you so?" He sized the outfits up before pulling one down and tossing it to Sean. "Get that on yourself. This is like a slice of my childhood, right here. Do ya ken what a fulling mill is?"

"If you mean do I know what it is, then nope," Sean answered. "Never heard of them."

"Such sheltered wee lives you live," McCloud said, sitting on a changing bench on one side of the room. "A fulling mill produces heavy woolen cloth. It's old as the hills, is fulling. First, the cloth is cleaned of dirt and oils, then shrunk to tighten and make it as waterproof as possible. Thankfully, by your time they'd stopped using urine as the cleaning agent. The Romans actually taxed urine because it was so valuable to the process. Can you imagine having your wee taxed?" He laughed loudly enough to send the sound echoing through the entire first floor. "Aye, I can still remember the women of the family fulling. They made a game of it. Even had songs to help pass the time faster."

"Sounds a bit antiquated, doesn't it?" Sean asked.

"Probably why this one is the worse for wear," McCloud said, taking in the shabby interior. "I doubt it lasts much longer here. But it served its purpose well for many years. And it was a staple industry for us Scots. Like I said, no coincidences."

Sean adjusted his new outfit. Deep brown trousers and a green shirt of sturdy wool. It was surprisingly comfortable. He found a pair of rugged work boots under the bench and put them on.

"A little big, but I can make do," he said, stomping his feet to get a feel for the new footwear. "Okay, I'm dressed for the sixties. Now what?"

"Now we wait, my friend," McCloud settled into his spot in the bench. "Now we wait."

"For what?" Sean replied.

"Not what. Who," came the answer.

After an hour and twenty minutes of rehearsal, with Noodle watching it all with an open sketch pad in his lap, Rebecca called a ten-minute union break and the cast scattered to check their phones, grab some water, or just natter away in a corner. Brandy and Ken corralled Noodle, who had been chatting with Haydn and Page.

"Noodle," Brandy said, guiding him to a quiet spot by the door. "What gives? You never said a word about being here."

"Trust me," Noodle replied. "I'm as surprised as you are. Two days ago, this wasn't on my radar at all. One phone call from Mr. Pettirosso, and I find myself on a train this morning with a pretty hefty drawing project and an even heftier payment deposited in my account. That man is persuasive."

"Yeah," Ken agreed. "We've seen him in action. Formidable."

"And you're really going to draw everyone? The entire cast?" Brandy asked.

"Not just that," Noodle said. "Drawing the creatives, some of the staff. It's a lot. And not really what I normally do, but the paycheck was attractive, and the theatre seems to be on the upswing. Can't hurt to get to know them now. And, you know? Lancaster is a pretty little town. Should make a nice quiet break from the city."

"Yeah, about that..." Brandy began, before being interrupted by stage management calling everyone back to rehearsal. "More on that later."

The rest of the day's rehearsal flew past, and when the clock struck five backpacks were grabbed quickly and the hall emptied in under five minutes.

Noodle found Brandy and Ken. "I have a short meeting with Mr. Pettirosso. Can I meet you somewhere?"

"How about Rural City Taproom?" Ken suggested. "Half a block up King. Should be quiet."

"Perfect," Noodle said. "I'll get a round when I make it over."

"You'll need it when we fill you in on some of the latest developments," Brandy replied.

Noodle shot a questioning look over his shoulder as he followed the director out the door to the rehearsal room, while Brandy and Ken headed for the elevator.

"That wasn't fair," Ken chided Brandy. "Poor guy is going to wonder through his whole meeting now."

"Well, I thought he should know it's not all Cabot Cove around here," Brandy said, grabbing her bag.

"Wrong state," Ken answered.

"Shut it. You know what I mean. Meet at the door in ten?"

Ken nodded as they left the elevator and parted ways, headed to their respective apartments.

Sean and McCloud had spent a short while exploring the mill. It was in a general state of disrepair, and though it clearly still saw some activity, its days were obviously numbered. Sean had found some literature and paperwork in an office and was taking the quiet time to look them over, trying to get a sense of the nature of the work.

The two had returned to the anteroom by the front door. They sat on benches on opposite sides of the room, legs sprawled out in front of them. Sean rolled his shoulders and felt a satisfying crack. He was tired. More tired than he expected to be. The simple, sturdy clothes he'd acquired were surprisingly warm, especially given the chill in the autumn air and the lack of heat in the mill.

McCloud fixed him with a searching look. "There's no reason you can't just shut your eyes and get a quick kip in while it's quiet. Time jumps can take it out of you. Especially your kind. Not many humans have had the experience, so you've just joined an exclusive club."

"I am tired," Sean acknowledged. "I thought I was just getting old. Glad to hear it's more than that."

"Och, lad, you just leapt sixty years. It's not natural. Even my kind finds it unsettling. And not many more of them have done it than your kind. There is only one of me, after all."

Sean swung his legs down to the floor and faced McCloud, ignoring the pop that erupted from his left knee when he did. "Yeah, so what's it like?" Sean asked. "Is it lonely being one of a kind? Do your people respect it? Fear it? Both? Humans tend to fear the things they don't understand, so I can see them going to either extreme if they knew about you."

"Aye, that's true for my kind as well. I've been around so long, many of them have likely forgotten about me. No one has called on me for a long time, so hearing from Kallan and Pettirosso was a pleasant surprise.

My kind is practically immortal, as it is, so traveling through time is a bit of a niche skill."

"Not many calls for Peripherals to escape back in time?" Sean said.

"Nay, not much. I jump on my own every once in a while, just to keep in shape. It's a dangerous business, jumping. I keep it to vital instances, beyond my own personal jumps."

"It's funny," Sean mused. "Humans spend a lot of time thinking about immortality. Probably because we know it's out of our reach, and it's the one mystery we will never understand until we're beyond sharing the answer—death. The brief span of our time here. Most of us would probably jump at the chance to walk in your shoes. Long life. Life beyond our imagining. And the ability to visit other times. Being able to see loved ones who have gone. The temptation to go back and fix past mistakes. Right past wrongs. I'm not sure my kind would handle it well. We find a way to corrupt most things."

"It's not the pure blessing you would imagine," McCloud replied, his eyes straying to a window looking out onto the green pasture behind the mill. "It's shockingly lonely, at times. My kind doesn't pass on quickly, but when it happens, the pain is all the more for it. I've lived long enough to see nearly all my loved ones leave. And despite the ability, and temptation, to go back and visit them, jumping without a specific reason can be—a bad idea. Living in the present, whatever that may be and what it seems to cost, is truly the only way to *live*."

"I've never thought about it that way," Sean said, quietly. "That must be unbearable at times. Do you have anyone close to you? The newest members of your family?"

"Not really," McCloud answered, still looking through the window. "I *know* many people. But not many of them really know me. I've given up on close friendships, let alone anything more intimate. I've lost...too much. Too many. The pain has been...a lot. This conversation is probably the most personal I've had in centuries."

"And, given that, you still are able to resist the temptation to jump backward to visit your loved ones?" Sean turned fully to McCloud. "I can't fathom the self-control needed for that. Don't you ever want to go back to them and just—stray?"

McCloud let out a small, bitter chuckle. "Oh, very often. But our history is littered with cautionary tales of Timestriders who gave in to those urges. Jakob Ludhaven is probably the most famous. Or notorious, depending on your perspective. He fell in love. But rather than allow her to age and live her life, he decided to take her with him and disappear into time. No one knows exactly what happened to them. If she survived, or eventually perished in some far-flung era. There are many ways to abuse my gift. I may wear down eventually and someday just…jump away. But not yet. Not today."

"The pressure must be incredible," Sean said. "Being one of a kind. At least one at a time. Do you think others may have your gift but choose to hide it. Out of fear. Or selfishness?"

"An interesting idea," McCloud answered. "It's possible. But we are identified early. Our elders know the signs. And we are trained and educated to follow a strict code. I suppose, if the elders sense that a Strider lacks the willpower to see it through, they may turn a blind eye to one slipping away. But I've never heard of such a thing."

"All credit to you, McCloud," Sean said. "I don't think I would be able to do it."

"You have a different burden to carry, youngster," McCloud replied, finally turning to look squarely at Sean. "And by all accounts, you have acquitted yourself beyond anyone's expectations." The Scotsman stood and stretched. "And now, I'm afraid, we must put this discussion aside. At least for now. Our hosts are nearly here, if I'm not mistaken."

Sean became aware of a growling motor drawing near. He peered out the window and saw a Volkswagen van, the classic style from the sixties, rumbling along the dirt road toward the mill.

"And remember," McCloud continued, "let me speak. And keep that scarf around your neck." At a worried glance from Sean, McCloud laughed. "Not to worry. All will go fine. And if not, you're with a Timestrider. We'll just find a friendlier time, if need be."

Sean pulled his scarf tighter around his neck as he heard the engine sputter and die, and the doors open and shut.

***

Brandy and Ken were halfway through their beers when a visibly stunned Noodle came through the door. They waved him over and he made his way slowly to their corner of the bar. The manager of the bar, Lance, ambled over, a tall, muscled, chestnut-bearded fellow. Pretty much exactly what you would imagine a taproom manager to look like. He stopped in front of Noodle. "You look like you could use a beer."

"That's an understatement," Noodle mumbled. "I'll have what they're having." He hadn't even glanced at the beer board. Brandy glanced at Ken. This was very un-Noodle-like behavior.

"Let me guess," Brandy said. "Pettirosso must have brought you up to speed?"

Noodle turned glazed eyes to her. "I hope I'm up to speed, because if there is any more, I don't think I can handle it. My head feels like it could explode as it is."

Lance returned and put a hazy IPA in front of Noodle. "I'm Lance. Shout if you need anything, but I'm gonna give you some space to talk. I'll be nearby."

"Let me see if I have this all straight," Noodle began, stopping short when he took a sip of his beer. "Damn, that's good."

Ken shot Brandy a look. That was more like the Noodle they knew.

"Okay, priorities," Noodle reminded himself. "So that theatre is haunted. And the basement holds an immensely powerful portal that can transport folks and magnify whatever superpowers they have. Speaking of superpowers—you all have them. Harkening back to the days of troubadours and—what did he call them? — the seanachie? When spoken and sung word carried great strength? And the written word, too? And Sean is being hunted by evil spirits and creatures because he may be the strongest of all, so they had to send him off somewhere while they try to broker a deal? Oh, and you all have had adventures lately," he looked pointedly at Ken. "Adventures in Montauk and North Carolina where you became friends with some of these paranormal, supernatural, immortal folks? And Sean fell in love with one? Is that up to speed?"

"Wow, he really did fill you in," Brandy said. "Just three things. They're not immortal. Not really. Just really long lifespans. Trout fell in love, too. And yes, they sent Sean away, but somewhen, now somewhere. They sent him back in time."

"Back in time," Noodle mumbled. His head didn't explode, but he did down half of his beer in one gulp and motion to Lance he'd need another.

Marcello Pettirosso sat at his desk, his fingers steepled in front of him. Deep in thought. The windows behind him were closed to the light from Prince Street. He was weary of peering out over the gathering darkness over Lancaster, both literal and figurative. The shadows had begun to heave and slither along the edges of the light thrown by flickering street-lamps. He could feel the city, his city for so long, falling under the thrall of their foes. He felt no fear. As so many other Fae, he had faced count-less challenges through the years. And he was in his own home. Whoever was behind this challenge to the Fulton would soon discover the Fulton was not to be trifled with. He wasn't afraid. But he was tired. The years stretched long and hard into his past. This persona, Marcello Pettirosso, was fairly new. Too new to abandon. But he needed a jolt. A spark. Inspiration. It was ironic because he had more companions now than in a very long time. His secrets, held tightly for so long, had been shared more freely than ever before. And yet, this new threat felt more significant than any other had been.

He touched a button below the lip of his desk and a panel on the right-hand wall slid silently open, revealing a small sleeping area. Little more than a bunk on which to lie down. An incredibly luxurious bunk, to be fair. But a bunk. One of the advantages of the recent remodeling had been to design everything to his taste. He slept little in recent years. Like many of the Fae, he required less sleep than humans. He maintained a home across town, more for appearances' sake than anything else. But truthfully, he spent most of his time now in the theatre. The custom shower and sleeping accommodation in his office were new, and he availed himself of them often.

But tonight. Now. He was tired and allowed himself to fall wearily into the bunk nook. He drifted instantly into a dreamless state. Lying perfectly still.

Two hours passed quietly. But at nine o'clock, something disturbed his slumber. He stirred and sat quickly. All was not well. He felt—something else in the office. He silently slipped from the bunk. Darkness had fallen completely since he'd lain down, but his eyes acclimated and he stood motionless, allowing his senses to expand throughout the room.

There. Stealthy movement. Surely invisible to most. But not to him. There. One, no two, sets of footprints leaving an impression in the deep carpet. Moving toward the doorway. Not human prints, though. One canine and one feline. Large. Larger than any found in nature.

Pettirosso knew instantly what he was seeing. The Wayob, in their animal forms of jaguar and grey fox, had used his sleep to enter his office, slinking in through his dreams. The presence of the Mayan spirits here remained a mystery to him, as so much swirling around the theatre at this time. His instinct was to stop them, confront them, imprison them. But they were attempting to leave and had done him no harm. Had not approached him at all, as far as he could tell.

The prints reached the door and passed through, while the door remained closed. He searched the room. Nothing had been disturbed. Nothing had been removed. But there. In the center of his desk. A piece of fine linen stationery. Even from across the room, he could see the large, florid writing on its front. *Pettirosso.*

He pressed a button on the control bank atop his desk. He knew Deborah would arrive within minutes even at this hour. And she did.

When she arrived, tapping lightly on the door, and entering at his invitation, she found him, brow furrowed, sitting at his desk with the note open in front of him. She knew instantly that something was amiss, and at her questioning look, he explained to her what had happened. And telling her that the letter was an invitation for him to meet with their unknown adversary. As the only true Fae present at the Fulton, only he was allowed. Only him.

After he finished, Deborah paced the length of the room, pausing periodically as if she were about to say something only to remain silent and resume her pacing.

"Deborah," he said. "Please sit. There really is nothing else that can be done. The message was clear. I am the only one they will consider as negotiator. I must go. I will do everything I can to return quickly. With an agreement in place, hopefully."

"But, sir," Deborah protested, taking a seat, "you haven't left the theatre for..."

"Over two hundred years. I'm well aware. I leave you in charge during my absence. I'll go soon. Now. This will take very little time. I should be back before our visitors awaken. They will never know I was away."

"Of course I'll stand watch," Deborah replied. "Drew will be here, of course. And the spirits. I'm sure you've considered the possibility of a trap?"

"Yes." The director stood and moved to the window. "If they should dare, they will bitterly regret any duplicity."

"I know you declined, but will you consider once again taking me with you? Or even one of our guests?"

Pettirosso turned back to the desk and lifted the piece of rich paper, reading it aloud. "'Come alone. We will not tolerate the presence of any but a pure Fae. Any other will be considered a betrayal of the conditions of this parlay.' They are quite clear. Further, I need everyone here should anything go wrong. If I don't return, Kallan and Bayard will know, I have no doubt, that they are needed here. Do not underestimate our guests, either. Rouse them at the slightest sign of danger. They have all been chosen quite carefully."

"Yes, sir," she said. "But you will be back. I refuse to accept any other possibility."

"I will be back," Pettirosso agreed.

He rose and walked to the center if the room where he stretched his arms and neck. He seemed almost lighthearted, expectant.

"It's been so long. It will feel good to stretch unused muscles," he said, turning a brighter gaze on her than she'd seen in some time. "See you very soon."

With that, he blinked out of sight. The atmosphere in the room charged briefly, and then settled. Quiet. Too quiet.

***

Sean and McCloud watched from the window in the anteroom where they had rested. They saw two figures, tall and lanky, climb out and face the mill. One, slightly taller than the other, lifted his face toward the sky and seemed to lean into the easy breeze that swept through the small basin that formed the entrance area. Sean could have sworn the figure was sniffing the night air. The other figure, slightly shorter and muscular, leaned through the open window of the passenger side door that remained ajar. Even in the darkness, it was after nine o'clock, Sean couldn't escape the feeling that the stare the individual fixed on the mill was more specifically aimed at him, and he stepped back from the window before his common sense told him there was no way he could be seen in these conditions.

At a nod from the taller individual, the pair started toward the front entrance. Their gait was long and loping. Easy, athletic. Sean suddenly felt small and very inadequate,

McCloud turned to Sean. "Remember, let me do the talking. If the signs are as I read them, we should be in no danger. If I do my job, it should be quite the opposite. D'ye ken?"

"Sure," Sean replied. "Whatever you say. I'm just along for the ride. But I hope you know what you're doing. Those two look intimidating."

"Ach, you're with a Timestrider. And a McCloud, at that. They'll be the ones intimidated, don't you fret."

Sean followed the Scotsman toward the front door and hoped that the stone he felt in the pit of his stomach was nothing but residual unease from his trip through time.

They reached the entryway in time to see the front door swing slowly inward. The two figures they'd seen arrive in the Volkswagen van stood there, silhouetted by the rising full moon behind them.

McCloud stepped further into the front room; palms outstretched in a conciliatory gesture.

"Look, lads," he began, "we're not here to cause any mischief. In fact, I'm damn glad to see you."

The taller of the two newcomers entered the room. He stood well over six feet, sported a shaggy head of chestnut hair that descended into an impressive stretch of sideburns. He wore a flowered shirt, unbuttoned nearly to his waist and a pair of well-faded bellbottom jeans. His features were sharp, and his movements precise and measured. His air was languid, and he took his time before acknowledging the two trespassers. Brilliant green eyes flashed around the room, before settling on McCloud.

"Nice accent there, pops," he said. "Sounds like you know you shouldn't be here. That's a start. But we're not interested in you. We know what you are. No surprises there."

"I doubt that very much," McCloud said quietly.

The newcomer gestured to Sean, still halfway in the anteroom and trying, unsuccessfully, to conceal himself behind McCloud. "Man, stop hiding back there, boss. It's you we're interested in. So come on out."

Sean flashed a panicked look to McCloud, who seemed as surprised as Sean. This was not going the way they had anticipated.

"Best do what he asks," the Scot said. "It's their turf. I'll be right here."

The second figure in the doorway stepped forward now. Shorter and squatter, he was just as agile and powerful as his companion. Dressed similarly, but with a leather vest. His hair was midnight black and long enough to be tied back in a ponytail. His eyes were dark and gave nothing away.

"Look geezer, he wasn't asking," the second man said. "Just get out here and give us your reason for crashing our place. I'm not in the mood to mess around with some strangers squatting in our spot. If you're looking for scratch, you probably already know we're skint. Nothing here to snatch, so fess up before I lose what little cool I have."

Sean took a tentative step into the front room. He glanced to his left, where the doors led further into the building and eventually to a back door. Another way out. For a fraction of a second, he considered making a dash in that direction, until he saw two more figures emerging from that direction.

The first figure put a hand out to his companion. "Don't flip your wig, Donal. You caught a whiff of what I noticed. I know you did." He gestured to the figures who had joined from further in the mill. "Carolyn, love. Craig. Come out here. Let's get this off to a friendlier start, yeah?"

Sean relaxed just a bit. This sounded more promising. The obvious leader of the group stepped to Sean and seemed to sniff the air around him before fingering the scarf around Sean's neck.

"It's real," he called to his companions, before facing Sean and looking him straight in the eyes. "Now, howsabout you tell me exactly where you got this scarf? Because there's no way you should have it. But here you are."

McCloud let out a grunt, drawing looks from everyone else in the room. His face wore a beaming grin.

Sean put his hand slowly out, in a conciliatory effort. "Hey. I'm Sean Curley. This scarf? A friend gave it to me."

"He lies, man," Donal said from the doorway. "You know he lies. This flake is gone or crazy."

"I don't think so," the leader responded, before addressing Sean again. "Who was this friend of yours?"

"Duncan Wulliver," Sean answered cautiously. "Nice kid I met in Lancaster. Helped him out of a jam and he gave me this to say thanks."

The group's leader looked closer at Sean. Sniffed again and shook his head. "Well, I think we have some things to chat about. "Nice to meet you, Sean. My name is Finlay. Finlay Wulliver."

Back in Pettirosso's office, Deborah found herself pacing the floor once again. This was the first time in years that the Director had been off site. She knew that the theatre, its history, and all it stood for was so much more than one person, but somehow the entire building felt emptier than it should. As she watched the clocks creep closer to midnight, she couldn't escape the knot in her stomach. She had hoped Pettirosso would be back quickly. Ideally, he would have been back before now, but she knew that was asking for too much given the severity of the situation.

She felt woefully inadequate to be entrusted with the safety of the complex. She was a simple woman who had found her place here with the Fulton and...never left. It had so quickly become the center of her life. Her friends were here. In fact, a gloriously revolving series of friends that cycled in from show to show. The sadness of saying goodbye to each cast as their shows finished, was tempered by the arrival of the next cast and a new group of pals, both old and new. She imagined it was, in some ways, not dissimilar to what the actors felt with each passing show, although she did have the Fulton to provide her with a home. Something most actors were never able to enjoy.

But none of that had prepared her to be the solitary guardian on a night when everything was hanging in the balance. She knew Pettirosso would be in no personal danger himself. She had seen him work miracles both large and small. But the tide of events felt bigger than any one person. Bigger than anything she had ever considered coming to quaint little Lancaster. She had grown up in a traditional home in the county and had become familiar with many of the hexes her ancestors had employed. Not the ones made famous on souvenirs sold to tourists throughout Amish country. No, the hexes she had learned were used by farmers, craftsmen, true believers throughout the centuries from the homelands they had left to the rich fields of Pennsylvania. But those hexes were meant to safeguard against common worldly events—drought, illness, fire. She had no idea what would happen if they were put to the test by some of the forces lining up against them.

She stopped at the window and looked out over Prince Street. She felt like an imposter. This was Pettirosso's place. Not hers, no matter how much she had wanted to share it with him.

The street was silent. An occasional truck rumbling through the town, delivering its load to a neighboring town or county. As she watched, she realized that to the left, toward the Ware Center, the night had grown blacker, almost impenetrable. She concentrated on that area and felt more than saw movement within it. Shadows. Deeper and darker. Thick with numbers and oozing their way toward the alley along the side of the theatre.

As she watched, the inky darkness divided, and began to slide across the front of the building, like an obsidian river, flowing around and encircling the Fulton. She thought of the many actors and artists sleeping quietly, vulnerable, toward the far side of the complex, and felt her greatest fears were about to be realized. She thought of the Grumbles and Pettirosso's advice to trust them.

Before she could reach the phone on the desk, determined to wake them, but as few others as possible, the alarms started to ring. First, the stage door on the near side of the building registered an attempted entry. Next, the loading dock behind the stage door sounded. And then the doors to the rear of the building. Soon every alarm was sounding inside the office, but only audible in that room. Pettirosso had always considered himself the first and last line of defense. The only one needed.

But he was not here. And the warnings rang through the office. She lifted the phone to call Brandy's apartment, hoping she could rally the others, but as she did, a more ominous sound broke through the cacophony. The interior warning system shrieked above all the others. Someone, or something, was trying to enter the theatre through the portal in the basement.

CHAPTER 12

Sean found himself back in the changing room that he and McCloud had relaxed in earlier. This time, though, he was surrounded by the Wulliver family. Finlay was clearly the leader of the clan. He was married to Carolyn, who brought a gentle, nurturing air with her. Craig was Carolyn's brother, and her equal in temperament. Donal was a cousin to Finlay, and clearly the firebrand of the group. He observed Sean and McCloud from a distance and wore his doubt openly in every comment and expression he wore.

The entire family bore a striking similarity in appearance. All had dark hair, varying in color from a coppery chestnut to coal black. Their eyes were similarly brown, from deep chocolate to a bright hazel on the part of Finlay.

But it was their physicality that was most distinctive. They didn't simply walk, they prowled. Each step seemed deliberate. There was an economy of effort to their movements, but beneath the surface lay the promise of strength and speed. They were incredibly in tune with each other, their actions. Almost as if everything was choreographed in advance. A group mentality that informed all they did. Sean found them fascinating, and wondered how they could be connected to the awkward youth, Duncan, he had encountered being assaulted in the Lancaster alley. It was only a few days ago, but already felt like a lifetime ago.

Finlay had taken charge and looked intently at Sean. "You claim to have received that scarf from a Duncan Wulliver, but we have no Duncan in our clan. Yet that is a design and fabric that signals membership in our family. Can you explain that?"

The penetrating gaze Finlay had fixed on Sean was startling. Disconcerting. It set him back, and he found himself stammering to answer. He knew the hesitation made him look bad, and even though he had nothing to hide, he felt his face flushing with embarrassment. "It's like I told you, I gave a hand to this kid—"

"Duncan," Donal interjected from the far corner of the room.

"Yes," Sean replied. "Duncan. He'd been cornered by some other guys, was outnumbered, and I jumped in to even the odds. Turns out the others weren't much more than bullies and turned tail at the first sign of trouble."

Finlay held out a hand to stop Donal's biting response. "And these *guys*. Why were they hassling this Duncan?"

"The kid said they had been bullying him for years. Said there wasn't any one reason, just always been that way," Sean answered.

Carolyn stepped closer to Sean, and after a quick glance at Finlay, asked, "Did you happen to hear any names for them?"

"Names?" Sean replied. "Oh, man, it's been a crazy couple days, not sure. One was something Stubbe. I remember that because it was odd. The others? One was...Verdun? And the other...Bur-something. Sorry, that's all I can remember."

The Wullivers shared a glance. Donal and Craig let out guttural noises that Sean could only think to call growls.

"How could he possibly know?" Donal muttered. "He can't know. He must be here on their behalf. I say turn them out."

Craig seemed to be of the same mind, but Carolyn and Finlay clearly disagreed.

"No," Finlay said quietly. "Something else is going on here. I just don't know what."

McCloud took this opportunity to step forward. "I think I can help clear this up, if you all are willing to listen?"

Again, Donal and Craig reacted with low growls. And again, Finlay cut them off, this time with a sharp motion of his hand.

"Look, man," Finlay said. "We see you. We know you. You're a Fae. We get it. Our family has seen your kind for as long as we can remember. Honestly, the fact you're from Scotland gets you a little more leeway with us. Our roots are there, too. But I don't think you should get any more involved than you are. We don't exactly have cozy feelings for the like of you."

"Ach, Finlay," McCloud answered. "You know just the smallest bit about me. But I know you, too, which I would have told ye if you'd given me a chance. I'm no run-of-the-mill Fae, though."

Donal had reached a breaking point and surged toward the Scotsman, forcing Finlay to hold him back.

"Your kind has been at our heels for too long, Fae," Donal hissed. "We don't need to listen to one single word from you."

"Would it make a difference if you knew I was a Timestrider?" McCloud asked, grinning. "And that Sean here is under my protection? Because I think it should matter."

The entire Wulliver family stopped, still.

"There's no such thing—" Donal whispered.

"Wives tales," Craig added.

"Sometimes those wives should be listened to," McCloud said, laughing. "Let's cut all of this ridiculousness and talk like civilized Fae. We should be helping each other."

"Helping each other?" Donal hissed. "Your kind did nothing when our family was persecuted, demonized, and chased from our homes. Why would we ever help you, man? Get outta here with that kumbaya crap. We've been on our own for a long time and we sure as hell don't need help from you or any treacherous Fae. And don't get me started on the useless humans."

Finlay held his hand out. "Enough," he said. "If he is what he says he is, we at least need to listen. A Timestrider? Dude, did you ever think you'd see the day?"

Carolyn stepped to Finlay's side and grasped his hand. "He's telling the truth," she said quietly. "I know it, and you all know it, too. No one pretends to be a Timestrider. No one. The scarf, the names. It's too much to be coincidence. Stop letting ancient hates blind you. Wullivers don't turn their backs on anyone in need."

Donal and Craig looked chastened and faded back against the wall. Finlay and Carolyn presented a more generous air toward Sean and McCloud.

"Aye, well that's more like it." The Scot chuckled. "Sit yerselves down. It's quite a story I have to tell you."

Sean, looking confused, placed a hand on McCloud's arm. "I'm confused," he said. "I know that's par for the course, but who exactly are they? How do they know about the Fae? Timestriders?"

"First things first, Sean. Let's get them up to speed and then we can let them share their own story with you. We'll see that we all have a lot more in common than any of us realizes."

With that, McCloud took the floor and explained to the Wulliver family how he and Sean had found their way into the mill by Cocalico Creek. Sean was surprised as he heard the Timestrider leave nothing out. He told them of the mysterious dream attacks in Lancaster. He shared the story of Pettirosso, who in this year was known as Nathaniel Hager. This raised more than a couple of Wulliver eyebrows. McCloud explained the growing animosities between the Fae factions, the discovery of unexpected powers among Sean, and, to a lesser extent, his companions. He described the Wayob, the Hide Behinds, the Shadow People, Red Caps. All of the forces gathering to capture or destroy Sean and exploit the long-protected powers of the portal that lay shielded and guarded below the Fulton. He even, to Sean's dismay, revealed that he knew of the earlier adventures in New York City, Montauk, and the Outer Banks.

He shared the involvement of Fae—or Peripherals, in Sean's mind—from the world over. The noble Japanese Yokai Kitsune, the indigenous wise man Kelphit. The vicious native Wendigo. However, it was the evil Dullahan who drew the most attention from the family. McCloud painted the picture clearly and let the Wullivers fully understand the gravity of the situation.

"So you see," he concluded, "not only does this shadow coalition want to either erase or enslave the humans, they are clearly determined to create a new order among the Fae. One that I think it's safe to say would not be the ordered, peaceful existence we've maintained for so very long."

Donal, from his place along the wall, chuffed, before saying, "Maybe that's not such a bad thing. The old way didn't do our family any favors."

"Lad," McCloud replied, "I lived the old days with your family. As bad as things were—and they were bad—it was nothing compared to what will be unleashed if the world order is shattered."

"Look, geezer, let it shatter," Donal pushed himself off the wall aggressively. "Burn it all down."

Finlay whirled and was on Donal in less than the blink of an eye. He threw Donal to the ground, pinning his shoulders, while Donal cowered beneath him. Sean's immediate thought, once he accepted the speed and strength of Finlay, was that Donal would have tucked his tail between bis legs if he'd had one.

"That's not how Wullivers do things. And you know it. Despite what was done to us, we have honor. We help those who need it. To do any less—*be any less*—would give those that wronged us reason to justify what they did. Wullivers are better than that. And we always will be."

Donal offered no resistance to Finlay. His head hung in shame, and he looked up toward Finlay with pleading eyes.

"Unless, of course," Finlay growled, "you would like to go it alone. How would your life look without the family?"

And now real fear spread across Donal's face. He looked close to tears and Finlay gave him one last shove into the ground before rising gracefully to his feet.

"Right, then," McCloud went on, as if nothing had happened. "You know our story. I think it's time you shared the Wulliver story with Sean here, so we all know what's at play."

Carolyn stepped silently to Sean's side and guided him to one of the benches on the side of the room, gently lowering him onto it.

"Yes," she began. "I think we owe him that. And we owe you"—she nodded to McCloud—"an apology. You clearly are what you say you are. We are humbled to meet you. We, who've been shunned for so long. We want to help."

McCloud nodded and sat his considerable bulk on the bench next to Sean with a smile. "Let's have it, then. Let's see if we all remember it the same way. Because I was there. And I stood with Titus Wulliver and your family when the days were darkest."

Carolyn turned her bright hazel eyes to him with surprise before she began. "It's like this, Sean..."

***

Brandy's sleep had been fitful, filled with startling images of violence and danger. She was racing through a rainforest, pursued by a large cat, unseen but audible crashing through the undergrowth behind her. Roots along the forest floor grasped for her, trying to trip and clutch her. Low-lying branches whipped her face and arms, which she raised in a futile attempt to protect herself. A divot in the soil, shaped as if something large had rushed through recently, caught her shoe, and she went cartwheeling across the ground. Before she could right herself, she sensed her pursuer upon her. She flipped onto her back to find a massive jaguar, unusually colored black and white, leap from the brush. As it flew toward her, her mind inexplicably recalled that jaguars have the strongest bite force of all cats. She realized she was about to experience that fact firsthand.

Before the cat landed, the sounds of the forest were disrupted by the sound of the Rolling Stones' "Beast of Burden" echoing through the trees. Brandy found herself sitting abruptly up in her bed, unsure if the dream had awakened her or what she now realized was her phone's ringtone.

She glanced at the screen and saw that it was midnight. Her first thought was that something had happened with the Sean experiment in time. However, when she answered, she was greeted by a calm but clearly stressed Deborah speaking loudly but precisely.

"Brandy, rouse your friends and meet me in the basement. Something is coming through the portal, and I don't think I'll be able to hold it shut alone."

"Shit, okay," Brandy replied, shaking the cobwebs from her mind. "Can't Pettirosso handle this? I thought this was his domain."

"I'm sure he could," Deborah said in a strained voice. "But he's not here. Please, hurry. And come prepared for violence. I don't know what to expect."

The line went dead, and Brandy swung her legs over her too-tall bed, her bare feet not reaching the cool wooden floor. She grabbed a pair of jeans, slipped a sweatshirt over her sleeping t-shirt, and started for the door. Before it closed behind her, she had a thought and raced back into the room, tossing the contents of a duffel bag across the floor until her hand found what it was looking for—an indigenous war club given to her in Montauk by the ancient wise man Kelphit. She hefted it once and raced back to the door.

She emerged into the hallway, and turned to her left, stopping to pound on each door as she moved toward the elevator at the end of the corridor. One by one, the doors opened and bleary-eyed Grumbles poked their heads out. Nick, Trout, and Ken all set eyes on her and prepared to complain to her about their interrupted sleep, but when they spied her war club they knew something was up.

"Deborah called me," she called. "Trouble in the basement at the portal. Worst part is Pettirosso isn't here, so she's on her own. Until we get there, at least."

"He's *gone?*" Nick said, incredulously. "Where the hell is he at midnight?"

"Well, we can ask him when he gets back," Brandy answered. "Grab your gear. Let's move."

"I don't have any gear," Ken lamented. "What do I do?"

"Find something heavy and get to the elevator," Brandy said. "Deb is down there, like, now."

Ken's head dipped back into his apartment and a moment later he reappeared, swinging a cast iron pot. "I made pasta tonight," he announced. "First thing I saw."

Nick appeared wielding a war club similar to Brandy's, acquired at the same time as hers. A moment later, Trout emerged from his apartment with a vicious-looking tomahawk, also gifted by Kelphit in Montauk.

"Let's do this," he said, and started toward the elevator.

Before they had time to assemble, another door opened, and Dante Gugliomo popped out. "What's up, gang? Everything okay?"

The Grumbles stopped in their tracks and looked at each other. None of them had considered that there were other actors on the hall.

"Uh," Trout said, stepping toward Dante. "All good. Just headed to the basement to help Deborah with something. Not a bother."

"Mhm," Dante replied slowly. "That must really be a bad something for you all to be carrying weapons." He spied Ken's pot. "Well, weapons of a sort. I think I'll tag along if you don't mind."

Dante disappeared into his apartment and the Grumbles huddled up.

"What are we going to do?" Ken asked. "We can't bring him with us. He'll get in the way, at best, and get slaughtered, at worst."

"I don't know about that," Nick replied. "He's a big guy. Might be of some use. And I doubt Pettirosso would have anyone here if he didn't think they could be of use."

At that point, Dante emerged from his apartment. In one hand he held a golf club, and in the other he held an enormous scythe that equaled his more than six feet in height.

"My 'Ghost of Christmas Future' scythe," he explained as he was met with incredulous stares from the others. "I was practicing some moves for the show. It's surprisingly sturdy."

"Dude, that is sweet," Trout said, clapping the big Italian on the shoulder. "Let's go find out what the problem is. Happy to have you along. Just be prepared to be surprised."

Brandy opened the door to the stairwell next to the elevator and pointed the others downward. "Stairs will be faster. Dante, watch your back and try to save questions for after. It won't be easy, but try. Let's go! Deb is alone down there."

They filed onto the staircase and rushed toward a basement filled with the unknown.

———

As Carolyn began to tell Sean about her family, the other Wullivers arranged themselves around the room and settled in like children expecting a favorite story. Even Donal seemed to have calmed himself and waited in hushed anticipation. The night outside was silent. The slight breeze that had whistled through earlier had stilled. No one passed on the road and the moon was arcing across the sky sending shadows from the surrounding tree branches like spindly fingers reaching toward the mill.

"The Wulliver family traces its roots as far back as can be followed," Carolyn began. "We called the Highlands home and lived largely on our own. As is often the case, our solitary nature eventually drew attention, and then suspicion. Though we avoided contact with others, we were eventually harassed and pushed out. The family remained together and moved north. Repeatedly. Each time forced out by locals who mistrusted the strange clan that stuck to itself."

"Persecuted, is more like it," Donal muttered from the far corner. His face shrouded in shadow. "Dim-witted, small-minded little men."

Finlay turned and huffed at him, shutting the other man down.

Carolyn resumed. "Over time, we drifted as far north as we could and settled in the Shetland Islands, hoping against hope that we had finally found someplace isolated enough to live quietly and in peace. But sadly, that was not to be. A few years of peace was all that we could claim before the islanders began to turn on us. Our patriarch, Titus Wulliver, finally made the difficult decision to leave our homeland. By that time, America was becoming a haven for many fleeing persecution. We hoped to lose ourselves amongst all the other pilgrims. And finally, we seemed to have found a home. We settled in this area, where the Amish are also very insular. Our family has always included millers. If you had told me I would end up here as a miller myself, it would have made sense. Our particular talents were suited to the fulling mills here, and we quickly made a name for ourselves with our craftsmanship— suits, shirts, and yes, scarves. The Amish appreciated us for our diligence and left us largely to ourselves. The example they set allowed us to be ourselves and to claim a place for ourselves free from the hatred and vitriol of neighbors who hated what they couldn't claim as their own."

"But why?" Sean asked. "If all you wanted was to live peacefully and alone, why did the others push you out? I don't understand."

"I can help to answer that," McCloud said, sitting forward on his bench. "I knew of the Wullivers and traveled to the Shetlands to give what little aid I could. Their family is not exactly what they seem. You and your friends would consider them what you call Peripherals. To me, they are simply fellow Fae. But their gift, if one can consider it that, is one that is difficult to conceal. At least at times. The Wullivers have always been shapeshifters. And while they control their shifting, their second form taps into very primal fears in most people. Especially the superstitious Highlanders of centuries ago."

"Hold on," Sean cut in. "Shapeshifters? Here in Lancaster County? What kind of shapeshifters? They seem perfectly normal to..."

Sean's voice trailed off as he turned back to Carolyn and found himself face to face with a startlingly beautiful woman with the head of a wolf. A wolf with caramel-colored fur and the same bright hazel eyes he had watched while she began her story. He jumped back on the bench in surprise and found himself bumping into Finlay. He turned quickly, and found Finlay had shifted also, and now wore the head of a dark brown wolf.

The wolf spoke to Sean in Finlay's voice. "Sean don't be afraid. You are here under McCloud's care and even if that weren't the case, you've nothing to fear from us."

"Yeah, okay," Sean said. "Trying to make that jump. Never been in a room full of werewolves before."

From the far corner, Donal leaned further into the light, revealing a squat, midnight black wolf head atop his powerful frame.

"See, that's the kind of uninformed bull we've had to deal with forever. We aren't werewolves, man. Far from it."

"He's right," McCloud agreed. "That's what I meant by primal fears. The Wullivers are something far different than werewolves. They shift at will, to begin with. And, ach, they've been a true friend to their neighbors whenever allowed. They're quite benign and have been known to protect those around them and even share their crops or catches with them. But man will be man, and fear often needs little excuse to rule the day."

"I'm sorry," Sean replied. "It's all new to me, and I'm still in a bit of shock after the whole time travel thing."

"No need for that," Carolyn said. "We've dealt with much worse, believe me. We're not lycanthropes. Nothing bit us or turned us. We aren't cursed. We don't turn into mindless beasts. We were just made this way. Like you humans, there are good and bad of our kind. But we Wullivers have always chosen a path of peace. Other shifters, other families, have made different choices."

"Other families?" Sean asked. "It's not just you?"

"No," Finlay answered. "There are families scattered throughout the world. We do our best to stay out of sight and to ourselves. Some do little to conceal themselves. Still others prefer to prey upon the weak. Use their strengths to inflict pain on the defenseless. Some have even allied themselves with werewolves. Chaos agents, at best."

"Wait." Sean held out his hands, palms out. "You all reacted strangely when I said the names of the bullies who attacked Duncan. Were they—?"

"We know them," Carolyn said, "we've got certain families that just don't get along. And yeah. Those names you listed are some of our least favorite shifters. They've been hounding us for as long as the family memories stretch back. Not surprised they were still at it in your day. I'm sure if you asked them, they'd say we deserve it. But from our point of view, they're the worst of the worst."

Donal leaned in to speak. "Man, what really bites is that means we still haven't snuffed them out in sixty years."

"On the other hand," Craig, who had remained largely silent, said, "it also means they haven't put us down, either. Sixty more years of this? Knowing that just is a flat-out downer."

"It's not great, that's for sure," Finlay agreed. "But the good news in there is that there's a new family member. Duncan. That's damn good news."

Carolyn was nodding. "It's a rare thing for us to add to our family. We live longer lives than you," she gestured to Sean, "and not as long as you," she gestured to McCloud. "But we bear few young. To know we add someone, and a boy, in the near future—it's very welcome news."

"Yeah, but sounds like he's a bit of a wuss, getting pushed around like that," Donal complained. "Can't be my pup."

"I wouldn't say that," Sean said. "I got the impression he was holding back. I'm guessing he could have done some damage if pushed much farther."

McCloud stood and crossed to the window. "Too bad he's not here right now," he said. "Sounds like you all are about to have company."

Silence fell over the room as everyone paused, and faintly through the night came the sound of a howl. And soon after, a chorus of howls. The howls of a wolf pack. A pack on the hunt.

The Grumbles, followed closely by Dante, came plunging out of the stairwell onto stage right. The stage lay beyond, dark and silent. Full of so many stories. And possibly more.

But the group didn't slow one bit. They skidded to the left, making a full U-turn and dashing down the old staircase that led to the original greenroom a flight below. The part of the building that harkened back to the earliest days, when the structure served as the jail for a much younger Lancaster.

As they emerged into the large room, the green furniture that had filled the room was scattered, tossed to the walls where they lay in heaps. There was a black shadow stretching from out below the stage, from the small door that had held so much fascination for the group when they'd gotten their original tour of the theatre.

Deborah stood before that door. Alone, she was chanting in a language none of the newcomers recognized. The various drawings she had made around the entrance glowed with a silver light. That light pulsed and stretched across the floor, along the walls, forming an argent web that enclosed the doorway.

The black tendrils creeping from the doorway crept among the strands of Deborah's web, grasping, and pulling the shield. The midnight coils continued to surge outward and soon Deborah, who looked so small standing alone against the onslaught, would clearly be overwhelmed.

Brandy, first to enter the room, called to Deborah. "We're here, Deb! What can we do?"

Deborah couldn't spare a backward glance, but called, "I won't hold much longer. Be ready! I expect the Red Caps and Hide Behinds will be here in large numbers. You'll know what to do. But remember—don't let the Hide Behinds get past us. Once they are out of our sight, they can be almost impossible to stop."

Brandy held her war club before her and took a defensive stance. The others did the same with their weapons, giving Dante a wide berth to wield his massive scythe.

As Deborah's protective spells and hexes further weakened, it became obvious that she would be devoured by the blackness before the weapons could begin their work.

Suddenly, Ken stepped closer to Deborah. His sad pot hanging limply at his side. He placed a hand on Deborah's shoulder and turned to look back at Brandy and the others.

"I've never really done this," he called back. "Definitely not without Sean, but we can't just leave her here."

He began to sing, wordlessly, sending out a clear, warm baritone note. Dante looked at him as if he had lost his mind, planting his feet firmly where he stood, thrusting his scythe toward the shadow arms.

Brandy saw what Ken was trying to do and stepped to him, a hand on his shoulder. Trout and Nick also clued into the idea and did the same, forming a human chain leading away from the doorway to the portal. Each of the Grumbles added their voice to the music. Nick's crystal tenor, Brandy's velvety alto, and Trout's rich, rumbly bass. It was clear they had done this together before.

Much to Dante's shock, as they sang, a clear white nimbus appeared around them, growing in size and strength as their chord did the same. The cloud extended down Ken's arm, reaching Deborah and encircling her just as her chanting faltered.

With her weakening, the silver web she had woven began to fray and snap. The black coils seized on the opening and began to tear the web apart. Before Deborah was lost, Ken began pulling her back into the safety of their musical spell, where she collapsed, completely spent, in the center of the Grumbles.

Dante approached, shaking his head. "You all have a lot to tell me. That's the damndest thing I've ever seen."

"We'll get to that, but care to help out? The more voices the better," Brandy replied.

"I can't do anything like that," Dante protested. "Not sure how you all are doing it. I'll just stick to my fake scythe."

"Trust me," Brandy said. "Just give it a try. You'll be surprised."

Nick, eyes on the doorway, broke in. "Gang, we may want to get ready. Look."

All eyes turned to the doorway. It was entirely engulfed in blackness now. Deep in the center, and seemingly from a great distance, an orange flicker appeared. It grew brighter and larger as it approached.

From the floor Deborah stirred. "They're here," she whispered. "Oh, Marcello, where are you?"

Dante, still shaking his head, moved to the circle of Grumbles. As they all steeled themselves for whatever was coming their way, he joined their music with a deep, powerful bass. Trout, hearing the new voice, turned to him flashing a wicked grin and a thumbs up. With the addition of another note, the white aura grew stronger and began to claim back some of the room that had fallen to darkness.

The orange light was relentless, though. It grew larger. Larger. Until finally it had supplanted the darkness and filled the entire doorway. As that happened, the defenders began to see shapes moving within the doorway, Shambling creatures, with red caps atop their heads. Along with them were shadowy forms, vague and difficult to bring into focus.

Trout and Dante, the largest of the portal guardians, stepped to the front, allowing the others to fill in behind them, which they did, taking up positions around Deborah, who was still recovering.

The orange light flickered into the room, shoots of it licking the walls and the ceiling, and as it did so, the first of the attackers poured forth. Surging toward the group. The first to emerge were massive, with dark, wine-red caps on their heads that hung over their faces, adding an even greater sense of menace. As they lined up inside the room, they began to lift their gazes and revealed eyes glowing a bright red. Their spindly arms ended in long, vicious talons. They had filthy, lanky, colorless hair hanging past their shoulders. Each of them held a long pike in their left hand and wore boots of iron.

One Red Cap, clearly a leader of some sort, pounded his pike once on the floor. At that, a great cry erupted from the invaders, and they surged forward. The scythe and the tomahawk flashed through the first to arrive and they fell, before dissolving into clouds of ash that settled to the floor.

The music strengthened, the white light growing brighter and clearly slowing the advance of the attackers. Despite the numbers arrayed against them, the Grumbles and friends were holding their own. The door was throttling the advance and for a few moments, it seemed the tide of the battle was with them. But suddenly shadows began to flicker behind the Red Caps, flitting about just beyond their ability to sight them clearly. They shielded themselves behind the goblin-like aggressors. They had entered the room and were probing where to slip behind the guardians. It seemed only a matter of time before they succeeded, with the sheer numbers of the Red Caps demanding attention.

"No," Deborah shouted. "Hide Behinds. If they get past, we are finished!"

Scythe and tomahawk did their jobs. The war clubs of Brandy and Nick joined them. Ken's pot was surprisingly effective, clearing swaths through the assailants. The floor around them was now littered with small piles of ashes where the raiders fell.

But the numbers continued to be against the Grumbles. Their attention became divided, as they sought a way to prevent the Hide Behinds from reaching their goal. It seemed inevitable that the defense would begin to falter, and it did when Nick received a nasty slash from one of the pikes. He fell to his knees, clutching his arm and dropping his war club.

With Nick down, the group lost both his club and his voice in the music, which dimmed noticeably. The shadowy Hide Behinds surged at the sign of weakness and things looked grim for both the defenders and the hallowed Fulton.

At just that moment, a tiny sliver of green appeared from the direction of the portal, deep within the angry orange light that had consumed the doorway. It grew quickly, a brilliant verdant streak that became larger and larger until the orange was nearly entirely eclipsed. The new color was lush, alive, pulsing with a brilliant verdigris.

Within the light, a figure strode purposefully toward them. It moved quickly, gracefully, confidently.

The Grumbles fell back slightly, unsure what to make of this new arrival. Deborah, however, got unsteadily to her feet and a look of over-whelming relief flooded her face. At that moment, Pettirosso swept into the room, anger emanating from every movement he made. The green light came with him, surrounded him, driving the orange light from the room. It found the faltering light of the Grumbles' music and swept around it, strengthening it and lifting it up.

Pettirosso's eyes flashed with the same light. He seemed to be floating above the floor. His movements more graceful and controlled than any choreography that had appeared on the stage upstairs.

He swept his arms in a full circle, executing a perfect pirouette. As he did so, he cried out. "Not here! Not in my theatre! Not ever again!"

The room exploded in light. The attackers in their entirety were pulled inexorably backward through the door. All signs of orange, or black, were gone, replaced by Pettirosso's brilliant, life-affirming light. As the last of the Red Caps flew through the door and out of the portal, the door slammed shut and sealed itself. The alarms throughout the building fell quiet, and the entire theatre filled with a deafening silence.

With that, Pettirosso sank to one knee and caught his breath. "It's much worse than we could have known," he said.

"Okay, can we deal with this first?" Brandy called from across the room where she was sitting on the floor next to Nick, whose arm hung limply at his side, a pool of blood getting larger below it. As they all turned in that direction, Nick slumped onto Brandy's shoulder and lost consciousness.

CHAPTER 13

Within moments, the mill was surrounded by a racing, circling pack of powerful creatures. Bodies of humans, sinewy and lean, with the heads of wolves. They were dressed similarly to the Wullivers. Loose jeans, patterned shirts. Sturdy leather boots that had seen much use. Tongues lolled out of open maws, revealing massive canine teeth. They loped easily around the building, flashing in the moonlight between the shadows cast by the tree branches. Their howls echoed off the bowl of land formed by the path coming down from the bridge and held an almost mocking, mirthful tone. These were predators on the hunt, secure in the knowledge that they were the apex in their environment and therefore able to enjoy the physical exertion and the pursuit of whatever drew their attention.

After a few moments, the pack outside slowed and a wolf, much larger than the others, stepped to the door of the mill. He held his nose aloft and drank in the scents of the night. And of the mill and its inhabitants.

"Mongrels!" it called into the building. "Come out, Wullivers! We all know how this has to end. Gotta say, we didn't think even you lot would be stupid enough to be caught out here late at night. But we dig that maybe you lot just want this all to be over, and we're here to grant that wish." The wolf stopped and raised its nose again. "Man, I feel sorry for whoever you talked into hanging in there with you. But I guarantee that human will regret the choice. And whoever that other one is—we don't exactly shake at a single Fae. Let's do this. Come on out here and get it done."

Inside the mill, McCloud was at the window watching the pack outside.

"Ach, that one's a cheeky gadge, yeah? What's his story?"

Finlay joined the Scotsman at the window. "Max Stubbe. The worst of the worst. Even his own family fears him and follows his lead more out of fear than anything else. Don't get me wrong, they're rotten, too. But he takes it to new levels."

"But why do they hate you so much?" Sean asked from his bench. "What could possibly have caused a centuries' long feud. Most people would get tired of it and move on."

"Most people would, yes. But we are shapeshifters. Fae, of a sort," Carolyn answered. "Time moves differently for us. And sometimes a hatred of others becomes so ingrained in someone that it gets passed on from one to another. After a time, it doesn't even matter what caused it. It becomes a reason for being unto itself. Hate for hate's sake. I'm guessing if one side eventually wins, the other will be lost without the object of their hate to drive them. So stupid, when you think of it. Pointless."

"Coming to America was our chance," Craig added. "We could have wiped the slate clean. Chosen to help each other. Gods above, we could have used more help, more friends. Especially of our own kind. But it all went the opposite way."

Donal paced to the window, shoving his nose on the air. "And as long as that miserable cur, Max, is in charge of their side, there will be no choice but to fight. First chance he gets, he'll take us down. One by one, if he could. Coward that he is."

"Well, he hasn't caught you on your own tonight," McCloud said. "I think we can help. At least for tonight. What do you say, Sean? Want to teach some puppies a lesson?"

Sean looked at McCloud, who seemed to be thoroughly enjoying the situation. "Teach some...What are you talking about? I can't do anything to help. Did you see them? There must be at least fifteen of them out there."

"Sean-o, you took three of them without even trying in that alley. And now you have me," McCloud almost vibrated with excitement. "That lot doesn't stand a chance."

"No," Finlay said. "We can't have you fight our battles. We need to handle this ourselves."

"C'mon, dude," Donal said to McCloud. "You won't be here forever to fight for us. And if they smell fear on our part, we're done for. We gotta do this ourselves."

"Oh, ye, of little faith," McCloud replied. "Sean and I can handle this *and* make you look good in the process. Not the first time I've had to deal with bullies."

Finlay cocked his head, curious. Within five moments, Sean and McCloud were by the front door, prepared to take on a pack of shapeshifters.

***

Deborah rushed to Nick, where he lay motionless on the floor. She examined his arm, checked his pulse, and began to draw more of her hexes on the floor beside him.

"It's a serious injury," she said, "but he should recover. At least physically. Hopefully, the Red Caps' pikes weren't poisoned. Only time will tell us that."

Brandy was still crouched worriedly on the other side of Nick. "Damn, I wish we had Stewart here. Or Sandy Dale. They know their healing arts."

Ken crossed to where the others were attending to Nick. Michelangelo could not have created a more poignant scene of a fallen warrior. "We could call Stewart. He said he'd come if we needed him."

"Not for nuthin'," Trout called from across the room, "but I think we should let Stew stay the course in New York. Unless, of course, Nick takes a turn for the worse. Seems like Stewart's doin' a lot of good up there. Plus, not even sure we could, or *should*, bring him into this situation. Stew's always been a gentle soul. He should stay out of this. I think it's about to get messy here."

With that, all eyes turned to Pettirosso who had caught his breath and gained his feet again.

"First things first," the diminutive director said. "Let's get Nick someplace comfortable and dress that wound. I suggest we take him to my office. I have certain resources there. We'll need to leave someone here to watch the portal. After what I've learned, I can't be confident they won't try that again."

"I'll stay here," Deborah replied. "I belong here. I should have held it the first time and then none of this would be happening."

"That's a load of bull hockey," Trout said. "No one else could have done what you just did. And look at you. You're plenty tired, and rightfully so. No, you go with Nick. He'll need you. I'll stay here."

Deborah began to protest but was interrupted by a new voice. Drew Brindig had descended the stairs behind them unnoticed, and stood with his head down, clearly despondent.

"I'm so sorry, boss," Drew began. "I should have been here. I was up top in the grid. I picked up on some activity there that seemed out of place. Then the alarms. I didn't know what was happening down here until too late. I failed you."

Pettirosso looked to Drew and his voice was gentle when he responded. "Drew, there is no greater champion of this theatre than you. You have no reason to hang your head. We will all play a part in what lies ahead. Why don't you stay here with Trout. Watch the portal. There is no greater task right now than that."

Drew raised his head, a determined look in his eyes. "Yes, boss. I won't let you down again."

"You never have," Pettirosso answered. "Before we part, I need you all to know what I have learned. Our instincts were correct. The Wayob, Red Caps, Hide Behinds—are all foot soldiers in a much larger army. Even the mighty Dullahan you have faced was simply a lieutenant. They are led by none other than Balor, the ancient foe of the Tuatha. We had thought him long dead. It seems he has been biding his time. The most frightening aspect, though, is that he has convinced some of our kind, Fae, Tuatha, Peripherals—however you name them, they have aligned with our enemy. War is coming."

"Well, shit," Brandy said. "Not exactly the result we were hoping for. So that attempt at diplomacy?"

"Rejected out of hand," Pettirosso answered, his brow creased with concern. "I was fortunate to make my way back here, at all. Balor is one of very few who could have any chance of imprisoning me. And he nearly did."

Dante, who had been silent in the corner throughout, stepped forward. "I'm just hearing about a lot of this for the first time. Can I suggest that we enlist some of the others to help out? I know Bobby Smalls would want to help. Cory, Lina, Adriane...can they help?"

"We'll get there," Pettirosso replied. "I suspect we will need every artist—every sensitive soul—before all is said and done. The writers, singers, artists. The feelers. They will lead the way in this. We will need to rediscover the old ways. Recall them from the past."

"Yeah, we can help with that," Ken said. "Maybe, though, we need to deal with this first?" He pointed toward the doorway to the portal. Though closed again, it had begun to seep a blue light around its edges, and the light was growing brighter by the moment.

"You have got to be kidding me," Brandy muttered.

"We got this," Trout declared. "Yo, Dante. Shall we?"

"We shall, my friend," Dante replied, stepping to Trout's side and taking a few casual swings of the scythe.

Pettirosso passed between them and approached the door, a curious expression on his face. He placed his palm flat on the door. He pressed his forehead to the wooden frame, before standing up suddenly and throwing the door open.

"Pettirosso, what are you—" Ken called, as the room filled with the azure light.

A figure appeared in the light, coming closer. As it neared, another, smaller, figure appeared at its side. A four-legged figure.

"You can lower your weapons," Pettirosso said, turning to Trout and Dante.

Before any could reply, the Peripheral Bayard emerged from the light into the room, his faithful companion wolf, Cinder, at his side.

"You better check the seal on that portal," Bayard said, laughing. "You never know who might wander in."

"Well, you're a sight for sore eyes!" Brandy cried. "We were *just* saying how much we needed you. Welcome back. We have a lot to tell you."

"And I a lot to tell you, friends," Bayard answered. His hair was tousled, and he seemed weary. Exhausted. His sleek black clothes were dusty, torn in places. The others noticed that Cinder was limping and had sunk to the floor, her head resting on her paws.

Ken, seeing Bayard's distress, came to his side and helped him to one of the easy chairs after setting it back on its legs. The Grumbles, minus Nick, all stepped to Bayard, concern on all their faces. Bayard was a Peripheral, which to them meant that he was powerful beyond their understanding. What could have done this to him?

"I have answers," Bayard began. "Or the beginnings of answers, at least. I did find Breena. It's as we feared. She is being held by her family. A response to her relationship with Sean. What I don't know, is if her family is simply against such a relationship, or if they have aligned with our foes."

"Well, that's not great, but not exactly a surprise," Brandy said. "She would have been here, especially at Sean's side, if she were able."

"True," Bayard replied. "I strongly suspect her family is divided. Like so many others. My greatest fear is war among the Fae. But I have more news. Kallan is gone. Captured or enslaved, I don't know, but he is beyond my reach."

"Okay, that one is a surprise," Brandy muttered.

———

The front door of the mill swung slowly open, spilling a golden light out onto the moonlit yard between it and the dirt roadway. Eyes reflected the glow, encircling the building. One set of dark, almost black, eyes detached from the others and danced through the light until a powerful figure stalked into view.

This shifter was massive, larger than any of the Wulliver family, who watched from the windows of the mill. Over six feet tall and thickly muscled. The wolf head atop it was a startling silver, with flecks of black throughout. It stopped at the edge of the pool of light. Snarled. And snapped its jaws.

McCloud stepped into the doorway, nearly eclipsing the glow from within the building. He held up a hand surreptitiously, keeping Sean behind and out of sight. His laugh echoed through the yard.

"Max Stubbe, I presume? Probably best you call your lot to heel and shove off before things get messy here."

The wolf huffed once and turned its face toward the night sky and howled, long and firm. The surrounding eyes answered in kind and the collective clamor echoed throughout the mill yard and bouncing through the wooden bridge at the top of the hill.

The wolf spoke. "Nice to see that my reputation precedes me. Our fight isn't with you, Fae." The massive snout thrust itself forward and sniffed the night air. "You shouldn't even be here from what I smell. So step aside. Our beef is with the bums inside, but we don't mind tasting some Faerie flesh tonight if you insist."

"You're missing a golden opportunity here, friend. I convinced the family to let me try to talk you out of getting your tails whipped. I suggest you take that opportunity."

"I'm not your friend," Max answered. "And we aren't afraid of you *or* those mutts inside. If you want to make this your fight, we have no qualms including you in the fun. You're not the first Fae we've had to deal with. And your human friend back there won't come as a surprise to us. We can smell his kind a mile away. Surprised he hasn't hightailed it outta here already."

"Normally, I'm against cruelty to animals," McCloud said. "But in your case, I may just have to make a wee exception."

Without warning, Max took a mighty leap straight at McCloud, but the Scot was more than ready. Before the wolf could sink its teeth into him, a massive fist backhanded the shapeshifter and sent it flying back in the direction it had come from.

The other wolves howled and barked and began a coordinated advance toward the door and McCloud. Two of the wolves peeled off to check on their leader, who shook his head while regaining his feet, and howled long and high.

"Kill," Max called out and the wolves increased their pace, with McCloud sending his own howl to the moon.

The pack crept into the ring of light, circling back and forth across each other, trying to confuse McCloud with fents and nips as they drew closer, but the massive Scotsman remained rooted to his spot, unfazed. A deep brown shifter was the first to make a full leap at McCloud and was rewarded with a meaty fist around its throat. McCloud used the first wolf to bludgeon the next one to give a try before sending the first attacker across the yard where it skidded along the ground and into the darkness.

After the first two aggressors were so easily dispatched, the pack changed tactics, abandoning direct charges for quick lunges from the sides, all the while continuing to circle and mislead. McCloud was unbothered, swinging whenever any shifter left itself too close for too long.

Sean, watching from the doorway, was impressed at the lack of tension in his friend. It was as if fighting a horde of wolf shapeshifters was something he'd done countless times before. No wolf came even close to hurting the massive Timestrider. The longer he watched, though, Sean began to see the wolves' strategy emerge. They quick strikes and bluffs weren't meant to cause any damage, but to wear McCloud down. The shifters were counting on wearing their opponent down. Their stamina and advantage in numbers would eventually take a toll.

Sean noticed two of the wolves slink beyond the light thrown from the doorway, and followed their eye shine as they tried to silently approach McCloud from the rear while two others occupied his attention by striking in quick succession from the front.

Sean knew McCloud likely didn't need any help. It certainly hadn't been in the plan they'd cooked up. But he also saw that there was a possibility that the pack could eventually break through and do some damage. And, frankly, he couldn't allow McCloud to take any more risks. Not when Sean himself was the reason they were here in the first place. When he saw the two shifters slipping behind and drawing closer than any of the others had been able to do, he had seen enough.

Pushing himself off the door frame, he strode purposefully toward the two ambushers. They paused and looked in his direction before dismissing him as no threat. Sniffing the air, they considered the human not worth their effort and turned back to the Scot. That was a mistake.

Sean stopped and planted his feet. He began to sing, quietly at first, then with rising intensity, producing a clear, high tenor note that swelled and soared. He began to glow. Golden and pure. His light grew brighter. And brighter. Even McCloud, who turned at the sound, had to shield his eyes as Sean exploded in a resplendent globe of incandescence. The wolf shifters all froze, stunned. In that moment, Sean gestured with one hand toward McCloud, emitting a beam of focused energy that encircled the Timestrider, cradling him gently and lifting him off the ground, then slowly drawing him to Sean, where he was placed on the ground, safely out of reach of the wolves.

Once McCloud was within Sean's golden orb, Sean turned his full attention to the shifters. He drew an enormous breath, and drew his arms to himself, before throwing them outward, as if clearing a path of low hanging branches. His light burst forth and the glade exploded in golden brilliance. The wolves were lifted in the air and thrown clear to the roadway that led down from the covered bridge.

They had seen enough and ran wildly in all directions.

Only Max Stubbe paused and glared back at Sean, ignoring McCloud completely now. Fury was in his eyes, but also curiosity, and he gave a last snarl before backing out of the receding light that Sean had thrown.

McCloud turned slowly toward Sean. "Well, that was unexpected. Pettirosso told me you were unusual, but he didn't do you justice."

Sean was shaking his head. "It's getting easier. More powerful. I barely had to exert myself for that."

"I mean, I would have been fine on my own," McCloud insisted, before grinning. "But that was impressive. I doubt we'll see that pack again. At least not for a very long time."

"The whole thing makes me uneasy," Sean answered. "I don't want this. I just want to make music. Go back to life before. This is all way over my head."

McCloud placed a massive hand on Sean's shoulder. "Lad, I understand your feeling that way, but this genie is not going back into the bottle. If you ask me, and I know you didn't, the best thing to do now is face forward and make the best of it. If it's getting stronger, that means you're unlocking more potential with each effort."

"It just feels wrong," Sean said. "Music to me was always about nurturing, learning, communicating. Expressing what words alone couldn't. And now I'm using it to harm others. It's not at all what should happen."

McCloud put a corner of his beard into his mouth and sucked on it while allowing himself to consider what Sean had said. "I can't fault a single word of yours. Let's face it, you're a thinker. Me not so much. And I don't pretend to have answers for you, or even to understand how you feel. But I would simply say that there are two sides to every coin. Music does all of the things you mentioned. But the other side of things is that music has always been used to inspire, to inflame emotions, whip up a frenzy. And sometimes, no matter how much we hope to avoid it, there are those who respond only to power and, ultimately, violence. That pack you just saw off wasn't going to listen to logic. To words. The only thing their like understands is strength. It's the only thing that they will respect. The only thing to turn them away. While I know you are not a man of violence, you have the ability to protect those you care about in a world that seems to be hurtling toward confrontation. Like it or not, I'm afraid you'll be smack in the middle of it. And how you respond will go a long way in sending us all in one direction or another."

"Not much of a thinker?" Sean noted. "That's some bollocks, there, to put it in terms you understand. But I know, deep down, that I can't wiggle my way out of this without acting. I just wish it wasn't like that."

McCloud boomed out a trademark laugh and wrapped Sean in a tremendous bear hug. "Ach, I didnae doubt you for a second. I think in the morning, I'll pop back to 2024 to see where things stand. If those diplomatic meetings went well, this may all be a moot point." With that, he began to shake Sean up and down. "You just did that, Sean-o! You ran a pack of wolf shifters off without breaking a sweat. That's the stuff of legend there."

Sean noticed the Wullivers had emerged from the front door and were regarding him with decidedly different attitudes than when he had left them inside. While Finlay and Carolyn seemed intrigued by what they had witnessed, Donal and Craig were most definitely wary, the fur along the napes of their necks standing on end.

Sean understood. It's good to have powerful friends. But it's intimidating to have friends so powerful they could dispatch you with little effort. He would need to assure them they could trust him. No easy task when he didn't entirely trust himself.

CHAPTER 14

Pettirosso led the group up to the fourth floor and his office. Dante carried Nick before placing him gently in the director's sleeping drawer. Nick was weak and drifted in and out of consciousness, but neither Deborah nor Pettirosso sensed any fever or other side effects. Thus far, it seemed the pike that had dealt the blow had not been poisoned.

"I think it best to leave him here for the rest of the night," Pettirosso said. "I'll not be sleeping tonight, and this is as secure a location as any in the building. I would ask those of you who feel able to stay and stand watch over him. And Deborah, who needs to recover."

Every person in the room stepped forward, and Pettirosso nodded with a gratified grin.

"I expected as much," he said. "Bayard, you and Cinder are most welcome. Please, use tonight to rest. I suspect we will be needing you in the days ahead. Tonight, I will put the call out that Lancaster's sensitives —all those in tune with the unseen, the other realms—should gather in the morning. We will meet in the theatre itself. There is no more appropriate place to join together to face what now is coming."

Ken stepped forward. "Can we do anything else? Until then? It just seems we should be preparing somehow. Barricading doors, filling sand-bags. Something."

"Thank you, Ken," the director answered, setting a hand on Ken's shoulder. "We have been preparing for quite some time. I had hoped confrontation could be avoided, but I am not fool enough to rely entirely on hope. Your being here, in fact, is part of the defense. Your castmates. Noodle. Bayard. Even Deborah and Drew, who have been here for long years, were always part of a plan we hoped would never come to pass."

"Right," Brandy said, moving to Ken's side. "So—what? We just sit here all night?"

Dante spoke from the far corner. "I'm afraid it is something like that. I've worked with Pettirosso more times than I've stopped to count. If he says wait and rest, we should do exactly that."

"Thank you, Dante," Pettirosso answered, relief in his eyes. "I need you to rest now while I do not. We will all need to be at our best in the morning. And when Balor arrives, as he most certainly will."

"That's good enough for me," Brandy announced. "Priority one is fixin' Nick up. Priority two is getting our ducks in a row for when we get some unwelcome visitors. Roger that."

"Thank you," Pettirosso said. "It's an enormous relief to know you are here to help. It will take every one of us to see this through."

"Mr. Pettirosso," Deborah, slipped back into her more deferential tone toward the director, as she spoke quietly and stepped to his side. "You're just as tired as I am. As the others. You need to rest, too. We need you. Maybe more than anyone else."

Pettirosso turned to her and surprisingly reached out to clasp her hand. "Faithful Deborah. What would I have done without you? Thank you for your concern. My time for resting is done. This situation is exactly why I was placed here. I will rest again when it is done. One way or another. Now, I must go to the grid to investigate what Drew sensed. That something is off within the theatre. He is too familiar with this place to have been mistaken about something like that."

Deborah clearly wanted to say more, but all that escaped her was a simple, "Yes, sir," as she looked at her hand in his. Quite likely for the first time ever.

Pettirosso took his leave and the room sat in a tense silence. Nick was still drifting in and out of consciousness. Deborah, exhausted, took a place by his side, watching him closely. Brandy stood by the windows, looking out over the street, where every shadow and corner suddenly seemed to hold a menace she was only beginning to understand. Dante had placed himself in a seat by the door, his scythe resting on his knees.

Ken stood alone, observing the others. There was concern in his eyes as he turned from one to the other of his companions. If any of the Grumbles had not been injured or lost in their own thoughts, they would have noticed a difference in his demeanor. A short time ago, he was all but unrecognizable to them as ambition had driven away the caring friend they had grown to love. Now, something else had replaced that ambition. But for all the distractions, they may have noticed their friend reach a decision. Whatever that decision was, it remained locked inside Ken, and only time would reveal it.

———

When Sean returned to the mill, the Wullivers had given him a wide berth. Craig and Donal had moved to another room, while Finlay and Carolyn, seemingly more curious than wary, made sure he had someplace comfortable to bed down among the clothing that had been left by the workers, before giving him space and thanking him again for his help with Max Stubbe.

McCloud tutted as he watched them move away. "Lad, you've turned many of their beliefs upside down with your show out on the lawn. Ignore the other two. Finlay and Carolyn are the ones that matter, and they respect what happened. And they're more than a little intrigued. You being here changes—everything. For them. At least, as long as we're here."

"They seem like good folks," Sean replied. "As long as I can, I'll help out. But I guess we know that the feud continues into my time. My real time. So, I guess I don't solve everything." He yawned then. Long and deep. "I'm sorry. I think I need to get some sleep. That time travel stuff takes it out of you."

"Well, tackling a pack of shifters doesn't help," McCloud said, with a gentle cuff to Sean's head. "Kip in and rest. I won't leave in the morning until you wake. With luck, you'll be a Wulliver family legend and back in your rehearsals by midday tomorrow."

"From your lips—" Sean muttered, before sleep claimed him, and he was gone.

Sean slipped downward. Inexorably drawn deeper and deeper into his subconscious. Even as he slept, there was a corner of his mind that remained aware. Aware that he was now enjoying a restorative, peaceful sleep as he hadn't in days. He drifted into a place of silver, green, gold, and blue lights. Clean and safe. Gone were the blacks, oranges, and reds that he'd found himself enmeshed in since his arrival in Lancaster. There was no sense of peril. No sense of being stalked or watched from creatures just beyond his perception. No terrible decisions where he was forced to choose which of his friends to save while watching all the others perish.

Then, in the midst of this blissful calm, she was there. He couldn't see her, but he could feel her. Breena. Bright and clean and beautiful. Reaching out. To him. To him only. Her crystalline voice echoing through his sleeping self. The words playing like music in him, though she merely spoke. Spoken words he had so badly wanted to hear. Needed to hear.

"Sean. Love. I have tried so hard to reach you. To tell you. Tell you all that is happening. There are so many obstacles between us now. I am being held. Far away. Deep in the realm of my people. Beyond your knowing. They have guarded me. Imprisoned me. And you have been surrounded. Even in sleep, they prevented me from reaching you. Creatures of the dark realms, infecting your dreams. I don't know how I am able to reach you now, but I am so relieved to feel your presence. You seem to be—somewhere beyond their reach. I don't understand it, but I take great joy in it. My time is short. They will find me out soon, but you must know—trust no one. Perhaps the Grumbles. Perhaps. No one is what they seem. War is marching closer. Even I can't say who will fall to our side and who will choose the other."

Sean struggled from deep within his sleep to speak to Breena, but he was too immersed in slumber. The corner of his mind that was alert could not take control. His struggle became more frantic. There was so much to say.

"Do not panic, Sean," Breena continued. "I don't know if I can break free. Others will come to aid me. I think. I must go. They will know. But remember—trust no one but your Grumbles."

She faded away. In his sleep/wake state, Sean knew instantly that she was beyond his reach again. He reached for consciousness. He reached for where he wanted her to be. He reached. But achieved nothing. The blissful, serene rest swept over him again and he knew nothing else until the dawn arrived. When he opened his eyes, McCloud was there. Patiently waiting for him to rouse.

Sean leaned up on his elbows, wiping the sleep from his eyes and taking a moment to focus on the morning. The Scotsman took a long look at him and began to nod his shaggy head.

"You've had a visitation, I see. Not uncommon after a time jump. Especially for a first-time strider. You shed the worries and preoccupations of your time. Leave them behind. That first sleep is often one of the deepest in a very long time. Am I right?"

Sean swung his legs over the side of the makeshift bed and stretched his arms, feeling a satisfying pop as his joints joined him in the new day.

"Yeah, that pretty much sums it up."

McCloud took an even closer look. "Was it Breena? I would be shocked if it was anyone or anything else."

"It was," Sean affirmed, nodding slowly. "She said she was being held somewhere. Somewhere I couldn't reach. And she told me—" He caught himself before finishing, thinking on what she had said. He considered the Timestrider before reaching a decision. "She told me to trust no one but my friends, the Grumbles. But if I can't trust you, well I think the damage is already done. You haven't stabbed me in the back yet and I can't get back to my today without you, so—all in with you, I guess."

"I'm flattered," McCloud replied, laughing. "Wise words, for the most part. Trust those you know the best. Too many shifters and dream hijackers around for my taste. I would say that you can trust Pettirosso, too. He's an ancient and has held true longer than most of us can remember. And also consider that, even here, it's not impossible that one of the Wayob could reach you. Unlikely, but not impossible. So, trust with caution. It likely was Breena, but just in case—"

"I hear you," Sean said. "My guard is basically perpetually up at this point. What's the plan now? Any chance we get back to the right time today?"

"A chance?" McCloud asked. "Yes, of course. I just need to nip back there to check on the state of things. Once I get the all clear, back across the bridge we go. Neat as you please."

"Well, let's get that going then, yeah?"

"And don't look just to the bridge for me. I could return from anywhere. It does help me on my way, and why spend excess energy if it's nae needed. And we're here, so why not? I'm set to go. Just remember there are many places where the veil between realms, and that includes times, is thinner. I told you about the bridges, especially the covered variety, aye? But also, the forest stairs to nowhere. And caves. Caves are a big one, too. Remember, the Tuatha went below the surface when they retreated from mankind. I've no idea if your music will help you cross the time veil, but we don't need to find that out just now. I'll be back before you know it, so just giving you the information. Be mindful."

Sean walked with McCloud up the hill to Zook's Mill Covered Bridge, only stopping when they reached the entrance.

"Good luck," Sean said. "Let's hope Pettirosso set everything right and we can just—go home."

"My money's on exactly that," McCloud answered. "Not that I'm a betting man. See you soon, my friend. Stick close to Finlay and Carolyn. They're good people."

"I think you're right," Sean replied. "And I will."

Sean stood back and watched as McCloud crossed onto the bridge. He shimmered for a moment; a swirling green light seemed to open on the bridge. The Scot passed into it, not breaking stride, then slipped from view and was gone.

Sean could see through the far side of the bridge again. He turned and faced the mill again and realized that he felt truly alone in a way he'd never experienced before. Hands thrust into his pockets, he cast a glance back over his shoulder onto the bridge before starting back down the path.

———

At a quarter to ten in the morning, the Grumbles, along with Dante and the newly arrived Bobby Smalls, sat in the front rows of the theatre. Any minute now, they expected to be joined by whomever had sensed Pettirosso's silent call of the previous night. There was tense expectation in the air. They hoped to see many of their colleagues respond. What they didn't know was if anyone else in the community would appear. Lancaster was a city of history and intrigue. It would be foolish to think that the theatre was the only enclave of, as Pettirosso had called them, sensitives.

They sat in the plush, upholstered seats in the theatre. They were deep red, reflecting the color of some of the intricate gilt work that adorned the box seats that flanked the stage. The scrollwork then stretched across the facing of the mezzanine and reached the ceiling itself, high above. The theatre harkened back to another era when architecture was more inspired and decorative. An art unto itself. Modern theatres now were more utilitarian and spartan in their approach. The opulent and dignified Fulton was a throwback to a time when the arts were an event and the artists were respected, at times revered, in their communities and farther abroad. It somehow seemed appropriate that this meeting, where the creative types of Lancaster, would meet to rediscover some of that lost respect and the power that had always lain inside them.

As the minutes passed and the clock inched closer to ten, the Grumbles became more fidgety. Squirmy in the seats that had suddenly begun to feel less comfortable.

"Where is everyone?" Brandy whispered loudly, despite them being the only ones in the auditorium. "Shouldn't *someone* have shown up by now?"

"Dunno," Trout answered. "Maybe the doors aren't open yet?"

"Or maybe, it's just us," Nick, his injured arm bandaged, and in a sling, said. "Maybe there are a few special folks around, but they just don't want to get involved. Can't blame them."

"They'll be here," Ken assured them. "I have faith. Not sure why. I just do."

They sat in silence for another few minutes before Dante broke the silence. "I hope you're right. If this Balor guy can take on Pettirosso, I wouldn't mind some help."

Bobby Smalls turned in his seat to take in the others. "If you all weren't so somber, I'd think you'd made the whole thing up." He turned to Dante. "And I'm still mad you didn't wake me up to help last night. Not cool."

"No time," Dante replied. "And trust me—we're deadly serious."

Smalls fixed him with a dubious glare. "Well, we shall see. But if Pettirosso walks onto that stage, then I'll start to believe."

All of their heads swiveled toward house right when they heard one of the doors to the lobby begin to open. Ken even began to rise from his seat, so sure that they were about to be greeted by a host of folks ready to join the struggle.

Instead, only one figure appeared in the doorway, their face obscured by the backlight streaming in from the lobby beyond. They all instantly recognized the arrival, and Ken sat quickly back in the seat.

"Noodle!" Trout called out. "Nice of you to join us. We hoped you'd show up."

The artist shuffled slowly into the theatre. "Well, I gotta admit I'm a bit confused. Just heard from Pettirosso to show up this morning. I mean, I know there's a lot going on, but this made it sound more imminent."

"Yeah, you could say that," Brandy replied. "Take a seat, pal. There have been some developments overnight, but we'll let the boss man fill you in."

"Developments?" Noodle said. "Is there news on Sean? Is he back? That time travel thing has me freaked. The sooner he's back the better, I say."

"Sadly, no," Nick answered, sitting forward in his seat to see Noodle, cradling his arm gingerly. "Maybe Pettirosso can shed some light on that, too. Uh, did you happen to see anyone else out in the lobby? We were hoping for a bigger turnout. No offense."

"Hey," Noodle said. "What happened to your arm? And none taken. I still have no idea what I'm doing here."

Nick shared a quick look with the others, before replying. "Yeah, this happened last night. You'll hear."

"Okay," Noodle said. "You all are being very mysterious. Even for you. But I'll just sit tight, I guess."

"Like the rest of us," Trout said, and they all settled back into their seats.

Before long, Cory, Lina, and Adriane walked onto the stage, having taken the elevator from the artist village down. They jumped down into the house from the lip of the stage and took seats behind the others.

Cory leaned forward between the seats. "So—any clue why we're here? Ten o'clock is pretty early considering I was at Rural City until last call. Lance was generous if you know what I mean."

Ken laughed. "He does that. We were there earlier but headed out before things got to that point."

Dante turned toward Cory. "And, yes, we do know what it's about, but I think we should leave it to Herr Direktor. He probably has a lot to say that we know nothing about."

"Fair enough," Adriane said from the row behind. "That old stoat keeps more secrets than anyone I know. And I say that with love."

Once again, everyone settled into their seats. Phones were pulled out of pockets, email checked, headlines perused. At five past ten, the back doors to the theatre were opened and a steady stream of people began to head down the aisles.

Brandy saw many of the theatre's employees among the crowd. She spotted Rebecca Chapel and Dani Landau, the two stage managers, instinctually taking charge, guiding the newcomers to the closest available seats. She also spied Kerstin and Kirsten, two of the wardrobe staff. Word was that they were expert stitchers and, more than that, designers. Behind them, came a parade of current and former employees. Stephanie Joseph, who was a performer, but had also joined the staff. Ben Naboe and Sam Grosse, two of the conductors who led the orchestras. Local performers were also represented. Brandy spied William Green, Cherisse Lyon, Randolph Peter, Kevin Farinacci, Mickey Pallucci, Randy Prizzado. The stage crew was represented, as well. She saw Liza, the wardrobe supervisor taking a seat. Behind her, he saw Dominico, one of the former stage managers, and some of the stagehands—Sophia, Isabella, Samuel, Kai... Bringing up the rear came Haydn and Page, the eminent writing team, confidently taking seats.

The greater surprise to Brandy was the number of locals who appeared that seemingly had no connection to the theatre. She saw Sean's friend, Kat, in the rear of the auditorium, hanging back and looking confused. A tall, lanky young man with long chestnut hair and a decidedly lupine air to him led a group of what seemed to be family members down the aisle. More than one generation were present in that family, and bringing up the rear was an elegant couple with brown hair streaked with white. They prowled down through the house, alert, tense. When Kat saw the family, she rushed down the aisle to join them, and Brandy thought she heard her call out "Duncan!"

They even spotted Jen, the woman from Ric's Bread at the market, who sold them the coveted pepperoni bread.

At the last minute, Bobby Smalls spotted a disheveled older man with an unruly shock of white hair entering quietly and alone. Bobby couldn't contain an "I'll be damned."

"What?" Dante asked.

"Probably nothing," Bobby replied. "Only...Brett Billson just crept in. Haven't seen him in years. Used to dabble here, but I always thought of him as more of a mad scientist type. Hey, whatever. I'll take anyone willing to help."

When everyone was finished arriving and was seated, there were a good fifty people seated throughout the first few rows of the audience. Rebecca and Dani closed the doors to the lobby and took seats in the back, ready to guide any latecomers.

An expectant silence settled over the assembly. The first row of occupants, The Grumbles with Bobby and Dante, were the only ones with a real idea of what to expect.

The sound of steps reached the audience as Pettirosso and Deborah made an entrance from stage left. Brandy saw Drew Brindig silently take the stage behind them, keeping an eye on the wings, especially stage right, where the staircase down to the portal stood. He was poised to leave at the slightest hint of trouble below.

Pettirosso cleared his throat and took a deep breath. "I can't begin to thank you all enough for being here. The fact that you are, means you are sensitive to certain things that make you...extraordinary. And it also means that you can help the Fulton, in fact our entire city, in what is sure to be a challenging day, and night, ahead."

He then began to tell them exactly why they were here. He left nothing out and was particularly precise in explaining how they could all contribute. To convince them that their presence here meant they held within them talents they had never suspected. He explained the nature of the danger they faced, and that every person there had a role to play. He told them of realms beyond their imagination, and the beings who lived there and had existed beyond their senses for so many centuries.

When he was finished and those in the audience reacted in their myriad ways—some with silent disbelief, some nodding as if a long-held secret had been revealed as true, some with anger and denial—Bayard and the wolf, Cinder, blinked onto the stage, seemingly from nowhere. At that point, Pettirosso allowed himself to rise off the floor and emit a gentle golden light that stretched across everyone assembled. That was the moment the truth descended over the crowd like a shroud. That was the moment the defenders of the theatre began to believe.

Sixty years in the past, Sean stood silently contemplating Zook's Mill Covered Bridge. He knew it could be a while before McCloud returned, but he had hoped to be able to get back almost instantly. After ten minutes perched at the end of the bridge, watching the Cocalico Creek burble past underneath, he stood up and, heaving a sigh, slowly made his way back to the mill.

The Wullivers were preparing to head back into Lancaster to sell some of their wares at the Central Market. The Market was the oldest running farmers market in the country, having opened in 1730, and had grown over the centuries to become a hub of industry and commerce in the city, but also a major tourist attraction. Sean felt a pang when he thought of his Grumble friends shopping there. A few short miles away as the crow flew, but decades away from where he stood now.

Sean let himself into the mill, trying to stay out of the way of the family. Carolyn came to sit by Sean in the changing room they had adopted the night before. She pointed to a far corner where she had arranged some of the excess work clothes into a bed, of sorts. Sean couldn't help thinking it resembled a modern dog bed, which seemed appropriate and amused him simultaneously.

"I'm sorry we have to leave you here," she said. "Fridays are an important market day for us. The mill here is winding down. I doubt it has more than a few years left in it. The old ways of doing things are on the way out. Not sure what we'll do when that happens. This is all we know."

Sean thought back to what Duncan had told him about his family. Only a few nights in his past but now six decades in the future. He knew the Wullivers, at least some of them, remained to run a successful woolen business. He subconsciously touched the scarf that was still around his neck.

"I have a feeling you all will find a way," he said quietly. "I've always hated change, but the older I get the more I realize it's inevitable. But, hey—you all are clearly survivors. You'll be fine."

"Ah, Sean," she replied. "Such a gentle soul. You're kind. And that scarf you're wearing means you have some idea of what happens to at least a few of us." When Sean began to speak, she held up hand to stop him. "It's cool. I don't actually want to know. We're sort of a 'go with the flow' kind of family. I'd rather life happen to me than I sit around knowing what's in store. If that makes sense?"

"Yeah, it does," Sean said. "Not sure I would have the strength to turn down a glimpse of my future, but I bet your approach is healthier. If it's any comfort, I don't really know much."

"And that's all I need to know," Carolyn answered. "Sean, I don't know how these things happen, but I don't think it's an accident we met each other. Finlay and I will be back tonight. I can't speak for the others. But we're committed to seeing you safely back home. You saw us through last night with the Stubbes. They won't be back anytime soon. Not after what you did to them. That means we're bonded."

"No, need. Really," Sean said. "I was happy to help. And honestly surprised at how it worked out. But no need to look after me. I'll be fine."

"I don't doubt that for a second," she chuckled in response. "But I think our paths lie together. At least for now. So we'll be back. No arguments."

"You're the boss," Sean said. "I'll be here, until I can go home. That was McCloud's plan, and I intend to stick to it. If I'm not here when you get back, look for me in the year 2024 and we can continue this talk."

"Oh, Sean," she placed a hand on his face. "Nothing would make me happier. Both today and in the future. Say, I pulled an old transistor radio down from upstairs and plugged it in over by the bed. Might be nice to have some company today. Even if it is over the airwaves."

"Thanks, Carolyn. You're the best. A living time capsule. I love it. And I really appreciate it."

"C'mon, man," Donal called from the entryway. "We have to jet if we're going to unload this product before market closes."

"On my way," she called. "Ignore him. He's an ass. But he's harmless and a softy when you get past that crusty outer shell."

"I'll take your word for that," Sean said with a skeptical cock of his head. "Hope market goes well." He poked his head into the entrance room where the rest of the family waited. "Thanks again, everyone. Good luck today."

Finlay shook his hand. "No sweat, Sean. We're all cool. Just take a load off and Car and I will see you later."

"Enough of this shmoopy junk," Donal chirped. "Let's move. This loser is on his own now."

Carolyn shot him an apologetic look as she followed the Wulliver clan out the door.

Sean stood by the door, watching as they climbed the short hill and took the bridge back toward Lancaster. He stayed in the entrance, soaking in the cool autumn air. Quiet. So quiet. He enjoyed it momentarily, before the silence began to close in again. He wandered into the changing room and settled himself into the makeshift bed, leaning against the wall.

He sat quietly, but inevitably his thoughts turned to Breena. If he tried to sleep, would she return to him? Had that even been her? Here he was, in a strange time and place, unsure of pretty much everything, and still, he couldn't keep from thinking of her.

He turned to the radio Carolyn had left him and switched it on. He moved the dial up and down, searching for a station that caught his attention and thinking of childhood rides in the car when he and his brother and sister would vie for the right to control the radio.

He settled on a station that was playing the latest top songs for the month of November 1964. The first song played was "Time Is on My Side" by the Rolling Stones. Sean remembered the song from years ago and shook his head at its title given his current predicament.

He rose to his feet. Restless. Unable to settle in one spot. He looked hopefully out the window, scanning the bridge and the approaching road, but McCloud was still nowhere to be seen. Not to worry. It had been less than an hour.

In the distance, he saw the Wullivers, loping along the path toward town. As he watched them, the song on the radio changed to the number one song for the week. "Leader of the Pack," by the Shangri-Las. Sean shook his head in disbelief. He wouldn't have believed it if he hadn't heard it himself. He didn't believe in coincidences. So what exactly could this mean, other than he had somehow arrived at the right place and time.

CHAPTER 15

McCloud had returned to the present time without any problems. He'd walked across the covered bridge feeling the familiar shiver as he crossed through the time veil and stepped back into 2024. He paused, taking in his surroundings. Not surprisingly, there was no traffic nearby, as the bridge had fallen off the main road as time and commerce passed it by for larger roads. Easier thoroughfares. He began his walk back to town, keeping an eye out for a friendly driver who might take pity on him and give him a lift to Lancaster. He thought it unlikely, given his size and rather gruff appearance, but to his pleasant surprise, a farmer in a beat-up pickup truck slowed down as he passed, and offered a ride. McCloud gratefully accepted and found himself walking up to the Fulton a mere twenty minutes later.

Prince Street was unusually quiet as he entered the theatre. Fridays were quieter than Saturdays at the Market across the street, so foot traffic was quieter, and Lancastrians had begun the migration indoors with the arrival of autumn.

McCloud spotted Pettirosso's Land Rover parked in the loading dock down the side alley. Good. It was just after ten in the morning, the director should be in his office alone. The actors arrived later, along with most of the employees, so he could grab a few moments alone with Pettirosso without interruption.

Entering through the stage door, the Scotsman made his way to the elevator that would take him to the fourth floor and walked the hallway toward the office. The door was closed, and he stopped to knock quietly on the massive door, which had been salvaged from an Italian palazzo. Presumably, it was a sentimental reminder of Pettirosso's homeland. In fact, though, McCloud could sense that it had been fortified many times over with runes, hexes, and magic almost as old as he could recall.

"Come in, friend," he heard Pettirosso quietly call to him through the doorway.

Pushing the entrance open, he approached the massive desk across the floor. Pettirosso was in his familiar position, peering out over Prince Street and the infrequent pedestrians. The windows, as they so often were, had been shaded, allowing the director to look out while concealing him from curious passersby. The light from the desk threw up a glare and in the reflection, McCloud could see a pensive look upon Pettirosso's face.

"You seem troubled, pal," McCloud said. "Should I take it that the news you brought back from the peace meeting wasnae what we had hoped for?"

"Oh, what I have to tell you will most definitely not be to your liking, Timestrider," Pettirosso answered.

Something in the set of the director's shoulders and the tone in his voice struck McCloud as off. Something was wrong. He began to back away and noticed a flash of motion reflected in the window. Someone was behind him. Two someones. From the corner of his eye, he caught a third, but the first two were on him before he could react. Impossibly, he saw the shapes of a large cat and a smaller canine leap toward him and, as he realized he was seeing the Wayob dream stalkers, he felt their hands on the sides of his head and an inescapable weariness descended upon him.

The figure at the window turned to him and shifted, and he saw clearly now how easily he had been fooled, Before him stood a Naga, half human atop the coils of a massive snake. Traditionally, they would never be seen in this part of the world, let alone in league with the evil Wayob.

"You shouldnae be here," McCloud spoke haltingly. "You should not be my foe." His mind succumbed to the power of the Wayob, and while he was far too ancient and powerful for them to vanquish, they were able to send him far away, to the corner of the underworld where sleep ruled. The last thought he had before he slipped into a slumber beyond the reach was of Sean, trapped sixty years in the past, alone.

The Naga turned a stony gaze on the Wayob. "I have done as I was told," a sibilant voice echoed through the office. "I will leave now. No more will I aid you."

As the snake shifter began to shimmer and fade, the two Wayob had their attention stolen by a movement behind them near the massive wooden door. Drew Brindig stood there, his mouth agape. The three looked at each other before all of them raced into action.

The Wayob leaped toward the handyman, but he proved to be surprisingly elusive and was off like a shot down the hallway before they could grab him and send him to the land of sleep and nightmares, as well. Before they even could fling the door open and emerge into the hallway, he had fled to the stairwell and the stage below, where the meeting of sensitives and creatives had been under way for some time.

With an unspoken understanding, the Wayob stopped their pursuit. There was nothing the meek human could do now. They had banished the Timestrider and trapped Sean, the only human of consequence in the approaching war. With nods to each other, they shimmered and were gone. Seeking new victims to torture in their sleep and more tasks to carry out for their master.

On the floor of the office, McCloud lay still. His eyes were closed and occasionally twitched, as if some unknown dreams were sending jolts of fear through him. After a few minutes, he lay still. Beyond reach. The Timestrider had been banished.

"Thank you," Pettirosso said to those seated in the audience. "I understand that this is a shock. I understand, also, that many of you will either deny the truth of this or feel the danger is too great. I recognize that many of you have families, lives, priorities. And risking so much would mean placing those you love in danger. There is no shame in leaving. Now. But remember us. Hold the Fulton, and your fellow creatives in your thoughts. Or prayers, if you are so inclined. We must succeed in this fight, or you will find these enemies at your doors. The best chance is for us to win. Here. Now."

At this, a few scattered individuals rose and strode out of the theatre. Some slowly, weighed down by shame. Or responsibility. Others walked out with purpose, seemingly confident that what Pettirosso described had nothing to do with them.

As the doors closed behind them, Pettirosso looked over those who remained. "I have to admit, I thought we'd lose more than that. Thank you. To all of you still here, thank you. We have a long day ahead. I will leave you in the capable hands of Rebecca and Dani. They will instruct you on how your time will be best spent today. All of your unique talents will be needed if we are to have any hope."

As the director and Deborah turned to exit stage left toward the backstage offices, Drew Brindig came sliding onto the stage and rushed to Pettirosso's side.

"Sir, we have a problem," Drew whispered. "There's been an—incident—in your office. You'll need to see this. Sir. Boss."

Pettirosso shot a glance to Deborah, who in turn looked out to the Grumbles, who had been watching the interchange with interest. As Pettirosso and Deborah exited the stage and hurried toward the elevator that would bring them to the office, the Grumbles dashed to the stage, up the escape stairs, and followed in their wake.

Drew was already back in the office, and surprisingly un-winded, when they arrived minutes later. Dante and Bobby Smalls had tagged along, sensing something was amiss. Bobby, in particular, was determined not to miss out on anything else.

Drew stood beside the prostrate form of the enormous Timestrider. McCloud remained as he had fallen—silent, unconscious, unreachable.

Deborah knelt beside him and began to speak quietly words that none of the others had heard before. She laid her hands on McCloud's face, closed her eyes. There was no change.

Drew was pacing the room, clearly agitated. "I'm so sorry, boss. So sorry. I got here too late. Not sure what I could have done, anyway. Maybe warn you sooner?"

"Easy, Drew," Pettirosso soothed, as he examined the room. He knelt behind his desk, touching the floor, then stood at the window. "Naga. Without a doubt. Our worlds are on a collision course. All of the worlds. Once again, a creature who should not be here, yet was."

"Wait," Brandy said stepping forward to confront Pettirosso. "Our pal here is in a coma, yeah?" At a solemn nod from the director, she continued. "And that means—Sean is trapped in the past somewhere? We don't even know when, do we? Because we just *had* to keep things secret. If I've got this straight, we have no idea when he is. And even if we did, we have no way of getting to him. Yeah?"

"Well, sheeeyit," Trout uttered, stepping next to Brandy. "This was *your* plan, Pettirosso. So, what is the solution? Because Sean's the strongest of us, and with trouble on the way, we sure could use him. Plus, there is the fact that *our friend is trapped and alone and we can't do a damn thing to help him!*"

Pettirosso stood behind his desk. He was about to speak when an unexpected voice interrupted.

"Um. I may have an idea," Bobby Smalls said, tentatively. He glanced to Dante who shrugged a "what have we got to lose" look back at him. "It's a long shot. Like a really long shot. Like a Hail Mary. Like a Doug Flutie Hail Mary."

"We get the picture," Ken replied. "Just lay it out for us and let's see if we can make it work, okay?"

"Yeah, yeah," he answered. "Sorry, I get nervous when I'm the center of attention."

"You're an actor, for the love of..." Brandy said.

"I know. Weird, right?" Bobby answered. "Anyway, this is going to seem way crazy, but it's like this."

***

Sean had a sinking feeling. It had been four hours now since McCloud had left for the present. Four hours. The Timestrider had said that it should only seem like a few minutes to Sean, if things went well. If. And here it was hours later with no sign of the Scot's return.

Left to himself in the mill, Sean's mind raced to all of the worst conclusions. Had the peace meeting gone wrong? Had McCloud somehow been lost in time? Sean had no idea how this time travel worked. What if he'd lost his way? Had something happened to his friends? To Pettirosso?

Cycling through all of the worst-case scenarios, he still kept coming back to something unexpected happening to McCloud. Even with those other possibilities, he should have been able to make his way back to Sean. If things had really gone sideways, wouldn't they want Sean back with them? *Need* him back to help. This line of thinking led him to another worst-case thought. What if the price of the peace overture had been leaving Sean in the past? What if the solution was that the only way forward was without Sean being in their world, in their time?

No. Sean had to reject that out of hand. They wouldn't do that to him. The Grumbles would never stand for it. Neither would Dante, Bobby Smalls, or the others. He was one of them They were some of his dearest friends.

But what if his freedom was the price to save the world? And what would they be able to do against the likes of Pettirosso if the decision was made? They were discovering their own powers, yes, but nothing compared to what he suspected Pettirosso was capable of doing. What if

Pettirosso was willing to sacrifice *all* of them if it meant peace for every other person in the world?

He stopped his thoughts. He had to. There was no good that would come from this. There was no way he could know what was actually happening in his time. He considered trying to sleep in the hopes that Breena would appear to him again, but he knew his mind would race away again and he would not rest. And what if it wasn't actually Breena who had visited him? There were too many questions. Too few answers.

He reached for the transistor radio and turned it on. Maybe music, always such a haven for him, would distract him from his worries. The Righteous Brothers' "You've Lost That Lovin' Feelin'" was playing and Sean immediately changed the station. There were too many questions in his head about Breena. He needed something else.

Dusty Springfield caught his attention on another station. She was singing "Wishin' and Hopin'." That seemed appropriate. And the catchy melody brought the slightest of smiles to his face. He let it play and wandered over to the window.

The day was bright and crisp. A perfect autumn day. He let the song play out and then left the mill, walking toward the bridge. He knew the old adage about a watched pot, but he had nothing else to do. The Wullivers wouldn't be back for hours still. He hadn't intended to go past the bridge, but after a few minutes of pacing, he crossed the bridge and ambled up the far side of the hill. He wouldn't go far, but he needed to find some peace of mind. Somehow.

Once Dante and Trout had lifted McCloud and placed him in Pettirosso's sleeping drawer, the group settled about the room. There was no change in the Scot. The room was tense, and tempers were running close to the surface.

Eventually, everyone in the office looked expectantly at Bobby, which made him very uncomfortable indeed.

"Look," Bobby said. "I'm sorry I said anything. It probably won't work. We should just do whatever Mr. Pettirosso says."

"Hold on, hold on," Dante cut Bobby short. "You haven't even told us your idea. Unless I'm mistaken"—he shot a look to Pettirosso—"we need any idea we can come up with."

Pettirosso nodded in agreement. "As you all know, McCloud is one of a kind. Timestriding is an incredibly rare talent. It could be centuries until we see another. And that is the only solution I can think of, other than finding a way to wake him up."

"He's beyond my abilities," Deborah said. "That's not saying it's impossible. My talents are homegrown family legacies. There is certainly much stronger healing to be found. Just not from me."

"Bobby." Dante turned again to his friend. "We got nuthin'. Even if your idea doesn't work, it's *something*. Let's hear it and make a choice."

"Okay. Sure. Yeah," Bobby stuttered. He took a deep breath. "So downstairs, in the crowd? I saw Brett Billson. It's been years since he's been around. I never thought of him as sensitive in any way, but what do I know? He showed up, so he must have felt the call."

"Get to the point," Brandy barked. "We don't exactly have much time here."

"Right, sorry," Bobby replied. "Back in the day, he was rumored to be involved in a lot of crazy scientific experiments. That's what I meant when I said he was more of a mad scientist. One of those rumors, and bear with me here, was something to do with time travel."

Brandy and Trout audibly groaned at that information. Ken quietly shook his head. Pettirosso and Deborah received the information with no reaction. Nick, of all those present, seemed to be the most intrigued.

"I know," Bobby pushed on. "The stuff of science fiction. I know. But there was a story, from back in the sixties. A group of scientists had devoted themselves to a kind of time travel. I mean, people have been chasing that as long as mankind has been around, it seems."

"Yeah," Brandy replied brusquely. "And never accomplished a damn thing. We don't need crazy people. We need a way to save our friend."

"Listen," Bobby continued. "The scientists involved included a former Nobel Prize winner in physics, a Benedictine monk from the Vatican, and a former Nazi mastermind. These were not lightweights. The rumors were old man Billson was an assistant to one of them back then. Can't hurt to ask, right? I mean, he's right here in the building."

Silence fell over the group. Skepticism was written all over Brandy's face. Trout seemed more dubious, and the others simply seemed defeated.

"Thank you, Bobby, for the suggestion," Pettirosso said. "I find it highly unlikely that the solution to this problem will come from mankind. You've been chasing time travel, as you said, forever. And this seems a uniquely Fae situation. Of our making, and therefore our responsibility to solve. That said, I see no harm in speaking to Mr. Billson. As long as it doesn't distract too much from what we need to achieve today in preparation for tonight, I think it's worth a conversation."

Nick, who had his nose buried in his phone's screen, sat up straighter in his seat. "Actually, it may be more than just a wild idea. I've been reading about it. They supposedly came up with something called a chronovisor. A helmet thing that let them look at moments in the past. Not so much travel there but take a snapshot. I don't normally like having anything to do with the work of a former Nazi, which one of these scientists definitely was, but maybe this is a chance to reclaim it for something good. Rumors everywhere that the CIA and Vatican are in cahoots, keeping these visors secret and away from the public. Yikes."

"But a snapshot doesn't really do us any good," Ken broke in. "We need to get there ourselves to bring him back. And we don't even know *when* he went." He gestured to the slumbering McCloud in the bed. "And he sure isn't going to be helping us out on that score."

"Yeah, about that," Nick said. "We know they used the Zook's Mill Covered Bridge to help cross the years. I ran a search on that area, and it seems that sixty years ago last night, there was an unexplained light phenomenon reported in that vicinity. Apparently, the locals reported a golden ball of light, bright as day, sometime around midnight. No explanation, but the local papers thought enough to report it. They chalked it up to a meteorite, but even they didn't think that could be right."

"Sounds an awful lot like one of Sean's song lights to me," Ken pointed out.

"And that tells me two things," Brandy said. "First, we just might have found when he went. It fits. And second, whatever he found when he got there, it was bad enough that he had to use his voice. Between that, and sleeping beauty over there, it sure sounds like the sooner we find him the better."

"True. Although 'sooner' is relative, given that it was sixty years ago. It's the best we have," Pettirosso agreed. "Bobby, will you talk to Mr. Billson for us? At least you are familiar with him."

"Yessir," Bobby said. "Happy to."

"Hot damn," Trout crowed. "Let's go get fitted for some time hats!"

"Let's hope it's as easy as that," Dante replied. "But it's never that easy."

***

Afternoon was creeping toward dusk, and Sean found himself still wandering aimlessly in the area of the bridge. There was no doubt in his mind now that something seriously wrong had happened to McCloud. There was no way he would have left Sean alone for this long. His stated plan was to be back within minutes. Those minutes had now stretched to over seven hours.

Sean knew the Wullivers would be back at the mill soon. At least some of them. Irrationally, he now felt that his continued presence would be both an imposition and a sign of some sort of failure on his part. Abandoned here in a time not his own. He knew he was not thinking straight, but the emotional part of him would not be denied.

He slowly made his way back to the mill. The sun had begun its descent, and the shadows began to stretch along the ground. Sean was reminded of the feeling he'd been constantly watched in Lancaster. He knew now that he had been right. But even those feelings were preferable to the complete isolation he felt now. There was no one alive, not a soul, who could comprehend what he was experiencing. And a precious few he could even discuss it with in any detail.

Over the bridge, the still-silent bridge, he went and down the hill to the mill. The mill which sat dark and silent below. He let himself in and turned on the transistor radio. He turned to a news station, hoping the sound of another voice would be some comfort. It wasn't.

He listened to news stories on the recent election win by Lyndon Johnson. He heard of nuclear tests in France, and a proposed "no first use" nuclear agreement with China. There was unrest in Congo and an attempted rescue of hostages that had drawn anger in various countries, including Egypt, where an American library had been burned. Twenty-four thousand books had been lost.

It was all too much. It sounded too familiar. Echoes of things that were happening in his own time. Unrest. Violence. Distrust. He turned the station after just a few minutes. He found no comfort in the words the voices were speaking. In fact, he felt his malaise deepening and he searched for some solace in music, something it had given him many times.

"Mr. Lonely" by Bobby Vinton was the first song he found, and he quickly turned the dial. He settled on "I'm into Something Good" by Herman's Hermits. Better. He sat on a bench by the window, and watched the sun slide beneath the tree line. He let the music work its magic, as it so often did, and when he saw Finlay and Carolyn approaching from the bridge, his mood was greatly improved.

He rose to meet them, realizing that he had let darkness fall without turning on a light. The mill would look empty to them, and they would assume he had left with McCloud. He flipped the light switch and saw them pause on their way as they realized someone was there.

He opened the door and stood in the doorway, slowly raising a hand to greet them. They picked up their pace. Finlay stopped a few paces away, a look of concern on his face. Sean was surprised, and more than a little disappointed, to see that Donal was following behind them, and began shaking his head when he spotted Sean. Carolyn, though, increased her steps and, with a look of compassion on her face, walked straight to Sean and wrapped him in a knowing embrace. Maybe he wasn't so alone, after all.

<hr>

Bobby Smalls led the group of actors back down to the theatre. In the time they'd been gone, everyone had swung into action. Rebecca and Dani were directing people to various departments. The stage was swirling with activity. Carpenters had begun building platforms and barricades to fortify the doors. The costume staff were hard at work, stitching subtle designs similar to Deborah's Pennsylvania Dutch Hex drawings. Both Kerstin and Kirstin had grown up in the area and were well versed in the local traditions. The lighting staff had climbed into the grid, high above the stage, and were moving lighting instruments about the space.

Most noticeable, and dominating the scene, was the rehearsal that was taking place center stage. The cast of *A Christmas Carol* was there and had been joined by the local performers who had answered Pettirosso's call. Haydn and Page were at the center of it all. Page's fingers flying across the keys while Haydn perched next to him, making corrections and additions to the sheet music on the piano. They were creating something new. Something for the situation. All thoughts of the show had taken a back seat to the cry for help. As they taught the new music to the assembled singers, a clear brilliant golden light glowed and ebbed around them.

As they entered the auditorium, Brandy couldn't help but note that it felt very much like the last frantic hours before a big opening night. The energy in the space fairly crackled. She shot a look to Dani, questioning why the music was being learned onstage instead of in the Castagna rehearsal room. Dani caught the look and hurried over.

"Yo," Dani said to the group, before turning to Brandy. "The consensus was that the rehearsal space felt too exposed. Even with the shades down, those floor to ceiling windows don't let you hide much.

Given what we were told about the critters running around the city right now, everyone was more comfortable in here."

"I get that," Brandy replied.

"Also, the stage is directly over the doorway downstairs," Dani continued. "I'm not real into that stuff, but folks felt like they were closer to the heart of the theatre here. More in tune with energy of the place. No pun intended."

Trout, still watching the music being created onstage, nodded to the rising light that enveloped the singers. "Hard to argue with that reasoning when they've got that going on."

Bobby Smalls stepped forward, and broke in. "Dani, sorry to interrupt, but do you have any idea where Brett Billson is? Older guy? White hair?"

"Oh, Brett," Dani said. "I know Brett. We're friends online. We critique horror movies together. Yeah, he's"—she scanned the audience —"there. Over with Kat and her friends."

Bobby followed her gaze and spotted a group huddled toward the back of the seats. Kat, who everyone seemed to know as one of the city's most popular bartenders, sat surrounded by Duncan Wulliver and his family. A few seats away, Noodle sat with his face buried in a sketch pad, working furiously.

Bobby approached the group. Cleared his throat to get their attention. "So, um, hey. Brett, I don't know if you remember me. Bobby Smalls. We worked together a while back."

Brett turned to Bobby, his long white hair drifting over his face. He brushed it out of the way and took a long look at Bobby. "Well, shit," he said. "Bobby. We did *Kismet*. Seventeen years ago. I'm old, but I'm not that far gone. Yet. What's up? I'm feeling about as useful as an inflatable dartboard, so I hope you have something for me to do."

"Well, as a matter of fact," Bobby answered. "Mr. Pettirosso sent me down to ask you a favor."

"The man himself," Brett said. "Must be good. Hit me with it."

Kat and Duncan's family rose and made their excuses.

Brandy noticed Drew Brindig coming toward them, but when he saw

Kat and the others stand up, he changed course and walked away. Something about his expression struck her as odd, but she had more important things to worry about right now than the well-meaning but awkward handyman.

"This sounds serious," Kat said. "I think I'll go see if anyone can use me. I recognize you, by the way." She nodded to Bobby. "Small pitcher of lager and bourbon wings. I never forget a regular. Brandy, Trout, Ken, Nick, Dante. Good to see you. Whoda thunk, huh?"

Duncan was next. "We're moving out, too. Dani asked us to check the perimeter for weaknesses. I'm Duncan Wulliver. These are my parents, Finlay and Carolyn. And my uncles Donal and Craig Marks. We'll be around if you need anything. I hear you're Sean's friends. That makes you my friends."

Bayard appeared suddenly, blinking in next to the Wullivers. "Mind if I join you?" he asked. "Perimeter security is a specialty of mine. And my friend"—he nodded to the wolf, Cinder, at his side—"needs a stretch."

"Of course," Duncan answered, giving Cinder an ear scratch. The wolf nosed his hand and turned her hazel eyes to Bayard, tail wagging.

"Right," Brett continued. "Now that you've scared off the good-looking babe and my new wolfy friends, this better be good."

"We wanted to talk to you about the chronovisor," Bobby blurted out.

"We're in a little bit of a jam," Brandy broke in.

"Not us, specifically," Trout added. "A friend of ours."

Brett let out a long low whistle. "Chronovisor. Now that's a word I haven't heard in a very long time. I said it better be good. I didn't mean suicidal. Ah, what the hell. Whaddaya want to know?"

Despite Carolyn's assurances that she and the others would watch the bridge throughout the night, Sean couldn't relax enough to find sleep. He sat in his makeshift bed, his back against the wall, and ran countless scenarios through his mind. He couldn't just sit here, waiting for a rescue that may never come. In the morning, he would have to take things into his own hands. He would have to find his own way back to his today.

What had McCloud told him before he left? To remember that the covered bridges made crossing the veil easier. At least, easier for a Timestrider, which Sean most definitely was not. What else? Something about forest stairways to nowhere. He didn't have the slightest idea on how to find those. There must be some around, though. Why else would McCloud have mentioned them.

Of course, the strongest point to try to pierce the veil would be the portal itself. Presumably, it was just lying there. He imagined he would find accessing it easier than in his own time, when Pettirosso had created so many safeguards. Of course, Pettirosso himself would be there, just in another persona. That meeting could be interesting if it happened. Probably best to avoid it if possible. The Director was one of very few people around who would still be there in Sean's own time.

He made a decision. He would try some of the covered bridges in the morning. He wasn't a Timestrider, but he was something they had never encountered before. Maybe his music would do the trick. It hadn't let him down yet. Barring that, he would ask around about the forest stairways. If they existed here, someone would know.

He felt better. Some little relief from the simple act of making a plan. He was far from helpless. He could do something to set things back on course. He had to.

He settled back into his bed and closed his eyes. He heard the stealthy movements of the Wullivers in the other rooms, trying to give him space and silence to try to rest. He wanted to sleep. Hoped that Breena would visit again. He drifted along in a semi-conscious state. Neither awake nor asleep. Dreams eluded him. And without dreams, Breena did not appear.

Sometime in the night, he was aware of Carolyn, backlit in the doorway. She stood silently, watching him. Concern in her eyes. Finlay joined her. And finally, surprisingly, Donal joined them. The trio of shifters observing their guest.

"Poor sod," Donal whispered. "Not much anyone can do for him. Do you think this was their plan all along? Just dump him somewhere in time and avoid the whole situation?"

"Nah," Finlay answered. "Easier ways to lose someone. And that Timestrider could have taken him a lot farther back in time than this if he really wanted Sean to disappear."

"I agree," Carolyn said. "McCloud struck me true. Something must have happened to him. Though I thought nothing under the moon could harm a Timestrider. No, this was not intentional, which means Sean is under our care until we somehow find a solution."

"Or he does," Donal pointed out. "We all saw what he did last night. He can probably handle anything that comes his way."

"Anything but being lost in time," Finlay replied. "Let's leave him be. Maybe he'll rest."

"Goodnight, Sean," Carolyn whispered through the doorway. "I know you're listening but try to sleep. We'll all deal with this together tomorrow."

Sean smiled to himself. Of course, wolf shifters would know if he was awake. They could probably hear his breathing or maybe people smelled differently when they slept.

"Goodnight, Carolyn," he answered her. "Thank you."

She closed the door and the shifters settled in for a night of watching the covered bridge. Hoping against fading hope, to see a giant Scotsman striding toward them through the darkness. But dawn came. And McCloud did not.

Brett Billson sat in the back of the auditorium, surrounded by a rapt audience of actors. It was easy to see how he had wound up on the stage. Less easy to see how this character with wild hair and a wilder vocabulary, had started out as a scientist.

"Jeez o flip, the chronovisor. Now that piece of junk was an unmitigated disaster from the get-go. One of my mentors, Enrico Fermi, drafted me to basically be his man Friday. I was the dogsbody—did all the grunt work and got none of the glory. Honestly, in hindsight, that's a good thing. Most people have no idea I was involved at all."

Bobby leaned forward in his seat. "I've only heard it rumored. You didn't even talk about it when we worked together."

"Well, why would I?" Brett asked. "That was a lifetime ago. A very different lifetime. I realized after the experience that, even though my brain *could* work scientifically, I was much happier playing the guitar and singing a song. Doing shows. Actors are more fun than scientists, too. Generally speaking."

"You wrote books, too, didn't you?" Bobby leaned further up in his seat. "Horror?"

"Yup," Brett confirmed. "Lots of things based on my time with the eggheads. Don't tell the CIA, though. Writing was too lonely, for me. I like company. And a paycheck. Both of those were lacking. At least as far as I wanted."

"A regular Renaissance man," Brandy said.

"Bridging the gap between art and science," Dante pointed out. "Might be exactly what we need."

"So, the chronovisor," Trout said, getting back on track. "Can you help us? Is it a dead end?"

"Funny phrase that. 'Dead End,'" Brett answered. "It just so happens I have a few of the old prototypes back at my place. If I was the office drone, my buddy Kelvin Cevasco was the guinea pig. They had him try things they wouldn't dare. Well, he was the last one to try the chronovisor. Last one because he disappeared and was never seen again. Not in our time anyway. Rumors had him popping up in different spots in history. All nonsense, of course. The damn thing didn't work, and I lost my friend because of it. Anyway, after that they shut the whole thing down. I never saw Fermi and the other bosses again. Showed up one day and the offices were cleaned out. Like it never happened. I knew there were a few prototypes in a warehouse nearby. I picked them up before the Feds could. Hoped if I figured something out, I could bring old Kelvin back. No dice."

"Can we see these prototypes?" Brandy asked quickly. "Our friend seems to have gotten himself in a bit of trouble. In time."

"You know what?" Brett replied. "I don't even want to know. Magic singers, bad guys at the door, Pettirosso gathering an army of artists. I'm just gonna take you at your word. And, trust me, you don't want me to know any more. If the G-men do ever pick me up? It's better I can't tell them anything. I will say this. One of these models is useless. Junk. The other three showed promise. But they're old. And have never *actually* worked. Just big ol' question marks."

"We'll take 'em," Ken said. "Best chance we have."

The group rose and Brett agreed to take them to his house in Elizabethtown to get the visors. On a hunch, Nick saw Noodle, still sitting alone, and asked him to join them.

"What's up," the affable artist asked as he approached.

"How are you with impromptu sketching?" Nick asked. "Just a quick squiggle based on something someone says?"

"Ah," he replied. "Quick squigs are my favorite. Don't get to do them much anymore."

"Wanna take a ride?"

"I'm just noodling on my own, right now," he answered. "As long as I can be back in time to help when things get going here, I'd love to.

As they all moved toward the front of the theatre, Brandy took a head count.

"Hey, there's eight of us. I still have the keys to Sean's car, but we'll need another," she said. "Trout, you okay to fire up that snazzy Bronco?"

Before Trout could answer, Dante stopped as they reached the front door.

"Actually, gang," he said, haltingly. "I think I need to stay here. Sean's my pal and all, but we can't all go. And there's a lot that needs to be done here. If things get rough in the theatre, or you all get held up out there, I'd hate to leave everyone shorthanded here."

Trout paused with his hand on the door, a troubled look on his face.

"Well, doggone it," the Montanan said. "Dante has a point. They're going to need all hands on deck here, and he and I have some of the biggest hands. His scythe and my tomahawk would be missed if we were gone. The fact that Sean isn't back means anything can happen back there. Hurts my heart to say it, but I think I should stay, too. Like the man said, there are only three visors."

The entire posse stopped in the lobby. Caught between staying and leaving. Torn between loyalties.

Nick finally broke the silence. "Okay, let's break this down. Dante and Trout should stay here. They'll be needed. Two of the biggest, strongest in the building. I've got a broken wing," he held up his bandaged arm. "I'm not a candidate to time travel, anyway. Who knows what's waiting back there. Brett, you obviously have to go. At least to retrieve the visors at your house. Bobby, you should go since it was your idea, and you know Brett best. Probably shouldn't send you back in time, though. Sean doesn't know you as well as some others. Noodle, If I'm right, we'll need you on this side of the time jump. Pencil in hand. So the Crosstrek should take us, minus the two big guys, to try the visors. Process of elimination means Brandy and Ken should be the ones to jump. Only three visors and we'll need one for Sean to come back. That makes you two the chrononauts. Congratulations."

"Chrononauts," Brett muttered. "How did we never come up with that?"

Everyone took a moment to look around the circle of friends. Splitting up, even in the name of saving Sean, just hadn't been in the plans. But it made sense. If anything in this insane situation made sense.

Trout grabbed Brandy. "Just make sure you make it back here. And bring Sean with you."

"Oh, don't you worry about me, Boze-man," she replied. "Just be here when we do. And try to keep the theatre standing. And, you know, everyone alive."

"Piece of cake, sweet cheeks," Trout said with a grin.

"Okay," Brandy growled. "That's enough of that. Chrononauts

assemble. The Crosstrek will fit us now, so let's go do some time jumping."

The hours stretched into days. The days melted into weeks. Sean felt his hopes dwindling the longer he stayed in 1964. He took to long days of rambling the countryside. McCloud's words had stuck with him, and he had come around to thinking that he had to find his own way home or be resigned to spending the rest of his days here in the past.

He walked everywhere in the county. He visited Erb's Mill Covered Bridge, Hunsecker's, Kurtz's. Even as far as Lime Valley and Baumgardner's covered bridges. He repeated his experiment at each location. He stood at one end of the bridge. Waited for there to be no traffic in sight, and then began his song. Wordlessly, he'd weave his music. If a passing car or horse-drawn buggy noticed a strange glow, none stopped to explore what it was.

Always, the results were the same. He would draw his power to himself, and as he began to cross the span of that day's bridge, he would see a swirl of energy begin to form at the far side. Each time, his heart began to hammer. Could this be the one? The one time he could break through and go home?

But at least so far, it had never happened. He would draw close to the swirling ball of energy, different colors every time, and it would fade and disappear before he could reach it. Blue, green, yellow, silver, red. They had all eluded him. His power strong enough to call them, but unable to push him through. Each night he returned to the mill dejected.

Over time, his attention turned to Lancaster City. His curiosity grew. He'd been told to avoid areas where he may encounter someone he knew. But that had been when the plan was to be here for only a few hours. Minutes, even. Now he was imprisoned here. Possibly for the rest of his life. If that were the case, he couldn't be expected to remain isolated forever. Could he?

The Wullivers had proven to be remarkably kind. Carolyn and Finlay had become fast friends, and though they certainly pitied Sean for his situation, the friendship had become much more than that. They stayed up long hours, discussing their families and their lives. Sean's newly discovered gifts fascinated the shifters. And Sean, in turn, was equally intrigued by the abilities of the wolf family and their history. They asked questions and shared secrets late in the moonlit nights by the creek.

Even Donal and Craig, who had been so hesitant at first to interact with Sean eventually came around. With Donal both apologizing and explaining one night when they had all been sitting in the yard of the mill, bathed in the moonlight.

"Look, Sean, man," Donal began. "My bad for treating you the way I did when you first showed up. You've gotta dig, though, that you showing up unexpectedly, and in the company of a Fae, no less, just hit me bad."

Sean turned to Donal. This was one of the first times he had discussed anything of substance with him and he was afraid of doing anything to shut the discussion down. "I get it, Donal. You weren't what we were expecting to find here, either."

"Yeah, man," Donal answered. "I get that. But humans and Fae were exactly the folks who hounded our family out of Scotland. Chased us clear across the ocean here. When you two appeared out of nowhere—I wasn't inclined to give you the benefit of even half a doubt. Now I get to know you a bit...I can see you're not all bad. Not going to go nuts and become blood brothers or anything, but I guess you're not as bad as I thought."

"That's the most you've ever said to me, Donal," Sean replied. "And thanks for that. I get it. At least, I think I do. I had no idea what I was walking into. I see how we could have triggered some warning bells for you."

"Well, let's not get carried away and go hugging each other," Donal said. "But I'm glad to be proven wrong. You're not all bad. But that Timestrider better have a good excuse for abandoning you here. And if you're stuck here long-term, well—you're pretty much part of the pack now. That's all I'm sayin'."

"I appreciate that. I really do."

After that, they had all fallen silent. Watching the moon climb the night sky and listening to the creek sweeping past, completely indifferent to who was sitting on her banks.

It was then that Sean decided to force the issue. The Wullivers weren't bad. He was actually growing to genuinely care for them. But if he was going to stay here. To allow these friendships to take root in him. He had to know he had exhausted every pathway home.

In the morning, he would go to Lancaster. He would go to the Fulton Theatre. And he would visit the portal in the basement. If it was another dead end, he would accept his fate and make his home here. Sixty years. Before he had been born.

Eventually, they all drifted off to bed, the family having taken to sleeping in the mill with Sean. He was feeling better about his situation. Not happy, but better.

That was the second night that Breena came to him in his dreams.

———

Brett's long-suffering wife, Lauren, was still trying to make sense of their visitors as they pulled away from the Billson family home in Elizabethtown. They had spent forty minutes plowing through every box in Brett's "junk room," which was essentially an unfinished basement filled with memorabilia from every corner of his very fertile list of interests. DVDs of every imaginable western and horror film. CDs and cassettes of every jazz artist from Duke Ellington to Kamasi Washington. Books. So many books. Video games from Japan. Art from local craftspeople and movie posters from Hollywood's Golden Age.

And in among it all, tucked in a back corner, a box simply labeled Rico. They'd emerged carrying the box, marched past the bewildered Lauren, and climbed back into Sean's Subaru. As they made the short thirty-minute drive from E-town to Zook's Mill Covered Bridge, Brett worked furiously in the back seat. He rummaged through the box, examining and then discarding nearly everything he touched. He opened the security cover in the hatch to have a place to drop all the items. Finally, he let out a low whoop and lifted something that looked suspiciously like a colander with a chin strap and various wires jutting out at odd angles.

"This is the crap one," he muttered, tossing it over his shoulder into the hatch. "Aha! Now, this one...we're in business now."

He lifted another colander, this one with significantly more wires and a few protruding tubes. Then he lifted another. And another.

"Just like I remembered," Brett said. "We do need a power source. We used simple batteries. Is there a CVS on the way?"

"If I'm right," Nick said, "we won't need any. Just plow through to the bridge."

Nick fished through his pockets and pulled out a small length of wood that had been whittled down to a handheld size.

"This is from the post that Pettirosso showed us," he announced. "The original one he had moved to his office in the renovations. He gave me some scraps. I had thought to use them with my writing pencil, the one from the Outer Banks. I have a feeling, you—" he turned to Noodle, "can make equally good use of this. Can I see your drawing pencil?"

Noodle, looking very confused, pulled a pencil from a pocket in his jacket and handed it over. Nick took it and hollowed out the center of his piece of the theatre post until he could slip it over Noodle's pencil.

"Give this a shot when we get there," Nick said, handing it back to Noodle. "I don't think we'll need any batteries."

"I have no idea what you're doing, but I'll just roll with it for now."

They pulled up next to the bridge and all piled out. Brett carried the helmets under his arms, stopping short of the bridge and checking through the connections of the wires.

"That's going to have to do," he said, turning back to the group. "One for you, and one for you. Who gets the extra?"

Brandy stepped forward and took the third chronovisor.

"Now what?" she asked. "Where's the on button?"

"I'll get that," Brett said, stepping behind Brandy and Ken, flipping a small toggle on the back of each visor. "I've set these to a few weeks after we think Sean arrived in the past. They're not very precise, so I erred on the side of caution. Don't turn the other one on until you need it. Conserve power. This third one is the shakiest. The two you're wearing were at least tested. The last one, not at all. Also, keep in mind, the last guy to use one of these, and he had the new improved version, was never seen again. Kelvin Cevasco just—disappeared. It may have worked. We always hoped so anyway. Best-case scenario is that he's out there some-when. Just couldn't get back home. No clue, though. But these early versions? They're going to need a boost."

"What kind of a boost?" Bobby Small asked. "We should have stopped for those batteries."

"I don't think so," Nick said. "While we start our singing, Noodle, why don't you make some freehand sketches of whatever comes to mind when you think of time travel."

Noodle turned a highly skeptical eye to Nick.

"Trust me," Nick said. "Pettirosso said we were all here for a reason. I think this is part of yours. What have we got to lose?"

Noodle, shaking his head, began to draw with his hybrid pencil. First, a figure glowing, splayed out, with a helmet on its head and streaks of light surrounding it.

As Noodle sketched, Brandy and Ken began to sing. Quietly at first, and then with greater volume and urgency. After a moment, Nick joined them, and a silver light began to form around them. Growing in intensity. As it did, the group became aware of a light shining from the far end of the bridge.

A portal had opened. A spinning, swirling maelstrom of silver flashes spinning faster and faster. Brandy turned expectant eyes on Brett and Bobby. After a stunned moment, they joined in the musical chord.

The portal on the bridge grew brighter. And brighter. Brandy and Ken began to move across the span, but the closer they got to the portal, the dimmer it grew, and it appeared to shrink from them.

Nick, still singing, ran to Noodle's side, where he took the sketches Noodle had made of the travelers. He rolled each of them and approached the would-be chrononauts and slipped them into the brim of their helmets. He slipped a third drawing into Brandy's hand before she was out of reach. As he did, the glow around Brandy and Ken exploded outward and flowed firmly across the bridge. The portal pulsed brighter. Stronger. Faster. Green and silver making a whirlpool of luminescence.

With a backward glance, Brandy and Ken crossed the bridge. Entered the vortex. And disappeared.

"Man, I hope this wasn't a horrible mistake," Bobby said.

"I hope I drew the right thing," Noodle whispered.

"Time will tell," Nick replied. "Pun intended."

"Whatever happens," Brett muttered, "I'll tell you this. That was a lot cooler than the batteries we used back in the day. Powered by song and art. Bitchin'."

Nick, Bobby Smalls, and Noodle, once seeing Brandy and Ken off to what they hoped was a past where Sean awaited, had decided to return to Lancaster and the Fulton. There was nothing they could do now until their friends returned. If they returned. Their talents and energy would be better put to use where the action was set to occur.

For his part, Brett decided to wait things out at the bridge. His knowledge of the chronovisors may come in handy if things went sideways on re-entry. And, as he put it, "I'm too old to help out in a fist fight, much as I hate to admit it, but my brain might just be able to help out here." He arranged for his wife, Lauren, to drive over and wait with him. "We never were ones for a traditional date night," he said laughing.

When the time-traveling contingent arrived at the Fulton, they found that the day marched inexorably on, and the theatre throbbed with continued preparation for what looked to be a night of violence. When the afternoon began to become evening, Pettirosso had Deborah call everyone to the auditorium. She was still tired from her encounter at the portal, but did as she was asked, and within thirty minutes the seats were once again filled with the

Fulton folks. They sat, quietly speaking to each other, reviewing what had been accomplished. Suggesting what still needed to be done.

For a group of people whose entire world order had been challenged just this morning, they seemed remarkably focused. There was no panic, though some of the faces showed a degree of fear that was being buried with varying degrees of success.

In the midst of this, Nick was looking at his phone when he reached over and grabbed Noodle by the arm.

"Would you look at this," he said, handing the device to the artist to read.

"'Garland grabs New York by heartstrings,'" Noodle read. "'Stewart Garland gave one of the most consequential performances in recent memory last night at the Nederlander Theatre. In a sharp departure from the recent drift of events, Garland sang, and joked, and spoke from the heart in a seemingly successful bid to restore decency and hope to a weary city. And possibly beyond. Not to put too much on the experience, but this reviewer left the theatre feeling there just may be hope for us all after all.'"

Trout and Dante joined them in the seats just in time to catch the end of the statement and Dante shook his head while smiling. Trout let out a restrained whoop and laughed his trademark Big Sky-volumed laugh.

"I knew we were right to leave him to do his thing up there," Trout declared. "I actually feel like the tide is turning. No matter what happens here tonight, it feels like basic decency may actually be fixin' to set things to right."

"Wouldn't that be something," Dante said. "Been a long time coming."

"And simple, straightforward, good-hearted Stewart may be the messenger," Nick chuckled. "No better ambassador than Stew."

Bobby took them all in. "I hope you're right. I do," he said. "But all things considered, I'd like us to carry the night here *in addition*. You know? This theatre. These people. They matter."

"Damn straight," Trout agreed. "And I, for one, am fired up to make sure they see the morning."

At that point, Pettirosso walked onto the stage and took his now familiar spot down stage center. This time, though, he didn't sit casually on the lip of the stage. He remained standing and, taking in the assembled artists, slowly began to speak. Somberly and from the heart.

"I'm not sure if I can adequately express my thanks to you for being here," he began. "I find it remarkable that so many of you are willing to risk so much to defend this beautiful old lady." He paused to look around the ornate auditorium before making a full turn, also looking to the stage and backstage wings. "It has meant so much to so many over the years. I want you to know that I did not call you here lightly. Until now, I have always been enough to safeguard this sacred space, but I fear this threat goes far beyond my abilities alone."

"We trust you, Mr. Pettirosso!" a voice called from the audience.

"That means more to me than you can know," the director responded. "And I trust you. I always have. In the hours ahead, we will be tested. Bitterly. Those who seek to do harm here, seek more than that. The taking of the Fulton would be only one step in the destruction of much that we hold dear. But I believe we will be up to the task."

"I have placed certain—safeguards—in place. Those we love, our families and friends in the city, will be shielded from what happens here. To Lancastrians asleep in their beds, nothing will signal the struggle we will face. I, with the help of Deborah, have placed a protection over the theatre. Those of us within that sphere, though, will face grave danger."

Now he did sit on the edge of the stage, connecting more intimately with his listeners.

"I urge you now, in the remaining time before darkness falls and our foes arrive, to call your loved ones. Not out of a sense of foreboding, or to bid goodbye. No. To remind yourself why it is so important for us to prevail. To remember that there is goodness, and love, and value, everywhere around us if we choose to accept and embrace it. Fill yourself with what makes you whole and carry that with you tonight. Remember that. And think, also, on why you are here. Your particular talents that made you part of this family. The creative gifts you possess that make you unique. That will allow us to preserve this vital creative temple."

"I have always believed that creation is stronger than destruction. It takes no talent to tear something down. Hate is the refuge of the weak and the coward. True bravery is the father of creation. To build something from nothing and to set it free into the world? That is strength. This room is filled with creative warriors. Misfits and outcasts, all are welcome here. And have always been. Often, all someone needs is a place to be themselves. That is this place. Together, nothing will defeat us. As long as one courageous soul perseveres and gives life to their own vision of how things can be, there will be light in the world. Tonight, we will show, as creators have countless times through the centuries, that light shows the way. Not darkness."

Deborah stepped to his side and spoke. "Rest now. Grab a bite. Make those phone calls. Sunset is early now. By five o'clock it will be dark. Soon after, it will start."

Pettirosso and Deborah left the stage.

Sean woke earlier than the Wullivers, so he left them a note and began his trek into Lancaster and the Fulton Theatre. He'd told no one, not even Carolyn, of his plan. This felt personal. He still didn't really understand his own powers. He'd never tested their limitations, largely because he only used them when he was backed into a corner. This time he would be trying to use them for a completely different purpose—to open a portal and go home. Well, to his proper time.

The journey from the mill to downtown Lancaster was just over nine miles. Rather than trying to hitch a ride, as he had been doing lately, he chose to walk. He needed the air. He needed the chance to stretch his legs. He needed to think.

Breena had visited his dreams again last night, only the second time since he had traveled back with McCloud. Her words had not eased his mind.

She had appeared again out of an argent mist, beautiful as always with her blond hair cut short as it had been the last time he'd actually seen her, her blue eyes impossibly deep and clear. But her words had been anything but comforting.

"Sean, my love," she had said. "Stay where you are. Your time holds nothing but heartbreak for you. I have more chance of finding you here than back then. Worlds are in motion. Nations of Fae long silent are stirring. Your friends will not prevail. Your—our—best hope is to stash ourselves somewhere in time. The present, the future, promises nothing but pain."

This visit, Sean strongly suspected, had been a ruse. Someone had sent a false Breena to poison his thinking. The real Breena would have known that hearing those things would make him more determined than ever to find a way back. A way to help his friends. To change the course of events.

And so, he had awakened from a troubled sleep early and left on what could possibly be a fool's errand but was the only action he could imagine that was entirely within his control. He walked. And walked.

Eventually he entered Lancaster proper and made his way down Chestnut Street. He noted how similar some of the blocks seemed, even sixty years in the past. The Victorian row houses standing, stolid and true. Many of the mills and factories that in later years would be repurposed into trendy stores, and restaurants, and breweries, were in their earlier iteration. Traffic was lighter. People were friendlier.

Finally, he turned left onto Prince Street and, a few blocks down, saw the grand old lady herself, the Fulton Theatre, now called the Fulton Opera House. She was smaller now, decades before her expansion and renovation, but she remained proud and elegant. Her marquee was not yet the digital board of Sean's time, but a simple light board with letters placed by hand. The theatre itself was back to its original footprint. Narrower. Quainter. In keeping with the surrounding traditional architecture. A symbol, even now, of possibility and a beacon to all who would lend their talents to the community of misfits and misunderstood who found a home working side by side with like-minded colleagues.

As he approached, he saw someone out front washing the windows and made for them, hoping for a sympathetic ear and an easy entrance to the basement and the portal that could solve everything.

Moments after Sean left, Carolyn stood in the doorway of the mill. She had heard him moving when he woke but sensed that he needed some time and had left him to himself. She wasn't surprised to see him leaving on one of his solitary ambles. She was surprised, however, when she found his note and read that he was headed into town. They had agreed up until now that it was best to avoid large groups of people. No need to take unnecessary risks.

She roused the others and explained the situation. The general consensus was to leave him to himself. As Donal had pointed out, one of the dangers in pursuing him was the risk of exposing themselves to unwanted attention. They had spent generations keeping their profile low. The safety of the pack depended on not attracting suspicion. And the safety of the pack was paramount.

As the decision was made, the meeting was interrupted by an enormous crash coming from the direction of the mill. With a knowing look to each other, the pack rushed to the door where they expected to see the familiar figure of McCloud stomping down the hill and calling for Sean to be ready to jump.

But they all stopped short by what confronted them when they opened the door. Two very ordinary looking people stood in the middle of the road. The shorter of the two, a woman, planted her feet shoulder-width apart and surveyed the surrounding countryside. The other, larger, of the two, was bent over double and slowly sank to one knee in the dirt and retched onto the ground, a trail of bile slowly stringing from mouth to dust. The notable aspect of their appearance was what appeared to be two cooking pots on their heads, each with wires and tubing running in various directions. Both looked up when they heard the front door open, hopeful looks on their faces fading quickly when they were confronted by the family.

Carolyn, quickly surmising that what they were seeing was a rescue attempt, walked to the newcomers extending a hand in greeting. Even Donal, fighting every instinct in his body, managed to keep his hackles down and follow the others to the new arrivals.

The pack ushered Brandy and Ken, as they were now known, into the mill where Ken was seated and given a glass of water. He seemed very unsteady on his feet and confused. Brandy, on the other hand, was all business and got directly to the point.

"Thanks for the welcome, but we're here to meet up with a friend of ours," she announced. "Name of Sean. Red hair, medium height, overly earnest. Probably more than a bit panicky that we haven't been here already."

"We know Sean," Finlay answered. "You missed him by just a little while. He took a walk into town. Should be back soon. Ish. Maybe."

"Yeah, no offense," Brandy answered, "but we need to find him, like now. He needs to get back—home. It's a kind of emergency."

Carolyn placed a hand on Brandy's arm. "We know. We were here with Sean and McCloud, and we've been sitting with Sean since McCloud left. You're right. He's worried. Scared. He went to the theatre to try to use a portal there to get back."

"Ah, great," Brandy allowed herself to drop to one of the benches. "That portal is dangerous. And he definitely shouldn't come through it back in our time. It's protected by spells, and guards, and who knows what else. We need to get to him. Can you help?"

Donal surprised everyone by stepping forward. "Sure we can," he said. "Let's take my van. We can be there in twenty minutes. By the way, what happened to McCloud? He said he'd be right back."

"I'll tell you on the way," Brandy promised. "It's...complicated."

Ken looked up at the others. "We made it right? We're in 1964?"

"You are," Donal answered. "The next thing we want to know is how the hell you managed that? We've always been told its impossible for anyone but Timestriders."

"Not anymore, I guess," Ken said, shaking his head. "We've only made it halfway, though. We need to get us all back before I'll say it was a success."

Donal stood. "I'll drive. You explain."

And so two Grumbles and a pack of shapeshifters piled into a Volkswagen van and chugged up the hill, across the bridge, and toward the Fulton.

Sean reached the front of the theatre and walked up to the man washing the windows on the front doors with a sponge and bucket of soapy water. Sean paused, hoping the man would sense him there and turn, but that didn't happen, so Sean cleared his throat. The man paused his work before turning.

"Can I help you?" the man said, an open, friendly smile lighting up his face.

Sean stopped dead in his tracks. The man now facing him was Drew Brindig, Pettirosso's handyman. But Drew looked exactly the same. He wasn't sixty years younger. He was *exactly the same* and Sean's mind could not reconcile what he was seeing with what he knew.

At that point, a slightly rusty Volkswagen van pulled up to the curb, belching smoke. The back door slid open, and Ken tumbled out, a chronovisor in each hand, and shouted, "Sean! Holy crap! It's really you!"

Brandy, on the other hand, slowly climbed down from the front passenger side door, her eyes not on Sean but on Drew Brindig standing in front of him.

"Carolyn, Finlay...that guy talking to Sean is from our time. But he's exactly the same age as when we left him. Something's wrong."

"Just remember not to say anything," Finlay warned. "There's got to be a reason, but he can't know what's happening. I don't sense anything unusual about him. Straightforward human. The less he knows the better."

They emerged from the van in time to hear Sean say, "Drew? Drew Brindig? What are you doing here?"

CHAPTER 16

As the sun set and darkness fell over Lancaster, Pettirosso rose from his desk. Deborah and Drew were with him. Dante and Trout were also in the room. Nick had just left, sent to the stage to collaborate with Noodle and other creators. Pettirosso had replenished his supply of chips from the original beam that now stood in the office, cut down to four pillars, placed throughout the room, a tangible connection to the long beating heart of the theatre.

"Friends, it is time," Pettirosso said quietly. "We must all do our best. If we do that, there will be no failure. No matter the outcome."

A bright light began to spill in through the windows from Prince Street. Orange. Red. The color of anger. Flashing and flickering.

"Deborah, you know what you must do," the director said, and she moved from one pillar to another, stopping to carve runes into each length of timber. "Trout and Dante, I'm afraid I have a favor to ask of you that I do not ask lightly. Our enemies will assault us from many directions. The front doors, obviously. The stage door on Grant Street. Even the new entrances to the artist village on King and Water Streets. But none are more important. None more vulnerable, than the doorway to the greenroom from Water Street. It lies next to the portal. The gateway under the stage. If you will, I ask you to make that your task. To preserve the portal. If we lose that, we lose all."

Trout glanced at Dante before answering. "You know it, boss. Chicago and Montana, scythe and tomahawk, fighting together. Don't give it a thought. We'll shut that down."

"You won't be alone," Pettirosso assured him. "The Fulton's spirits are awakening. The portal being here means that the veil between realms is thin here. And those realms include the spirit realm. I know you've felt them. They are like us—misfits, restless souls, those who have nowhere else they belong. They will rise to your side. Don't fear them. They may be our saving grace. Please go, now. It's time."

As the two left the upstairs office to make their way downstairs, they saw the light from the street intensify. It was as if the sun had risen again as soon as it had set. But this sun was angry, vengeful. Unnatural.

Deborah turned to Pettirosso. "I've done what I can, sir. It's up to you, now."

"Thank you, my friend," Pettirosso said, before stepping to the center of the room, between all of the pillars that now bore Deborah's handiwork.

"Boss," Drew said. "I'm sorry to bother, but do you have something for me to do? Where should I go?"

Pettirosso turned to Drew with genuine affection in his eyes. "Ah, Drew," he said. "My dear friend. You know where you need to be. I truly believe that your wait will soon be done. Find her. Find them both. Your loyalty has been a thing for the ages. Go with my thanks. And my love."

Drew, with tears in his eyes, turned and drifted from the room.

Pettirosso paused, and glanced at Deborah, who also had tears in her eyes. "If nothing else goes right tonight, I hope that does," she said.

"As do I," he replied. "And now, to work."

Standing between the pillars now, he began to weave intricate patterns in the air before him. Silver, green and gold orbs began to form around him. They, too, began to form patterns, and multiply, until the room pulsed and glowed, pushing back at the poisoned crimson light that flowed through the windows.

"They come," Pettirosso said, and his voice sounded distant, detached, as if it came from a great distance to reach the office. "Balor's army is here. The battle for the Fulton begins. I pray it is not the beginning of a Fae War. Stay with me, Deborah. We will need each other before the end."

Deborah cautiously crossed to the window and glanced to the street. A crimson whirlpool was forming in front of the theatre. It grew wider, taller, angrier. Black figures swirled within the flames, but it was the street itself that caught her attention, as shadows swarmed from every direction, silently surrounding the theatre. A host of red-capped figures followed them, pikes in their hands pounding the pavement and bricks below them as they marched. Behind them, flashing shapes of massive felines and foxes flitted from doorway to doorway. Far more than just the two that had been seen thus far.

Deborah's mouth fell open in dismay. There were so many. So very many here to take their beloved theatre. More than she could have imagined., More than she believed they could ever hope to defeat.

As she watched, something unexpected happened. The verdant, silver, golden light that had sprung from Pettirosso and the ancient wooden pillars, exploded through the roof of the theatre complex. It soared high into the air, before splintering into uncounted tendrils and falling to the ground, encircling the entire city block in a gilded luminous cage.

The attackers stopped in their approach, taken aback by their apparent prison, but when the light-cage simply settled in behind them, they began to laugh and turned their attention once more to the Fulton. They began their march on the building again.

Deborah turned to Pettirosso with panic in her voice. "They've started again. It's done nothing to stop them."

"It was never intended to stop them," he replied, in his distant voice. "I have placed us all beyond the reach of the citizens of Lancaster. They will sleep untroubled tonight. And within this light, we will decide the future of this place. And of the realms."

They heard the first sounds of the doors being battered on Prince Street.

The theatre itself was a hive of activity. Each different department operating at a fever pitch. When the first sounds of the doors being battered reached them, Dani looked to Paul White, the lighting guru, for a sign. At a nod from him, she hit a computer key, and the streets around the theatre, around the entire block, erupted in brilliant stage light. Every instrument that could be spared had been shifted to the roofline and focused outward.

Shadows disappeared under the brilliant glare of the LED lights, and as the shadows disappeared, the Hide Behinds, who dwelled in those shadows, fell back, desperate for a refuge. Someplace to launch their attacks on unsuspecting victims who came within their grasp. The man in the fedora led the way.

But the glare of the lights did nothing to slow the Red Caps, who came on, unwavering. There were hundreds of them, of all shapes and sizes. The smaller specimens wore caps of lighter shades, and many had no weapon in their hands, but the larger Red Caps wore hats of deep, blood-red hues and used the massive pikes they carried to inflict senseless damage on anything they passed.

The antique gas lamps exploded in showers of glass and gouts of gas-fueled flame. Cars unlucky enough to have been parked on the street fell to pieces under the hail of blows. Windowpanes on neighboring businesses shattered.

Inside the theatre, panic was being held at bay. Barely. These were artists. Actors, singers, painters, musicians. They were poorly suited to withstand the terror now facing them. Terror born in a realm and from a power they had not known only hours before.

Haydn and Page, the composing team, had gathered a band in the center of the stage. Scott Snug was there, along with many of the regular musicians, and as they began to play from sheet music the writers had given them, a glow began to rise from the stage. Silver and pure and healthy, the glow rose and surrounded the artists, the sensitives as Pettirosso had called them, and they took heart from it. It was almost as if it gave them a physical assist, and a steel began to appear in their eyes. The Fulton—*their Fulton*—needed them. This space was sacred to them. Pettirosso's words echoed again in their minds, and they began to act.

Improbably, it was Bobby Smalls who took charge. He stood on a rehearsal block downstage and began to direct people in different directions. Kerstin and Kirsten, the wardrobe staff, were passing out tabards and shirts stitched through with symbols directed by Deborah. As each person slipped one on, they felt themselves bathed in a protective shield. Isabella, one of the dressers, helped everyone to wear them properly.

Sophia and Kai, from the stage crew, were passing out props from various past productions, anything that could be used in defense of the Fulton. There were swords from *Treasure Island*. Staffs from *Robin Hood*. Rifles from *Les Mis*. Everything that could be repurposed, had been.

With a cry from Bobby, the assembled, as motley a group as ever sought to defend a place, lined up in the aisles and began to move toward the front doors, with the music of the band ringing behind them.

Outside the theatre, Bayard and Cinder prowled the exterior of the theatre complex. The Wulliver pack, now revealed fully in wolf shape, prowled along with them. The bulk of the attackers seemed to be focused on the façade of the building, which immediately raised warning bells for Bayard, who had fought the likes of these opponents too often to take them at face value.

He led the newly formed pack down the side of the building, along Grant Street past the stage door. It was relatively quiet here. A handful of Red Caps were easily dispatched and the way down to Water Street behind the theatre opened and lay empty. More warning bells.

Together, they approached the corner of Grant and Water Streets, peering around the corner, where they stopped short.

Water Street was entirely full of attackers. Red Caps, all of them the larger more seasoned fighters, stood shoulder to shoulder, facing the back door. Even Hide Behinds could be seen lurking in doorways, finding any small shadow they could to conceal themselves and focus on the theatre. The Fedora Man again there. Still. Silent. Waiting for some sign.

And then it appeared. A second vortex of fire appeared, and deep within it they could glimpse a figure. A figure mounted on a horse. A figure with no head on its shoulders. Bayard knew immediately and hissed a curse. And then a warning. A foe he had thought gone, had returned.

"Dullahan," he snarled through gritted teeth.

Beside him, Cinder's hackles rose, and she growled long and low.

"Hey, Ginge!" Brandy called, approaching Sean and Drew on the sidewalk. "We've been looking everywhere for you!" She raised her eyebrows, hoping Sean would take a hint, but Drew noticed, also, and his look of confusion grew deeper.

"I'm sorry," Drew said. "Do I know you? I recognize you all," he gestured to the Wullivers. "But I don't think we've met," he turned to Sean and Brandy. "I'm sorry. I don't mean to be rude. Could you maybe have met me up at Musser Park? My wife and I are there with the kids pretty often."

"Oh," Sean answered, realizing the predicament he'd created for himself. "Yeah, that must be it. I used to stay up on Orange Street. Dremmel House. Must have met you at the park sometime. Didn't mean to be presumptuous."

"Oh, gosh," Drew said. "No apology necessary. And we live at Dremmel now! Maybe we crossed paths there, too. My wife and I still have baby brain. Our youngest is ten months, so we don't sleep much. I'm sure I did meet you. It's my fault." His smile was guileless. Honest.

"Well, no need for apologies from anyone. Just a neighbor saying hi," Sean backpedaled.

"I hope you'll say hi again if you see us up at the park," Drew continued. "My wife's name is Katie if you see her. She's usually got our little ones hanging off of some part of her." He chuckled. "She's just the best Mum ever."

Sean paused, something tickling the back of his mind, but he couldn't quite get a hold of it and Brandy broke in to move things along.

"Well, we'd best get back to the mill, yeah? Need to run those tests and get along *home*."

Sean took the cue. "Oh, right. Of course. Drew, I was going to ask for a little backstage tour, but maybe we can save it for next time?"

"You betcha, Sean," Drew said. "I'm new here, so I probably shouldn't be giving tours just yet anyway. If I make a good impression and they keep me on, I'd love to show you around. Beautiful old place. I'd be happy if I could stay here forever."

"I'm sure they'll love you," Brandy cut in. "He'll take a rain check."

Ken, finally catching on to what was happening, held the back door open for Sean, who climbed in.

"Holy crap," Ken muttered when Sean had settled. "That's Drew. Like *DREW* from sixty years in the future."

"I can see that," Sean said. "More importantly, how the hell are you guys here? Is McCloud with you?"

"Well, no," Brandy answered. "He's out of commission. Possibly for a long time. We took an alternate method of transport."

"And we'd better get out to the mill and fore these up," Ken lifted the two chronovisors he held. "Not really sure how long they'll be functional."

Sean turned to the Wulliver family and addressed Carolyn directly. "Thank you. You all have gone way above and beyond here. I don't know how to repay you."

"Get home, Sean," she answered. "Get home and set things to right. And take care of our Duncan if we're not around. That's how you thank us."

"I absolutely will," Sean said, and then turned to Brandy and Ken.

"Now tell me what is happening. How you're here and what we need to do."

Bobby Smalls was leading a phalanx of ill-equipped but determined theatre artists toward the lobby of the theatre, where the doors were shaking from the pummeling of the horde of attackers. It seemed only a matter of time until the doors gave way and the Red Caps and Hide Behinds rushed into the theatre.

Their weapons were sad. Clearly no match for what they faced. But they took up positions by the doors, waiting to tackle whatever came through them.

Suddenly, the lobby shimmered and shifted. Where there had been simply carpet and show posters, there now grew barricades. Wooden barricades with vicious wooden poles, sharpened to a point, facing outward toward the attackers. Bobby watched it all grow up from out of the floor but could see no reason for it. He turned and looked back into the theatre to see Nick and Noodle, working side by side on the stage, one writing and one drawing. They looked up and met Bobby's eyes. Using their enchanted pencils, crafted from the chips of the original Fulton beam in Pettirosso's office, they were calling their artwork into life.

"We're writing and illustrating the story of the siege of the Fulton," Nick called. "How're we doing?"

"It's amazing!" Bobby called back to them, and when he turned back to the lobby defenders, there was a renewed determination. This impossible army of peaceful artists actually now believed they could carry the day.

That's when the doors exploded inward, and a sea of violence flooded them all.

As they drove back to the mill, Brandy and Ken told Sean everything that had been happening back in 2024. Specifically, they focused on the failed attempt at diplomacy, the ambush of McCloud by the Wayob when he returned for news, and the impending assault on the theatre. The recounting of the chronovisor and the introduction of Brett Billson was a longer telling, and they described the marriage of science and magic that had occurred when Noodle's artwork pushed the chronovisors into action.

"The problem though, well one of them, is that they aren't incredibly precise. We had to overshoot your arrival here to make sure we didn't arrive before you," Brandy explained.

"Honestly," Ken said, "I would have made the best of it. No one knows you. Nothing to live up to. Or to make up for. Could be worse."

"Well, let's just all get back and help everyone at the theatre, okay?" Sean replied. "You've come this far. Let's get it done with."

Crossing Zook's Mill Covered Bridge and arriving back at the mill, Sean felt a surprising tug at his heart as he realized he would soon be saying goodbye to Carolyn and the Wullivers, and he was surprised to find that they had become close in a short amount of time. Extreme situations could do that, he supposed.

As Brandy and Ken looked over the visors, Sean pulled the family aside.

"I don't know what to say," he began. "Thank you seems so inadequate. I don't know what I would have done without you."

"Just get home," Carolyn said, stepping closer to him. "Take care of Duncan for us. Save that theatre. We have some experience with the cruelty of the Fae. The world needs more places where everyone is welcome. Go. Be safe."

The Wulliver pack, even Donal and the reticent Craig, crowded him for a hug. Apparently, the feelings of friendship were mutual, and Sean fought a lump in his throat. He knew he had to leave. The only way to help his friends and the theatre, was to be there. The only way to discover what was really happening with Breena, to bring her home to him, was to go back. Everything that mattered to him was there. But the heart is infinite, and he knew that this time with his new pack would always be a part of him.

He turned to Brandy and Ken. Brandy, after making sure that Noodle's drawing was tucked into the lip of her visor, set it on her head.

Ken was a bit behind her. Checking both his visor and the extra they had brought for Sean. He paused for a moment, checking the connections on the extra. He looked up to the others and smiled. Sean could have sworn for just the slightest moment he had seen a sadness in Ken's eyes, but it was gone quickly, and Sean assumed it was simply nerves at having to make a jump again so soon after the last one that had left him sick to his stomach.

Ken approached him and held out a visor. He settled it onto Sean's head and made sure it was secure. Lastly, he checked for the Noodle doodle. All seemed in order, and he placed a visor on his own head.

With a glance at the ground, Ken turned to Sean and Brandy. "I just want you to know, you two, the Grumbles, are the best friends I could have ever dreamed of. You've put up with so much from me, and I have so much to make up for. I would do anything for you. Anything."

"Enough of that," Brandy barked. "We're going back and we're going back together. We can be maudlin when our next Broadway show closes. Let's hit it."

Ken grinned. "Yeah, let's hit it."

He hugged them both. It was so out of character, that Brandy recoiled for just a second. It was then that she saw it. Ken was wearing the extra visor, the one they'd brought for Sean. But it's lights weren't blinking. It lay lifeless, shut down on Ken's head.

"Hey, wait. Ken, you're visor is—"

"Not working. I know. It's broken...I love you guys. Go save the day. See you in the funny papers."

Ken tapped the activator button on the back of both the other visors and stepped back to watch two of his closest friends shudder and shift. He sang a clear, beautiful tenor note. The finest he'd ever hit if he did say so himself. He stepped back from the lip of the bridge, and the portal at the far side widened, deepened, and flowed outward to envelop Sean and Brandy, who were still shouting soundlessly as they disappeared. As Ken watched his best friends disappear forever and turned to face his new life. A life he could never leave.

CHAPTER 17

Kat had followed the others to the lobby, unsure of what else to do. She was no fighter, but she lingered on the back lines of the fighting, pulling the injured to safety and warning anyone of impending danger. She had wrapped a chain from her bike around one fist but hadn't had any use for it.

The defenses from Nick and Noodle were holding. The fierce defense of the sensitives was remarkably potent. The Red Caps and Hide Behinds had been unable to penetrate the line, and it seemed that the momentum was on the side of the defenders.

But then, a murmur swept through the lobby. Stealthy figures flashed through the crowd. Feline. Canine. Massive. They surprised the defenders and, placing hands on their heads, sent them screaming into a waking nightmare where all sense left them. As the nightmares took hold, the attackers gained a foothold and rushed through wherever one of the creatives fell to the floor, clutching themselves and thrashing with terror.

Some good people were lost then. Cody Jones fell under a Red Cap's pike. Randolph Peter was the next. Then Kevin Faranacci. Charisse Lyon was in danger of the same fate, torn between the hellscape that had been placed in her mind and the massive Red Cap that faced her. She proved surprisingly resilient in the face of the terror, more than many of the others, but when a Hide Behind circled her and approached from behind, her fate seemed sealed.

Kat leaped into the fray, striking the Red Cap square in the face with her chain-bound hand. The result was little more than a snarl from the evil creature. Now, with Charisse incapacitated, and Kat standing between the Red Cap and its target, all seemed lost for both.

Suddenly, a figure appeared between Kat and the aggressor. Drew Brindig, from out of nowhere, faced the Red Cap, and somehow seemed to grow larger.

"Leave my granddaughter alone, you bastard," he cried. "In fact, leave this place—NOW!"

His voice echoed throughout the lobby. It rattled the doors. It stopped everyone in their tracks.

Bobby Smalls rushed to Drew's side. "Drew, leave this to me!" he said, hoisting a ceremonial blade from *Brigadoon.*

But Drew was having none of it. He turned to Bobby and said, "Bobby, trust me when I say I've got this. I've been waiting for this a long time."

"Granddad?" Kat whispered, kneeling over the injured Charisse. "But you're...How—?"

Drew turned to Kat. "Yeah, kiddo. I could never leave you. Best watch your eyes now. It's about to get awfully messy."

Drew turned then toward the attacking horde and raised his voice again. "Spirits, the time is now! Fulton, I call your spirits to me. Protect our Lady! Spirits of Lancaster, to me!"

And with that, the spirits of the theatre appeared. They rose from the floor. They streamed through the closed doors. They flew in through the ceiling. They seemed innumerable. They were dressed in every style and every period imaginable. There was the one they called the Whistler, who whistled to whoever he encountered. There was Mary Cowhill, who had never been able to truly leave the stage behind. The parent who had returned time and time again after death to watch her son take the stage. There came a parade of stars from years past. M.B. Curtis. Henry Dickey. Emmet Davenport. James Young. Sally Hellman. Coursing into the lobby, sweeping the invading army ahead of them. And then behind them, the newest spirits of the Fulton. There came Cody. And Randolph Peter. Kevin Faranacci. They appeared as they had been in their youth. Now forever a part of the theatre they loved so well.

And then, from the street, came the ghosts of Lancaster City. They answered the call to protect their own, the grand lady of Prince Street. Thaddeus Stevens. Samuel Haldeman. And countless others whose names were lost to history, but who held the city in their hearts.

The attackers were cut off. Those that could, fled to the portal in the street. The portal that still swirled and roiled with fire and smoke.

Out of the crowd of city spirits, a woman stepped forward and approached Drew. She was young, beautiful, jet-black hair tied back in a ponytail.

"Andrew," she spoke, quietly. "Finally. It's been so long."

"Katie," he said, stroking her face.

"Grandma?" Kat said, barely able to catch her breath. "Grandpa?"

"Your call finally freed me from the house. I was afraid I would be stuck there forever."

"We made it, love. You're here," Drew said to Katie. "What now, Mum?"

"Now, we make sure no harm will ever come to our grandchild, husband."

With that, they turned to Kat, who remained on the floor, cradling the injured Charisse. Drew and Mum stretched their hands out to her, and she took them, rising to stand.

"We've been waiting so long," Mum said. "To get back to each other, but also to see you safe. We've never been far from you. Our precious grandchild."

"That's why I always felt I was being watched when I passed Dremmel House," Kat said quietly.

"Yes," Drew said. "And now we will never leave you again."

With that, the two spirits embraced Kat. Holding her close. And then they simply—melted into her. When she lifted her head, and once again saw the lobby around her now quiet and still, there was a light in her eyes that hadn't been there before. It was as if she could see things now that no one else could see. And she glowed from within.

<hr>

Trout and Dante faced the doorway to Water Street and watched as it pulsed and bowed before finally exploding inward. They lifted their weapons—tomahawk and scythe—and prepared to meet the onslaught.

They were surprised, when the dust began to settle, to see the doorway filled with the shape of a massive steed, black as night, with eyes fire red. Atop the horse sat the Dullahan, a being from the depths of horror-filled legend. A headless rider, his head held under one arm, while a flaming whip snaked back and forth in the other.

At the rider's back, a sea of Red Caps and Hide Behinds swarmed. So many that they had to wait to enter through the doorway.

"You have got to be joking," Trout said. "This guy again? What does it take to kill you, you cheesy-smelling loser!"

The Dullahan laughed then. A sinister, rasping sound, much like fingernails on a chalkboard. It dismounted then, and entered the green-room, the whip carving the air in front of it.

"The likes of you will never kill me," it rasped. "Your pathetic existence is nothing to me. You are a fly to be swatted. Nothing more."

"You'd better be a bit more polite to my friend here," Dante called from Trout's side. "This scythe is for more than show."

As the two closed on the Dullahan, the street outside became a frenzy of cries and shouts. Through the doorway, massive shapes fell upon the assembled army. Wolves. A pack of wolves large enough to cleave their way through the throng. Red Caps and Hide Behinds wilted before the attack.

Next, another group pf wolves, the Stubbes, Verduns, and Burgots threw themselves on the Wulliver pack from behind, hoping to catch them unawares. For the first time, and in no small part because of the inspiration drawn from Bayard and Cinder, the local bullies were thrashed and sent on their way. Humiliated. As with all bullies, in the end they were exposed as cowards.

Bayard, barely out of breath, watched them flee. Laughing. "All bark. No bite," he said, shaking his head.

Soon the street was empty, while inside the Dullahan stood alone, facing Trout and Dante.

"Oh, you are so screwed," Trout laughed at the horseless rider, and stepped toward the ghoul.

"You have no idea how true that is," came a familiar voice from the doorway.

Trout paused to see who the newcomer was. Bayard, Cinder at his side, leaned on the doorframe, tossing two knives in the air as he considered the Dullahan. The Wulliver pack stood silently just behind him.

"I suggest, pretty strongly actually, that you run. Now," the Peripheral snarled.

And the Dullahan did. Dashing forward through the greenroom, then down a hallway to the left, and up a staircase.

Trout began to make chase, when Dante grabbed his arm.

"The portal," he said to the Montanan, with a jerk of his head back toward the doorway under the stage.

Bayard reached them then and, shaking Trout's hand, looked back toward the portal.

"I think that's covered," he said and directed their attention behind them.

The spirits of the Fulton, all of them now, had arrived and stood watch over the entry to the portal. No one, not even the Dullahan, would pass through them.

With that, Trout, Dante, and Bayard raced down the hall in pursuit of the Dullahan.

The trio raced up the stairs. They caught a glimpse of the Dullahan rounding a corner above them. A moment later, they spilled out of the stairwell and into the lobby. The door to the theatre was swinging shut before them and they dashed through it. What they saw next stopped them in their tracks.

The Dullahan was slowly making its way up the aisle in the theatre moving toward the front lobby and Prince Street. What stopped them, though, was the entire Fulton contingent. All of them, as if by unspoken agreement, had stepped back to watch the Dullahan. The creature gnashed its teeth and flicked its whip as it walked, but the gestures were empty, lacking any real menace. The crowd filled in behind the Dullahan as it moved along so that by the time it reached the lobby there was a mob pushing him out with their collective will.

Along the way, the defiance of the Dullahan ebbed. Its shoulders sagged. As it realized that it held no sway over these mortals, it began to move quicker. Eventually it was running again, and the jeers and laughs of the Fulton creatives mocked it out the door and into the street, where it sprinted to the fiery portal and cowered behind it. Its steed, left behind the theatre, did not appear, and the Dullahan was greatly diminished having to carry itself alone.

The crowd followed onto the sidewalk and collected there, eventually falling silent as they faced the whirlpool of flame and anger, still churning and billowing. In the midst of the gateway, a figure appeared. A man. Of no particular stature or menace. Simply a man. He walked toward the crowd, emerging onto the street. He was tall, but not overly so, standing just over six feet. His hair was of flame, dancing and flicking atop him, and occasionally slithering down his arms to snap in the air around him. His eyes were fiery red, also, although his face was otherwise unremarkable, neither good nor evil. He was dressed simply, all in black. Trout and Nick were reminded of the clothing the Peripherals most often wore. Functional. On his head, couched in the seething flames, lay a simple circlet of gold, and on the circlet was a red, unblinking eye. The eye moved of its own will, and wherever it cast its glance, fear followed.

The fiery eyes stared down at the assembled crowd, and the creatives felt suddenly exposed, as if this man could see straight through them to their darkest secrets. They shrank back slightly, seeking cover under the theatre's marquee and they looked down and away, ashamed of themselves but for what they could not say.

The man looked them over and spoke in a voice deep and rough, as if the earth itself had opened and seen fit to make itself known. "Yes, look away. Hang your heads in shame. What you have done today is as nothing. You are as nothing, and all your works will fall to dust and be scattered before the might of the armies I am assembling. Tremble, humans. Tremble as you realize that your time on this earth is come to an end. Tremble at the sight of Balor, King of the Fomorians, and Lord of the next epoch on earth."

The Dullahan, emboldened by its overlord, began to slink from behind the portal. Dante had seen enough, and with a bellow, stepped into the street, swinging his scythe high, caring not who he struck, but meaning one of these two monsters to fall.

The being now known as Balor, barely moved. With the slightest glance, Balor shattered the scythe and sent Dante flying backward, skidding along the pavement until he reached the theatre wall and was still.

Trout felt his rage rising and as he raised his tomahawk, his attention was drawn to the roof of the theatre. The golden done that had encompassed the entire city block was intensifying. It grew brighter and brighter until all, even Balor, had to look aside and shield their eyes. When the illumination began to fade, Pettirosso appeared, floating gently down on beams of light. He crackled with energy, streaks of gold, and green, and blue snaked around and through him. His eyes, every bit the match of Balor's, shone clear and clean and bright.

"Balor," he spoke, and his voice had changed. The director now sounded as if he spoke down through the ages, clear and strong and ageless. "You have lost this war once before and were banished long ago. You will not win now. You cannot win. Go. While you still can."

"You?" Balor sneered at Pettirosso. "They dare send a puka to confront *me?* The flimsiest of the Fae to face *me?* Your body will be scattered to the winds before you even know you have fallen."

"You are wrong on many counts, Balor," Pettirosso responded. "I am more than I once was. I have learned. Grown. Unlike you. And, also unlike you, I value those around me. You and your kind seek to subjugate each other, making each other weaker. We"—and here he took in all those assembled around him—"seek to make each other better. Destruction versus creation. Creation always wins in the end."

"Fool," Balor spat, and snapped his fingers. At that, two Wayob emerged from the portal. One led Breena by the hand. Her eyes were entirely black. She showed no knowledge of where she stood but swayed slightly. Helpless.

The other Wayob, the larger of the two in the shape of a jaguar, held Kallan splayed in his arms. The mighty Celtic warrior lay motionless, but whether he was dead or merely unconscious was impossible to tell.

"Weak," Balor said. "Love. Your *attachments* are what will be your downfall. *Family.* Look what good it did these two. Look what dealing with the likes of you has done to them."

Bayard cried aloud and would have thrown himself at Balor, but Trout held him tight and tried to calm him. Pettirosso cast a glance at Bayard and Trout and nodded.

"You have learned nothing, Balor," Pettirosso said, dismissing Balor. "You have no power here. You are nothing to us."

"Fool," Balor rasped. "Your friends will all die and wither. I give you notice. The Fae War has now begun. Your lot now lies with the mewling humans. When next you see me, it will be on the field of battle as I stand over you and end your miserable existence."

Pettirosso looked once more at Balor with what could only be called pity, before turning his back on him and beginning his ascent back to the balcony outside his office. As he did, the band on the stage inside began to play. A new song, written by Haydn and Page, for this moment. And as the opening chords drifted out over the sound system set up under the marquee, the Fulton creatives began to sing. The song was simple. Direct and clear. And pure. As it swelled, the entire block, still under

Pettirosso's golden dome, began to shimmer with its own light. The power of dozens of voices, united, caught hold and set the night ablaze around the theatre. The words, the notes.

When windowpanes are edged with frost
And frigid winds do howl
When skies are bleak, all warmth seems lost
The dogs of winter prowl

But spring will break
The world still spins
Let not your spirit quake
For sure 'tis true that in the end
Love wins, love wins, love wins

Balor glared at the crowd now assembled around him. They had moved closer throughout the song. Their golden light washing over him and his minions in waves, each one taller and stronger than the last. Finally, he could bear it no more and with a shake of his head, he stepped into the portal. The Wayob, still bearing Breena and Kallan, followed, along with the Dullahan. As the portal closed, the few remaining Red Caps and Hide Behinds rushed to join their master, but the portal closed with many still trapped on Prince Street. As they turned back to the crowd, it seemed that some of them bore a look of realization as the gateway closed and they fell into dust and were carried away on the breeze.

Pettirosso, from his balcony, rose once more into the air and with a few graceful but economical motions of his arms, allowed the golden dome to slip away, restoring the night to itself. The citizens of Lancaster slumbered on, completely unaware of what had happened.

Moments later, a dark blue Honda Fit came trundling up Prince Street and stopped, idling in front of the theatre. The back doors opened, and Sean and Brandy tumbled out, each holding a chronovisor under their arm and looking about, expecting to see a battle raging.

Instead, they were greeted by a somber crowd, many of them familiar faces.

"Dammit," Brandy cried. "I finally got the visors to pinpoint a time, but then we got held out by that giant dome thing. I'd say we could have helped, but it looks like you all did okay."

Sean surveyed the street. "Maybe they didn't need me, after all," he said quietly.

Trout and Nick rushed to their sides, expectant looks on their faces as they checked the car for anyone else but finding only Brett Billson's sheepish smile and his saintly wife, Lauren, behind the wheel.

Nick looked to Sean. Then Brandy. "Ken?"

Brandy shook her head, a grim set to her mouth.

"He's dead?" Trout whispered.

"No," Sean answered. "But he's not coming back, either."

The next week moved slowly. Rehearsals for *A Christmas Carol* continued, but the mood was bleak. Ken's absence cast a pall over the proceedings and the Grumbles, in particular, were melancholy. The following Thursday arrived, and with it, opening night of the show, but the proceedings felt empty.

Nick's arm had shown signs of infection, and he had made the difficult decision to postpone the one-man show he had been writing for Trout. As a result, Trout moved over to take Ken's place as the understudy on the play. Nick was being treated in town, and was in the audience for the performance, but an alternative course for his arm was needed. He was getting worse.

Sean went through the motions, and by all accounts acquitted himself very well as Bob Cratchit, but his mind was elsewhere. He was overwhelmed with guilt at the decision Ken had made, sacrificing himself for the good of the others.

He also was preoccupied by Breena's fate. Pettirosso had sent messages to the leaders of the Tuatha, informing them of developments, but there had been no response as of yet. Sean spent a great deal of his time with the Wullivers. He had become particularly close with the now mature Carolyn, and they often went for long walks through the farm country, and she told him of Ken's early days in the past before he had left the pack for the city.

Trout was restless. Being an offstage understudy, while necessary under the circumstances, didn't suit him. He needed to be in the middle of things. He longed to see the woman he loved, Eleanor, who remained confined to the Outer Banks in North Carolina. It had been too long since he'd seen her. But his mind was also on the fate of Kallan, their erstwhile leader through some of the most dangerous recent episodes. Torn in two directions, he was unhappy with his options.

Brandy was the most affected of them all. Ken's absence felt like a personal failing to her. She had led him back in time, she should have been the one to stay behind. But he hadn't given her that choice. She worried about Breena and Kallan. She worried about Nick's arm. She worried about Sean. What if he took it upon himself to rescue Breena? It was exactly the type of thing he would do. So she stayed close by him. Watching and fretting over him.

The others involved in the defense of the Fulton fared better.

Dante had recovered fully and given a masterclass of a performance as Ebenezer Scrooge. It was being hailed as a triumph, and his star was on the ascent.

Bobby Smalls, as nephew Fred, had also garnered positive attention. His actions while leading the defense of the theatre made him the toast of the Fulton community.

Bayard, too, found himself spending time with the Wullivers. He had been alone for so long, that the sensation of belonging to something, to a pack, was comforting. And that surprised him. Cinder, too, had become fast friends with the wolf shifters, and would take to the forests to run for hours with Donal and Craig.

The play ran its course, and at the end of December it was time to close and for the company to move on. After the final performance,

Pettirosso, as stalwart as ever, invited the Grumbles, and Bayard, to his office.

With all present, and the director in his customary position, looking out the window over Prince Street, Pettirosso addressed the group.

"It has been an interesting time" he said. "There have been turns even I couldn't have anticipated. And with them, many questions still to be answered. But first, an announcement. My dear Deborah has decided it is time to see the world. She will retire from the theatre, and she goes with my love and respect. I did my best to dissuade her, but she is set on it and I respect that."

Deborah, from the far corner, nodded uncomfortably. "Thank you, sir. Time to see some new things. I've done all I can for this place. A fresh face and perspective will do you all good. New perspectives are always necessary."

"You will be missed," Pettirosso answered. "Deeply. And maybe now you will finally stop calling me sir."

The Grumbles gathered around Deborah and hugs were shared along with tears.

"With endings come beginnings," Pettirosso continued. "And so, I would like you to meet my new assistant, Kat Brindig."

Kat rose from a chair in the corner and smiled brightly at everyone. She walked to Sean.

"I literally wouldn't be here without you," she said. "Thank you. For being a friend. For welcoming me. For—everything."

"You did it all yourself," Sean replied. "You're a remarkable person, Kat. You deserve it. And...you seem different."

"Yeah, well, I am," she said. "I see things differently now. Clearer."

For just a moment, her eyes flashed gold. So fast, that Sean doubted it had happened at all.

"And with the departure of Drew," Pettirosso said, pushing a button on the underside of his desk, "I want you to meet the new jack-of-all-trades, Joseph Coon."

The door opened and a nattily attired young man entered, a question in his eyes.

"Yeah?" he asked.

"Just wanted you to meet the outgoing cast, Joey," Pettirosso said.

"Oh, gotcha," Coon said. "And, actually, I prefer Joseph, if you don't mind."

"Duly noted," Pettirosso said, nodding, and when Coon had left, he continued. "Obviously, there will need to be some adjustments made."

And finally, they all took seats around the office. There was much discussion of what had happened, and priorities were drawn up. And, in the end, difficult decisions were made.

Nick, with his injured arm, would accompany McCloud, who remained comatose, north to an island off the coast of Maine. It was renowned as a haven for artists. And for Fae. There would be healing there for both of them. If healing was to be found.

The others, Sean, Trout, Brandy and Bayard, would go in search of Breena and Kallan. They would need to travel into the Fae realms, something no human had done in untold centuries. It would be perilous. Perhaps deadly. But no amount of argument from Pettirosso would turn them from the task.

The Grumbles, what remained of them, would go their separate ways.

Before they left, Pettirosso pulled a large envelope from his desk and slid it across to the others. Across the front was written, "Grumbles, January 1, 2025."

"This has been in the theatre archives for decades," he said. "No one ever knew what it meant. Until now. It bears this date, the day after your show closed. I believe you have mail."

Brandy picked up the envelope and showed it to the others. Ken's writing was instantly familiar to them all. With trembling hands, she opened the letter and began to read.

"My friends. I hope that this finds you healthy and well, whenever it may find you. Please, don't mourn for me. I made the most logical choice under the circumstances. Sean is needed to save the world. And to find Breena. Brandy, you are the rock of the Grumbles. We would fall apart without you. Trout, you have Eleanor now, and your mom in Montana.

Nick, you've only just scratched the surface of your writing. You will change the world. And that mutt, Bunsen, would be lost without you. And Stewart? Well, he's the best and brightest of us. I have a feeling he will make decency sexy again.

No, it had to be me. I burned so many bridges with my foolishness. My own family doesn't know what to do with me now, but I have a chance to change things for them. And to show you all that, deep down, I am the friend you all knew I could be. I lost my way for a bit but found it here in the end.

Now, I'm free to start again. Be myself. I can be the star I always knew I should be. No one can hold my past against me because it hasn't happened yet.

I'm going to bet on the '69 Mets. And the '04 Red Sox. And Reagan to become President. Look for some unexpected windfalls along the way.

My family will never want for anything. And neither will you. My dearest friends. I say farewell for now. With so much love in my heart."

The Grumbles sat in stunned silence. Even Brandy wept.

"To that end," Pettirosso said after a respectful silence, "I want you to know that this morning, we received a cashier's check for a very handsome sum. As a result, the upstairs studio theatre will now be named the Ken O'Carroll Theatre. I wanted you to know before you left. Now go. And Godspeed to you on your journeys.

As they left, Nick did a quick online search for 'Ken O'Carroll' and hooted when he saw the results.

"Damn if he didn't do it," Nick told the others. "I've searched each day from something about him online. This is the first day something showed up. Ken enjoyed a successful career in TV and film throughout the late 1960s and 1970s. He invested wisely and retired in the early 1980s. There is no record of him after 1998. I'll be."

EPILOGUE

Pettirosso stood at his window and watched as the Grumbles left.

"In the end, I'm not exactly sure who saved who," he said to Kat.

"Well, we're not out of the woods yet," she replied. "The veil between realms has been weakened by everything that has happened. With the Grumbles gone, and Dante headed back to Chicago, we'll need that help we discussed."

"We will," he agreed. "In fact, they should be here any moment. Our newest cast, and also our most potent creatives. Joseph "Sticks" Capp, James Masterson, Camille Romano and Marian Elizabeth Donagher are all on the same train. Arriving," he checked his watch, "right now."

"And are you sure of them?" Kat asked.

"Very," he answered. "The Fulton chapter of the Ghostlight Brigade will ensure our safety throughout what's to come. And the women may be the most powerful we've seen yet. They may eclipse Sean in the end."

"His fixation on Breena may be his undoing," Kat said quietly.

"I just hope it is not ours, as well," Pettirosso mused.

"When I first met him, for a moment..." Kat's words trailed off.

"I know. And I'm sorry."

"Don't be," she answered. "This is the way it had to be. I see that now."

"I'm afraid you are right," the director replied.

He darkened the windows and got back to work.

The End

The Peripherals Will Go On

If you enjoyed this book, please take a moment to visit Amazon and provide a short review. Every reader's voice is important for the continued life and growth of a book or series and vital in helping authors find their audience.

Look for *Book Four, Beyond Darkness*, soon and the first books in the Brethren of the Sea and Ghostlight Brigade series.

Keep up to date on all things Peripherals at

www.markaldrich.net

where you can also sign up for a mailing list. Rest assured it will be used sparingly and only for announcements about the books.

GLOSSARY

You should know that this glossary may include spoilers, so it is best to finish reading first, if you are so inclined.

PLACES

First, the Fulton Theatre. It is very much as described in the book. I've been fortunate enough to perform there on a number of occasions, and it is a place near to my heart. It does have a colorful, and at times tragic, history, and is reputed to be one of the most haunted theatres in the United States. Which is saying something. If you are familiar with a few of the more renowned ghost stories there, you will find nuggets alluding to them in Chasing Today.

Dremmel House has been renamed for Chasing Today as it is no longer used as housing for the Fulton.

Dreams. I wanted to introduce a dream realm as it is so prominent in folklore around the world. The dreams that Sean experiences are very similar to dreams I have had myself.

The paranormal encounters in Dremmel House are related from personal experience. Make of that what you will.

Zook's Mill Bridge also exists and stands today. It still spans the Cocalico Creek in Lancaster County, Pennsylvania. It is sometimes also referred to as The Wenger or Rose Hill Covered Bridge. It was constructed in 1849 by Henry Zook and is 74 feet in length. The bridge is one of few that survived Hurricane Agnes, despite filling with over six feet of water. There was a mill on either side of the bridge. I've combined them for the story. The last mill there closed in 1970.

I did quite a bit of research on the covered bridges in the area. The combination of proximity, topography, and timeline made Zook's Mill my choice. Covered Bridges have long had a mystique about them, and I wanted to tap into that.

The Rural City Taproom does exist just a short walk from the Fulton Theatre. They are fine folks and make some excellent beer. Pay them a visit and, if you're lucky, you may run into Lance.

THE CREATURES

In Mayan mythology, **Wayob** (plural of Uay or Way) are spirits that are able to shapeshift, frequently taking the form of jaguars and, less frequently, grey foxes. In the Yucatan Peninsula in modern folklore, they have become known as evil sorcerers.

The word Wayob is translated as "to sleep" or "to dream", which suited the dream subplot perfectly.

Redcaps (sometimes known as Powries), are evil, often murderous, creatures from the folklore of the Anglo-Scottish border. They are known for soaking their headwear in the blood of their victims and are described as goblin-like, with prominent teeth, long fingers, eyes that glow red, and wearing iron boots while wielding large pikes. They are more normally considered solitary creatures, but for the purposes of the events in Chasing Today, I have altered that behavior.

They are sometimes referred to as Red Comb and Bloody Cap.

The Hidebehind is a fearsome nocturnal creature from American folklore. They are said to be able to conceal themselves and if someone does lay eyes on them, they quickly shift to hiding behind any nearby object. They use this ability to stalk their prey, often wanderers in the forest, and drag their targets back to their lair to be consumed.

They are reputed to have a violent aversion to alcohol, which made for the scene at the Dispensing Company.

Despite no one being able to see them, they are described as large, shadowy, animal-like figures.

In Irish mythology, **Balor** was the leader of the Fomorians, evil supernatural beings who were the adversaries of the Tuatha De Danann. He is described as a giant with one eye, who causes destruction wherever he passes and is often likened to other mythological creatures such as Cyclops. His strength is sometimes compared to the scorching power of the sun. He was considered the most powerful of his kind.

TIME TRAVEL

The concept of the **Timestriders** is purely my own. I researched quite a bit to find time travel folklore to suit my narrative. I was not successful. The first instance where I didn't find the mythology or folklore that filled the role I was looking for. I enjoy the research aspects of my books, but this time came up empty and created my own folklore. I enjoy the idea of very rare time hopping Fae. I hope you do, too.

Interestingly, the **<u>chronovisor</u>** *is* an actual device. Whether it worked or not is an entirely different matter. The visor is said to give the wearer the ability to see through time. A book published in 2002 by a Vatican priest claims that the device was real. It was reportedly developed by a Benedictine monk, a famous physicist, and a former nazi scientist. Supposedly, the team was able to chronicle many significant events of the past. The researchers were active on the project in the 1960's and 1970's, and though the claims are dubious, some of those involved insisted the device was real and functioned.

Conspiracy theories swirl around the chronovisor, including claims that it was deemed dangerous by the Vatican and CIA and hidden to prevent it doing any lasting damage.

The lyrics to **<u>"Love Wins"</u>** are original, and an homage to the late playwright Terrence McNally. I was fortunate to work with and get to know him. He often included the phrase in his posts and messages. His voice is missed greatly, and I wanted to carry that message forward in some small way.

ACKNOWLEDGMENTS

No author is an island. We plow forward through the help of family and friends, colleagues, and collaborators. The list of those for this book is long, and I am deeply appreciative.

Once again, I begin with my family. My brother, Stephen Aldrich, and sister, Cindy Vollmer, have been sounding boards, cheerleaders, critics, publicists, and, above all, friends. I can't imagine this book coming to fruition without them.

Thanks, also, to my father. He introduced me to reading very early in life, sharing favorites of his long before I was of an age to appreciate them fully. Somehow, though, I found something in them to inspire me, beginning a lifelong fascination with storytelling. He's not here to see my books being published, but I know he would have been thrilled. Somehow, somewhere, he knows. My very own Peripheral.

Thank you to my mom. I know she knew I had a flashlight under the covers to read by long after I should have gone to sleep as a child, but she let me read on. She took me to the store to get the latest comic books and to the bookstore where she would let me roam and discover and dream. Look where it led. Thank you doesn't seem enough.

Teachers. They impact us in so many ways and for our entire lives. I renew my thanks to three outstanding teachers who, to this day, inspire and encourage me—Ken Link, Brian Nelson, and Tom Watson. All were ahead of their times, and we students knew and were grateful.

Amy Gillespie has become a vital part of my author process. Thank you for your keen eye and tackling these manuscripts with intelligence, humor, and alacrity.

Profuse thanks to Chris Sorensen for his formatting and his cover design. Once again, he was able to create something that so wonderfully captures the tone of the book. He is a magician.

Gretchen Douglas, proofreader extraordinaire, once again provided invaluable insight both grammatically, logically, and thematically. She is a boon to anyone fortunate enough to work with her.

A heartfelt thank you to my beta readers, who took this latest venture seriously and offered excellent ideas, corrections, suggestions, and encouragement. Stephen Aldrich, Cindy Vollmer, Robin Lee-Thorp, Amy Gillespie. Thank you is not nearly enough.

Once again, I single out two individuals for special thanks, Nick Sullivan, and Chris Sorensen. From practical help to encouragement to ridiculous banter via text or over a nosh and beer, they have been invaluable. Not just helpful, but friends and part of a burgeoning author network. Thank you.

Without doubt, my biggest thanks are reserved for my wife, Jennifer, and our new daughter, Stephania. Jennifer has encouraged me throughout, pushing when needed, handholding just as often. Stephania for opening my eyes to all the possibilities still surrounding us all. The gift of being able to watch her grow and discover the world around her is the most magical journey I've ever taken. She's the sweetest.

Lastly, I thank you, the readers, for taking another journey with me. I've always told stories, whether on a stage, a screen, or a page. None of it would have been possible without people willing to come along. People like you. Thank you for loving stories. Thank you for sharing mine.

About the Author

Mark Aldrich was born in Massachusetts and raised in Virginia. Most of his adult life he has made New York City his home while traveling extensively as an actor and singer. He has appeared in television, film, and theatre, including Broadway and many of the world's most famous stages. However, some of his favorite performances were given in village pubs late at night on the wild West Coast of Ireland.

Mark has written extensively for web publications, periodicals, and industry journals. After helping to tell others' stories on stage, he decided to commit some of his own to the page. *The Peripherals* marks his debut novel and combines his love of history, travel, folklore, music, and his decades-long knowledge of the inner workings of live theatre and the artists working there.

Please feel free to follow and keep in touch at markaldrich.net and @marktheginger on Instagram and Twitter.